Changing

Fortunes

Book 2

A One Way Ticket

By

Carole McEntee-Taylor

Published by CaroleMcT Books

Edited by Jules Davies

Jacket design/kindle cover by Flintlock Covers

Additional material Bob Young, Bill's son

Other books by the author

Non Fiction
Pen and Sword Books Ltd:
Herbert Columbine VC
Surviving the Nazi Onslaught
A Battle Too Far
Military Detention Colchester from 1947
The Battle of Bellewaarde June 1915
From Colonial Warrior to Western Front Flyer
The History of Coalhouse Fort
A History of Women's Lives in Scunthorpe

The Weekend Trippers
My War and Peace
Biography of John Doubleday: The Work

The Re-Enlightenment
The Holiday From Hell

Fiction
Secrets
Lives Apart: A WW2 Chronicle
Obsession
Betrayed

Dedication

To my brother, Stephen William Young, who started me on
this journey.

28 October 1959 – 6 August 2020

Bob Young

Characters

Bill Young

Nora – Bill's sister

Alan Finch – Bill's friend

Chris Belton – Bill's Friend

Danny Cowl – Bill's friend

Taff (Bryn Caddell) – Bill's friend

Mary – Bill's mother

Joseph – Bill's father

Abigail Saunders – Bill's girlfriend

Tom Carter – Bill's Friend

Gerry Smith – Bill Friend

Jacob Goldsmith

Emanuel Goldsmith – Jacob's father

Suri Goldstein – Jacob's cousin

Ezra Goldstein – Sura's father

Yael Goldstein – Sura's mother

Levi Herstein – Sura's husband

Aaron Herstein – Levi and Sura's son

Rebecka Herstein – Levi's sister

Niklas Konig – Jacob's colleague

Clemens von Landau – Linus/ Jacob's boss

Eva von Landau – Linus/Jacob's girlfriend

Harald Backer – SS Officer

Matilda Weber - Tilly

Dot Weber – younger sister

Gladys Weber - mother

Georg Weber – father (deceased)

Francis Marshall – Special Branch

Tim Gregory – assistant

Joren Varwijk – Tilly's friend and co resistance worker

Sturmbannführer Drescher

Clarissa/Desiree - Dowager Countess of Westbrook

Clive, Earl of Westbrook (deceased)

Nathanial, Earl of Westbrook - Son

Tristram Cook – Clarissa's friend

Major Heinz Kessel/Jonathan Creighton

Paul King – Heinz' assistant

Mrs Jean Enderby – housekeeper

Sammy Halliday - ENSA

June Halliday - ENSA

Renee Drolet - ENSA

Part 1

July 1943

Chapter 1

Warrington

Nora gazed in the mirror and blinked back tears. Fortunately, nothing showed at the moment, but another few months and she wouldn't be able to hide her growing stomach. She would have to tell her parents. The thought made her feel sick. What was she going to tell them? That she had been raped but never bothered to say anything? Nora thought back to the night that was rarely out of her mind. She had no idea how she had found the strength to walk into the canteen the following day, let alone walk home. She had eventually made herself leave the hut, lied to the guards on the gate, saying she'd had an extra shift and somehow reached the safety of her home. Fortunately, her parents were in bed and she had managed to creep in without waking them. She had washed herself repeatedly in the wash basin, not daring to run a bath in case it woke her parents, but however much of their precious soap she used she still felt dirty and disgusting. Eventually she gave up and lay in her bed, but she couldn't sleep, and she was almost grateful when the alarm went off.

She had left without breakfast, not wanting to speak to her parents, to have to explain why she was pale, her eyes ringed from lack of sleep. Painstaking steps took her ever closer to the base, a camp that somehow, she expected to be different, to reflect her pain. But on the surface nothing had changed, the canteen was packed, full of Americans fliers and to her relief, no British soldiers. Nora survived the day feeling like she was in a dream, or some kind of nightmare.

****

Berlin

Jacob pulled up outside Clemens' house, climbed out and walked up to the front door. Clemens had suggested that he also act as his driver now that his regular man had been sent to the Eastern Front. It suited Jacob perfectly because it meant he could see more of Eva, even if it was only for a few moments each day. He was sure she felt the same as it was invariably Eva who opened the door.

'Good morning Linus. It's a lovely day.'

Jacob smiled. 'Good morning Eva. Yes its is.' His smile broadened as he realised he hadn't even noticed the weather until she mentioned it. 'Are you doing anything nice today?'

Eva shook her head. 'No not really, just the usual.' She sighed and wished she could tell him the truth. 'Sorry I'm very boring aren't I?'

'No, I don't think you are boring at all.' The words hung in the air, the tension grew as she stared into his eyes and then Clemens appeared.

'Morning Haas. Goodbye Eva.' Clemens walked swiftly to his car.

Jacob gave the obligatory Hitler salute and then smiled at her. 'Goodbye Eva, enjoy your day whatever you're doing.' He hurried after Clemens and opened the back door of the car. Clemens climbed in a slight smile on his face. He was tempted to say something to Jacob about Eva but then changed his mind. From the little he could see things were progressing nicely. It was probably best he didn't interfere.

While Jacob climbed into the driver's seat Clemens glanced casually across the road and grimaced. As he'd expected Harald Backer was standing in the shadows on the ruined house further down the street watching. He was convinced Backer wasn't suspicious of him and that he was only interested in Eva, but it was best to be sure, hence his decision to encourage Linus to court his daughter. Unfortunately Jacob was rather slow to act. It was obvious he liked Eva but he still hadn't asked her out.

Harald watched the car drive off and clenched his fists. He was sure there was something going on between Linus Haas and Eva and he was finding it difficult to control his anger. He had liked Eva for ages and had even asked her out a couple of times several months earlier, but she had turned him down. Rather than putting him off her refusal had spurred him on, determined that she would go out with him. If she'd been seeing someone else he would have backed off but she hadn't been, not that he'd seen anyway. But now… now it looked like she was getting much too friendly with Linus Haas. He turned his attention back to the house and cursed under his breath. As if to prove his point Eva was still standing there, watching her father's car drive off into the distance.

****

HMS Drake

Bill had spent the last couple of months on *HMS Diomede* while she did her post refit trials and was then deployed with the Home Fleet while the Royal Navy decided what to do with the ship. She was not allowed to do any interceptions of enemy shipping during this time because her age was against her, her surface armament was completely outdated and there was poor armour protection. But the Royal Navy had finally made a decision and she had been sent to Chatham for another refit, before being deployed to Rosyth as a Training Ship for Direct Entry Y Scheme officer candidates. Bill had been relieved not to be in action again and was enjoying the relative peace and quiet so when his next posing came through, to *HMS Drake*, he was delighted. Another shore posting, he would have plenty of leave to go and have fun.

'Are you coming ashore Bill?' Bernie Jackson put his head in the cabin and waited for an answer. Tall, blonde and wiry, Bernie drank like a fish and had an eye for the ladies, which had drawn Bill to him, kindred spirits.

'Try stopping me.' He grabbed his hat and followed Bernie off the ship. 'I'm going to call in on a certain young lady.'

'You will if she's not occupied!' Bernie laughed and Bill frowned.

'You're right. I think I need to find a better class of woman.'

'At least Pompey isn't full of yanks.' Bernie swung himself across the gangplank then looked back at Bill. 'Do you know why it's called Pompey?'

Bill grinned. 'Yeah, its because they used to write Pom P, short for Portsmouth Point, in the ship's log.'

Bernie shook his head. 'And there was me thinking it was some kind of drunken slang.'

Bill laughed. 'I'm going to go into town, see if I can find a decent girl.'

Bernie looked even more confused. 'You'll never get your leg over that way.'

Bill shrugged. 'Maybe I want something different for a change.'

Bernie sighed. 'Well how about one for the road?'

Bill hesitated then nodded. 'Go on then.' Bill followed Bernie into the nearest pub and waited while he went to the bar. The pub was full of sailors and women, ribald singing came from a group round the piano, a warm fug that reeked of beer, rum and cigarettes.

'Here, drink up!' Bernie handed him a pint of the watered down beer and Bill drank thirstily, his eyes scanning the room until he found what he was looking for. The girl was average height, brown hair curled in the latest wartime style with bright red lipstick. Bill wandered towards her, all thoughts of going into town and finding a decent girl forgotten. Bernie's eyes followed the direction of his friend's eyes and grinned.

****

Brussels, Belgium

Heinz Kessel left Army Headquarters and wandered slowly through the streets. Hopefully the man he'd had arrested would be ready to talk by the time he got back. Heinz was reasonably sure the man was a courier for one of the escape lines. The sooner they broke him the quicker they could pick up the rest of the resistance personnel involved in that particular route. Heinz shook his head. He couldn't understand why these people kept putting their lives at risk for men and occasionally women, that they didn't know, many of whom dropped their bombs indiscriminately on the Netherlands as well as Germany. His expression darkened. Not that arresting them would ultimately make any difference to Germany's fate.

Unlike many of his colleagues Heinz had become increasingly convinced that Germany would lose the war, and as the months wore on his conviction that Britain would prevail while his own country descended into chaos, became stronger. He said nothing to his companions, to have done so would have been treason, but he knew that at some point in the future he would have to make some difficult decisions if he was going to survive, and if Germany was to recover and become great again in the future.

After the debacle with Hess, Heinz had escaped England and made his way back to Germany via Ireland and Denmark, only a few steps ahead of the British security forces. He was still seething that Clive had messed up his plans and he had every intention of taking ownership of Halford Manor when the war was over. Heinz had given his future considerable thought and had finally decided that with careful planning he should be able to return to Halford Manor and live there. From there he could continue with the preparations he was already putting into place to help Germany recover from losing the war.

Returning to England would mean changing his appearance of course, but that wouldn't be too difficult. Lord Westbrook had handed over the deeds to the property as security when Heinz had lent him the money, together with a signed note stating that if he didn't repay the loan within three years the property and estate would belong to him. Heinz had then agreed to pay Westbrook a certain amount for each of his men that Clive placed in positions where they would be useful. The number of men would equal the amount of money owing, thus cancelling the debt. But, because of the sensitive nature of that transaction there was nothing written down about the men, not as far as he knew anyway, so all Heinz would need to do would be to produce the deeds and the signed note and the estate would be his. The only problem was that he had signed the contract in his real name. If Germany did lose the war it was unlikely he would be able to return to England, certainly not immediately so he would provide proof of his death and leave Halford Manor and the other properties he had acquired to his half English, half Dutch friend, Jonathan Creighton, a name for which he had everything he needed in the way of forged documentation. It would have been better if he could have pretended to be English but he knew he still had a slight German accent so being half Dutch should cover that.

Lord Westbrook might have proved to be a problem, but he was dead, so the only person who knew of their arrangement was Heinz and he certainly wasn't going to tell anyone. Heinz would have to find a good reason why he hadn't claimed ownership straight after Clive's death, but that wouldn't be too difficult. He could say he had been a prisoner or fighting abroad somewhere and didn't know that he had been left the properties by his German friend until recently. Obviously having an old friend who was German was not something he would have talked about while there was a war going on between the two countries, and it had been years since he'd last had any contact with Heinz Kessel so the bequest had taken him completely by surprise. Jonathan would go on to state that he knew Kessel didn't have any family but he was still surprised that the German had chosen to leave everything he owned in England to him, surprised and very pleased. The end of the war would no doubt leave Europe in a certain amount of chaos so it would be very difficult for the authorities to check his story properly.

The only problem was making sure Clive had not written anything down about their arrangement. Although Heinz had not signed anything other than the contract it was possible that Clive had kept a record, just in case he needed it. He frowned and shook his head. No, even if Clive had written something down initially, it was unlikely that he would have kept it once their two countries were at war, it would have been too dangerous. But he would have to make sure that nothing existed.

Unfortunately, he couldn't do that until the war was over because it would be madness to go back to England now. He would just have to assume Clive had been careful and not left anything around for his widow to find. Heinz frown deepened. And if he had left something incriminating, what would Clarissa do if she found it? Presumably, if she'd had any sense, she would destroy it, but he couldn't leave anything to chance. Once it was safe, he would sneak back and make sure there were no nasty surprises before he arrived officially to take ownership.

****

Somewhere over Holland

The coastline was finally in sight and Chris breathed a sigh of relief. Not long now and they would be over the Channel and out of the way of the anti-aircraft batteries with only the Messerschmitt fighters to avoid. The coastline grew closer, the flak increased and he concentrated on trying to avoid the deafening explosions surrounding them. His hands gripped the controls as around them the sky was filled with smoke... and then to the left he was conscious of an aircraft bursting into flames, its engine screaming as it fell away towards the ground. Chris peered through the cockpit window, the aircraft was now in a dive below them, smoke billowing in the air. Chris bit his lip and looked away. He hadn't seen any parachutes in the sky, so it looked like none of them had made it out of the burning aircraft. He was still considering this when there was a loud bang, the aeroplane rocked dangerously, and he fought to control it.

'Shit! What's the fucking damage...?' He started to yell before falling silent. There was no point asking after the condition of the Lancaster, not when two of the engines had stopped, there were flames pouring from the third and only the fourth engine was flying the aircraft. They would never make it across the Channel and ditching in the sea was not a good option, especially as that would probably be on this side of the Channel. He turned the controls and the aircraft swung back towards Holland.

'We're losing altitude, everyone out as quick as you can. Don't forget to not open your parachutes too early or the bastards will shoot at you.' He fought hard to keep the Lancaster flying, hoping to give his men enough time to get through the tiny hatch. A few minutes later he left the controls, pushed Harry through the hole and eased himself into position. The escape hatch was much too small for any of them to make a quick exit, especially with a bulky parachute on, but they had all gone now except him. He fought hard and then he was clear, falling through the air, the sudden silence unnerving. He knew he didn't have long to open the parachute but to pull the chords too early would draw attention to himself. The Germans didn't treat downed allied pilots well, a heavy interrogation and then, if he was lucky, incarceration for the duration of the war. He preferred to get back home.

He had no idea how long he was free falling but if he got too close to the ground, he would break his neck so after offering a brief prayer he pulled the chord, the parachute opened abruptly, and he felt like all his breath had been squeezed out of his body. Then it was pulling him gently up into the sky before the slow descent began. Just as he began to relax he saw the ground rushing up to meet him and he landed in a heap before breathing a sigh of relief. He appeared to have judged it correctly, no broken bones or damage and no signs of any Krauts searching for him... not yet anyway. He cut the ropes on the parachute and looked briefly at his compass before putting it back in his pocket. He had no real idea where he was so it probably didn't matter in which direction he went. The most important thing was to try and find a friendly face to hide him before the Krauts picked him up.

****

Trent Park, London

The bombs were coming closer now, buildings all around him were collapsing, the ground shaking from the impact of the massive explosions. Levi could hear yelling and screaming but he was struggling to find his way through the mass of people filling the streets despite the sirens blazing. Thick acrid smelling smoke was filing his lungs and reducing his vision to virtually nothing, but he continued to push through the people and then the tube station was in front of him and he started to walk down the slippery steps. He had almost reached the ground when someone pushed him in the back, and he began tumbling downwards into the darkness. He could hear Sura calling him. but he couldn't stop…

Levi woke with a start, sweat pouring down his face, his heart pounding against his chest. He reached for the glass of water he kept by the bedside and drank thirstily. His heartbeat gradually returned to normal and he wiped his face with his handkerchief before climbing out of bed, walking towards the window and lifting the blackout.

Everything was quiet outside, no searchlights or enemy bombers overhead. Yet again his nightmares had woken him. He opened the window, closed his eyes and took a deep breath of the cool night air trying to visualise Sura in his mind as she had been the last time he had seen her. But the image wouldn't come to him and he clenched his fists in anger.

That night in March would never leave him. He had sat listening to the army wireless his heart beating wildly although he didn't know why until the raid had finally finished and then he had made his way to the hotel where he had been told that Sura had not arrived.

The telephone by his bed rang, interrupting his thoughts, and Levi cursed loudly before closing the window, replacing the blackout and striding back to pick up the receiver. 'Yes?' He barked, then his expression changed.

****

Portsmouth

Bill glanced at the clock over the bar and sighed. He had better get back on board or he would be late. He looked around but there was no sign of Bernie. Bill realised he hadn't seen his friend for a couple of hours, not since he'd waved drunkenly at Bill and left with one of the prostitutes. Bill had been too busy with a woman of his own to take much notice. He staggered to the door and peered drunkenly up the street. There were few people about and because it was dark he couldn't see properly anyway.

He stepped out of the pub and began walking slowly back towards the base. There was no point searching for Bernie as he had no idea in which direction his friend had gone. He stopped every few steps and turned back to check, but the streets were growing more deserted and there was still no sign of Bernie.

Bill finally reached the base and took one last look behind him. There was still time for Bernie to make it before he would be classed as late, but his friend would have to be quick. Bill passed the sentries and made his way down to his bunk a smile on his face. Obviously, his friend was having a very good time. Bill laughed, climbed onto his bunk and fell into a deep drunken sleep.

Chapter 2

Berlin

Eva watched her father's car disappearing down the street and sighed.
If only Linus would ask her out. It was so frustrating. He was much more
relaxed with her now he was calling every morning to pick up her father
and there had been a couple of times when she had been sure he was about
to ask her out, but on one occasion her father had appeared and on the
second Anton had come out to say hello. Oh well, tomorrow was another
day. Perhaps she should take the initiative and suggest they go to the
cinema. There was nothing on she wanted to see but that didn't matter. She
began closing the door, still wondering if she had the courage to ask him
out when she noticed a movement opposite. Frowning, Eva closed the door
then hurried up to her bedroom which faced in the same direction, strode
quickly to the window and tried to see out without getting too near the
window. It took her a few moments to make out the black uniform and she
paled. Why was Backer watching the house? Did he suspect something?
Her heart began to beat faster. She would have to warn her mother…

She was about to call her mother when she stopped and frowned. He
was leaving… She watched him stride down the road and disappear around
the corner. She leaned back against the wall and shook her head. Now she
had spotted him once she would keep a careful look out for him. In the
meantime she would change today's arrangements, just in case.

****

Halford Manor

Clarissa took one last look around her home, took a breath, and headed for the car which was waiting to take her to London and from there to Cairo and beyond. She glanced up at the nursery and smiled. Nathanial was sitting by the window waving to her. She raised her hand, blew him a kiss and turned away, not wanting him to see the tears that were already forming. Although she wanted to do this more than anything, it didn't mean she wasn't sad to have to leave Nathanial behind. But he would be safe at Halford with his nanny and although she would miss him, Clarissa knew she was doing the right thing. She couldn't sit at home while she had something to offer. It wasn't as if she could fight for her country, but she could help by entertaining those who were, giving them a few moments of happiness, brightening their lives, however briefly.

She climbed in the car, leant back in the seat and let the tears fall. She still missed Clive even though she was in love with Tristram. Clive had changed her life, given her Nathanial, a beautiful home and his name, which she had soon learnt was the key to open many doors.

The car swept through the gates and she took one last look back before focussing her attention on the future... and Tristram. Her lips curled up and her sadness faded away. For the next few months they would spend every day together and this time there were no barriers to their relationship. She could finally allow herself to love him back. For a brief moment she felt guilty. Clive had not been dead for very long; she should still be in mourning, but his death had shown her that life was too short to waste time. She would not only be facing the normal dangers of the sea, but if the information she had been given was to be believed, also that of U-boats and Stuka bombers. There was a chance they might never reach their destination, so she had no intention of waiting any more. When Tristram had stayed with her at Halford it had not felt right to share a bed with him. To have any intimacy in the house she had shared with Clive so soon after his death would have felt like she was being unfaithful. But being aboard the ship would be different and she intended to enjoy every moment of her new life. And as for the future, when the war finished... she would worry about that when it happened.

****

Amsterdam

Tilly walked quickly through the park towards the dead drop near the lake. The signal had been in place this morning when she had checked before leaving for work, some scrawled graffiti on the bottom of the wall that she would wipe off once she'd retrieved the message.

The park was quiet, but Tilly still kept her eyes open for the Gestapo or Waffen SS. Although there was no reason to expect the security forces to know about her, Tilly knew that complacency could be her worst enemy.

She stopped at the small fountain, glanced around to check once again and then moved towards a seat by some bushes near a stone wall. Tilly sat down, back to the wall and waited until she was absolutely sure there was no danger before reaching behind her and feeling for the loose stone. Her fingers clawed at it unsuccessfully for a couple of seconds before she felt it come away and she slipped her hand inside. The piece of paper was small enough to slide into her glove which she did, and then she was replacing the rock and relaxing back on the seat, her eyes searching the park for anything out of the ordinary. There was nothing so after a few seconds she stood up and made her way back to the apartment, taking care to wipe the graffiti off the wall on the way.

Once inside Tilly quickly decoded the message before placing it in the ashtray, flicking her cigarette lighter and watching the message burn to ashes. She then grabbed her bag and headed to the door. She would visit the address the following day as requested. On her arrival in Amsterdam Tilly had secured a job at the local newspaper as a junior reporter which meant she had the right papers to travel to Belgium and France when needed, perfect cover for a courier, but she needed to find a good reason to leave the office which would probably mean inventing a story. Fortunately, her employer knew exactly what she was doing so between them they would find something plausible for her to be reporting.

As she hurried to work Tilly wondered when the airmen had been shot down and how long they had remained hidden, guests of the underground movement set up to help them return back to Britain. All downed pilots were automatically checked with London first to ensure they weren't Nazi spies trying to infiltrate the network and then moved between safe houses to reduce the risk for the families involved. Her role was first to get photographs of the men so the forgers could make their false papers. When the documents were ready, she would pick the pilots up and take them on the first leg of their journey down one of the numerous escape lines through occupied Europe under the noses of their enemies.

****

Trent Park, London

'Myon, Ovid!' Levi stared at his friends in amazement then hugged them. 'I can't believe you are finally here.'

'Thanks to you Levi.'

Levi shrugged. 'I only did what I promised. I'm just sorry it took so long.' He had mentioned both Myon and Ovid to Francis when he had first started working at Trent Park, suggesting they could be of use and his employer had agreed to consider it. It had taken a while but both men had finally arrived back in England in April, just in time to support him through the worst time of his life.

'How's Aaron?'

'Growing bigger all the time. Rebecka is making a very good job of bringing him up. He's too young to miss Sura.' His eyes filled with tears and he turned away.

'His survival was a miracle.' Ovid patted him on the arm.

Levi nodded. 'Yes, I know. I still can't believe Sura managed to protect him... the last thing she did.' He blinked away tears angrily. 'If I hadn't asked them to come up to London Sura would still be alive.'

Myon exchanged glances with Ovid. 'It was a terrible accident Levi. It wasn't your fault. Did you ever find out why she was in Bethnal Green or what happened?'

Levi shook his head. 'No. I think she must have got lost and then the air raid warning sounded so she sought shelter. As to what happened, apparently, the locals had been expecting a raid after the one on Berlin and they also knew that the bombers are faster now. This meant they had less time to get to the shelters so when the sirens sounded there was a certain amount of panic. The report said that what really made it worse was that the local aircraft battery was new, and the people weren't used to the sound it made, they thought it was some new Nazi weapon. It had also been raining and the steps were slippery. From what they could gather someone fell and that was it, hundreds of people falling down steps in the dark.' He fell silent. Myon was right, Aaron's survival was a miracle, and he knew he should be grateful. But why couldn't Sura have survived too?

******

Portsmouth

Bill stared at the Captain and thought quickly. He didn't want to drop Bernie in it, but his friend should have been back by now. If something had happened to him and he lied in some mistaken attempt to try and keep his friend out of trouble... He made his decision. 'The last I saw him he was leaving the pub with a girl. I didn't see him again after that.'

'Give Number 1 the details of where you were and the time you last saw him and then get back to your duties.'

Bill saluted, followed the 1st Lt out of the office and told him the name of the pub they had visited. 'You don't think something has happened to him do you sir?'

'Probably not, but its unlike Jackson to be late back so we'd better check. The MPs will go and look for him. I wouldn't worry, he's probably just overslept.'

Bill nodded but he was beginning to feel increasingly uneasy. Bernie liked a drink, but he wouldn't have missed roll call.

Chapter 3

Berlin

Instead of waiting for the car to disappear around the corner as she normally did Eva waved goodbye to her father, closed the door quickly, hurried upstairs and rushed to her bedroom window. Yes, there he was. Harald Backer was standing in the ruins of the bombed house further down the road watching the house. As she stood there he turned on his heel and strode forcefully away. Eva shook her head. At first she'd been convinced he knew what they were doing and she had altered their activities but now she wasn't so sure. She had got up early this morning and watched out of the window and seen Backer arrive a few moments before Linus. He then waited for her father to leave before going. It didn't make any sense. If he was watching Linus or her father for that matter, why didn't he follow them? She had looked hard to make sure there wasn't more SS men around but there was no one. He was on his own. And if he suspected her of anything why didn't he stay there all day, or at least a little longer?

****

Amsterdam

Tilly smiled at the two men standing in the small room, noted the wary expressions on their faces, shook their hands and explained why she was there. The two men relaxed slightly, and she saw the sudden light in their eyes and guessed they were hoping that her presence meant that soon they would be on their way home. She began taking the photographs necessary for their papers, explaining how many sets of documents they would need and how it was important that they were correct in every detail. The men had been introduced to her as Chris and Harry, Lancaster pilots who had managed to escape their burning aeroplane and been lucky enough to have found their way to the resistance. Downed pilots had little option but to take potluck when they approached Dutch civilians. Several members of the population were pro German who would not hesitate to hand them over, others were collaborators because of what they could get out of the occupying forces, but fortunately there were still many thousands who would risk their lives for the allied cause.

'Have you heard anything about the rest of my crew?' Chris had smoked constantly since her arrival and she could feel the tension emanating from him.

Tilly shook her head. 'No, I haven't, I'm sorry. But that doesn't mean they weren't picked up. They could be with another group. For obvious reasons we don't mix too much.' She had not heard anything about their colleagues so she could only assume the others hadn't been so lucky, but she didn't want to depress them. 'I'm amazed you found each other.'

Chris gave a wry smile. 'Not as surprised as we were. This is my third stop. I knocked on one door and an elderly couple took me in before taking me to another house further up the street. I stayed there for several days until a girl brought me here by bike. It's a farm isn't it?'

Tilly frowned and didn't answer his question. 'Please don't think I am being rude but the less you know the better. If anyone asks you, no matter who they are or *say* they are, don't tell them anything about the people who have helped you. Even describing an elderly couple and saying you have been moved along the street can be enough with information from other escapees for the Germans to arrest helpers.'

'I'm sorry, we hadn't thought about it like that. We won't say anything, we both have terrible memories!' Harry laughed. 'It's just nice to speak to someone who's English.' He continued, before smiling and raising his hands in apology. 'Sorry, of course you can't answer that either, forget I said anything. I'll change the subject. Can you tell us how long we'll be here?'

This time Tilly smiled back. 'As I said we need to make sure that all your documents are as good as they can be. Once we've done that, we'll move you as quickly as possible. Can either of you speak Dutch or French?'

Both men shook their heads and Tilly tried to reassure them. 'Alright, we'll teach you some basics in Dutch and French so you can say the odd words as if in conversation, otherwise it will look odd. You don't have much else to do so make the most of the time you have here to learn what you can. Oh, and try and keep as fit as you can. I know its hard when you can't leave this room, but you can do some press ups, sit ups, that kind of thing to keep the leg muscles active. You have a long way to go.'

'Across the Pyrenees?' Chris met her eyes.

Tilly shrugged. 'I can't tell you that, I only deal with a small part of the journey.' She finished putting the camera away, her thoughts on their long journey ahead. From what she had heard, it was a hard slog, especially now the Krauts patrolled the smugglers tracks across the mountains regularly by aeroplane as well as on foot. But according to Francis the Spanish side was a bit easier now, less chance of the Spanish sending them back or sticking them in their prison camps. Tilly turned back to face them, smiled and held out her hand. 'I'll be back as soon as I have the necessary papers and your instructions.'

'Thank you.' Chris and Harry watched her go.

'I wouldn't do her job for anything.' Harry said thoughtfully. 'Its bad enough getting shot out of the sky, but what she's doing…'

Chris nodded. 'I agree. We'll just have to make sure we don't cause her any trouble.' Harry nodded and the two men settled down to wait.

****

Berlin

Clemens replaced the receiver and stared at his desk, a slight smile on his face. He had eventually decided that he needed to do something about Backer watching his house, things were moving quickly and he didn't need the SS watching his house for whatever reason in case they stumbled on something. But, to his surprise, the answer wasn't what he had been expecting. Backer's superior officer was an old friend and having checked he had telephoned back and told Clemens that there were no orders to that effect. Hearing that, and convinced his friend was telling the truth, Clemens had suggested that Backer was obsessed with his daughter and that was possibly the reason he had been there. His friend had promised to resolve the situation immediately and apologised profusely. Hopefully that would be the end of it.

****

Portsmouth

'Dead?' Bill stared at the Captain in disbelief. 'He can't be... I mean he was fine when he left the pub...' He fell silent.

'I'm very sorry Young. It would seem he was attacked and robbed on his way back to the base. The police found his body this morning but because his identity papers had been stolen it wasn't until the MPs contacted them that they were able to identify him.'

Bill was still looking shocked. 'I should have gone with him...'

The Captain shook his head, a wry smile on his face. 'I doubt he would have appreciated your presence in those circumstances,' he saw Bill's confusion, 'if he was with a woman.' Bill nodded, but he didn't feel any better. He should have looked more carefully when he left the pub. He realised the Captain was continuing. 'We don't know yet if she was involved or whether the person who attacked him was watching in the pub and targeted him that way. But it wasn't your fault, so please don't blame yourself.'

Bill didn't answer. How could he not blame himself? He had gone drinking with a friend and come back alone and his friend had been murdered.

The captain watched him, a thoughtful expression on his face. He had read Young's file, the boy had not had the best of luck. He made a decision. 'You're due some leave Young, some proper leave. Take it now. Two weeks. Go home to your family, have a rest and come back in two weeks. Number One will sort it out for you.'

Bill stared at him in surprise and then nodded. 'Thank you, sir.' He saluted and made his way out of the office, his thoughts back on Bernie. Yet another friend lost and this time he wasn't even at sea.

****

London

Clarissa stared up at the clock again and Tristram laughed. 'Time won't go any quicker if you keep looking at the clock.'

Clarissa smiled. 'Sorry, I'm just so excited. I can't wait to leave.' They had been told to arrive at the theatre at nine o'clock that night and not tell anyone where they were going. Relatives were not allowed to come and see them off as their departure was supposed to be as unobtrusive as possible. Their luggage had gone on ahead, but they still didn't know from which port they were travelling or exactly where they were going, although she was reasonably sure it would be Alexandria.

Tristram smiled back. He understood Clarissa's excitement, the thought of spending a whole year working with her was amazing and then hopefully they would remain together for the rest of their lives. He knew it was too soon to propose to her, so he planned to curb his impatience for at least six months. By then they would both know if they were meant to be together or whether their feelings were just a passing phase. 'How was Nathanial?'

'He waved to me from the nursery window.' She gave a wry smile. 'Fortunately, he's used to me not being there. I think he'd miss Nanny more than me.'

'He'll be safe at Halford which is the important thing, especially now there's much less chance of invasion.'

Clarissa nodded. 'If there'd been any chance of the Krauts invading, I would never have left him. But I know this is the right thing for me to do. I sometimes wish I was a man, then I could go and fight, but I'm not, so this is the best I can do.'

'I'm very glad you're not a man.' Tristram leaned closer, his eyes boring into hers. She stared back and moved towards him. Then his lips were on hers… and the clock chimed.

Clarissa pulled back and laughed. 'Time to go.'

Tristram sighed. 'Saved by the bell…'

'They'll be plenty of time for us to get to know each other.' Clarissa stroked his face tenderly before picking up her handbag and travelling rug and standing up. She took one last glance around the hotel room and walked towards the door.

****

Trent Park

Levi's heart started beating quicker and he almost forgot to write down what was being said. Unless he was mistaken General von Thoma was discussing some type of rocket. He finished writing and hurried up to the office.

'What do you think they're talking about?' Oscar Henderson had his own ideas, but he wanted to see what Levi made of it.

Levi frowned. 'Some kind of long range rocket, maybe a ballistic missile?'

'That's my take on it too.'

'It ties in with the information they learned at Latimer House doesn't it? The stuff that paratrooper said to his cell mate about the sloping launch ramps a few days ago.'

'Yes, only they weren't convinced he wasn't just repeating German propaganda about Hitler's secret weapons programme.' Henderson sighed. They had received information from two agents that the German were working on long range rockets the previous year, but so far they had not been able to verify it.

'But this is General von Thoma…' The General had been captured in North Africa. 'And he's discussing rockets he's actually seen at Kummersdorf West. It's the final proof we needed.' Levi could barely contain his excitement. Henderson thought for a few more seconds then he nodded and picked up the telephone. 'I agree. Get back down there and listen to the previous tapes, see if we've missed anything.'

Levi hurried back downstairs, his thoughts on what he had just heard. The thought of the Germans having long range rockets was terrifying, but the time scale was even worse. He knew the Second Front was being planned but this could affect the date. They could not afford to let the Germans rain rockets down on Britain, someone needed to get over there and find the launch pads and destroy them before they could become active.

****

Berlin

Jacob drove hurriedly towards Clemens' house with the papers his superior had asked him to drop off, his thoughts still on the latest directive stating that any postcards coming from German POWs in the Soviet Union after Stalingrad were to be destroyed and the families informed their relatives were dead. He could not see the point of that, but then he couldn't see the reason for anything the Nazis did. He reached the house, pulled up, climbed out and hurried up the path. He had barely raised his hand to knock when the door swung open, and a man and woman stepped out. Both were thin, their faces sallow, their complexions those of people who spent little time outside. If that had not piqued his interest, their immediate reaction to him, lowering their eyes and scurrying away, left him in no doubt that they were Jewish, although neither was wearing the Jewish star.

'Linus... I wasn't expecting you...' Eva was pale, her eyes wide and he could see the fear on her face. 'My father isn't home yet.'

'I know he sent me with these to drop off...' He knew he shouldn't say anything, but he couldn't help himself. 'Its alright... please don't worry. I haven't seen anything.' He flushed and looked away. Just saying that meant he was tacitly accepting she was breaking the law. He looked back and realised she had stepped aside, and he hurried inside while Eva closed the door.

'They used to work for us... we tried to help them leave the country, but we couldn't get them papers.' Eva gave a sigh of exasperation. 'You'd think someone in my father's position would be able to do anything wouldn't you?' She took his hand. 'You won't say anything will you?'

Jacob smiled into her eyes. 'Of course not.' There was a long silence while he fought with his conscience. He could probably get papers for the couple, but should he risk it?

'They are divers.'

Jacob frowned and Eva gave a brief smile. 'Its slang for Jews who are in hiding.'

'I might be able to help... with documents...' The words escaped before Jacob could stop them and his heart began to beat faster.

Eva's face lit up. 'Really?'

Jacob was still cursing his stupidity. 'You mustn't say anything to your father.'

Eva looked confused.

Jacob squeezed her hand. 'He has enough to worry about. Its best he doesn't know.'

Eva nodded. 'Alright, its our secret.' She smiled and Jacob leant closer. Eva put her arms around his neck and his lips found hers. Before he even realised what was happening, he was kissing her with a passion that she returned and everything else left his mind. All he could think of was how much he wanted to make love to her. He pulled her closer, his tongue exploring her mouth, his fingers sliding down towards her waist. A door banged upstairs suddenly, jolting him out of paradise and he stepped back and stared at her. 'I'm so sorry...'

'Why? Didn't you think I was enjoying it?'

Jacob smiled. 'Well, if you put it like that.' Then he frowned. Although the Major had seemed quite happy for him to chat to Eva in their cellar, he might not approve of anything else. As much as he liked Eva and wanted to get to know her better, he didn't want to alienate her father. 'Do you think your father will mind us being friendly.'

Eva smiled and shook her head. 'He wouldn't have invited you to our house if he didn't trust you and he virtually pushed us together during the raid.' She took his arm. 'Come on, let's go into the drawing room, he will be back soon.' She glanced around then lowered her voice. 'Will you definitely be able to get the papers for me?'

Jacob wished he could turn back the clock, but it was too late. If he said no now it would look suspicious. 'Yes. But remember, it's our secret.'

Eva nodded and Jacob sighed. Getting the papers was not his only problem. If he was going to start courting Eva he would also have to finish with Kara.

****

London

The roll calls commenced with each show being read out in turn and the artists heading out through the stage door to the waiting coaches. Eventually Clarissa and Tristram heard their names and they took their places on the cold coach. The engine started and they headed westwards, but no sooner had they reached Piccadilly Circus than the sirens began to wail. The coach turned down Piccadilly, crossed Hyde Park corner, through Knightsbridge and Kensington to Addison Road station, Olympia, where a train with several empty carriages was waiting. Clarissa and Tristram found themselves seats and she watched as several of her travelling companions investigated the lunchboxes they had been given by ENSA, together with a warning to make them last as they still didn't know their destination.

The carriages shunted up and down the railway, a seemingly endless limbo of sidings leading nowhere, and she began to feel bored. It was stuffy and uncomfortable and too dimly lit to read so Clarissa closed her eyes, leant back against Tristram and dozed off while around her the other entertainers played cards and discussed the war. Eventually the train began to move, jolting her awake, and as dawn broke she lifted the blinds and gazed out. The fields were covered with a delicate white mist hovering over dew sodden grass. In the distance she could see trees hazily outlined against the growing light and for a moment she felt homesick.

As the morning wore on her companions took bets on where they were going, but Clarissa had little doubt they were travelling north so she wasn't surprised when they arrived at Sheffield. She joined the stampede to the canteen hoping for a cup of hot tea, but there was not enough time so five minutes later, complaining bitterly, they were back aboard the train. A little while later they arrived in Liverpool, left the train and headed to a row of coaches where a large crowd was waiting.

As they climbed aboard and found seats Clarissa laughed. 'I thought our departure was to be unobtrusive!'

Tristram grinned. 'Obviously no one told them up here.' They sat down, and as the coach made its way to the docks, he put his arm around her and she snuggled into him while staring out the window at the funnels of ships peeping through the dreary grey buildings. A few moments later they were standing in a shed while officials took their ration books and then they were escorted quickly through customs before reboarding the coaches and being driven to the dockside where their ships were waiting.

Chapter 4

Berlin

Harald Backer stormed out of his superior's office, his face flushed with embarrassment and fury. He had just been told in no uncertain terms to keep away from Eva von Landau or he would find himself on the Easter Front, what was left of it. He wondered who had complained. It must have been Eva although it was unlikely anyone would have taken notice of her, so she must have complained to her father and Clemens had contacted his superior. He could hardly control his rage and as his speed increased so did the thoughts whirring around his brain. He had no intention of keeping away from Eva. She should be with him, she just hadn't seen it yet. But he would have to be careful. The Eastern Front was collapsing, it was the last place he wanted to be especially as he would not be able to keep an eye on Eva if he was thousands of miles away. He would just have to find another way of watching her that didn't involve standing outside her house every morning watching her flirting and batting her eyelashes at Linus Haas.

****

Warrington

'Over sexed, over paid and over here!' Bill finished his beer and glared at the two Americans.

'Look fella, we don't want no trouble, we're just out to have us a good time.'

'Then fuck off and find your own birds, this one's taken.'

The American raised his hands and backed off, but not quickly enough for Bill who lurched menacingly towards him.

Danny sighed. It was rare for their leave to coincide so he had been looking forward to a nice quite evening with his best mate, downing a few pints and maybe picking up a couple of woman, but it appeared Bill had other ideas. Danny had seen that his friend was struggling but had been hoping he could jolly him out of his bad mood. Obviously not. 'Come on Bill leave it, it's not worth getting into trouble for.' Danny grabbed his arm and tried to steer him away, but Bill wasn't interested in peace. He was still mourning Bernie and he'd had several pints of the pub's watered-down beer. The girl he had spent all evening chatting to was paying the Yanks more attention than him and he had gone beyond common sense. He pushed his friend's hand away. 'Fuck off Danny, I'm sick of these bastards stealing our women.'

'Well maybe you should treat them a bit better pal.' The American was no longer backing away. 'Obviously you don't have what it takes to keep them happy.' He grabbed his crotch, thrust his hips forward in a movement that mimicked sex and laughed loudly. His companion joined in and Bill lost it. He launched himself forward, his fist connecting with the American's chin knocking him off his bar stool.

'Enough Bill, we'll have the MPs here.' Danny pulled him back and tried to help the GI to his feet. He was too late. All around them the pub had erupted in chaos, several men were fighting, women screaming, chairs and tables being utilised as weapons. Bill felt a chair come down on his back, knocking him off balance. He spun around and grabbed the nearest thing to hand, a glass and smashed it on the bar.

'Come on then Yank, all fucking talk and late for the war again.'

The American's face contorted, and he swung wildly at Bill who ducked, his wiry frame moving backwards at the same time. For a brief moment common sense penetrated his drunken haze, and he dropped the broken glass and used his fists instead. The two men struggled, throwing punches at each other until eventually the fight spilled out onto the pavement. Bill finally got the better of his opponent, threw several heavy punches at the American before eventually connecting one with the man's chin and knocking him flat on the ground.

He was standing upright, admiring his handiwork when he realised the noise he could hear outside was the whistles of the rapidly approaching MPs. Bill stepped to the door, peered down the darkened street and could just make out several men heading rapidly towards the pub. He put his head back inside the pub and yelled 'Danny we gotta go…' He saw Danny look in his direction, nod briefly and wave his arm, encouraging him to go so Bill staggered back into the road before half running in the opposite direction.

****

Trent Park

Myon finished making the tea and handed Levi and Ovid a mug each. 'They've taken lots of photos of Peenemunde, it definitely appears to be the place where a new rocket programme is underway.'

Ovid nodded. 'I agree. The conversation between General von Arnim and the other German we couldn't identify does seem to back that up.'

'What do you think we'll do about it?' Levi sipped his tea.

'Hopefully get the RAF to bomb it to smithereens.' Myon stirred a spoonful of sugar into his tea. 'Although they may not be able to destroy it all if the main complex is underground.'

Levi stared at him in horror. 'Have you mentioned that?'

Myon nodded. 'Yes. but I think they are still going to try and bomb it first. If that doesn't work they'll have to send some poor sod in to sabotage it.'

'They'd have to know what they were doing though wouldn't they?' Ovid was thoughtful. 'It won't be easy to find an agent with scientific knowledge that also speaks German.' He grinned at Levi. 'I'd forget that you speak German if I were you.'

Levi laughed. 'I don't have the scientific knowledge though.'

'Ovid does. Science was his field don't forget.' Myon finished his tea and was about to say more when he saw the thoughtful expression on Levi's face. He shook his head. 'You have a son to bring up Levi, don't even think about it.'

Levi didn't answer for a few seconds then he looked at Ovid. 'Could you really teach me enough? Enough so that I could help…'

Ovid stared at him then nodded. 'Yes… I could. But Myon's right. Why on earth would you want to risk your life on what could be a suicide mission?'

Levi looked at him, his eyes cold with anger. 'Those bastards murdered Sura. We had to flee our homes, our country, because of them, and they still killed her. I owe them.'

Myon shook his head, then he remembered they were only speculating. With a bit of luck the RAF would finish Peenemunde. Levi stood up, took the mugs to the sink and begun washing up. When he was finished, he would speak to Oscar Henderson about going to Germany. If he couldn't help then he would contact Jacob's friend, Francis Marshall.

******

Berlin

The latest air raid had mainly targeted the factories and workshops in the south west of the city, but it was making life hard for everyone. Eva double checked the streets were quiet before waving Frau Liebersturm and her daughter out and closing the door quickly behind them. Eva had not told Jacob the whole truth about her activities. Two years earlier, Eva and her mother had joined an association of local women who were providing accommodation and food for Jews, and those hiding from the regime for various reasons. The evaders stayed a couple of nights before moving on to the next house and eventually receiving forged documents, so they were able to move around more freely. They were also providing food to a communal supply which was shared out amongst those hiding from the Gestapo. Eva knew they should probably tell her father what they were doing, but her mother had said no, that he might insist they stop, so Eva had said nothing. But things were different now. Linus knew what she was doing, and he had said he would help.

'Have they gone?' Ursula appeared from one of the doors behind her, making her jump.

'Yes Mutti.' Eva looked down and Ursula was immediately suspicious.

'What is it Eva?'

Eva glanced around and indicated the door Ursula had come out of before disappearing through it. Ursula followed, her misgivings growing. She shut the door and turned towards her. 'Eva, what's happened?'

'Linus arrived yesterday… he saw them leaving.'

Ursula paled.

Eva hastened to reassure her. 'Its alright, he said he can help… get us papers. I didn't tell him everything, just that the Ullmans were friends we were helping. He doesn't know about the others.'

Ursula breathed a sigh of relief that Eva hadn't been too careless then realised what her daughter had said. 'Papers? He said he could get papers?' She repeated. 'How?'

Eva shook her head. 'I didn't ask... I am seeing him tomorrow night.' She flushed. 'I could ask then.'

Ursula didn't answer for a moment. 'Be careful Eva. We don't know anything about him.'

'Vati bought him home so he must trust him, and he encouraged Linus to talk to me, didn't he?'

Ursula thought for a moment then nodded. 'Yes, your father does like him, and I can see that you do too, but be careful Eva.' Ursula could tell by her daughter's flushed face that her warning was probably too late. Clemens obviously trusted Linus but she was reasonably sure her husband did not know that his subordinate had access to forged documentation.

'I will, I promise.' Eva relaxed slightly. Now her mother knew she felt better, but she would still be careful not to tell Linus anything else, not until she was sure she could trust him.

******

Liverpool

The ship was enormous and filled to the gunnels with soldiers and sailors crowding up against the rails of every deck. The entertainers had waited for ages but were still unable to climb the gangplank because even more men were arriving, weighed down with heavy equipment. They had missed lunch and had left their ENSA lunchboxes on the train and were now starving. To their relief the dockhands began to distribute peanuts which at least took the edge of their hunger.

'Still excited?' Tristram was tired and he was beginning to wonder if they were doing the right thing.

'Aren't you?' Clarissa was enjoying herself despite her hunger. She watched as the dockhands continued to throw peanuts up at the soldiers packed against the rails and then as a sailor's hat fell into the water between the ship and quayside. One of the dockhands managed to fish it out and threw it back, but despite lots of hands reaching for it, they missed, and the hat fell into the water again. Another dockhand rescued it and threw the cap up, but again the waiting hands missed, much to every one's amusement.

Tristram laughed, his earlier melancholy gone. 'At least it passes the time.' He put his arms around her and she snuggled into him. As long as she was with Tristram, she didn't mind how long it took.

Finally, it was time for the ENSA entertainers to board the ship, and to Clarissa's delight each of the ladies was cheered by the sailors as they walked up the gangplank.

****

Trent Park

'Goodness Levi haven't you finished yet. Its late.' Oscar Henderson finished putting some papers in his desk drawer before turning his attention back to Levi and frowning. Levi looked on edge, as if something important had happened. 'What's the matter? Is there more information about the weapons?'

Levi shook his head. 'No, but it is connected to that.' He took a deep breath. 'It's possible the important part of the construction plant is underground. If that is the case then bombing from the air won't destroy it. The only definite way is to sabotage it from the inside. I would like to volunteer to do that. Obviously I speak German, but I also speak Polish.' Levi crossed his fingers behind his back. 'At Hay there wasn't much else to do so we set up a sort of university and I learnt several languages including Polish.' It was true, but he was nothing like as proficient in the language as he was making it sound, but if Oscar agreed Levi was sure he could resolve that problem. He carried on/ 'With Poland so close I am assuming that they are probably the only resistance near the island of Usedom. I know most will speak German, but it would be useful to be able to understand their language too. And Ovid was a scientist before he came here... to Britain I mean. He could teach me what I need to know... I'm a quick learner.'

Oscar stared at him in astonishment and eventually answered. 'Its very brave of you to volunteer Levi, but you don't know anything about being a spy, working undercover.'

'There's time for me to learn.' Levi leaned forward and spoke earnestly. 'The bombing might work in which case you won't need me, but if it doesn't you would have someone ready to send in.'

Oscar sat back and thought over the sparse information they had about Peenemunde... even with the photos. Levi was young, smart, intelligent and had obviously thought this through. 'Leave it with me, I'll pass your suggestion up the line.' His eyes bore into Levi's. 'In the meantime, it wouldn't hurt to get fit...,' he smiled, 'and perhaps learn some science.'

****

Warrington

Abigail had spent most of the evening in the pub staring at the good looking young sailor and wishing he would come and speak to her, but he had remained at the bar chatting to the factory girls. Eventually she had given up trying to catch his eye and, standing up reluctantly, she had decided to go home. Abigail had opened the door and was halfway into the street when she heard the row breaking out at the bar and she had turned back just in time to see the sailor hitting the brash American. Abigail watched as the fight escalated, before leaving and heading home, her thoughts on the sailor. Perhaps it was a good thing he hadn't spoken to her. Her mother and brother wouldn't approve of her getting involved with someone who liked fighting.

Abigail had almost reached home when she heard running footsteps behind her. Turning, she had seen the sailor racing towards her and forgetting her earlier thoughts she had seized her chance and opened her front door.

'This way.'

The voice was female, urgent and loud in the quiet street. Bill stopped and peered into the gloom.

'Quick this way,'

He realised she was holding open a door and he dived through before she quickly closed it and they were in darkness. He could hear her breathing, but he couldn't see anything, and he waited impatiently for his night vision to clear. Outside he heard running footsteps and then he felt her close to him. 'Shhh…'

His eyes were clearing now, and he could make out more. They were in a hallway of some sort. The girl had long hair but that was all he could see. 'Thank…' He began before she clamped her hand across his mouth.

'My mother…' she whispered urgently, and he nodded. Now his vision had cleared he could see her more clearly, long dark hair, brown eyes and a big smile. She looked to be about his age. He grinned back but remained silent. The footsteps echoed up the street and then all was quiet. The girl carefully opened the door and peered out. 'Alright. Its safe now.'

Bill stepped into the street and smiled at her. 'Thank you.' He took care to keep his voice low. 'What's your name?'

'Abigail… Abigail Saunders.'

'I'm Bill Young.' He glanced down at his watch, but it was too dark to see. 'I think I'd better go, but could I see you again?'

Abigail blushed. 'Yes, that would be nice. I work in the grocer's shop, at the end of the road.'

Bill grinned. 'I'll be in to see you later.'

He glanced up at the house and memorised the number before heading off down the street, a big smile on his face. Now all he had to do was to avoid the MPs, find Danny and get home.

Abigail watched him for several seconds before disappearing back indoors and closing the door. She headed slowly upstairs, a dreamy expression on her face. She would never sleep now, she was much too excited.

******

Liverpool

It had taken them ages to find their cabins and to Clarissa's disappointment she was sharing a four berth cabin with three other girls. She realised now that expecting to have a berth to herself on a crowded troop ship had been rather stupid, but it meant that finding time alone with Tristram was going to be more difficult than she had imagined.

'Bit crowded isn't it? I'm Samantha Halliday, Sammy, and this is my sister June and the other member of our act, Renee Drolet. We're the Swinging Sisters.' Sammy was in her late thirties, a well-built woman with coiffured auburn hair and a strong cockney accent.

'Clarissa. I'm a singer too.'

Sammy laughed and rolled her eyes slightly. 'Yes, we know. We're really excited about sharing with you, aren't we?'

June and Renee nodded, and after a brief hesitation Clarissa smiled back, deciding she must have imagined the sarcastic tone in Sammy's voice. June was a younger version of Sammy with darker hair and Renee was quite thin with dark blonde hair and appeared nervous. 'How long have you been singing?'

'June and I started in night clubs in the West End about ten years ago, when I was young!' She laughed. 'Renee joined us a year ago.' She opened her suitcase and began unpacking. 'As you and Renee are the youngest perhaps you wouldn't mind having the top bunks?'

Clarissa nodded. 'Yes, of course.' Renee nodded but didn't answer. 'Which side do you want?'

Renee looked surprised to be asked and shrugged. Clarissa tried again. 'I'll take this side then?' Renee nodded and moved her suitcase to her bunk and began unpacking. Clarissa did the same. There was very little storage space, a drawer and shelf each, but the cabin was freshly painted and smelt new and clean. She finished, climbed up onto her bunk and lay down. The berth was surprisingly comfortable, or perhaps she was just so exhausted that even sleeping on the floor would have been inviting.

'Don't leave your suitcase there Renee there's a good girl, or one of us will trip over it.' Sam's voice was quite firm, and there was an edge to it that hadn't been apparent in her early conversation with Clarissa. She opened her eyes and sat up in time to see Renee moving her suitcase to the side.

'Goodness, I'm sorry mine's in the way too.' Clarissa climbed down carefully and moved hers next to Renee's. She was about to say more when a bell rang.

'Dinner, thank goodness for that. I'll waste away if I don't eat soon!' Sammy was laughing again. 'Come on ladies, let's go. Apparently ENSA have the first sitting, together with the nurses and a small group of RAF officers, at least that's what I was told.'

Clarissa grinned. 'You're better informed than me.'

'Well, I bag at least one of the RAF officers.' Sammy continued. 'What about you Clarissa?'

'I'm alright thank you. I have Tristram to keep me company. He's my partner.' Clarissa was so looking forward to seeing him again she didn't notice the looks that passed between Sammy and June.

****

Warrington

'Have you worked here long?' Bill had been waiting outside the grocer's for Abigail to come out for lunch. He took her hand as he spoke and her heart beat a little faster. To his relief Danny had also escaped the MPs and had been waiting anxiously for him at home, concerned that he had been arrested. When Bill told him that he had met a girl Danny had burst out laughing, patted him on the back and offered him the remains of some scotch he had liberated from the pub under cover of the fighting. The two men had finished the alcohol and then gone to bed, Bill thinking about Abigail and Danny relieved that his friend seemed to have recovered from the anger and depression that had led to the fight that night.

'A couple of years.' Abigail smiled at him. 'Mr Rodgers is a friend of my older brother, Ernie.'

'Can I ask how old you are Abigail?' In the morning light she looked younger than she had the previous night.

'I'm eighteen.' She looked worried. 'I'm not too young for you am I?'

Bill laughed. 'No of course not, I'm twenty two. I hope that's not too old?'

Abigail shook her head. 'No, I think that's a good age. How long have you been a sailor?'

Bill chatted away as they walked to the park and by the time they had found a bench to themselves he was really enjoying himself. Abigail reminded him of Nora, the same innocent zest for life. He had forgotten what it was like to spend time with a girl that he wasn't paying for. He watched as she laughed, her face animated, her eyes full of life and for the first time in ages he no longer needed a drink to relax him.

'Is something wrong?'

Bill frowned. 'No, why? Should there be?'

'You were staring at me.'

Bill laughed. 'Sorry, I was just thinking how much I was enjoying myself. It's been a while…' He fell silent.

Abigail reached across and took his hand but didn't say anything. Bill squeezed her hand and stared into her eyes. 'Can I kiss you?' The request took him almost as much by surprise as it did her.

Abigail blushed. 'Yes please.'

Bill smiled and leaned towards her. His lips brushed against hers and she closed her eyes. He increased the pressure, and she opened her mouth, returning his passion with her own. Bill forgot the war, forgot everything he'd seen and disappeared into a place where there was no time, no pain, nothing except pleasure. Eventually he pulled back and smiled into her eyes which were now open. Neither spoke and he leaned forward again, lost in a paradise he had never known existed.

This time it was Abigail who pulled away. 'I have to get back to work or I will be late.'

He helped her up. 'I'll pick you up from the house tonight… if that's alright of course? We can go to the cinema or for a drink… whatever you would like to do.' They began walking back to the grocers.

'The pictures would be lovely. Do you know what's on?'

'No, but as long as I'm with you it doesn't matter.'

Abigail laughed. 'Does that line work with all the girls?'

Bill laughed as well. 'It's the first time I've ever said that and meant it.' He realised he was telling the truth. He put his arm around her and they walked the rest of the way in silence, Bill wishing his leave could last for ever, Abigail unable to believe someone as worldly and exciting as Bill was actually interested in her.

****

En Route

The dining room was several decks below their cabin and as they walked down the men on the lower decks came out to the staircases to watch.

'It must be awful being cramped down here in these airless conditions.' Clarissa spoke softly to Renee.

'I would hate it. Presumably they will be allowed up on deck to get exercise once we get underway?' Renee answered and then blushed.

'I would imagine so or they won't be in any condition to fight. I wonder why only the RAF officers are allowed to join us. I bet the Army officers aren't too pleased.'

'I suppose so. Still, it does mean they can have a lie in at breakfast.'

Clarissa laughed. 'That's true. Oh look, there's Tristram. I'll see you later Renee.' She gave Sammy and June a quick wave and made her way through the thronging crowd towards Tristram who was already looking for her.

'Hello Clarissa, how's your cabin.' Tristram smiled at her, his eyes alight with love. 'I'm sharing with three other men.'

'It's alright I suppose. I'm sharing with the Swinging Sisters.'

Tristram sighed. 'So much for spending more time together then.'

Clarissa took his hand. 'We'll just have to make the most of the days and wait until we get to Cairo, or wherever it is we're going.'

They made their way through the dining room and finally found a table with spaces. The meal was delicious, and Clarissa ate everything on her plate. Afterwards they went to the officer's lounge where they drank lemonade and played cards.

'I can't believe there's no alcohol on the ship.' Sammy's voice carried loudly across the room and there was a murmur of assent from everyone else.

Tristram smiled at Clarissa and leaned forward. 'I don't mind not having a drink, as long as I can spend time with you.'

Clarissa gazed into his eyes and felt the warmth flood her body. It was time to let go of the past and embrace the future and she no longer cared who knew. She leaned towards him and her lips touched his. Tristram was taken by surprise but he soon recovered and returned her kiss with growing passion. He was vaguely aware of the room growing quiet before the volume gradually resumed.

Chapter 5

Amsterdam

Tilly crossed the road and hurried towards the shops. She hoped the two RAF airmen were still following, but it was much too dangerous to check so she kept her eyes ahead and tried to look relaxed. Her job today was to take the two airmen to Brussels where someone else would collect them and take them on the next stage of their journey home. She had delivered the papers a few days earlier, along with the stories that went along with them. To her surprise the men had used their time well, both now speaking some Dutch, enough to make them sound like they could answer in conversations anyway. She had collected them today and once she arrived in Brussels, she would be leaving them in the capable hands of Pascal, providing he turned up of course. There was always the chance that something would go wrong, and if it did, she would have to improvise.

Tilly entered the station and made her way to the Brussels train. There was nothing unusual that she could see so she carried on towards the barrier. A few moments later she had passed through the security checks with no difficulty and was making her way along the platform to one of the benches where she sat down. She waited a few moments, then glanced casually behind her. To her relief Chris and Harry were sitting down on a seat near her. A few moments later the train eased into the station and pulled up amidst clouds of billowing steam.

Tilly stood up and made her way on board, found a seat, and sat down. She pulled out her newspaper and once it was open, she peered over the top and breathed another sigh of relief. Chris and Harry were seated on the opposite side of the carriage and studiously avoiding looking at her. Tilly glanced at the newspaper, but her attention was focused on the station, searching for any signs of the security forces. Eventually the train eased away from the platform and she relaxed slightly. Unless the Germans had boarded further down the train, out of her sight, they should all be safe until the next stop. She glanced out of the window and watched the flat countryside flash by. In the reflection of the glass she could see the two airmen, one reading his newspaper, the other apparently dozing. Harry glanced up and their eyes met briefly before she looked away and down at her watch. At least the airmen were English this time. The last two she had taken to Belgium had been American and had needed repeated reminders to walk and act more like European, their mannerisms were so different it invariably gave them away. The connecting train had been running late and to kill some time they had gone into a canteen where she'd had to remind them to use a knife and fork to eat instead of cutting the food up and then eating with just a fork.

Tilly allowed a small sigh to escape her lips before resuming her vigil. She wasn't sure what was more stressful, escorting escaping airmen and other *engelandvaaders* around the countryside or spying on German units and sending back wireless messages to London. A wry smile crossed her face. There probably wasn't much difference if she was honest. Day to day life in occupied Holland was nothing like living in England. There were so many things she had to be aware of, she could never relax.

****

Warrington

'Pleased to meet you Ernie.' To Bill's surprise Abigail's brother was also in the Royal Navy.

'And you Bill.' The two men shook hands then Ernie said what was in his mind. 'I hope you're going to treat my sister with respect.'

Bill looked horrified. 'Of course I am.' If his intentions towards Abigail hadn't been honourable, he would have finished it now he had met Ernie. He would never mess a fellow sailor about. 'I really like your sister.'

Ernie grinned. 'Good, it's your round.'

Bill laughed and ordered three beers. 'So what ship are you on?'

Ernie laughed. 'You know I can't tell you that. Loose lips etc…'

'He's an air gunner and wireless operator.' Abigail returned from the Ladies and began sipping her half pint of beer.

Bill frowned. 'Air gunner?'

'Fleet Air Arm, I'm an air gunner on a Swordfish, catapulting off merchant ships.'

Bill looked at him with renewed respect. He had heard about the Catapult Armed Merchant ships and their aircraft. 'Christ, that's a bit hairy isn't it?'

Ernie shrugged. 'Isn't everything?' He inclined his head slightly towards Abigail and Bill understood. Ernie didn't want to worry his sister.

'Yeah, even going out for a drink can be dangerous.' He winked at Abigail who blushed. Ernie was watching and he smiled.

'Right, I'll leave you two love birds to enjoy yourselves.' He downed the rest of his pint and stood up. 'Perhaps we could meet up tomorrow Bill, men only!'

Bill raised his glass. 'Yeah, I'd like that. Here, about midday?'

Ernie nodded. 'See you tomorrow. Night Abi, don't let him keep you out too late.'

Abigail stood up and kissed him on the cheek. 'Night Ernie.' She turned back to Bill. 'He obviously likes you. He's never wanted to go drinking with any of my boyfriends before… not that there have been very many…' Abigail flushed, and Bill grinned.

'Its probably the Navy thing, you know… having a connection.' Bill finished the rest of his pint and tried to ignore the voice in his head warning him not to get too close to Abigail or her brother or he might jinx them.

****

Tiergarten, Berlin

Clemens stared at the mounting paperwork on his desk, but his thoughts were elsewhere. His instincts had told him that Linus could be trusted, or he would not have taken him home and then encouraged a friendship between his subordinate and his daughter. But that was before he had found out that Ursula and Eva had been risking everything to help Jews and others escape the regime. That news had been bad enough, but Linus' offer to help furnish these escapers with paperwork was much more concerning. Had he been completely wrong? Was Linus a spy for the regime? Did they know what von Stauffenberg was planning? He shuddered.

The very thought that he could have been harbouring an SS spy… the pencil in his hand snapped and made him jump. He wanted to confront Linus but not here, not in the office which might be bugged. His home wasn't the ideal place either, but there was nowhere else… He smiled. Of course, their summer house by the river was secluded, shrouded by trees and the village was unlikely to be busy with its normal summer visitors. And if he didn't like Linus' answers…

****

Trent Park

Levi finished writing up one of the pile of tapes on his desk, sat back and stretched his arms above his head. Now he was spending an hour every morning running in the park he noticed how stiff he became just sitting at his desk for hours on end. But he didn't have any more time to spare as he was also spending two hours each evening studying with Ovid. His days and evenings were full, but he did still have one problem he wanted to address; the language. His Polish was probably much too basic to be of any real use despite what he had told Oscar, and if he was to work with the only resistance in the area, the Armia Krajowal who had provided the original information about Peenemunde, it would be really useful to improve and he needed to do so quickly. There were plenty of Polish soldiers in London and he could have made friends with them, but he was concerned that they would want to know why a German Jew wanted to speak Polish or that his quest for Polish lessons might reach Oscar and ruin his chances of being chosen for this mission. Ovid had suggested he find a Polish girlfriend which seemed like a much better idea, but so far he hadn't had any success.

'Afternoon Levi!' Myon put his head around the door. 'I think I have the answer to your problem.'

Levi sat back twisting the pencil in his hand. 'And what problem is that?'

'A Polish girlfriend of course… well maybe just a friend, but she is Polish.'

Levi grinned. 'Sounds perfect.'

'Good I'll take you to meet her tonight. See you at seven. I'll tell Ovid you will be late for your lesson.' Myon disappeared and Levi went back to listening to the latest tapes. Most of them were full of irrelevancies but every now and then something came up that was important. His biggest challenge was to forget anything to do with rockets and concentrate on what was actually being said.

****

Berlin

Jacob glanced at the clock and took a breath. Kara would be here soon and then he would have to tell her that he didn't want to see her anymore. Fortunately, she had made it clear that she was only interested in having some fun, so at least he didn't have to worry about breaking her heart. For a moment his thoughts drifted back to Nora and he wondered how she was getting on. He felt bad about the way he had ended things with her, but he hadn't been given a lot of choice. *Coward* his inner voice yelled at him and he sighed. He could have written to her saying that things were over, but instead he had taken the easy way out and used the war and his new job as an excuse. Hopefully, she was enjoying her life back in Warrington and had found someone to treat her with the love and respect she deserved.

As always when he thought of England and his past life Tilly came into his mind and he wondered what she was doing now. He couldn't see Francis letting someone as talented as Tilly go. He was bound to have found her something else to do, although he couldn't imagine what as he was reasonably sure the British security forces had found all the German spies and fifth columnists by now. He frowned. In which case there was a chance she was working somewhere else, maybe doing something similar to him. His heart palpitated wildly for a moment and he had to breathe several times before the beat returned to something resembling normality. The thought of Tilly being in danger scared him to death. He would rather die a hundred times than let anything happen to her.

Jacob gave a wry smile. He had thought he was in love with Eva, but obviously his feelings for Tilly had never really died. Was it possible to love two women at the same time?

****

Trent Park

Levi reached out a hand to shake that of the woman standing in front of him and found himself staring into sparkling blue eyes framed by long straight blonde hair. 'Hello, I'm Levi.' Marta smiled.

Levi swallowed nervously and tried to pull himself together.

'Marta Broz.' She shook his hand and her smile broadened. 'Myon says you wish to practice your Polish.'

'Yes, that's right…' He hoped she wasn't going to ask why as he didn't want to lie to her.

'Być może moglibyśmy wypić drinka?' *Perhaps we could have a drink then?* She had switched to Polish and it took Levi a couple of seconds to translate, not having heard the language for over two years.

'Tak, co chcesz?' *Yes, what would you like?* He said slowly.

'Some beer will be fine, thank you.' Marta smiled. 'You have very little accent which is good. I imagine its more vocabulary you need.' When Levi nodded, several second later after he'd translated it in his head, she continued, 'If we only talk in Polish from now on, you will soon find it automatic and you will begin thinking in the language.'

Levi nodded. 'Like I do in English.'

'Oh, you aren't English?' Marta looked surprised.

Levi ordered the drinks and then answered her. 'No, I'm German…' He saw her shock and hastened to explain. 'Jewish. We got out before the war.'

Marta sighed. 'I'm sorry, that must have been very hard for you.'

Levi paid for the drinks and steered her towards an vacant table before shrugging. 'I am happy here, well reasonably…' He fell silent not wanting to tell her about Sura, not yet. He changed the subject. 'What about you? Presumably you fled the Nazis too?' The language was coming more naturally now.

Marta sipped from her half pint glass. 'Yes, my parents were killed, and my brother and I escaped. He is in the RAF.'

'I'm sorry… about your parents.'

Marta stared down into her drink. 'The Nazis took hostages after the resistance blew up a railway line to one of their factories. My parents hadn't done anything…' She blinked back tears, sipped her drink and looked back at him. 'Let's talk about something else.'

Levi nodded. 'Why don't you tell me about your life before the war. That way I can listen and learn.'

Marta smiled. 'Where do I start?'

'Where did you live?'

Marta closed her eyes for a moment and then began speaking, telling him about her childhood and working her way forward. At first Levi had to concentrate hard to understand, and he had to interrupt her several times to make sure he had the correct meaning, but after a while he grew used to her accent and didn't need to ask as many questions.

****

Warrington

'Thank you for a lovely evening.' Abigail smiled up into his face and Bill leaned over and brushed a strand of hair out of her eyes.

'We didn't do much, perhaps we could go to the pictures tomorrow night?'

'I'd like that.' Abigail felt a thrill as she realised he wanted to see her again.

'Why don't you have a look and see what's on tomorrow.' Bill sighed. 'I know normally we wouldn't rush things, but I've only got a couple of days left and I don't want to waste it.'

'We could meet in the morning and go to the park and then have lunch together if you like? That way we would be making the most of your time.' Abigail blushed. She couldn't believe she'd been so forward.

Bill's face lit up. 'That would be wonderful. I wanted to suggest it but didn't want to make you uncomfortable... by pushing things I mean.'

'I don't want to waste any of your leave either Bill.'

He could see her lips in the light of the half moon and, forgetting all his intentions to avoid getting too close, he leant towards her.

Abigail closed her eyes and kissed him back. Bill eventually pulled away. 'I'd better walk you home.'

Her spirits dropped, but she nodded anyway. She turned away. Bill grabbed her arm and pulled her back towards him. 'On the other hand...'

****

Berlin

'You're finishing with me?' Kara stared at him in shock. 'Why? Is there someone else?'

Jacob hesitated before answering. It would not be too long before word got round that he was seeing Eva, but as it was none of Kara's business, he saw no reason to tell her. 'We've had lots of fun Kara, but it was never meant to be serious, was it?'

'There is someone else isn't there?' Jacob was surprised she was being so persistent. He really hadn't thought she was that interested in him. But Berlin was too small for his relationship with Eva to remain a secret, certainly in the circles he was mixing in anyway. And he couldn't afford to upset the Major so eventually he nodded. 'Yes. I'm sorry, I don't want to upset you, but I don't want to lie to you either.'

Kara didn't answer for several seconds. She was still in shock. 'Can I ask who?'

He shook his head. 'I don't think that's important, its not someone you know.' He was feeling guilty as she obviously cared for him more than he had realised, but it was too late now. He looked down at the floor and waited for her to leave. He hadn't wanted to hurt her, but he had no intention of trying to keep two relationships going, not when his feelings for Eva were so strong.

'We could still see each other occasionally... for old time's sake... After all we did have fun didn't we?'

Jacob looked horrified. Why on earth would Kara want to humiliate herself like that? 'I don't think that would be a very good idea Kara. It wouldn't be fair on either of you.'

'No, no of course not.' Kara walked slowly towards the door. Jacob breathed a sigh of relief and began to work out how he could persuade Niklas to provide forged papers for Eva's Jews. But first he needed to set up a meeting.

Kara walked slowly home, thoughts rushing around her head as she tried to work out how to tell Backer that Linus Haas had dumped her. If only Linus wasn't such an honest man. Her offer to see him only occasionally had been genuine. There would have been no need for Backer to know anything then. Kara shivered. Her dislike of Backer was not feigned, nor was the story of him raping her a lie. He terrified her. Maybe she could pretend a little longer, give her time to think or to get away before he found out the truth.

Chapter 6

Brussels

Heinz paced his office and tried to keep his temper in check. The courier was proving surprisingly resistant and he was no further forward. He sat down and glanced at the short message from the informer giving him the information about the man, but also stating that some more airmen were due to be moved within the next few days. Unfortunately, the informant had not given enough specific details for him to find these airmen without first breaking the courier. He stared at the writing and thought hard. The information had come from the Netherlands so he could assume that the airmen were also coming from there and the quickest way was by train. He had placed men at the station to carefully check anyone who was coming from Amsterdam, but he would prefer to know exactly who he was looking for. Perhaps he should take a walk down to the station himself.

****

US Burtonwood

'Are you alright Nora?' Jessica sounded concerned.

'Yes, I'm fine. Just tired. I didn't sleep very well.'

'Perhaps you should find yourself a boyfriend. Since you went out with that soldier you haven't been out with anyone? Are you missing him? I know he was with the men who were moved overseas somewhere, India I think.'

Nora paled. 'I didn't go out with him. He just offered to walk me home and no, I'm not missing him.'

Jessica stared at her for several seconds, but then the canteen filled up again and she didn't have a further chance to question Nora.

Nora concentrated on serving the airmen, grateful the American uniforms were a different colour to those of the regiment that guarded the air force bases, but she barely spoke to them.

'Are you alright ma'am?'

Nora started and looked up into clear blue eyes, a tall handsome man with a charming smile. She made an effort to respond, she was supposed to laugh and joke with the men, not snarl at them. 'Yes, thank you. What can I get you?'

He shrugged and ordered his meal before trying again. 'Are you quite sure you're ok? You can tell me to mind my own business if you like, but I hate to see someone as pretty as you suffering?'

Nora sighed. 'I'm fine honestly. Now, if there's nothing else?'

He smiled and gave a half salute. 'Message received and understood!' He picked up his tray. 'If you need someone to talk to, I'm a very good listener. My name's Hank, Hank Layman.'

Nora nodded but didn't answer. The last think she was likely to do was to trust another man, even if he was American.

****

Brussels

The journey from Amsterdam had been uneventful. Tilly alighted the train and walked slowly to the barrier. She was aware of the two fliers walking some distance behind her and she hoped they remembered what she had told them. They had practiced answering the usual questions several times, she would just have to hope the guards asked the normal questions. This was the second time she had brought airmen through the station and previously the guards had only given her own papers a cursory glance. As she moved forward she realised that the guards were taking much longer than they had last time to check documents. Tilly peered ahead, her eyes searching for Pascal on the other side of the barrier, but he was nowhere to be seen. It was possible he was late, but Tilly didn't think so. Her instincts were screaming at her that something was wrong. She took another step, her brain frantically looking for an alternative course of action. The train they had alighted from was not due to go anywhere else. It would just go back to Amsterdam. There was no way of reaching another platform without going through the barrier.

'Papers!' It was too late. Tilly was at the barrier. She handed over her documents and hoped her nerves weren't showing. Then her heart began to thump painfully. Tilly ignored the dizziness that threatened to overwhelm her and decided her only chance was to take control of the situation. She switched to German and called out loudly, 'Jonathan? Is that really you?'

****

US Army Airforce Burtonwood

'Are you sure you're alright Nora? You haven't been yourself for weeks.' The two girls were washing up and it was the first chance Jessica had to speak to her friend without anyone else being around.

'I'm perfectly fine, just leave it!' Nora snapped and then her face crumpled, and she burst into noisy tears.

Jessica immediately put down the drying up cloth and flung her arms around Nora. 'What on earth is it Nora? Is it your brother? Has something happened to him?'

Nora shook her head, but she was sobbing too much to speak. Her body was shaking, and Jessica felt helpless. 'Please tell me Nora.'

Nora shook her head, but Jessica persisted. Eventually she gave in. 'He raped me.' The relief of finally saying the words out was surprising, but short lived.

Jessica's mouth flew open in shock. 'The soldier?' She eventually gasped.

Nora nodded. 'Yes.' She wiped her eyes and stared at the ground. 'He pushed me into one of the huts…' She fell silent.

'Oh Nora, I'm so sorry.' Jessica held her tight.

'You warned me.' Nora gave a harsh laugh, then as she saw Jessica's horrified expression the tears started again.

'Did you report it?' Jessica spoke eventually.

Nora shook her head. 'He said he'd kill me if I told anyone. I didn't know he was being posted overseas… Then when I found out that they'd gone it was too late. I was terrified no one would believe me.' Her face crumpled again. 'I didn't even know his name…'

Jessica held her tight and didn't say anything. She had never seen Nora so desolate and she had no idea how to comfort her. Her friend had always been so happy.

'But that's not the worst of it.' Nora pulled away, blew her nose and wiped away her tears again before turning anguished eyes on her friend. 'I'm pregnant.'

****

Trent Park

'So they don't need me?' Levi stared at Oscar in exasperation and frustration.

'No, the RAF raids appear to have done the trick, although they took a lot of casualties. Its slowed up production considerably. The Americans will be carrying out raids on them too so there's no need to send in any teams to work with the local resistance. I'm sorry, I know you were hoping for a different outcome.'

Levi sighed. 'Obviously I'm delighted that the Nazis have been stopped but yes, I did want to do more. I feel like I am wasting my time here.'

Oscar shrugged. 'You're doing a very valuable job Levi.'

'But I'm not fighting Nazis, not stuck here.' Levi realised he wasn't going to get any further so he turned away. 'I'll get back to work then.'

Oscar watched him go, sat back in his chair and thought hard. Levi was an invaluable member of staff, but he could be replaced. It hadn't escaped his notice that Levi had been training to get himself fit, had taken science lessons and had even found a Polish girlfriend to help him improve his language skills. There had to be somewhere that a man of his talents could be used more profitably. He picked up the telephone.

******

Brussels

Heinz stared at Tilly in disbelief. 'Tilly?'

'Jonathan? I can't believe it's you.' Tilly grabbed her papers, shoved past the men at the barrier and stepped towards him, gambling that given his uniform the guards would not stop her. She was right. They were so confused by her actions that they did not move at all. 'I'm so pleased to see you.' There had been no time to warn the two airmen, but she could only hope they took the opportunity to disappear. She turned her full attention to Kessel and gave him the benefit of a beaming smile.

'I got hold of some false papers and managed to get out England after you disappeared, but I only got as far as Holland.' She shook her head in shock. 'I still can't believe you're here.'

Heinz was still staring at her in disbelief, his mind racing. Had Tilly been a plant all the time or was she really the person she had been pretending to be? She certainly seemed pleased to see him. 'Why didn't you tell the German authorities in Holland who you were?'

Tilly looked confused. 'I did think of that, but I wasn't sure they would believe me. I wanted to ask for you, but I only had your English name.' She gave a wry smile. 'Obviously its not your real name, but I didn't know who you were or who you worked for. I was scared they would think I was some sort of spy and lock me up.'

Heinz stared at her, she did appear to be telling the truth, but… 'Heinz Kessel… that's my real name.' He took her arm. 'Let's go to my office and we can have some coffee.'

'That would be wonderful.' Tilly sounded so enthusiastic his doubts began to fade. 'Now I've finally found you, you can get me something useful to do.'

'All in good time…' He let go of her arm and led the way out of the station. Tilly followed without looking back. She could only hope the airmen found their way onto the next train safely. They had been told the route, and also to continue on their own if their courier was arrested or the next one didn't turn up. She pushed them from her mind and concentrated on her own problem. She had to convince Kessel that she was a patriotic German and somehow get word back to Francis that she had found him, or rather, he had found her.

Chris watched with horror as their escort suddenly smiled at the officer in the black uniform on the other side of the barrier, began speaking German loudly and then walked off with him. He waited with baited breath for the Germans to arrest them, but nothing happened. Their courier disappeared out of the station with the German, still chatting away, the guards at the barrier accepted their papers and waved them through and Chris realised they were on their own. He couldn't speak to Harry because they dare not communicate in English, so instead he looked up at the departure board and hunted for the train they need to go to Paris. He exchanged glances with Harry, indicated the platform number they needed, and the two men made their way quickly to the next barrier where they produced their papers again.

Five minutes later they were on the train, unable to converse with each other and with no idea how they would find the next courier.

Chapter 7

Francis replaced the receiver and leant back in his chair. He was inclined to agree with Oscar that Levi was wasted at Trent Park. There were plenty of older men who could do what he was doing. He stood up, walked towards the filing cupboard, hunted for Levi's file and then returned to his desk with it. Levi spoke several languages, his time in Hay had been spent well. Having an active mind he had needed to do something to keep himself occupied, and learning languages had obviously appealed to him. As well as Polish, German and English he also spoke French, Israeli, Spanish, Greek and Dutch. Francis frowned. Perhaps he could send him to Holland to help Tilly. Then he remembered Kessel and shook his head. There was nothing to say that Kessel had ever seen Levi, but he couldn't take the risk. It was also much too dangerous to send him back to Germany although any occupied country would be a risk because he was Jewish. Francis shook his head slowly. No, perhaps it would be better to use Levi as a special agent, drop him in and out of places, not staying in one area too long. Francis smiled and picked up the receiver. He would have to make sure Levi had some proper training first.

******

USAAF Burtonwood

'You'll have to tell your parents.' Jessica sipped her tea. The two girls were sitting at the kitchen table in the canteen drinking the hot strong tea Jessica had made. Nora was calmer now and relieved that the truth was finally out in the open. For the first time in months she didn't feel alone.

'They'll be so disappointed in me.'

Jessica stared at her. 'It wasn't your fault Nora. They'll be shocked at first but I'm sure they'll support you.'

Nora stared into her tea and shook her head. 'I'm not sure they will. My father was born in Ireland. The church never takes a woman's side. Its always her fault.'

'But you couldn't stop him. He was much bigger than you...' Jessica fell silent not wanting to remind her friend.

'I didn't try. I was too scared. He said he would kill me if I didn't do what he wanted.' She sighed. 'I've gone over and over it and I wish I'd let him kill me now.'

Jessica looked shocked. 'Nora please don't say that.'

Nora shrugged. 'Why not? Its true. If I'd fought back he would have killed me and then I wouldn't be in this mess. Even if he had raped me, I couldn't have got pregnant if I was dead.' She stood up suddenly and began pacing up and down, her breathing ragged, her head swimming.

Jessica stood up too, grabbed hold of Nora and held her tight. 'Take deep breaths Nora, it will be alright I promise. I can come with you when you tell your parents if you like.'

Nora gradually regained control and her breathing lengthened out. 'Thank you, but not yet. I can't tell then yet.'

'Alright. Whenever you are ready, just let me know.' Jessica hugged Nora again and prayed she was right about Nora's parents. Nora really needed their support. If they blamed their daughter and didn't help her, Jessica didn't know what her friend might do.

****

Berlin

Jacob stared out of the car window and wondered where they were going. When Clemens had indicated that he wanted to talk privately, Linus had assumed that they were going to his house, so it wasn't until they turned off and began heading out in the countryside that he began to worry. He glanced at Clemens, but the Major's face was closed, his attention focused on the road and on frequently checking the mirror. Jacob frowned. 'Are we being followed sir?'

Clemens looked at him in surprise before returning his attention to the road. 'Why? Should we be?' He asked eventually.

Jacob shrugged and stared ahead. 'No reason sir, except you keep looking in the mirrors.'

'Habit. A sign of the times.'

Jacob gave a wry smile but didn't answer. He relaxed slightly and gazed out at the passing scenery. It was rare he had the opportunity to see the German countryside so he might as well enjoy it.

Clemens checked the mirrors again and then Linus. His subordinate appeared completely relaxed now he had said he was just checking behind him out of habit. He hoped he was wrong because he liked Linus and he knew Eva did.

Half an hour later he pulled up outside the small house in the isolated village. As he'd expected the place was deserted, the other holiday homes appeared vacant and the few residents who lived there were inside their properties.

'What a beautiful house.' Jacob climbed out of the car, stretched his legs and stared at the house and the river flowing rapidly behind it. 'When the sun's shining, I imagine it's even more stunning.'

'Thank you.' Clemens opened the door and the two men entered. Clemens headed towards the room backing onto the river and walked to the window. He waited for Linus to follow him then suddenly grabbed the younger man and flung him up against the wall.

'What are you doing?' Jacob gasped, trying to fight him off.

'You told Eva you could get her forged documents. How?' Clemens increased the pressure on his throat.

Jacob could feel his eyes bulging. 'I don't know what you are talking about.' He spluttered, his arms flailing around inadequately as he tried to free himself from the older man's grip. The punch in his stomach caught him by surprise and he would have crumpled to the floor if Clemens hadn't been holding him by the throat. He shook his head and the Major hit him again.

'Black market...' Jacob said eventually, hoping he had held out long enough that the German would believe him. The grip on his throat loosened slightly.

'How do you have contacts with the black market?'

'An old friend... someone I went to school with.'

Clemens stared into his eyes. Jacob held his gaze praying he wouldn't ask too much more. Even though he knew the Major was not a Nazi, and was probably in the process of planning to overthrow the regime, he couldn't tell him the truth. Overthrowing your own government because it was destroying your country was the patriotic thing to do, working with a foreign power to achieve the same ends was treason, at least he was sure that would be how the Major would see it.

Clemens let go slowly and stepped away. Jacob gulped in air as quickly as he could and tried to ignore the throbbing pains in his stomach. He straightened up and watched the Major warily.

Clemens walked to the window and stared out. He was sure Linus was lying but for some reason he was equally sure that his subordinate wasn't a

Nazi spy either. Which only left one other option. He turned back towards him, pulled out his gun and pointed it at Linus. 'Are you a British agent?'

****

Warrington

Bill and Abigail lay on the blanket on the grass in the park and stared up at the sky. 'I always think I can see things in the clouds.' Abigail frowned. 'Look at that one,' she pointed to their left, 'it looks like a bear.'

Bill concentrated and grinned. 'Yes, it does and that one looks like a ship.'

'Maybe it's a sign.' She smiled at the confusion on his face. 'Perhaps you're going to the Soviet Union… the bear?'

Bill didn't look very happy. 'Hope not, I've heard the arctic convoys are some of the worst.'

Abigail supported herself on one elbow and leaned forward to kiss him. 'I'm sorry. I was only joking. I didn't mean to upset you.'

Bill pulled her into his arms and closed his eyes. 'It doesn't matter.' He sighed. 'I'm really happy here, I don't want to think about going back.'

Abigail kissed him again. 'I don't want you to go back either.' She shook her head. 'I wish this bloody war would hurry up and end.'

'Me too.' Bill wished he could explain how he felt about going back to sea, but even if he could find the words, he doubted she would understand. He rolled her onto her back and stared into her eyes. When he was with Abigail everything was different. He didn't need a drink, the sneering derogatory voice in his head was quiet, and his mind felt calm, even when thinking about returning to Portsmouth.

****

Liverpool

'How long do you think it will be before we sail?' Clarissa and Tristram stood in the cold Atlantic wind on the top deck facing their appointed lifeboat station and waited for the first lifeboat drill to finish.

'Heaven knows.' Tristram put his arm around her. 'Are you warm enough?'

'Yes, I'm sure it will be much colder when we are at sea, even if it is early autumn.'

The inspection was finally over, they removed their life belts and headed back downstairs. 'My gas mask was easier to carry around all the time than this.' Clarissa laughed.

Tristram grinned. 'Not much of a fashion accessory is it?' His expression changed. 'Still its sensible to do what the Captain orders, even if they haven't had any problems there's always a first time and its best to be prepared.'

They had only just gone below decks when the engines started up. Everyone immediately ran back up to the deck and breathed in the fresh sea air as the ship steamed slowly out of the harbour. Waves crashed against the side and within a short time land appeared.

'Is that Ireland?' Clarissa peered at the grey mountains in the distance.

'Maybe, or Wales or even the Isle of Man.' Tristram turned to a member of the crew. 'Is that Ireland?'

'My middle name is oyster.' He winked and walked off. Tristram and Clarissa exchanged glances and she was about to say something about excessive security when the engines eased off and the ship sat idling in the placid water for some time before eventually turning around and steaming back to Liverpool.

'What on earth…?' Clarissa shook her head in exasperation. 'I thought we were finally underway.'

'It looks like they were just checking the engines, a trial run maybe.' Tristram took her arm. 'It means we'll probably be leaving soon.'

Clarissa sighed. 'Just not yet!'

****

Brussels

Tilly sat in Kessel's office and sipped her coffee, her eyes fixed on the desk while she waited for the axe to fall.

'So, when did you arrive in Holland?' Heinz lent back on his chair and tried to work out whether Tilly really was a German patriot or something more sinister.

Tilly decided to keep to the truth as much as possible, only leaving out any mention of the resistance. She began talking, only pausing to sip her coffee. Eventually she sat back, finished the last of her coffee and held her breath. She had done her best.

Heinz offered her a cigarette before lighting one for himself. 'And do you like writing for the newspaper?'

Tilly's face lit up. 'Yes. I love it. Apart from enjoying writing, it gives me the opportunity to travel.' Her smile broadened. 'I've come a long way from being a typist. I hope my father would be proud.' Her smile faded and she leant forward earnestly. 'That's why its so important that I do something useful for the Fatherland. There must be something I can do over here?'

Heinz thought for a moment. There was one way of finding out if she really was genuine. He inhaled deeply then spoke carefully. 'Do you think you could infiltrate the Dutch resistance?'

****

Berlin

There was a long silence while Jacob calculated his chances of overpowering the Major and escaping. Then he shrugged, took a deep breath and slowly nodded. If things went against him, he would attack Clemens, forcing him to fire. An instant death was infinitely better than facing torture. But the silence continued then eventually Clemens asked if he could prove it. Jacob stared at him in astonishment, not knowing what to say without giving anything important away. Eventually he shrugged and spoke in English. 'I'm English, my parents are German, we live in England, moved there after the war... the first one. I don't know what else I can tell you.' He fell silent.

'You have a radio?'

Jacob nodded again. If he was forced to use it, he would add the security letters to warn them he had been turned.

'Good. Can you send a message to England for me?'

Jacob was surprised but he nodded once more. Clemens slowly lowered his gun, moved to his desk in the corner of the room and sat down. Jacob watched as he wrote quickly. When he had finished Clemens handed the piece of paper to Jacob who read it carefully, then again as he was sure he must have misread it. 'Is this real?' He stared at Clemens in shock.

'Yes. Can you send it?'

'I can but do you have any proof?' He stared at Clemens.

'I am not saying anything else until I have seen the message go and we've had a reply.'

Jacob shrugged and stepped towards the door. 'Are you coming with me?'

Clemens smiled. 'Of course.' He shrugged. 'I realise this could all be an elaborate trap, but I don't believe you are Gestapo or SS.'

Jacob relaxed slightly. 'I'm not, but I suppose we'll just have to trust each other.'

Clemens' smile faded. 'Trust is probably too strong a word.' His voice was cold, and Jacob shivered.

****

Trent Park

'Well, it looks like you've got your wish Levi.' Oscar smiled across the desk. 'We shall miss you, but I think your undoubted talents will definitely find a better home now.'

Levi frowned in confusion, then his face lit up. 'You mean…'

'Yes.' He handed Levi a piece of paper. 'Report to this address tomorrow morning and you'll be given further instructions.'

Levi stared at the piece of paper. The address was in London… 'Well off you go then, you'll need to pack and hand over your papers to Myon and Ovid. Oh, and don't forget you can't tell them what you're going to do. Just tell them we're transferring you.'

Levi smiled broadly, he had no idea what he was going to be doing so he couldn't tell anyone even if he wanted to. He stood up and then remembered Marta and his face clouded over.

'Something wrong?'

'No… no nothing. Thank you, sir.' Levi hurried out of the room and back to his office. He was seeing Marta that evening so he could tell her the same thing. For some reason he felt sad and then it hit him. He had grown so used to spending time with Marta that he had hadn't noticed how fond of her he was becoming. He would really miss their conversations…

Perhaps she would write to him. The thought pleased him more than he expected, then he frowned. If his new job was secret, would she be allowed to write to him? He would have to ask when he got to wherever he was going. Levi reached his office and began sorting out his papers and notes ready to pass on to Myon and Ovid.

******

En route to Cairo

The ship finally sailed out of Liverpool and headed to Glasgow where it joined the rest of the convoy. Clarissa stood on deck with Tristram and stared at all the great grey ships assembled in formation.

'Its hard to believe they are all filled with people isn't it? They seem so quiet.' Clarissa watched as the armada steamed ahead and spread out on both sides of them. 'Goodbye Britain.' She whispered softly.

'Not regretting your decision?' Tristram put his arm around her.

'No, I will miss Nathanial, but I know this is the right thing to do.' She looked up at him. 'And we can get to know each other properly, can't we?'

Tristram leant down and kissed her. 'That sounds like my idea of paradise.'

Clarissa smiled. 'Mine too.' She put her arms around his neck and forgot about watching the ships.

Sammy pursed her lips and leant towards June. 'You'd think she would know better wouldn't you? Its not that long since her husband was killed.'

'It's over a year I think.' Renee answered, then flushed and looked away when Sammy glared at her.

'She's obviously no better than she ought to be.' June answered her sister as if Renee hadn't spoken.

'Disgusting behaviour I call it and she's got a young child too.' Sammy continued.

'Should have stayed at home to look after him.'

'The upper class don't behave like normal people. She's got servants to do that for her. Probably couldn't wait to get away from him so she could enjoy herself.' Sammy snorted in derision.

Renee leaned against the railings, breathed in the cold sea air and wished she'd never signed up with the Swinging Sisters. Sammy and June never lost an opportunity to let her know she was just there to make up the numbers. She glanced over at Clarissa and smiled to herself. She liked Clarissa and unlike Sammy and June who were jealous of her, Renee loved the fact that Clarissa was famous, well maybe not famous but certainly well known, especially in the north of England. She wondered if she should warn Clarissa about their animosity. Renee sighed and decided not to say anything. Clarissa was unlikely to believe her, not when Sammy and June were so nice to her face. And anyway, what harm could they do?

****

Trent Park

'I will miss you.' Marta looked so sad that Levi was suddenly leaning towards her and kissing her gently. He didn't know who was more surprised, but then Marta kissed him back and for a few moments he forgot all about his new job.

'I will miss you too.' He realised just how true that was and he kissed her again. 'Will you write to me? When I have an address, I mean.'

'Of course, I will.' Marta smiled at him. 'I thought you would never kiss me.'

Levi frowned. 'I think it took the thought of leaving you to make me realise how much you meant to me. I haven't thought about women, not in that sense, since Sura was killed.' He stared into her eyes. 'I feel guilty even thinking about having a relationship with you. It's like being unfaithful to her memory.'

Marta took his hand. 'I can understand that, but life does go on and yes, I know that's a cliché, but it's also true.'

'And I know Sura would not want me to be on my own, it's not fair on Aaron.' He sighed. 'Rebecka is a good mother to him but....'

'But she will want her own life, her own family?' Marta finished for him.

'Yes.' Levi shook his head. 'I'm sorry I didn't mean to talk about this, not on our last evening together. Perhaps we should do something different? Go to a night club?'

'Or we could go back to your flat?'

Levi stared into her eyes then reached for his drink. 'I can't think of anything I would rather do... as long as that's alright with you?'

Marta downed the rest of her beer, stood up and put out her hand.

Chapter 8

Berlin

Jacob left the office, the latest set of forged papers in his pocket and headed confidentially towards the Major's house. A lot had happened since Eva had told him the truth about her activities, but it had all worked out for the best much to his surprise and relief. He smiled and thought back to his first reaction, which had been horror followed by fear. What on earth had he got into? His life was already complicated enough. But by then it had already been too late because he had fallen deeply in love with Eva and would have done anything for her. The worst moment had been when Clemens had pulled his gun out and asked if he was a British agent. Jacob had realised that he had no choice but to take a chance and had told him the truth. He had passed Clemens' message onto Francis and had an acknowledgment, but he was still waiting for them to say what help they intended to send.

'Linus!'

Jacob spun around, heart pounding frantically then slowly relaxed. 'Kara? What are you doing here?' She looked awful, she had lost weight and was very pale.

'I have to speak to you.' Her eyes were pleading with him.

Jacob wanted to argue that he would be late, but she looked so pitiful that he couldn't bring himself to ignore her. 'I have to be somewhere now, but can you come back later?'

Kara nodded in relief. 'What time?'

'Come to my apartment at nine. Is that alright?'

'Thank you.' Before he could say anything, she turned and hurried up the road. Jacob watched her until she reached the corner and disappeared before turning back and continuing on his own way, his thoughts still on Kara. Her appearance had reminded him of the people he was procuring forged documents for, she had the same haunted expression in her eyes, the same fear... Jacob shivered. His job was dangerous enough without these extra distractions, but how could he not help his fellow Jews escape and how could he not help Kara?

Kara found a cinema, paid for her ticket, hurried inside and sat down gratefully. She would watch the film and the newsreels and that should be enough to kill the time until Linus was free. *And if he doesn't agree?* She quashed the voice in her head. Linus didn't have a choice. If he said no, he would leave her with no option.

****

Warrington

'Pregnant?' Joseph stared at Nora in shock.

Mary shook her head in disbelief. 'What the hell do you mean, you're pregnant? What have you been doing you stupid girl?'

'Mrs Young...' Jessica didn't get any further.

'I was raped!' Nora began sobbing.

'When? Why didn't you say anything?' Joseph's voice rose and he took a step towards her.

'He threatened to kill me if I told anyone.'

'What's his name?' Mary didn't look convinced.

'I don't know. He was shipped out to India the day after. I didn't find out that he'd gone until later.' Nora was almost beginning to doubt the truth herself, so she was not that surprised that her parents didn't believe her.

'We had to leave the Isle of Man because of your behaviour and you told us a load of lies then. Why should we believe you now? You're lying again aren't you?' Mary spat at her.

Nora's eyes widened in disbelief and she shook her head. She fought down the rising panic that always hit her when she thought about that night, collapsed onto the worn settee and tried to control the tears that were running unchecked down her face. 'I'm not. You have no idea…'

Jessica was listening to the conversation in bewilderment, how on earth could they not believe their own daughter? She finally managed to interrupt. 'Nora is telling the truth Mr and Mrs Young. She told me after it happened…'

'And you didn't think to make her to tell us?' Mary snapped at her.

'She was too frightened.' Jessica stepped towards Nora and put her arm around her friend's shoulder. 'She was terrified of that awful man…'

'You saw him then?' Joe was watching Jessica carefully.

Jessica nodded. 'I did. He asked Nora if he could walk her home and she said yes. He wasn't even asking her out on a date.'

Mary clearly didn't believe her. 'You would say that wouldn't you?' She sneered before turning back to Nora. 'How far gone are you?'

'About seven months…'

Mary gasped. 'Seven bloody months!' She peered more closely at Nora's stomach. 'Too late to get rid of it then.' She shook her head in disgust. 'You stupid girl. If you'd told us to start with, we could have sorted something out.' She thought for a couple of moments, then took a breath and added. 'Never mind. We'll just have to have it adopted.'

Nora's eyes opened wide in disbelief and she stared at her mother. 'But what if I don't want to have it adopted?'

Mary snorted. 'Don't be ridiculous. You don't have a say. I'll speak to the nuns.'

'No! I don't want my baby adopted.' Nora cried out, pain etched on her face.

'Like your mother said you don't have a choice. We can't afford another mouth to feed, especially a bastard.' Joseph glared at her. 'In any case, if you were raped as you claim, why would you want the child? I would have thought you would be delighted to get rid of it.'

Jessica opened her mouth to support Nora, but Mary took her arm and began leading her to the door. 'We can deal with this now, thank you.'

'Jessie...' Nora's cry was pitiful, and Jessica tried to prevent herself being propelled out of the room, but Mary was too strong for her.

Nora stood up but Joseph was blocking her way. 'Sit down. You're not going anywhere until we sort this out.'

'I have to go to work.'

Joeph hesitated. They needed Nora's money and fortunately she didn't show that much, not yet. She could probably get away with another week. 'Alright, but don't tell anyone there. We'll arrange for you to go into a mother and baby home and we'll think of something to tell the airbase. We don't want you to lose your job.'

Nora hurried outside before her father changed his mind. Jessica was waiting for her and immediately put her arms around her. She could feel Nora trembling, and although she was horrified by the things Nora's mother had said, she had to find something to calm her friend down. 'Perhaps they'll come round?'

Nora shook her head but didn't look up. 'I doubt it.' She sighed, pulled away, took a deep breath and stared into her friend's eyes. 'Maybe they're right Jess. Perhaps its best for the baby to be adopted. I haven't exactly made a great success of my own life, have I? And although I want the baby now, I might hate it when its born.' Her face hardened and she looked away. 'Anyway, I don't have a choice. I have no money, no one to support me. Its best this way.'

****

En route to the Middle East

The sea had been quite choppy for most of the way until they had approached the Straits of Gibraltar. The members of ENSA spent their time exercising, eight turns of the deck equalling a mile, playing cards, learning Urdu as the majority of troops and nurses were going to India, setting up a brains trust, spelling bee, and putting on impromptu concerts. As the weather became warmer sunbathing became the main activity with several ENSA members appearing on deck in bathing costumes, swimsuits and summer dresses.

'You look beautiful.' Tristram was having trouble keeping his hands off Clarissa, but it was hard to find anywhere private.

'Thank you.' She sighed and lowered her voice. 'I do wish we weren't sharing cabins with other people.'

Tristram squirmed uncomfortably, tightened his arm around her shoulders and stared out at sea without answering.

Clarissa smiled and gazed up at Gibraltar in fascination as the convoy formed into single file to allow it to pass through the Straits with the required amount of neutral water on either side. Then she transferred her attention to the opposite shore and the coast of Africa. In the distance she could see mountains standing proudly against the bright sunny skyline. 'I can't believe we are so close to Africa. It's like a dream.'

Tristram managed to briefly transfer his thoughts from making love to Clarissa to the scenery unfolding in the distance and smiled. 'It's incredible, isn't it?'

As they stood on the deck the sun sunk slowly into the sea behind them. The outline of the mountains turned black and forbidding, the temperature dropped slightly and Clarissa snuggled closer.

Tristram glanced around the ship and spotted Sammy and June sitting on some chairs in the moonlight. Renee was by their side looking miserable as usual. Further along the deck the men he shared with were also sitting on deck playing cards, coffees in hand. They would probably stay on deck for some time which meant their cabins were empty. His heart began to beat faster. Should they take a chance?

****

Scotland

Levi lay on his bed and stared at the ceiling. His first mission and it looked like he had failed. He knew it wasn't his fault, the Paris Prosper network had already collapsed before he had been sent over there, most of its personnel had been arrested by the Gestapo except their radio operator. Madeleine had somehow managed to stay out of Gestapo hands, changing her address every day, somehow lugging her heavy wireless set around Paris without being caught. But she had been the only wireless operator left in Paris so Levi's job had been to make sure the new radio operator arrived safely, and then to find Madeleine and bring her back home. But Levi had been too late. Despite the Resistance' attempt to protect her by providing a new wardrobe and hairstyle she had been arrested, betrayed by either Henri Dericourt or Renee Garry, he hadn't had time to work out the truth. Levi had been forced to leave before he too was arrested by the

Gestapo and although he had wanted to stay and try to rescue Madeleine, his superiors had deemed it too dangerous and unlikely to succeed.

Levi sat up and clenched his fists. The thought of the exhausted girl he had met briefly in a hotel room in the hands of the Gestapo was torturing him, even though he knew deep down that his superiors had been right to pull him out. Perhaps if this had not been his first mission, he would have accepted defeat more easily. Yes, he had delivered the new radio operator safely, and he had made a start on setting up the new network, but all he could focus on was his failure to save Madeleine. He lay back down, closed his eyes and wished he could sleep.

'Some post for you Germain.' Henri put his head around the door.

'Thanks Henri. Can you leave it over there? I'll read it later.' Levi indicated the small table by the window.

Henri shut the door, placed the letter as requested, and stepped towards him. 'It doesn't help to dwell on it Levi. You did a good job.' Henri was one of only two men in the house who knew his real identity. Everyone else knew him by his code name, Germain.

'That doesn't help Madeleine, does it?'

'Nor does you sitting here and replaying it over and over in your mind. There was nothing else you could have done.' Henri waited for Levi to get up and retrieve his post, but he was still laying on the bed. Henri sighed and made a decision. He shouldn't really say anything, but he needed to shake Levi out of his lethargy, or he would be useless as an agent, and probably get himself killed as soon as they sent him back. 'She made it easy for them in the end you know.'

Levi opened his eyes and stared at him. 'What the hell are you talking about? She was exhausted, I saw her… going from place to place, hardly any sleep, always looking behind her…'

'Don't get me wrong Levi. Her work was exemplary, she was a brilliant agent. But she had an idiosyncrasy. Her favourite colour was blue, and even though the resistance sorted her out new clothes she insisted on lots of them being her favourite colour. More than likely it was what led the Gestapo to her after she was betrayed.'

Levi shook his head, a look of horror on his face. 'No… surely not?'

Henri shrugged. 'We can't say for sure, but let's just say it didn't help. And it's a lesson for all of us. Don't have habits or idiosyncrasies. They will get you killed. You have to be anonymous, a nobody.' He retrieved the post from the table and handed it to Levi. 'Now read your mail, put the mission behind you, and come down to dinner.'

****

Boston, USA

Bill still couldn't believe he was actually in America. It was like a completely different world and he could almost believe there wasn't a war on… until he looked closer. American industry had been transformed to help the war effort. Food machinery plants were now making spouts for anti-tank guns, the Gillette razor plant was manufacturing tool posts and the Boston Navy yard was like a small town with over fifty thousand employees, apparently the busiest yard in the United States.

Bill was waiting with the rest of the crew for *HMS Keats* to be commissioned, and then who knew where they would be going. He was enjoying seeing America, but he was missing Abigail badly. Without her calming influence he was drinking more, anything to stop the pressure building up inside him. He was also wary of getting too close to anyone in his new crew in case he jinxed them. At least Danny was on a separate ship and Abigail was thousands of miles away. They should be safe from whatever curse he carried with him. Bill took a deep breath and tried to control the anxiety that was bubbling up in waves. Perhaps he should write to Abigail. It might help to relax him. He reached for some paper.

My dear Abigail

I hope this letter finds you well. I am really missing you and it seems ages since we were laying on the blanket in the park staring up at the sky and watching the clouds. I can't tell you where I am, but its completely different to anywhere else I have ever been. How is life in Warrington?

He stopped. What else was there to say? He wanted to describe America or tell her about their new ship, but he couldn't because of censorship. And he couldn't explain how he preferred to be at sea because at least then he was concentrating on staying alive, something he was trained for. Inaction was worse than anything else because it gave him time to think about the friends he had lost. It also gave him time to think about his own mortality. It could only be a matter of time before he was killed. While he was at sea and on constant alert he could cope with that, but once he was safe his thoughts wouldn't shut down. He dreamt of ships sinking, his friends drowning and broken bodies. But that wasn't the worst of it. When he was awake he was haunted by the screams and cries of the wounded, together with the sounds of bombs dropping, the roar of aeroplanes overhead and the constant shriek of Stukas diving at him. It was as if he was still there, not sitting safe in a friendly harbour. How could he explain that to anyone? They would think he was mad. Perhaps he was?

'We're going ashore, you coming Young?' Tom Jarvis was short and wiry with clear blue eyes, blonde hair and a strong Geordie accent that Bill struggled to understand sometimes.

Bill nodded in relief, grateful to have his chaotic thoughts interrupted. He shoved the letter under his pillow to finish it later. 'Yeah, why not?'

'Writing to your girl?'

Bill nodded. 'Difficult to know what to say though when we can't say where we are.'

'I tried to write to me Mam, but same problem and I'm running out of questions to ask. There's only so many times you can ask how they're doing.'

Bill nodded and wondered briefly if Tom felt the same as him. Maybe one day he would ask...

Chapter 9

Scotland

Levi reread Marta's letter for the third time, a smile on his face. He was so pleased to hear from her, and grateful he had explained in his letter that it might take a while before he was able to reply. She had written in Polish which was good because having to concentrate to understand the language pushed Madelaine and France out of his brain for a while.

'Dear Levi

I was so pleased to get your letter as I was already missing you even though it was only a few days since you had left. I don't have much to say because nothing has happened except there is a big hole in my heart. I was thinking that when you get some leave we could go to the Isle of Man and you could introduce me to your sister and your son. But only if you are comfortable of course. I have not been out of London since I arrived here. My brother always comes to London when he has leave so it will be really exciting to see something of this wonderful country that has given me a home and a life, when I thought I had nothing left to live for.

I never told you that when Myon introduced us I was feeling very low, I hadn't seen my brother for months, I was mourning my parents and I was so lonely. Not that people hadn't been friendly to me, but I needed something more and you provided that. You gave me back my life and, whatever happens between us, I will always be grateful to you for that.

So, what else is there to tell you? Nothing really. Now I am trying to find things to tell you I wonder what on earth we found to talk about for hours every evening. Maybe it's because holding a face to face conversation is easier than writing to you, but writing to you makes me feel close to you so I keep putting off the moment when I say goodbye.

Unfortunately, I have run out of things to say now so I must concede defeat. I will stop writing now and post this. Hopefully, you will be able to reply before you are sent abroad or wherever it is you are likely to be. If not, I will wait patiently to hear from you.

With lots of good wishes

Marta

Levi folded the letter up and put it back in the drawer of the bed side cabinet, pulled out some paper and a pen and began writing.

My darling Marta

I have just read your letter and I had to reply straight away. Yes of course I will take you to see my son and my sister. They will love you as much as I do. I have just realised that I have said love and hope this doesn't offend you because I do love you, very much. I hope you too feel the same.

Well, goodness... my secret is out now, and I feel wonderful. I don't know how much longer the war will last but when it finally ends, and if we are both still alive, perhaps we could get married. Well! That's another secret out! You don't have to answer straight away and no doubt you would like your brother to make sure I am good enough for you so I will have to meet him first.

I have just reread this letter and I am now not sure whether I really should send it. Perhaps these things are best said when we are face to face, not in a letter.

Levi sat back and reached for the bottle of whisky he had bought from the bar downstairs. Perhaps he should start again? On the other hand, if anything happened to him on the next mission, he might never be able to tell Marta how he felt about her. He sipped his drink and sighed. If anything happened to him would it really be better for Marta to know how he felt? Might it not be kinder for her to be ignorant of his true feelings?

Then at least she would be able to get on with her life without any guilt that she was being unfaithful to his memory.

****

US Burtonwood

'There has to be another way, Nora.' The lunchtime rush was over, and they were on their own in the kitchen, Nora washing up and Jessica drying the plates.

Nora shook her head. 'No. There's no point trying to find another solution. I should have told my parents to start with, then I could have had an abortion. At least this way the child will be well looked after and be with someone who truly wants a baby.'

'But what about you?'

Nora shrugged and concentrated her attention on the pile of dirty plates in the sink. 'I'm not able to look after a baby Jess. I can't even look after myself. No one else was stupid enough to let that maniac walk them home, except me. He must have known I would be easy. I couldn't even fight him off. It's my own fault I'm in this mess but the baby didn't have a choice. He or she deserves a better life than I could ever give them.'

Jessica slammed the cloth down and grabbed her friend's arm. 'That's ridiculous Nora. He was much stronger than you. How could you possibly have stopped him?'

'It doesn't matter because that's what everyone else will think.' Nora turned to face her. 'I've had enough Jess. Once I have given birth I can get back to enjoying my life. And believe me I will! My parents think I'm a slag so I might as well be one. At least that way I'll be punished for something I *am* doing.' Nora reached into the sink, pulled out a plate and slammed it down on the draining board for Jessica to dry.

Jessica stared at her in shock. 'Nora...'

'Just forget about it Jess. Mum will speak to the nuns today so I might as well make the most of the last day of my freedom. No doubt I won't get much of that in a mother and baby home. Let's stop off in the pub on the way home.'

Jessica wanted to argue, but she could see Nora was not likely to listen to her while she was in this mood. Perhaps she would be in a more receptive frame of mind tomorrow. 'Alright.'

Nora finished the last of the cutlery, emptied the sink and dried her hands on a towel. 'Come on then. We're finished here, let's go and have some fun.' She turned away so Jessica couldn't see the tears in her eyes. She had known her parents would be shocked and angry, but she had expected them to believe her. Their attitude had almost been worse than the rape, but she wouldn't let them see that. She was fed up with everyone walking all over her. She had loved Alan, but he had chosen the Navy over her and then got himself killed. She had loved Jacob, but he had left her without a second thought. She had loved her job on the Isle of Man, but she had lost that because she had risked her life for her country. What was the point of doing the right thing? All she had done was to accept a man's offer to walk her home. For anyone else that would have been all that happened, but not for her. What had he seen in her that made him think it was alright to rape her? She was obviously such a terrible person that she didn't deserve the normal happiness other people expected. Well, she wasn't going to hide away. If everyone thought she was a bad person she might as well enjoy herself doing all the things bad people did.

For a brief moment Nora wished Bill was there. Maybe he would be able to explain to her why her life was such a disaster. But he had left her too. Like Alan he had chosen the Royal Navy over her and now he was off in America enjoying himself. She knew Bill shouldn't have told her where he was going but, knowing how much she loved everything American, he hadn't been able to stop himself. Well one day she would go to America and leave this dreary island behind, along with all the narrow minded people who lived here. In the meantime, she would make sure she put herself first, look after number one as the Americans said, and stuff what anyone else thought.

****

Berlin

Jacob watched Kara finish her schnapps and place the glass carefully on the table. He had handed Eva the documents, spent an hour with her and then hurried back, telling her he had an early start the following morning. Fortunately, Eva appeared to believe him and hadn't questioned him.

Kara fixed her gaze on him. 'I suppose I had better tell you why I am here?'

Jacob nodded but he didn't speak.

'I need your help.' Kara took a breath and stared down at the table. 'I lied to you. I went out with you because Backer ordered me too.' Jacob, who'd been in the process of drinking his schnapps, choked and began coughing. Kara didn't appear to notice. She carried on talking, her voice a monotone. 'I didn't lie about him. He did rape me but only because I refused to do what he wanted. He wanted me to spy on you, I don't know why, but once I started going out with you, I liked you, so I didn't tell him anything, not that I ever saw anything to tell him anyway. I didn't tell him that we weren't going out anymore because I was terrified. I pretended that we were still seeing each other but I can't keep lying to him. I think he's suspicious…'

Jacob had listened to her monologue in growing horror. He didn't care that she'd used him, to a certain extent he had used her too, but to find out that she had been working for Backer was terrifying. He tried to pull his thoughts together. 'Why does Backer want you to spy on me?'

Kara still didn't look at him. She shrugged. 'I don't know, he didn't say. And I didn't ask... You know how it is... with the SS.' She finally raised her face towards him. 'That's why I wanted to see you occasionally... so he didn't know you'd dumped me.'

Jacob was still thinking furiously. 'What do you want from me?'

'Just pretend we're still going out, so I can report something back. I am running out of lies and I'm sure he doesn't believe me anymore.'

Jacob stared at her. How did he know she was telling the truth? What if Backer already knew and this was some kind of trap? He thought back to what she had said about not reporting anything about him anyway and wondered if he should believe her. Then he realised he had no option but to go along with her. If he refused and she was telling the truth it would probably only be a matter of time before Backer managed to find an excuse to arrest him. If she was lying the outcome would probably be the same. There was an alternative, but he wasn't sure if he had the stomach for it. Then he thought about Eva and young Anton, Clemens and Ursula and the bigger picture.

****

Amsterdam

Tilly finished sending her latest radio message and quickly dismantled the equipment. Not that she needed to worry too much about the detector vans. With the Nazis thinking she was working for them, there was little chance of her being picked up. Although she still had to be careful as she wasn't yet an official member of the resistance as far as the Germans were concerned. If she was picked up she would just have to improvise, pretend she had just been recruited and this was one of her first messages and that she hadn't had a suitable opportunity to notify them without making her new friends suspicious. Tilly gave a wry smile as she thought back to the day Heinz had asked her to infiltrate the Dutch resistance. She'd nearly fallen off her chair in shock and then delight as she had realised she could use that to her advantage. The difficulties of being a double agent hadn't really occurred to her until she'd agreed and was on the train back to Holland.

Heinz had given her a codename, *Butterfly*, and the name of the officer in the Nazi administration in Amsterdam she would be working for and said that he would soon be in touch with her. Tilly had met Sturmbannführer Bruno Drescher in Amsterdamse Bos a few days later and taken an instant dislike to him. In his early thirties with short blonde hair and piercing blue eyes, Drescher was quite handsome, but unfortunately he reminded her of her father, the same bullying, sneering manner, the way of looking down on anyone he considered his inferior.

Drescher had given her a list of names he believed were involved in escape lines and somehow Tilly had hidden her shock. She recognised some of those on the list, but she'd kept her face impassive and said she would make contact with them.

Once back in her apartment Tilly had tried to decide the best way forward. If she warned the resistance Drescher would soon realise she was not working for them and they would all be arrested. But if she didn't warn them, the result would be the same and she would be a traitor. At the same time there was a good chance that at least one person on that list was already working for the Nazis, a trap set up by Kessel to make sure she was genuine. It was only then that she realised how complicated her life had become. Whatever she did, she couldn't protect everyone.

****

En route to the Middle East

They were just about to leave their cabins for dinner when the air raid signal went. Clarissa, Sammy, June and Renee put on their Mae West life lifebelts and looked at each other rather self-consciously. Two minutes later they heard the roar of aeroplanes overhead and then the ship's guns began firing, the noise so thunderous that they shrank back against the walls of the cabin in terror.

The noise of the engines changed as the ship speeded up, zigzagging from side to side while above them the guns continued to fire. Then there was a massive explosion, and the lights went out. Renee screamed and Clarissa sank to the floor, her heart pounding frantically against her ribs. At any moment she expected water to begin seeping under the door, but nothing happened and a few moments later she could hear people talking and moving around outside the cabin.

Clarissa stood up and opened the door.

'Quick, you need to get to the next deck,' someone yelled at her. Clarissa stared briefly at the thronging mass of people fighting their way up the stairs before leaving the cabin. The others followed quickly. Once outside they were swept along with the crowds in total darkness up towards the decks, until they came to some sailors who advised them to stay where they were because the aerial barrage was still heavy.

In the distance Clarissa caught a brief glimpse of an angry sky, red hot with explosions, the silhouette of an enemy aeroplane and puffs of smoke from the ship's guns, before the crowds swept her forcefully back down to her cabin again.

Chapter 10

Amsterdam

Tilly decoded the latest message from Francis and breathed a sigh of relief. The two airmen she had deserted in Brussels had arrived safely in Spain and would be on their way home soon. She read on and frowned. Francis was still concerned about her situation and wanted her to come home because he felt it was much too dangerous for her to remain in Amsterdam. Tilly stood up, walked over to the window and stared down at the near empty streets. It was tempting to go home, to be safe, but she hadn't completed her mission yet. Her job had been to find out who amongst the resistance was working for the Nazis, and she hadn't done that yet. Tilly frowned as a thought crossed her mind and then her face broke into a smile. She had been looking at this from the wrong angle. Instead of thinking about the difficulties, it could be the opportunity she had been waiting for. Now she was working for the Nazis she might be able to find out exactly who the Dutch traitors were. But how? Her mind explored various possibilities, but none of them seemed particularly feasible except the last idea, the one she really didn't want to use. Tilly thought hard but finally conceded defeat. She had no option, she would have to get closer to Drescher.

****

En route to the Middle East

'I think its disgraceful, all those people trying to force their way up on deck. I'm sure we haven't really been hit, probably just a bomb dropping in the sea, not on the ship at all.' Sammy pursed her lips and stared at Clarissa with disapproval.

'I agree, some of them were even saying that we would have to leave the ship. Absolute rubbish.' June joined in. 'We should have waited here.'

'I'm sorry.' Clarissa looked embarrassed. 'I heard them outside the cabin and when I opened the door and saw them going up to the decks it seemed sensible to follow them. I didn't want to get trapped down here if the ship began flooding.' She reached for her big coat and specially packed panic bag. If anything did happen at least she would be ready.

'Which of course it is not going to do if it hasn't been hit.' Sammy shook her head and murmured under her breath. 'I always thought the upper class were made of sterner stuff.'

'I didn't hear that, sorry?' Clarissa waited for Sammy to repeat it, but instead she just shook her head again. Clarissa began to feel annoyed. 'Look, I have no more idea of what's going on than you do…'

She didn't get any further before the door flew open and someone yelled. 'We've got to get up on deck, they're evacuating the ship.'

'Oh, for goodness sake, not again.' Sammy replied loudly. 'I'm sure there's no real danger.'

''course not Miss, the jerries are only dropping butterflies.' The sailor outside their cabin was in his late thirties with a weather-beaten face and dark brooding eyes. He wasn't smiling.

Sammy glared at him but didn't respond. Clarissa grinned, grateful for the release of the tension that was building inside her and for the sailor for putting Sammy in her place. They started to follow him up the steps and Clarissa began to look around for Tristram, but she couldn't see him anywhere and she couldn't stop because the weight of people behind her was pushing her upwards.

By the time she reached the deck women were already being helped over the side into the lifeboats and within a short while she too was seated in the cramped lifeboat. With fifty in each, they were packed so tightly Clarissa couldn't move, but even worse she hadn't seen Tristram at all.

****

Tiergarten, Berlin

'Linus…' Clemens was standing by his desk looking awkward. Jacob stared up at him, his heart beginning to beat a tattoo and he tried to keep calm. 'Yes sir?'

'Its about Kara Meinen. There's no easy way to tell you, but she was killed in the raid last night. I know you two were close… before you started seeing Eva of course.'

Jacob's first instinct was relief that it wasn't anything serious, then he felt terribly guilty. Kara had been a friend, fun to be with and a welcome relaxation and now she was dead because of him. Well not entirely because of him, that was Backer's responsibility. But Jacob had ordered her death like some underworld crime boss in an American gangster film and Niklas had obliged. 'That's awful.' He finally spoke. 'I haven't seen her for a while, but she was a nice girl.' He fell silent.

Clemens patted him on the shoulder. 'Come into the office and have a drink. You've had a shock.'

Jacob stood up, followed him into the main office and waited while Clemens poured them both a drink. He waited while Jacob downed the fiery schnapps before speaking. 'Come to the house tonight. Eva will be pleased to see you.'

Jacob looked at him, but Clemens had his finger over his lips warning him not to say anything untoward. Jacob stared at him in horror. Had Clemens found his device? Even though Clemens knew who he was Jacob wasn't sure how he would react to knowing that Jacob had bugged his superior's office, so he hadn't said anything. Or maybe Clemens was just being ultra-cautious in case the SS or Gestapo had planted listening devices in the office? Jacob felt cold. Perhaps he should remove his own device in case the Gestapo found it. That would be a disaster. He didn't really need it anymore; he just hadn't had an opportunity to remove it. He nodded and then found his voice. 'I'd like that. I'm very fond of Eva.'

'Good. I was hoping your intentions were honourable.'

Jacob flushed. 'Its not the best time to get married…' He saw Clemens' expression and realised that could be misconstrued if anyone was listening. 'I mean being so busy and with the war and everything, but I would like to marry Eva if you approve?'

Clemens reached for the bottle and poured them both some more. 'I would like that very much. Prost!'

Jacob clinked glasses and downed the schnapps, his thoughts whirring around his brain. Clemens knew who he was, why on earth did he want to risk Jacob to marrying his daughter? If anything went wrong Eva would be arrested too; and getting married would mean producing his papers so they could check his lineage, make sure he wasn't Jewish. That would mean extensive checks that might go wrong, especially if the SS were already interested in him. Obviously, Clemens was assuming his papers would survive any investigation, but Clemens didn't know about Backer. Perhaps he should tell Clemens that Kara had been working for the SS? But not here. He would wait until they were in the car. Then he changed his mind. If he told Clemens about Kara, his superior might suspect that Jacob had arranged her death and he wasn't sure how Clemens would react to that.

****

En route to the Middle East

The lifeboat was slowly lowered, at one moment bumping against the side of the ship and nearly tipping them all in the water. Below them, on the inky sea, another lifeboat drifted under them and for a few frightening minutes it looked like they would land on top of it. The other vessel moved out of the way just in time and then they were safely in the water. Clarissa looked around the boat, frantically trying to identify those on board. It was mainly women, although there were a couple of ENSA men, but there was no Tristram.

'Geoff!'

The elderly pianist opened his eyes slowly and looked in her direction. His lips curled up slightly in an attempt at a smile. 'Clarissa, are you aright girl?'

'I'm fine. Have you seen Tristram?'

He shook his head. 'No luv, I haven't. We got separated as we were coming up the steps, but I'm sure he's on one of the lifeboats. Don't fret.'

Clarissa nodded, but didn't answer. It was easy for Geoff to say she shouldn't worry, she doubted he had a romantic bone in his body. She couldn't think of anything other than Tristram, to lose him now when they could finally be together would be unbelievably cruel. She stared out at the chaos going on all around them and wished there was enough light for her to see into the other boat. There seemed to dozens of them, bobbing up and down on the choppy water. Not far away she could see their ship, motionless, like a beached whale, an open invitation to any returning German aeroplane. The motion of the boat was beginning to affect some of the women, and the sound of their retching echoed around the boat. Clarissa was trying to ignore it when the boat lit up suddenly.

'Put that bloody cigarette out.'

'Put the fag out you prat!'

Darkness resumed. Clarissa could no longer see the other boats and for the most part they drifted in silence until eventually she was able to make out the outline of another ship heading towards them. The ship came alongside, and then she heard American voices.

'When the destroyer dips down to you, jump up and cling tightly to the net. We'll pull you in.'

The passengers went up two at a time. Clarissa clutched the net with one hand, her panic bag firmly in the other and almost immediately felt helpful hands pulling her over the rails and onto the deck. Once there the men encouraged her to stand up and move out of the way. Clarissa was beginning to feel like she was in a film, an impression helped by the various American accents around her, *'come on sister'; move along honey*; *step on it sister,';* Eventually she was further along the deck and escorted down below into a packed saloon where strong coffee was being ladled out and a tall petty officer with tired eyes handed her some chocolate.

'Thank you.' Clarissa suddenly felt ravenously hungry. 'Do you know what happened to our ship?'

'She's still afloat at the moment Ma'am. It seems she was hit by an aerial torpedo that went right through the ship. Luckily no one was killed.'

Clarissa breathed a sigh of relief. If that was the case, then Tristram must be alright. 'Is everyone who was rescued on board this ship?'

'Only those in the first lifeboats Ma'am. We couldn't get you all onboard, not enough room. The other ships will be picking up the rest.'

Clarissa thanked him again and then began a slow walk around the saloon, searching for Tristram. There were people everywhere and she knew the chances of finding him were slim, but she couldn't just sit down and do nothing. Half an hour later she was ready to give up. No one had seen him leave the troop ship and she was beginning to despair.

'Clarissa.'

She stopped, her heart pounding and turned slowly around. 'Tristram!' Then he was beside her, his arms around her, holding her tight. 'I was so worried, I thought you'd drowned.'

Clarissa snuggled into his arms and closed her eyes. At last she felt safe.

****

Rouen, Northern France

Levi lay quietly in the woods and peered silently through his binoculars. In front of him were several local workers, under the control of the Todt Organisation, building a large concrete construction. In front of the building there was the beginning of what appeared to be a ramp, which according to his compass, was pointing in the general direction of London. Levi watched for several minutes then put his binoculars away, glanced at the plans his informant had given him before standing up and making his way back to the bicycle he had left by a tree deeper in the woods. Once there he took out his map and studied it for a few moments before putting it away and heading towards the nearest road.

Levi checked in both directions, but everything was quiet, so he mounted the bike and headed northwards. That was the tenth ramp like structure he had seen, the majority pointing in the general direction of London which supported the intelligence they had learned at Trent Park. Intelligence reports from the Pas de Calais region had suggested there were several more there. His job was to cycle around the Normandy area, spot as many possible ramps as he could and report back. Their locations would then be given to Bomber Command. From the little information the scientists had received, they had decided these weapons weren't rockets because they didn't leave the atmosphere, but were pilotless fuel propelled flying bombs. Levi wasn't sure whether the distinction was that important. A rocket or a bomb, both caused casualties and both were a threat that should be taken seriously.

Levi had suggested remaining in the area and arming the local resistance group with explosives to blow up the construction sites he had discovered, but he had been rebuked. Everything was in hand, but that wasn't his job. His role was to travel around the area finding as many storage buildings and ramps as possible, not remain in one place doing something other people could do.

Levi sighed, leant forward and put his head down into the cold winter wind. If he could find all the bomb sites the RAF would destroy them before the Allies opened a second front. If he couldn't it might affect the outcome, and the last thing he wanted was for the war to go on any longer.

Chapter 11

Philippeville, Algeria

Clarissa gazed out at the whitewashed red roofed houses clustered around the quayside and the terraces behind them, their thick green vegetation seeming to rise up out of the sea. 'It looks beautiful doesn't it? I can't wait to explore. How much longer to you think it will be before we're allowed off the ship?'

Tristram shook his head. 'Heaven only knows.' They had already been in the harbour for several hours, apparently waiting for permission to land. Breakfast on the American ship had been sweet cereal, waffles and hot coffee served by waiters while the ship's loudspeakers played a Thanksgiving service. Then they had congregated on deck and waited.

Clarissa closed her eyes and leant back, enjoying the warmth of the sun on her skin. She was just dozing off when the engines suddenly started up and the ship began to sail slowly towards the harbour. Tristram helped her up and they joined the others waiting by the gangplank. It was several hours later before they finally disembarked onto the chilly dockside and were then taken to a rather pungent shed and served some soup and buns from a NAFFI van. Having only eaten a sandwich for lunch they were all ravenous.

After they had eaten they were divided into groups, and while some were taken to a hotel, Clarissa and Tristram were taken to a hostel. The town was nothing like as inviting as it had appeared from the ship and with no clothes except those they were wearing Clarissa began to feel more and more depressed. The hostel was even more of a disappointment. It had previously been a brothel, so a guard had to be posted on the door to prevent clients trying to enter.

'I'm sure we won't be here too long; we'll just have to make the most of it.' Tristram hugged her.

'I know and there are thousands of people worse off and at least we survived the journey.' Clarissa forgot her depression and hugged him back. Cairo wasn't going anywhere, they would soon be there and at least she had Tristram for company. It would have been awful to be stuck with just Sammy and June for company. Poor Renee. She smiled. 'And just think of all the exciting things I'll have to tell Nathaniel when he's older.'

****

Manchester

At first Nora decided that the mother and baby home was not as bad as she had expected, not once she had settled in. Her parents had arranged for her to be cared for outside of Warrington so that nobody knew about her disgrace, so she had ended up in Manchester.

On arrival Nora had been tested for venereal disease and warned that she would not be accepted if she became pregnant again. Nora had stared at the nun in charge in astonishment and growing disbelief. 'Do you really think anyone would choose to be raped and made pregnant?'

'Don't be rude to me my girl, or you'll find yourself back out on the streets.' Sister Bartholomew, a tall thin nun with cold eyes and a narrow mouth spat back, her face contorted in anger.

Nora frowned. 'I wasn't sister. I was just…'

'Enough! Any trouble with the police?'

Nora gave up arguing and shook her head.

'Your parents can't pay towards your upkeep, so you'll have to work.'

Nora shrugged. She had been working for years, so that was nothing new. Sister Bartholomew glanced down at the paperwork and continued.

'You'll have your baby and then look after it until we find a couple to adopt it. Then you will leave.'

Nora frowned. 'Look after it? But surely it will be adopted immediately?' The thought of having to care for a baby that was then going to be snatched away from her, a baby that she would never see again, was appalling.

Sister Bartholomew ignored her. 'Angela!' Another girl came running awkwardly into the room. From what Nora could see she was about the same age as Nora and in an advanced state of pregnancy. 'Take Nora up to the dormitory and show her where everything is.' She stood up and left the room.

'Hello, I'm Angela. Pleased to meet you Nora.'

'And you Angela.' Nora was still in shock. 'Is it true we have to look after the baby until its adopted?'

Angela's face fell. 'Yes. I'm dreading it. Jo, she's one of the other girls, says Its part of the punishment. To stop us having more babies out of marriage.'

'It's barbaric!' Nora exclaimed loudly and Angela's fingers flew to her mouth in horror and she looked around nervously.

'Sshhh, they'll hear you.'

Nora was about to say more when she thought twice about it. There was no point causing herself more trouble, not until she had to. She followed Angela up the long winding kitchen stairs to the dormitory and collapsed gratefully on the bed Angela indicated. The long room was clean and quite bright, winter sun streaming through the windows, and the other girls seemed friendly. Her only worry as she fell asleep was how she would cope with looking after her baby knowing it would be taken away from her.

****

Berlin

Jacob finished sending another message asking Francis what they were going to do to help Clemens and the other German Generals, switched off the wireless and quickly put everything away. Francis' original reply had said he would pass on the information and get back to him with a response. But Clemens was fed up waiting and Jacob could understand why. He was also concerned about his own standing and credibility.

He had finally managed to remove the listening device from Clemens' office and had supplied Eva with several sets of false documents. After careful discussion with Clemens Jacob had not told her that he was a British agent. There was no reason for her to know. He hoped she would understand when he eventually told her. He had also finally realised why Clemens wanted him to marry his daughter. To protect her when the war ended.

****

Amsterdamse Bos

'Well? What have you found out?' Drescher glared at her.

Tilly shook her head. 'Nothing yet. I have to get them to trust me first.'

Drescher frowned and stared at her for several moments without speaking. 'Our mutual friend speaks very highly of you. Please don't let me down.'

'I won't I promise.' Tilly hoped she sounded sincere.

'Good. We are struggling since the British found out about the radio operator we had turned. We badly need someone inside to put a stop to the escape lines.'

Tilly's heart began to beat faster. Surely it wasn't going to be that easy to find out who they had working for them. She frowned. 'I thought you already had someone, that I was just an extra precaution?'

Drescher shook his head. 'We don't. That's why it's so important you hurry up.'

Tilly could hardly believe her luck. If they didn't have anyone inside the resistance she could speak to the others and come up with some kind of plan. Somehow, she kept her face expressionless and nodded. 'Understood. I will be in touch as soon as I have anything…' She hesitated. 'You won't arrest them immediately will you or they might guess its me and then I won't be able to get any more information?'

Drescher laughed. 'Of course not. We aren't stupid. We will warn you in advance of any arrests.' He glanced at his watch. 'You'd better get back or the curfew will be on.'

Tilly nodded, climbed on her bicycle and began pedalling towards the city. Her brain was working overtime as she began planning how they could confuse the Germans and protect the resistance at the same time.

****

Manchester

Nora soon adapted to the routine of the mother and baby home. Her day began at seven and, once she had finished all her chores, she was able to go and rest or go out for a walk if that was what she wanted to do. Feeling exhausted most days Nora was in bed by seven or eight at night having spent the day dusting, cleaning and sweeping floors. Occasionally she helped with the laundry and carried coal from the cellar to the upper rooms of the large house that had been converted into accommodation for unmarried mothers. As her time grew closer Nora's panic also grew. She was becoming more and more convinced that she would never be able to give the baby up, but what else could she do? Having wracked her brains, she suddenly remembered Tilly. Her friend might not be able to help but she might have some ideas. It was worth a try.

'Dear Tilly

I hope this brief letter finds you well. I am sorry to bother you, but I don't know where else to turn. I am pregnant and my parents have put me in a mother and baby home. When the baby is born they will take it away from me and have it adopted. I can't bear that to happen but have no idea how to stop it. I have thought of running away, but I don't know where to go. You are the only person I could think of it ask for help. If you can't I will understand, but I had to ask.

Nora read what she had written several times and decided it was probably too short. If she was asking Tilly for help, she should at least tell her why she was in this mess and that it wasn't her fault. Nora stared at the paper for several minutes unable to find the words to explain her ordeal without reliving it in her mind.

I can't ask the father for help because I do not know who he was. I was raped by a soldier on the camp where I work. He said he would kill me if I told anyone, so I didn't say anything. Then I found out he had been sent overseas the day after so I could have reported him, but it was too late by then. I was pregnant. My parents don't believe me, especially because I want to keep the baby. They think I'm lying about the father and that I was behaving badly.

I know this sounds crazy and that I shouldn't want anything to do with the baby. But its been inside me for so long it's a part of me. The baby was the only person I could talk to for months because no one else knew. You may think I am mad too, but I can't help how I feel.

I have put my address at the top and I hope to hear from you soon,

Best wishes

Nora

Nora read the letter again before putting it in an envelope and writing Tilly's name care of Francis. It was the only way she could think of reaching Tilly as she didn't have an address for her.

She climbed off the bed, reached for her coat and hat, and headed downstairs. If she hurried, she could catch the post.

****

Berlin

Jacob smiled into Eva's eyes. 'I think you already know what I am going to say but...' He took a breath. 'Will you marry me?'

Eva leaned forward and kissed him gently. 'Yes, of course I will.'

Jacob relaxed, put his arms around her and hugged her tight. 'Thank goodness for that.' He laughed. 'Sorry, I forgot to give you the ring.' He reached into his pocket and pulled out a small box containing a beautiful solitaire diamond. 'Your father gave it to me, he said it was your grandmother's.' He slipped it onto her finger.

Eva stared down at the heirloom that had been in her family for so many years and blinked back tears of happiness. 'Thank you.' She smiled at him and indicated the sitting room. 'Shall we go and tell them?'

Jacob nodded and then the siren began wailing. The sitting room door opened, Clemens, Ursula and Anton came out and they all hurried down to the cellar.

'Well?' Clemens waited until they were all seated.

Jacob laughed. 'I am delighted to say that I have asked Eva to marry me and she has said yes.' Ursula hugged her daughter and then Jacob. Anton also hugged his sister and shook Jacob's hand. 'You will be my brother then?'

'Yes Anton, I will be.' Jacob thought about Sura and his parents and wished they could be with him to celebrate. He hoped they would accept Eva after the war was over. It wouldn't be easy for Eva to come and live in Britain after years of fighting between their two countries, but he was sure she would settle eventually.

'Where will you get married and when?' Ursula was looking happier than Jacob had seen her before.

'We don't know yet, we'll have to sort it out.' Jacob was still worried about whether his own paperwork would stand up to extensive scrutiny.

'All in good time. I think we should just do our best to celebrate now.' Clemens stood up and disappeared into the depths of the cellar, reappearing with a rather dusty bottle of champagne and some glasses. Outside the bombs began dropping, the cellar shook, dust and bits of paint flew off, but for once Jacob barely noticed.

Chapter 12

HMS Keats

The ship had carried out several sea trials off the coast of America, but they were now on their way to Bermuda to check on any final things that needed doing. Having survived so many ships that had sunk Bill had made it his business to find out more about their Captain and been rather impressed and relieved to find that Commander Israel was a very experienced seaman who had first gone to sea as an apprentice at the age of fifteen and subsequently sailed all around the world on various ships. But it was his war service that had finally satisfied Bill he was in safe hands. When war broke out the Captain had immediately joined the RNVR, was commissioned as a Lieutenant and sent to Bombay to serve as gunnery officer on *HMS Hector* in the Pacific and Indian Ocean until the ship was sunk by Japanese dive bombers off Columbo in April 1942. He had then returned to England, served on the sloop HMS Sandwich before being made commander of the Corvette *HMS Dianthus* where he had been awarded the Distinguished Service Cross and Mentioned in Dispatches for sinking a U-Boat and rescuing one hundred and twenty Merchant Seamen.

Bill was enjoying the warm weather, away from freezing cold Boston and know it all Yanks who got on his nerves, and he loved being back out in the open sea again. He had received a letter from Abigail just before they sailed so he had something to keep him warm at night. Although U-Boat activity had diminished they still had to be on their guard, but it was much safer than any of the other places he had been. The plan, according to Tom, was to spend a few days in Bermuda making any final repairs that were needed before waiting for a convoy to attach themselves to and make their way back to Boston. From there they would begin escort duties and that meant crossing the Atlantic with all its dangers.

Bill looked up at the blue sky, pushed away thoughts of convoy duty and thought about Abigail instead. Hopefully, once they were back in Britain, he would be able see her again. He was surprised by just how much he missed her. Perhaps when the war was over, they could get married. Bill frowned. Married? What on earth had made him think of that? His lips curled up slightly and then broadened. Why wait for the war to finish? He would ask her when he got back to England. He would ask for a forty eight hour pass. Providing he behaved himself there was no reason for him not to get it. Then they could get married and he would always have someone to come back to. For the first time in years Bill felt at peace and was looking forward to the future.

****

En route to Tunis

'Thank goodness we're finally leaving this filthy place.' Sammy settled back on the wooden seat in the lorry and breathed a sigh of relief.

Clarissa nodded and stared out the back of the lorry at the sun rising behind them, a fiery red glow covering the countryside, the hills standing out in sharp relief. 'I've been to better places, but at least we're on our way now.' She reached out a hand to Tristram who put his arm around her.

'Its going to be a long journey so I'd get some sleep if I were you.'

'I'm not going to close my eyes; I'll miss all the scenery.' Sammy shook her head dismissively.

'Look we're in the hills now.' June called out.

Clarissa stared back as the road wound higher and higher, behind them there were numerous desolate hills with rich green valleys in between. 'There's so much space out here. Makes you realise how small Britain really is doesn't it?' She sighed.

'Are you alright?' Tristram looked down at her in concern.

'Yes, just feeling homesick for Halford and Nathanial. I'm sure I will feel better once we get to Tunis.'

'I don't know how you can leave you son with a stranger for months on end.' Sammy pursed her lips disapprovingly.

Clarissa stared at her in astonishment. 'Firstly, he's not with a stranger. Secondly, we all have to make sacrifices; we're at war.'

'Yes, but you didn't have to come all this way, just to do your bit.' June smiled at her, but her eyes were cold. 'Wanted to make a name for yourself, did you?'

Clarissa was shocked at the unprovoked attack, but then anger took over. 'Its none of your business why I chose to come out here June, but I'll tell you anyway. My husband died in this war and I can't sit at home in luxury while men are dying to save my life and that of my son. Nathanial will be perfectly happy at home with familiar surroundings and people that love him. I made the decision that I can do more for the war by raising morale than I can by joining the WVS or the Women's Institute. And if that meant having to leave my son for a few months, then so be it.'

Tristram interrupted. 'I would suggest keeping your views to yourself June. I know you're jealous of Clarissa, but you are making a fool of yourself.'

'How dare you?' June tried to stand up, but at that moment the truck ran over a particularly large bump in the road and she fell back abruptly.

'Leave it June.' Sammy glared at Clarissa and Tristram. 'You might fool everyone else with your false patriotism, but I know the real reason you're here. Its so you two can be alone together.'

Tristram pulled himself up and stepped towards her. 'How dare you…?'

'If we wanted to be *on our own,* we could have stayed in Britain. I own a country estate, more than enough space for us to be alone!' Clarissa snapped. She reached up and pulled Tristram's arm. 'Just ignore them, they aren't worth the trouble.'

'ENSA won't want you causing them any bad publicity.' Sammy gave an unpleasant smile.

Clarissa stared at her with loathing, then shook her head and looked away. She would take her own advice and just ignore them. There were enough other people on the tour for her to find other friends. She glanced at Renee and their eyes met briefly before the younger girl lowered her gaze. Clarissa wanted to say something disparaging about the sisters to her, but unlike Clarissa, Renee was stuck with Sammy and June. Clarissa showing friendship towards her would only cause her new friend more trouble. Clarissa moved closer to Tristram and wished she could do something to help Renee.

Sammy watched Clarissa and Tristram chatting and fought down her anger. She would love to find a way of cutting Clarissa down to size.

******

London

Francis reread the letter from Nora to Tilly and let out a heavy sigh. He felt really sorry for Nora, but Tilly certainly wasn't in any position to do anything to help her. It could be months before she was back in England. He wished there was something he could do, as he still felt responsible for the girl losing her job on the Isle of Man. But he had more important things to worry about.

He sat back in his chair and lit a cigarette, his thoughts on the mounting problems landing on his desk. Tilly was refusing to come home despite the precarious position she was in. Francis couldn't understand why she was so adamant about staying there. He understood that she had worked hard to insert herself into the resistance, and that as far as Tilly was concerned she hadn't fulfilled her mission. But they couldn't have foreseen that Kessel would turn up in Brussels. Francis was seriously thinking about going over to Holland himself and dragging her back to England, except there was no way he would ever get permission to do that and he wasn't actually stupid enough to really go back into the field. He knew too much to put himself at risk.

Then there was Jacob. Francis had passed on his message about the importance of Pervitin, an addictive tablet form of methamphetamine, to the German population and their armed forces. Jacob had suggested the air force target the factories making the tablets, a suggestion which had amused Francis. He had passed the intelligence on, but he doubted the allied air forces would take it seriously. They had other plans for their bombs and targeting drug manufacturing companies probably wasn't likely to be very high on their list.

Jacob was also waiting for some help with the Generals' plot to assassinate Hitler, and his messages were becoming increasingly urgent. Unfortunately, no one in authority was willing to do anything. The Allies were determined that the war would end only when German surrendered unconditionally. There was to be no negotiation, no armistice, not this time. If the Allies supported the assassination of Hitler, the Generals would want terms so they could end the war as soon as possible. But Francis hadn't wanted to tell Jacob that for fear of causing him a problem. Francis was fast running out of time and he would have to tell Jacob something soon. He inhaled deeply, closed his eyes and thought hard. Maybe there was something he could do unofficially.

****

Berlin

The number of bombing raids had grown over the past months and the previous night had been one of the worst ever, despite the Germans tracking and shooting down twenty three RAF Lancasters over Holland and Northern Germany. Several hundred aeroplanes still made it through to Berlin causing considerable damage to the railway system and delaying hundreds of wagons filled with war material from travelling to the Eastern front. The National Theatre and the building housing the country's political and military archives had also been destroyed. According to the reports crossing his desk nearly a quarter of living accommodation in the city was now unusable. Unfortunately, from what Jacob could see, it didn't appear to be affecting the morale of Berlin's citizens. The number of parties had grown, alcohol flowed freely, the citizens determined to enjoy themselves, treating each day as if it could be their last. Their euphoria was aided by increased sales of Pervitin. Clemens had offered Jacob some, but Jacob had refused, wary of the effects and becoming addicted. He needed to be in control, not out of his mind, his life depended on it. It had been some useful intelligence to send to Francis though and he wondered if the British and Americans would act on his suggestion.

'Looks like those wagons could be delayed for up to a week.' Clemens put down the report and interrupted his thoughts. 'Claus, my son, could be relying on that material to keep him alive.'

Jacob didn't answer.

Clemens shook his head. 'I'm not blaming you my friend, I just want the war to be over so my sons can come home and we can begin living our lives again. Have you heard anything yet?'

Jacob shook his head. 'No.' He hesitated and then said what he was thinking. 'I don't think they are going to do anything to help you, not unless you succeed. Then you will have more chance of them talking to you.'

Clemens nodded. 'I think you are right.' He shrugged. 'Its our mess, there's no reason for them to get involved is there? And you?'

Jacob sighed. 'I am in enough danger already, but you know I will do anything you ask.'

Clemens nodded. 'Good. Then this is what I am asking you to do.'

****

Warrington

The pains had started early, she wasn't due for another couple of weeks. Nora had called the nuns and been rushed to another room where she had finally given birth to a girl. The nuns had asked her if she wanted to hold the child, but she had refused, knowing that if she took the baby in her arms, she would never be able to let go. And that wasn't an option.

'You know you have to feed and look after her until she is adopted.' Sister Bartholomew snapped, her eyes blazing. Nora had soon realised that the nun had no empathy for the girls she was looking after and she knew arguing with her was pointless, but she couldn't help herself.

'I can't.' Nora shook her head, tried to get out of bed and was immediately pushed back. The baby was shoved towards her, her shoulders held back until she finally took the tiny bundle in her arms. Nora tried hard not to look down, but it was like an irresistible force drawing her in and she couldn't stop herself. The baby's eyes were closed and then they opened and stared directly at her. Nora shook her head and fought back tears. The damage was done, the baby's face imprinted on her brain and she instinctively took its hand.

'It's a girl by the way.' The nun walked off, a satisfied smirk on her face.

Nora kissed the baby's forehead and spoke softly. 'Hello Jennifer. Welcome to the world.' Her eyes filled with tears. 'I'm not allowed to bring you up or even spend much time with you. But I will never forget you and I hope you have a happy life.'

She cuddled the baby in her arms and closed her eyes. She would never forget how she had been treated either.

****

Amsterdam

'You're serious?' Joren Varwijk, Tilly's employer at the newspaper, sat back in his seat and stared at her in disbelief.

Tilly smiled. 'Its perfect. I can give them the names of anyone we suspect of collaborating. They might not believe all of them, but it will keep them busy. For a while anyway.'

Joren thought for a moment. 'Do you think they will try and turn these people or just arrest, torture and then shoot them?'

Tilly frowned. 'I don't know. Why?'

'Because you're right, they will eventually realise what you are doing. Then they will arrest you. It will work better and longer if we also give them some real resistance workers. But we can only do that if the Boche want to turn them. Our people can then allow themselves to be *turned* and we can use that to our advantage.'

Tilly's smile broadened. 'That's even better. Inspired!'

Johan sighed. 'Only if they want to use our people. We can't do it otherwise.'

Tilly thought for a moment. 'Perhaps we can find reasons to make the Germans want to use them.'

'Like what?'

'I don't know… 'She wracked her brains. 'If they were from different groups the Germans would want them because I couldn't feed them information about escape lines outside my own group. I could make that quite clear when I gave them those names.'

Joren thought hard. 'That might work. We need to have a meeting and see what everyone else thinks.'

Tilly nodded. 'Will they trust me after this? I had to lie to everyone about the airmen after Kessel turned up.'

Joren shrugged. 'They can do their own checks with London if they have to. This is too good a chance to pass up.'

Tilly tried to ignore the butterflies in her stomach. If they didn't believe her after Joren's assurances she could be in trouble. If only she could let Francis know what she was doing before they held the meeting, but that would make the message much too long and too dangerous to send.

****

Warrington

Abigail had read Bill's latest letter so many times that she virtually knew it by heart. She closed her eyes briefly, held it against her heart and replayed the words in her mind again.

My darling Abigail

I am missing you so much. I didn't think it was possible to fall in love so quickly, but I think that's exactly what I have done, and I can only hope you feel the same way. I know it has been a rather rushed relationship, but wars have a tendency to make people concentrate on the really important things in life, so here goes. I already feel like I know you more than anyone else I have ever met, and I want to spend the rest of my life with you. I know we haven't known each other very long, but who knows how much time we have left in this world. So, I am asking you, in my clumsy way, if you would do me the honour of becoming my wife? If your answer is yes (and I hope it is), we could get married when I finally get some leave? It might be difficult to arrange it when Ernie is home too, but we could try. I would like my best friend Danny to be my best man and he is on another ship so I will have to make sure he is available too.

I will look forward to your earliest reply. Please don't keep me in suspense. If your answer is no, then I will understand, but I would hope we can still write to each other.

Well my darling, its now time to catch the post before we leave port. I am scared to send this in case you say no, but I am also filled with excitement because I am sure your answer will be yes.

With all my love

Bill

xxx

Abigail smiled. As if her answer would ever be anything other than yes. Despite the short time she had known Bill she was missing him just as much as he was said he was missing her. She couldn't wait for him to be back in England. Bill had not said anything in his letter about when he was coming home, just that they would get married when he did. But perhaps that was just because of censorship?

She put the letter down and picked up her own piece of paper and began writing.

My darling Bill

Thank you so much for your letter which arrived today. Of course, my answer is YES. Yes, yes yes! I am missing you so much that I can't wait for you to be home again. If we are going to marry on your next leave you will have to give me a date so I can arrange it. (Goodness, don't I sound bossy!) I will also need a date so I can ask Ernie to try and get his leave at the same time.

I am so excited I can't think of anything sensible to write. The daily trials of home life in Warrington that I thought were so interesting and would make fun things to tell you, suddenly seem so unimportant. All I can think about is getting married and being together.

I haven't met your parents yet or your sister. Have you told them about me? Can you let me have their address then once I have a date for the wedding I can invite them properly? You haven't met my mother either, but she will be happy because she knows Ernie likes you. As you know, my father died when I was a child. I still remember him though, and I am sure he would have been so pleased to see me this happy.

I am not going to write anymore in this letter because I want to post it. I will write again tomorrow with proper news, well I will if I can calm down enough. But for now, goodbye my darling. Look after yourself my love and I did say yes, yes, yes, yes YES!

With all my love

Abigail

******

Berlin

Jacob sat in his office and thought back to Clemens' instructions. They weren't what he'd expected, and he was trying to work out whether they were in contradiction of his orders from Britain. Clemens had told him not to get involved with the plot to overthrow the Nazis at all. Clemens would pass Jacob any information he thought was useful for him to pass on to the Allies, but Jacob was to have nothing to do with the assassination attempt. If it went wrong Jacob was to take Eva, Ursula and Anton to the Allies. Clemens would prepare papers nearer the time so they could leave Berlin and travel towards the west.

Jacob sighed. It was this part that was worrying him. His orders were to stay in position unless his safety was threatened. Then he frowned. If Clemens was arrested, he would be at risk and should therefore leave. If he hadn't known about the attempt Jacob would have remained blindly in position, not knowing Clemens was involved. He should be grateful. He had been given a lifeline and he should take it. Having resolved that problem his next concern was whether the papers drawn up by Clemens would be enough to get them out of Berlin if things went wrong. It probably wouldn't hurt to get some alternative documents.

His thoughts turned to his forthcoming wedding and he smiled. His paperwork appeared to have gone through with no problem. His only concern was that the wedding wouldn't be legal because Linus Haass wasn't his real name, but hopefully that could be sorted out once they reached Britain.

****

Amsterdam

Tilly guessed there must have been a massive raid on Germany given the number of downed aeroplanes over the Netherlands. At least she hoped that was the reason and it wasn't just a really bad night for the British. Then she shook her head. No, the Germans hadn't increased their air security over the Netherlands, if they had she would have heard about it and reported back, so her first assumption must be correct. She hoped the raids had been successful and destroyed whatever the target was. Sadly she would never know which made it very frustrating. Unless one of the pilots told her of course and that was very unlikely and totally against their orders. Tilly smiled to herself, bent her head into the wind and pedalled faster. She needed to hurry, her job was to go from house to house collecting the information about the downed Lancaster pilots so it could be checked with London and new papers could be drawn up.

Unfortunately, there were Germans everywhere, all presumably looking for any survivors from the numerous aeroplanes they had shot down. Tilly sighed. She was delighted so many had been rescued by friends of the resistance, but it would be hard to get them all out when the Germans were actively looking for them and had increased security at the train station and checkpoints. That was the only problem with large raids, it drew too much attention. It might make more sense to hide them in Amsterdam for a while until the Germans gave up their search. She would suggest that when they all met later. Well, she would if everything went to plan. She was dreading this particular meeting in case the other resistance workers didn't believe her, not that she thought Joren wouldn't be able to persuade them eventually. And then they would be able to make proper plans to disrupt local German intelligence. But time was running out, and this latest raid had placed her under increased pressure because of the extra crews at large in the country. If she didn't give Drescher someone soon she had little doubt that she would be arrested.

******

Manchester

Nora finished changing Jennifer's nappy and cuddled her tightly in her arms. She couldn't believe how protective she felt towards her daughter, and she hoped Tilly would answer her soon. Sister Bartholomew was already talking about inviting prospective parents to visit the home and see Jennifer. Nora had been told to make something, a gift that she could send with her daughter, but she hadn't done anything yet because what she really wanted to do was to write Jennifer a letter explaining the circumstances of her birth and how much she had wanted to keep her, and she knew that wouldn't be allowed.

Nora walked over to the window and watched as a young couple walked down the lane pushing a baby in their large silver pram. The looked really happy and Nora didn't know how she felt. A part of her was pleased for them, they obviously really wanted a baby and for some reason they couldn't have one. But what about the mother? Nora thought about what she knew and tried to decide how she should really feel. The boy belonged to one of the other girls in the dormitory, Jacqueline, a small mousy girl of about fifteen with pigtails. Jacqueline hadn't said who the father was, but she didn't seem to want the child. She had to be told repeatedly to feed and wash her son and had been pleased when some parents had been found. Nora had heard the rumour that the boy's father was Jacqueline's older brother, but she didn't know if it was true or not. Jacqueline had already packed and as she stood there an older couple came to the front door and a few moments later Nora saw Jacqueline walking down the lane with them. Nora could tell the girl didn't want to go with them. She kept pulling away from the older man Nora presumed was her father, but he was too strong. Perhaps the baby *was* better off and perhaps Jacqueline was too…?

She turned away not wanting to see any more. She had her own problems. Just because that baby was better off being adopted, it didn't mean Jennifer would be. Jennifer murmured and wriggled in her arms and she began showering her with kisses. 'Don't worry my love, I'll always be your real mother whatever they tell you. I won't let them take you away, you're my daughter.' She blinked away tears as she realised the enormity of the task facing her. The nuns would never let her keep her daughter. The money they earned from selling the children, and supposedly looking after the wayward girls, helped to keep the convent going. 'And if I can't stop them, I'll never forget you I promise.'

Chapter 13

Amsterdam

'Why should we trust her? She could be working for the Boche.' The man in charge of one of the other escape lines was short and wiry, a sceptical expression on his pale face. Tilly only knew him as Siert.

'I've told you how it came about.' Tilly spoke patiently. 'You can check with your contacts in London if you aren't sure. I don't blame you for not trusting me, but I need to give the Germans something soon or they will arrest me. I want to start off with someone we know is a collaborator, but we need to agree on who, and I need to have a plausible story about what he is doing.'

'I will vouch for Juliette.' Joren spoke as soon as she had finished. 'She told me what was happening as soon as she found out that the Boche don't have any spies amongst us. Until then it would have been suicidal to say anything.'

'Alright, let's say she is genuine, who do you suggest we turn over to them?' The speaker was in the shadows, but Tilly could just make out a tall thin man in a raincoat, his face hidden by his homburg hat and a thick scarf. She remembered Joren introducing him as Martijn.

'Henk Imenschot.' Joren said without any hesitation.

A collective gasp went through the cellar. 'The Germans will never believe he is working against them.' Siet shook his head.

'He is one of the biggest manufacturers of machine parts. We have a man in there who will sabotage some of those parts. Juliette will tell the Germans that he is only pretending to work for them and if they go to his main factory they will find evidence to prove what she is saying.'

'And they won't be suspicious?' Siet didn't sound convinced.

'The sabotage has been going on for months. If they double check with the factories in Germany, they will be able to confirm that. Our man was careful not to overdo it, so the ruined parts were just put down to natural problems or damage during transit, but if someone tells them it was all deliberate they aren't likely to disbelieve it.'

'Perhaps she should give them two names at the same time, one being the collaborator and the other... How about me?' This time it was Martijn, the thin man in the raincoat, who spoke.

There was an immediate outcry.

'You're too important...'

'If she's wrong they won't try to turn you...'

'And if she is a traitor....?'

Objections reverberated around the damp cellar and Tilly was about to raise her own when he raised his hand. 'I'm not prepared to hand over my men and women to the Gestapo precisely because of those reasons, not unless I know its genuine.'

Tilly shook her head. 'I can't guarantee they will try and turn you, it's a theory. If I'm wrong... No, I am not prepared to take that chance.'

He smiled. 'The very fact you are objecting gives me more confidence that you are not a Nazi spy, but we can't afford to miss this chance to misdirect them, so I am going to volunteer.'

Tilly looked at Joren for support, but he shrugged. 'If Martjn is happy...'

Martjn laughed. 'Not sure happy is the right word, but we have to try this out at some point. I will warn all my people to leave the area for a few weeks. We are operating a tight cell system so the most I can give is one name. I don't know any of your real names and obviously you won't be meeting here again, so even if they break me, I can't give them anything of use.' He turned to Tilly. 'When will you tell them?'

Tilly thought for a few moments. 'I'll give it a few days so you can make preparations.'

Martijn nodded. 'Good. In that case I think I will go as I have lots to do. Can you take care of my airmen?' He reached into his pocket, wrote some addresses down and handed it to Siet.

Siet memorised the addresses. 'I'll move them immediately.'

Tilly watched as the men said their farewells and the cellar slowly emptied. 'I hope to Christ this works Joren. What if I can't convince Drescher?'

'We'll make sure you are prepared.' A glint of amusement appeared in his eyes. 'I publish newspapers under German occupation, if anyone can make up plausible stories its me!'

****

Tiergarten, Berlin

'Nothing?' Clemens swore. 'We're on our own then.'

'Will they still go ahead?' Jacob still didn't want to mention anyone's name even thought he'd double checked that there were no listening devices in Clemens' office.

'Yes. And then we'll push for an armistice.' He frowned. 'You don't think the Allies will refuse do you? I've heard them say that they won't accept anything except unconditional surrender.'

'Would that be so bad?' Jacob held his breath.

Clemens stared at him in shock. 'I doubt the Generals will ever accept that.'

'Even if there's a danger Germany will be overrun, not just by the British and Americans, but the Soviets too?'

Clemens shook his head. 'Things are looking bleak in the east, but I can't see the Soviets getting that far. And the British and Americans haven't even opened up a second front yet, other than in Italy and that isn't going very well.'

Jacob shrugged. The Italians had surrendered a couple of months earlier but the British and their Allies were struggling to completely liberate Italy from German control. 'Its only a matter of time.'

'Maybe.' Clemens conceded. 'If things get worse then you could be correct about unconditional surrender being the right thing to do. But I don't think we have reached that stage yet.'

Jacob sighed. Unfortunately, Clemens was probably right which meant he was stuck in Berlin for a bit longer. But that wasn't his biggest concern. 'Every day the war continues more Jews are being murdered.'

Clemens frowned. 'I'm sure the reports are exaggerated. I can't really believe we are systematically exterminating an entire race of people.' He saw Jacob's expression and was about to say more when Jacob interrupted.

'I could go and find out sir.'

Clemens stared at him. 'Go to one of the camps you mean?'

'Yes. If it is true it might encourage the Allies to support you. If not… then it doesn't really matter, does it? The war will run its course.'

There was a long silence, Clemens sat back and lit a cigarette. 'Alright. I'll find a reason for you to go to one of them. You will have to be careful though. They are run by the SS.'

Jacob nodded, his heart beating faster at the thought of throwing himself into the lion's den. Ever since he'd read the dreadful reports and passed them onto Francis he had wondered if they really were true. Now he was about to find out.

******

Manchester

'No!' Nora screamed, pushed the novices away and tried to grab hold of Jennifer before Sister Bartholomew could pick her up. But she wasn't quick enough.

'For goodness sake, she'll be back after the prospective parents have seen her. Stop making such a fuss.' Sister Bartholomew snapped before reaching into the cot and picking up the baby. Jennifer immediately started wailing loudly and a brief expression of satisfaction crossed Nora's face. 'Now look what you've done! You've made her cry.' The nun headed for the door with the baby in her arms, Jennifer still screaming at the top of her lungs.

'Well done Jenny. Keep crying!' Nora yelled after Sister Bartholomew's retreating back. 'Then perhaps they won't want you.' She struggled wildly against the two novices who were now holding her back.

'Don't be so silly Nora.' Angela was looking horrified. 'Even if this couple don't want her the nuns will soon find some more who are interested. Its not as if you can keep her, and the longer you try and stop the adoption, the worse it will be.'

Nora stared at her friend in disbelief and shook her head. 'I don't understand how you can be so callous.' She turned her attention back to the novices, finally shrugged off their hold and pushed them angrily away. 'I'm not going to do anything so you can let go of me now!' She yelled before throwing herself on her bed and sobbed uncontrollably. Why hadn't Tilly answered her? If she didn't reply soon it would be too late. Her precious daughter would be taken from her and Nora would never see her again.

****

London

Levi stretched out on his bed and closed his eyes. It was nice to be home, to feel safe and not have to keep looking over his shoulder. He would make the most of it, as he doubted he would be back in England for very long. His thoughts immediately switched to Marta and he opened his eyes, sat up and glanced at his watch. He could rest later, if he hurried he could get to the pub before they closed. Even if Marta wasn't there Myon and Ovid might be, and anyway he fancied a drink.

The pub was crowded, men and women in various uniforms gathered around the piano singing the latest songs, the loud buzz of conversation and laughter filling the small space, the air smelling of beer and tobacco. Levi smiled to himself. It was surprising how much he had missed this. He bought a pint and searched the bar for Marta. A few seconds later he was making his way towards her, a beaming smile on his face. 'Marta!' He had to shout to make his voice heard over the talking and singing all around him. 'Marta!'

Marta was in the middle of a game of chess with Myon but something made her look in his direction. She jumped up and pushed her way through the numerous people. 'Levi! You're back!' She threw her arms around him and he hugged her tight.

'Levi, when did you get back?' Myon patted him on the shoulder.

'A few hours ago.' The two men shook hands.

'Successful trip?' Ovid lowered his voice and Levi nodded.

'Yes, very, tell you later.' He turned away and hugged Marta again.

'Don't worry, I'm not going to ask where you've been or what you've been doing.' She kissed him passionately, then spoke into his ear. 'I hope you are going to stay with me tonight?'

Levi nodded. 'I can't think of anything I'd rather do.'

'Then let's sit down and finish our drinks.' Marta indicated the table and Myon grabbed another chair.

'So… who's winning?' He concentrated his attention on the chess game.

'Me of course.' Marta laughed.

Levi looked surprised. 'Really?'

Marta looked affronted. 'Why? Do you think I'm stupid?'

Levi laughed. 'No of course not, it just that Ovid is….', he was about to say a scientist and stopped himself just in time, 'the best player I know.'

'Well, he's not that good!' Marta laughed. 'My grandfather taught me. He was a Polish champion.'

Levi stared at her in surprise. 'I didn't know that.'

Marta shrugged. 'No reason you should is there?'

Levi laughed. 'No, no reason. I can't wait to learn all those little things about you that I didn't know.'

Marta reached over and took his hand. 'I'm sure there are lots of things I don't know about you too. When the war is over we will have a lifetime to get to know each other.'

Levi leaned over and kissed her, then finished his beer. 'Who wants another drink?' As he went up to the bar Levi thought about what she had just said. He had been planning to ask her to marry him, but now he was having second thoughts. Not because his feelings had changed, but because he didn't know if he would survive the war. His current job was nothing like as secure as working in Trent House had been. Anything could happen to him and it wouldn't be fair to Marta if he left her a widow with Aaron to look after and maybe a child of her own. Perhaps it would be better to wait until the war finished and then get married.

'Are you alright?' Marta looked concerned.

'Yes, I'm fine,' he saw she wasn't convinced, and he smiled, 'honestly.' Levi knew he would have to tell her how he felt, but not now, not when he had just got back. He put his arm around her and leaned closer. 'Let's finish this and go back to my flat. I want to spend some time with you, on our own.'

****

En route to Cairo

Clarissa stared out of the aircraft window and smiled. Finally, they had arrived. Tunis had been a lovely change after Philippeville, and she had enjoyed walking around the large town with its civilised pavements and streets. The shop signs were written in French and there were rows of trees down the centre of the boulevard although not much to buy. But it seemed deliciously French and was so much nicer than Philippeville had been. Even the people were friendlier there although Tristram had suggested that perhaps being under German occupation might have influenced Philippeville's attitude to the British.

Clarissa was relieved to finally get to Cairo as at one point it had seemed they would be sent back to Phillipville and put on a ship again. The RAF had not been able to fly them to Cairo but one of the girls had met some Americans who had offered to arrange passage for them from their own airport. To her amusement the Americans appeared to have far fewer rules than the RAF. They had picked the entertainers up in jeeps, raced at breakneck speed to the aerodrome and helped them climb aboard the American troop aircraft.

The flight took eight hours, mainly because the pilot insisted on taking them over the coast so they could enjoy the view. Eventually they were flying over the Libyan desert. Strangely, from the air it appeared slimy green and grey, with oily rivers flowing slowly towards the sea. Clarissa had no idea why and no one else seemed able to answer her. They had finally landed at Tripoli and spent the night in a hotel. The following day they had flown to the Western Desert, landing at El Adam to refuel and drink tea made with salty water. Night had fallen soon after they had taken off and they had flown the rest of the way in the darkness. Eventually the glittering lights of Cairo had come into view and then finally they were landing.

'Thank goodness.' Clarissa smiled tiredly up at Tristram who was unshaven, his eyes red rimmed with exhaustion.

'I was beginning to think we'd never get here!'

Clarissa was about to answer when Sammy and June pushed passed them in a rush to leave the aeroplane.

'Sorry...' Renee flushed with embarrassed, but Clarissa winked and smiled at her.

'Don't apologise Renee, its not your fault. If it ever gets too much, you can always come to me. I can find you something to do.'

Renee smiled and nodded before leaving but Tristram looked at Clarissa in horror. 'You can't do that Clari. The acts are set. The management will go potty if the Swinging Sisters can't go on because you've pinched one of their members. In any case what are you going to do with her? You're a soloist unless you are performing with me.'

Clarissa shrugged. 'We'll find something for her if it comes to that. I felt sorry for her. Would you like to be stuck with those two?'

'No, but...'

Clarissa smiled. 'No buts... Come on, let's get off this bloody aircraft or we'll find ourselves walking into Cairo.'

******

Belfast, Northern Ireland

Bill hurried back to his hammock; Abigail's letter clutched tightly in his fist. He sat down and stared at it, suddenly frightened to open it. What if she said no? What if she hadn't got his letter and he had to write it all again? Sweat broke out on his upper lip and he wiped it away nervously with his shirt cuff.

All around him he could hear men opening their mail, accompanied by laughter, delight and occasionally anger and moans, but still he stared at it.

'Aren't you going to open yours Bill?' Tom sat down opposite him and began opening his own letter.

'Yes, yes of course.' Bill finally took the plunge and opened it slowly. He unfolded the paper, read the first few words and his face broke out in a smile.

'She said yes…'

Tom stared at him in confusion then he grinned. 'You proposed?'

Billy nodded. 'Yes… and she said yes!'

Tom laughed. 'Hey lads… Our Billy's got himself engaged.'

Within seconds he was engulfed in men patting him on the back, congratulating him, offering him rum, cigarettes and cakes from their parcels and it was a good half an hour before he was able to read the rest of Abigail's letter.

When he'd finished Bill leapt off his hammock and hurried along to the Captain's cabin. He would ask when they were going to get some leave and then he could write back to Abigail and she could start arranging their wedding.

Bill smiled to himself. Fancy him being married. Even saying the words made him feel warm inside. He couldn't wait to make love to Abigail, but that wasn't why he wanted to marry her. He loved her. Abigail was the person he wanted to come home to, she made him feel safe and soothed his fears, when he was with her he had fewer nightmares and he didn't need to drink. With difficulty he pushed her out of his thoughts and concentrated on more practical matters. Once he had spoken to the captain, he would write to his parents amd tell them his good news. He hoped they liked Abigail and that she and Nora would soon be friends. Bill frowned as he realised it was ages since Nora had written to him. That wasn't like her. Perhaps she had a boyfriend? His frown deepened as he wondered briefly if everything was alright, then the door was open, and he was busy explaining why he needed to know about his leave to the Captain.

Chapter 14

Berlin

'Konrad!' Eva flung her arms around the tall well-built Hauptmann in army uniform standing next to her mother and Anton in the Town Hall and hugged him tight. 'Jacob, this is my oldest brother Konrad.' She turned her attention back to her brother. 'I can't believe you are actually home. Its been so long since we've seen you.'

'Pleased to meet you Linus.' Konrad disentangled himself from Eva's arms, shook Jacob's hand and gave him a wide smile.

'And you Konrad.' Jacob smiled. 'Your father will be very pleased that you are here.'

'He certainly is.' Clemens hugged his son tight. 'They must be feeding you well, you've put on weight!'

Konrad laughed. 'I am lucky, I have a very good billet in Paris.' He glanced around. 'Is Claus here too?'

Eva shook her head. 'We had a letter from him saying he had applied for leave but nothing else.'

'I'm sure your brother will be here if he can Eva.' Clemens patted her shoulder.

'I know.' She sighed. 'It would just be nice to have the whole family together.'

'Then you're in luck little sister!'

Everyone turned to the door and Jacob blanched. The man standing there was obviously Eva's brother. He shared the family colouring and resembled Clemens quite strongly. But what Jacob hadn't been prepared for was the uniform. Claus was wearing the uniform of a Hauptsturmführer in the SS. Jacob glanced at Clemens and saw his own shock reflected in his superior's face. As his gaze travelled around the rest of the family, Jacob realised he was not the only one in shock.

'Claus?' Eva recovered first. 'I'm so pleased to see you, but what on earth are you doing in that uniform?'

Claus' face darkened. 'You say it like it is an insult Eva. I'm sure that's not what you meant.'

'No of course it isn't.' Clemens stepped towards Claus and hugged him. 'I can't believe you're here. Your letter didn't sound very hopeful.'

'Last minute change of mind by my superior.' Claus smiled. 'Is this the man who's willing to take my sister on?'

'Yes… yes this is Linus Haas.'

'Linus…,' Claus held out his hand and Jacob shook it, his heart pounding frantically.

'I'm delighted to meet you Claus. Eva will be so happy you could come to her wedding.' Jacob hoped his nervousness wasn't showing.

Claus turned to Eva and smiled. 'Don't I get a hug then?'

'Yes of course.' Eva flung her arms around him. 'I didn't mean anything… about the uniform. I was just surprised. You were in the army the last time we saw you.'

Claus stepped back and smiled into her eyes. 'I was offered the chance to join the SS. It meant promotion…,' he hesitated, 'and getting away from the front line.' His face darkened momentarily, then cleared. 'Not that I minded fighting for my country of course, but this way I could serve the Fatherland better.'

'So where are you based now Claus?' Ursula stepped forward, put her arms around him and closed her eyes. 'I can't believe you're actually here. We've been so worried about the reports coming out of the Soviet Union.'

'Well, you can stop worrying now Mutti. I'm in Poland now, in a place called Majdanek near Lublin.'

'Thank goodness you are no longer on the front line.' Ursula was busying hugging her son so she didn't hear the slight gasp that came from Clemens or see the expression of horror that crossed his face. 'I've missed you so much son. I just wished you'd told us you weren't in danger anymore.'

Jacob glanced at Clemens who still hadn't said anything, but Jacob could see that his face had paled. Clemens seemed to sense him looking and he glanced briefly across at Jacob, his face now expressionless, before transferring his gaze back to his son. He spoke eventually, his voice calm and not betraying his inner turmoil. 'You're actually based in the camp at Majdanek?'

Claus nodded. 'Yes, that's right Vater. I wasn't sure you would have heard of it.'

'Yes, yes… only in passing though.' Clemens looked up at the grandfather clock and, with relief, changed the subject. 'We'd better get going or we'll be late. We can finish catching up later.' He stared at Jacob again and gave an imperceptible shake of his head which Jacob took to be a warning not to say or do anything to make his son suspicious. Jacob nodded. What on earth did Clemens think he was going to do?

****

Somewhere in the Atlantic

Bill was furious that he was still waiting to be given some proper leave, but there was nothing he could do. He had been hoping he could go home for Christmas, the first one he would have spent with his family since 1937, but it wasn't to be. The war didn't stop for Christmas or for

Bill's wedding. It was even more frustrating knowing that Abigail and Ernie were meeting in London in a couple of weeks. Normally Ernie would have gone home to Warrington for his leave, but he had a new girlfriend, Catherine Henderson. She worked in Westminster and Ernie wanted to spend his time ashore with her. He also wanted to check on Abigail and his mother though, so he had invited them both to spend a few days in London where they could have a break and meet Catherine. He had booked them into a very nice hotel and Abigail had promised to tell Bill all about it. Not that he was particularly interested. He just wanted some leave so he and Abigail could get married. He glanced down at her letter again and tried to forget his anger. It wasn't Abigail's fault he couldn't get leave and he loved reading her letters, it was almost like being with her. Bill smiled and imagined her sitting in her room thinking of things to tell him, things she thought would make him laugh. He wasn't entirely sure they were all true but it didn't matter. Knowing she cared so much about him that she wanted him to be happy gave him a warm glow inside. He reread the part about her going to London and his smile broadened. He could almost feel her excitement. He hoped she enjoyed herself. When they were finally married and this bloody war was over he would take her to lots of places. If he began saving up now he could take her to America or Bermuda. If she thought London was exciting, wait until she saw some of the places he had been. Bill lay back, placed her letter over his heart, closed his eyes and started planning their future.

****

Cairo, Egypt

Clarissa loved Cairo with its traffic crowded streets and smart shops, the rich properties of the wealthy that overlooked the Nile and the grinding poverty and dirt that existed side by side. She spent hours walking through the narrow streets of the Mousky bazaar staring at the brightly coloured silks and expensive jewellery and inhaling the heady fragrance of the oriental perfumes. The bazaar was full of sheep, donkeys, heavily veiled Arab women in their black flowing robes and bare footed street urchins, and then there were carved Arabic houses and statuesque mosques all leading to the domed citadel with its minarets on the hill above them.

'I love this view.' Clarissa gazed out over the town and the Nile to the pyramids rising majestically in the distance.

'Its certainly stunning.' Tristram held her arm and glanced out over the ruins of the past. 'You could almost believe there wasn't a war on.'

Clarissa laughed. 'Well, you could if you ignored all the uniforms from various different countries. It's a real mixture isn't it? Look at those wealthy Egyptians in their European suits over there and then you have all the poorer people in their traditional robes. I just love being able to do the simple things again. You can even hail a taxi here without any difficulty, they were like gold dust in London.'

Tristram frowned. 'I don't like the poverty though. I find the beggars a depressing sight, especially the children and those with withered limbs.'

'One of the girls was saying the children are hired out specifically for begging.' Clarissa's face screwed up in disgust. 'Do you think that's true?'

Tristram shrugged. 'I suppose its possible. They must make a good living out of it if that's the case.' Sensing her mood dropping he changed the subject. 'I'd love to have dinner at the restaurant in Opera Square one night, the rooftop one. We could look out over the city and enjoy the night sky.'

'That sounds wonderful.' Clarissa forgot about the beggars and gazed up at him. He leant forward and kissed her. She closed her eyes and gave a long contented sigh. 'I'm so happy. Is that wrong?'

Tristram looked astonished. 'Why should it be?'

'There is a war on and we're enjoying ourselves. I've left my son thousands of miles away and although I miss him, I wouldn't be anywhere else.'

'You are allowed to be happy Clari. The war would still be raging even if you were miserable. Why shouldn't you take whatever happiness comes your way? We never know when things will change so we should make the most of every moment.'

'You're probably right, I just can't help feeling a bit guilty.'

'Well don't. We're here to do our bit, and don't forget we were torpedoed on the way here, that wasn't fun was it? We are lucky we weren't killed, so just relax and enjoy yourself while we can.' Tristram leant forward and kissed her again, with growing passion this time and eventually Clarissa forgot about feeling guilty and gave herself up to the warmth that was engulfing her.

******

Berlin

'I'm sorry if you are disappointed in me.' Claus sipped the expensive French brandy that Konrad had bought back from Paris.

Clemens stared at his son in astonishment. 'Of course I am not disappointed Claus. You have done very well.'

Claus didn't answer for a moment as he tried to work out whether to tell his father the truth. He swallowed the rest of his drink and stood up suddenly. 'I just couldn't take it anymore. You have no idea what it was like there. You never knew when you were safe.' He clenched his fists. 'They came at you when you least expected it... and the cold... I've never known anything so miserable. It seeps into your bones until you never think you will be warm again, men were dying, freezing to death in the snow.' He fell silent, not wanting to tell his father about the summary executions of those who had tried to desert, unable to continue taking part in the brutal massacres and torturing of civilians. Nothing had prepared him for the images that were now ingrained in his mind; women and children impaled on wooden crosses in retaliation for helping the Soviet guerrillas, mutilated bodies lying bleeding to death in the icy wilderness, children shot when their parents wouldn't cooperate. He had accepted the invitation to join the SS because he had been naïve enough to believe he would no longer have to carry out atrocities. But he had soon learnt that they had only invited him because of his interrogation skills and then it was too late. Majdanek was a thousand times worse than fighting on the front line. The only bonus was that no one was trying to kill him there.

He sat down abruptly and tried to remind himself of what he had been taught; that he was part of a superior race and it was his duty to rid the word of the scourge of the Jews. He realised his father was talking to him. 'Sorry?'

'I was just saying that it can't be easy to be a prison guard.'

Claus stared at him. 'No... no it isn't. I mean it wasn't at first, but I know where my duty lies.'

Clemens watched him in increasing concern. 'I know its probably silly, but I've heard some strange rumours about the camps in Poland.'

Claus stare darkened, his leg began twitching and he stared drumming his fingers on the arm of the chair. 'What rumours?'

Clemens hesitated. 'That people are being systematically killed there.'

There was a silence. Clemens expected his son to deny it, so he was shocked when Claus suddenly broke down, tears streaming down his cheeks. Clemens hurried over and hugged him. He could hear Claus muttering under his breath, and in between the heaving sobs Clemens could make out just enough to confirm his worse fears. He paled, wanting to stop his son from talking, but he didn't interrupt because he realised that Claus needed to tell someone, needed to unburden himself, even if there was nothing they could do about it.

****

London

Levi lay on his back in the single bed in Marta's flat and hugged her tightly to him. It was his last night of freedom before he was due to return to Scotland, but he hadn't told Marta yet. Nor had he told her how he felt about getting married, even though he could almost feel her waiting for him to propose.

He took a breath. 'I have to go back to work tomorrow.'

Marta sighed. 'I thought you wouldn't have much longer. Why didn't you tell me earlier?'

'I didn't want to ruin our time together by having you count down the days.'

'And you didn't think I was doing that anyway?' She shook her head and gave him a wry smile. 'Without knowing which day was the last I thought every day was, you silly sod!'

Levi grinned. 'I'm sorry, I thought I was being kind.'

Syli leaned up on one arm and kissed him. 'I do love you, Levi. I will miss you when you go back.'

Levi pushed her onto her back and moved until he was sitting astride her. He squeezed her nipples and then slid his hands under her bottom, lifting her up until he was back inside her. Marta groaned, arched her back, her arms reaching backwards for the headboard, her breasts rising upwards. As Levi began sucking her nipples, Marta closed her eyes and moaned, her body moving rhythmically against him. Levi increased his pace, thrusting harder and faster until he finally exploded. Marta opened her eyes, her cheeks flushed and smiled lazily up at him.

Levi fell back on the bed panting heavily. 'I think I'm going to miss you too Marta.

She laughed. 'I should hope so too.'

'I was going to ask you to marry me…' The words were out before he could stop them.

Marta sat up and stared down at him. 'Yes.'

Levi didn't answer for a moment. 'Thank you, you have made me so happy Marta but…'

Her face darkened. 'But what?'

'But not until after the war finishes.'

Marta frowned. 'What do you mean? It could be years before the war ends.'

Levi took her hand. 'And something could happen to me which wouldn't be fair on you.'

Marta shook her head. 'You want to marry me but not until the war ends?'

'Yes.'

Marta stared at him for several seconds without speaking then she climbed out of bed and began getting dressed.

'Marta? Where are you going?'

'I fancied some tea. Do you want a cup?'

Levi nodded and tried to feel relief, but he knew something had changed. 'Yes… yes that would be nice, thank you.' He watched as she boiled the kettle and put the milk in the cups.

'Marta… my love… are you sure you are alright?'

'Yes of course. Why wouldn't I be?'

Levi shrugged. 'I don't know… I mean… you do understand about not getting married until the war finishes, don't you?' He climbed out of bed, walked over and put his arms around her. She moved away.

'You'd better put your clothes on, you'll catch cold.'

Levi turned away, retrieved his clothes and began getting dressed. Marta was sitting at the small table, staring down at her cup.

'I'll write to you as soon as I have an address.'

'Yes, that would be nice, thank you.'

Levi sat down opposite her and tried to think of something to say. 'Marta…'

'It doesn't matter Levi. I'm sure you're right… about getting married I mean.'

'Its only because I love you so much. I can't bear to think of you having to cope on your own, with Aaron to look after and maybe a child of your own. It wouldn't be fair on you.'

Marta shook her head and then looked into his eyes. 'Don't you think that was my choice to make?' She stood up. 'I think you'd probably better go now. I hope everything goes well with you, wherever you go.'

Levi stood up and stared awkwardly, before moving towards her. Marta stepped adroitly aside. 'Good night Levi.'

Levi hesitated and then left, closing the door quietly behind him. He was sure that in time she would see his point of view.

Chapter 15

Manchester

Nora finished feeding Jennifer, put her back in her cot and lay back on the bed until the nun who was supervising had left the room. She jumped up, packed the few clothes and other possessions she had in the small bag, shoved it under her bed and lay back down. She was just in time as one of the other babies began to wake and the nun reappeared. She held her breath, but the nun made her way to the other girl and did not even glance at Nora as she passed.

Half an hour later it was quiet again. Nora pulled out her bag from under the bed, carefully picked Jennifer up out of her cot, grabbed her bag and made her way out of the dormitory and down the back stairs to the kitchen door. Fortunately, there was enough light from the half-moon through the small window half way down which didn't have a blackout curtain. After the couple had come to meet her daughter before Christmas, Nora had spent several days trying to work out how she could keep Jennifer. It wasn't until she started to think about running away that she realised her daughter was a prisoner. Nora could go into the city, leave the grounds and go anywhere on her own, but she could not take Jennifer outside the dormitory without one of the nuns being with her. She only tried once but was immediately questioned. Nora had pretended she hadn't realised she couldn't take Jennifer out and had not tried again. The last thing she needed to do was to make them suspicious.

Having decided that escaping during the day with her baby was impossible Nora knew she would have to get out at night. But that wasn't easy either. All the outside doors were locked and because women went into labour at all hours and babies needed feeding in the night, there were always several nuns awake.

There was no way of leaving by the front door, it was locked and padlocked, so her only option was through the kitchen. Nora had wandered out into the kitchen garden earlier that day and carefully removed the key hoping the nuns wouldn't be able to lock the door that evening. She didn't know if her plan would work, but she did know that her only chance would be tonight, before they called a locksmith in.

The kitchen was dark, the blackout tightly drawn, and Nora stopped by the door, waiting for her night vision to improve. Jennifer stirred in her arms and she rocked her gently whispering urgently. 'Shhhh my darling, you mustn't cry.'

Jennifer eventually went back to sleep and now Nora could make out the shapes of the cupboards and work surfaces. Nora took a cautious step forward and then another. The outside door was at the far end of the long room, so all she had to do was to make her way around the large table and turn right…

She was halfway across the room when it was suddenly flooded with light. Nora froze.

******

Amsterdam

Tilly gave Drescher the two names the Resistance had authorised her to deliver and waited for his reaction. She had given it a lot of thought and decided that the best way to get Drescher to do what she wanted was to flirt with him, distract him so he wasn't thinking clearly. The idea of sleeping with a Nazi didn't particularly appeal to her, but he wasn't bad looking so if she could get past his uniform and the resemblance in his manner to her father, it would probably be bearable. And if it meant she could secure the escape lines and find out information for the Resistance then it was worth it. She would just have to pretend he was someone else, someone like Jacob perhaps? The idea of pretending the Drescher was Jewish appealed to her sense of humour, although she had a feeling it would take a lot of imagination.

'Are you sure?' Drescher was staring into her eyes and remembering her plan she smiled up at him and nodded.

'Yes. The second one runs an escape line but it's a different group from the one I've managed to infiltrate so I can't tell you anything about them.'

'Don't worry we'll get the information out of him.'

'Its not up to me, but…' Tilly hesitated, her head on one side as if thinking, her smile more flirtatious.

'But what?' There was something about the way she was standing and looking at him… Drescher squirmed uncomfortably and looked away. For some reason he was suddenly attracted to her. On the other hand she was very attractive, and it wasn't as if she was the enemy. She was of good German heritage… He relaxed and smiled back. 'Go on Juliette.'

Tilly could tell immediately that she had his attention. 'Maybe you could turn him, get him to work for you. That way you'd have two escape lines under your control.'

Drescher looked surprised. 'I hadn't thought of that.'

Tilly shrugged. 'It makes sense doesn't it? If you close the line down they'll just set up another one. If you turn him you can find out where it leads and even let it run for a while until it suits you to close it down and then you can arrest them all.'

'I can see why our mutual friend thinks so highly of you.' He moved closer and stroked her cheek gently with his finger.

Tilly closed her eyes and pretended it was Jacob. She sensed him moving closer then felt his lips on hers.

Tiergarten, Berlin

Jacob looked down at the papers and documents he needed to visit Majdanek that were waiting on his desk when he arrived back from his brief honeymoon with Eva.

'Claus arranged them for you.' Clemens looked pale and Jacob could see dark circles under his eyes.

'Is everything alright?'

Clemens shook his head. 'No, not really.' He sighed and took a breath wondering how he could explain something that he himself couldn't understand. 'It would seem that the rumours are true… about the camps I mean. Claus told me.'

Jacob stared at him in shock. 'Claus…? How does he know?' He gasped. When Clemens had said that Claus had arranged the papers, Jacob had assumed it was in his capacity as an SS Officer, but now a considerably more unpleasant notion had come into his mind. 'Christ! He works there doesn't he?'

Clemens nodded.

Jacob shook his head. 'He is responsible…?' Words failed him.

Clemens couldn't look at him. 'He hates it, it's killing him.'

Jacob let out a sarcastic laugh. 'Killing *him*? Don't you mean *he's* killing the Jews? An entire race of people?'

'If you'd seen him… he was a shadow of his former self.' Clemens clenched his fists. 'This is Hitler's fault. He is killing my son as clearly as if he was murdered by the enemy on the battlefield.'

Jacob thought back to the wedding and the brief time he'd spent with Claus. It was hard for him to be objective towards someone wearing the hated black uniform and he hadn't known Claus before, but now he thought about it the SS Officer had seemed on edge. A horrible thought struck him. 'Did you tell him why you wanted me to visit Majdanek?'

Clemens looked horrified. 'Of course not. I just said that we... that is the German army... needed to know what was going on.'

'But not why?'

'No. My son is disillusioned, broken by what he's seen, but I wouldn't trust him.'

'I'm sorry. That must be hard.' Jacob didn't know what else to say.

Clemens let out a heavy sigh. 'We have learnt not to trust anyone in Hitler's Germany but when its your children....' He fell silent unable to put into words the pain he was feeling.

****

Amsterdam

Tilly let herself back into her apartment, closed the curtains and blackout, switched on the lamp and stared at herself in the mirror by the door. She couldn't see anything different on the outside but inside...

The most complicated thing had been that she had actually enjoyed sex with Drescher. Much to her surprise he had been a gentle, considerate lover and she had no idea how to deal with that. She had expected to hate it, had expected she would need to fantasise about Jacob to get her through, but she had forgotten him completely and now she felt guilty. Not because of Jacob but because Bruno Drescher was the enemy. Sleeping with him to get information was acceptable, sleeping with him because she wanted to, was not.

Tilly turned away from the mirror, walked into the kitchen and took out the bottle of cognac she kept under the sink. She took a large swig, but it didn't make her feel any better, so she drank some more. If she drank enough, perhaps she could persuade herself that she had just been doing her duty, that it hadn't meant anything to her. Unfortunately, she started to feel sick before she reached that stage, so she stopped, staggered into her bedroom, collapsed on the bed and fell into a restless, troubled sleep.

****

Manchester

'What on earth do you think you're doing?'

Nora swung around, clutching Jennifer tightly to her. The sudden movement woke the baby, and she began crying. Between Nora and the outside door were three nuns and the doctor.

'I'm leaving with my baby. You can't stop me.'

'Yes Nora, we can. When you first came here, you signed legal documents giving us the right to have your baby adopted once a suitable couple were found.'

Nora stared in astonishment, then shook her head. 'No, I didn't…'

The doctor waved some papers in front of her. 'Would you like to read them?' Nora stared at him in desperation but didn't answer. 'Let me hold your daughter while you read them.' He pushed the papers towards her. Nora backed away, her eyes searching for a way out.

'You can't leave here with the baby Nora, so why not hand her over.' Sister Bartholomew held out her arms. 'Come on, you're making her cry. You don't want her to get upset, do you?'

'You're the one that's making her cry.' Nora spat at her. 'Why don't you move out of the way and let us go?' As she spoke she put her free hand in her pocket and pulled out the gun she'd had since the attempted kidnap of the princesses. She was supposed to have got rid of it but she'd decided to hang on to the weapon just in case. She noted their shocked expressions with a fleeting feeling of satisfaction then repeated her demand. 'Move out of the way and let us go.'

'Do you want to end up in prison Nora?' The doctor spoke quickly. 'If you put the gun down now, we'll say nothing about this.'

Nora laughed. 'You might think you can keep this a secret, but *they* won't let you.' She waved the gun around, indicating the nuns. 'They're like the bloody Gestapo.'

'How dare you…' Sister Bartholomew began.

Nora stepped closer and pointed the gun in her face. 'Move out of the way.' To her immense satisfaction the nun paled, and Nora could see the fear in her eyes. A small revenge for the terror she had inflicted on vulnerable girls like herself.

'Nora you can't get away. Where do you think you can go with a baby and no money?' The doctor's voice was calm, almost mesmerising. Nora shook her head and turned the gun towards him. He raised his hands and tried again. 'If you do this you will have the police after you, you don't stand a chance Nora. Please put the gun down.'

Nora stared at him, tears forming in her eyes. She knew he was right, but she couldn't bear the thought of giving up Jennifer. She was still wavering when the doctor suddenly stepped forward and grabbed the gun. The next moment she saw the needle and then Jennifer was torn from her arms.

****

Portsmouth

Bill could hardly contain his delight as the ship finally sailed into the harbour. He had two weeks leave, but more importantly he could finally get married.

'So you'll be an old married man when you get back then Bill?' Tom Carter laughed as the two men hurried to the mail room.

'You bet.' Bill answered. 'I wrote to Abigail telling her I would be back this week so hopefully she's sorted out the wedding.'

'You'll be so hen pecked you'll be glad to get back on board!' Gerry Smith was several years older than Bill and Tom, had numerous children and a nagging wife, according to him anyway. Bill thought it was probably deserved as he had never met such a slovenly sailor. He often wondered how Gerry managed to avoid being on a charge most of the time as he was invariably late for everything, left his clothes everywhere and didn't wash nearly frequently enough.

'You're wasting your breath Gerry, Bill can't wait.' Tom laughed. They reached the post room and were handed their letters.

Bill frowned. There was nothing from Abigail, just a letter from his mother. It was ages since Nora had written but he was more concerned that Abigail hadn't. He opened the letter from his mother and began reading.

My darling son

Billy's frown deepened. His mother never addressed him in that way. His heart began beating faster and he started to feel dizzy as the next words floated in front of his eyes.

I am so sorry to have to tell you that Abigail, her mother and her brother were killed in an air raid in London in January. Their hotel was hit. I wish there had been some other way to break the news to you. Abigail was so looking forward to going to London, especially as she hadn't seen her brother for several months. I know Abigail couldn't wait to marry you, she was so excited and I know she would have made you a wonderful wife.

Bill stopped reading, staggered back against the stairs and collapsed.

'Bill? What is it mate?' Tom took the letter from Bill's hands and read quickly. His face paled and he shook his head. 'Oh Christ… I am so sorry.'

'What is it?' Gerry was watching them. Tom handed him the letter.

'Fucking hell Bill, that's awful. You poor bastard.'

Several other men offered their condolences, but Bill barely heard them. He couldn't believe Abigail was dead… and Ernie too… He felt sick. It was all his fault. He had allowed himself to relax and get close to them and now they had been killed. He would never forgive himself.

'Come on Bill, you can't stay here.' Tom was trying to help him up.

Bill shook his head. 'Its all my fault.'

Tom frowned. 'Don't be silly mate. How can it be your fault? It was the fucking Jerries.'

'You should keep away from me. I'm unlucky.'

Tom looked uncomfortable. Like most sailors he was very superstitious. 'Don't talk like that Bill. You're just in shock.'

'Let's get him some rum. The Captain will authorise it as he's had terrible news from home.' Gerry was also looking concerned. He leant closer to Tom. 'Don't let him say that to anyone else or they'll be hell to pay. We don't need that shit, not on a new ship.'

Tom nodded. 'Come on mate, let's get you a drink.'

Bill allowed his friend to lead him back down to their cabin, barely aware of his surroundings. It was only after the first rum went down his throat that he began to think clearly again. 'I don't know what to do Tom. I can't live without her…, knowing she was there was keeping me going.'

Tom didn't know what to say so he just poured Bill another drink and offered him a cigarette. Bill downed the rum and shook his head. 'No thanks, I prefer these.' He lit one of his Lucky Strikes. Knowing Abigail was waiting for him had kept away the nightmares, had even rid him of the desire to drink himself unconscious and how had he thanked her? The words of the popular Mills Brother's song, *You always hurt the one you love*, popped into his mind and he found himself muttering the words. *You always take the sweetest rose, And crush it till the petals fall. You always break the kindest heart...* It could have been written for Abigail. Only he hadn't just wounded her with words, he had killed her.

****

Manchester

When Nora woke up she was lying in a room on her own. Her head felt awful but her first thought was for Jennifer. She forced herself to sit up, but there was no cot beside the bed. 'Where's my baby?' Her voice was hoarse, and she cleared her throat, coughed and repeated herself. This time her voice was stronger and echoed around the empty room. There was no answer, so she tried again and then climbed out of bed and walked unsteadily to the door and opened it. The corridor outside was empty. Nora hesitated. She had no idea where she was, perhaps she should just go back to bed? But the thought of Jennifer spurred her on. She began walking to the end of the hallway.

'What are you doing out of bed?' Before she could answer strong arms dragged her back into the room.

Nora struggled but was unable to break free. Forced back onto the bed she looked up to see the doctor and another needle, then everything went dark again.

The next time she woke her arm was handcuffed to the bed and she realised she had wet herself. Tears ran down her cheeks and she began to sob. How dare they treat her like this? She was only trying to protect her daughter and they were treating her like a criminal. She stared up at the ceiling and frowned. This didn't look like the home. It looked like a police cell. Her heart sank and then she thought about Jennifer and her resolve strengthened. If they thought they could shut her up they had another thing coming. She sat up and began shouting. 'I want my baby. Where's my baby!'

Chapter 16

London

Francis was in the middle of deciphering Tilly's latest message when the telephone rang. Cursing loudly at the interruption he allowed it to ring several times before finally giving in and picking up the receiver. A few moments later he sighed. 'I'm on my way. Don't do anything else until I get there.' He replaced the receiver and sat back in his chair, Tilly's latest message momentarily forgotten as he thought about the phone call. He could do without another problem at the moment, but he couldn't ignore it.

Francis picked up the phone again and ordered his driver to be ready in half an hour. Then he quickly finished decoding the message, made some notes, wrote an answer, telephoned the radio operator and carefully read out the reply. 'Make sure it goes tonight at the usual time.' Once that was done, he stood up, grabbed his briefcase, coat and hat, hurried out of the room and down the stairs.

****

Majdanek

The camp was not far from the town and barely hidden from the road. After a short journey Jacob arrived at a large wooden gate, on either side of which were sentry boxes painted with black and white chevrons and manned by armed guards. He tried to ignore the uncomfortable feeling in his stomach, hoped his nervousness didn't show, and handed his documents to the guards.

After careful scrutiny the guards passed him through, and he drove into an inner compound. He was now surrounded by a double row of barbed wire fencing and encircling the compound was a line of eighteen watchtowers manned by guards with loaded machine guns, rifles and grenades.

In the distance Jacob could see a tall brick chimney belching continuous white smoke into the air from the top of a slope and although the car window was closed there was a strange smell in the air. He pulled over and was wondering where he could find Claus when there was a knock on the window.

'Linus, welcome!' Claus waited until Jacob lowered his window and shook his hand. 'I wasn't sure if my father was going to come with you.' He climbed into the front seat and directed Jacob deeper into the camp before staring at him and lowering his voice. 'You will have to be a little careful when taking photos Linus. Make sure you don't get any of the guards in them, just concentrate on the prisoners alright? A couple of years ago most of them were proud of what they were doing, but not now,' he glanced around nervously even though they were in the car with the windows firmly shut, 'not now the war is coming to an end.'

Jacob nodded. 'Understood. Your father wasn't able to leave Berlin, so he sent me on my own.' He pulled over near the building Claus indicated and parked up. 'Can you keep the guards distracted while I take photos?'

Claus looked uneasy. 'I suppose so. What are the Generals going to do with these photos Linus?'

Jacob shrugged. 'No idea. They don't tell the likes of me anything!' He smiled. Claus hesitated and then relaxed slightly. He glanced at his watch. 'Come on we're take a walk around. I've told the Commandant that the photos have been requested for some propaganda.'

Jacob looked surprised. 'Did he believe you?'

Claus sighed. 'Yes, it wouldn't occur to people like him that they need to hide anything.' The two men exchanged glances. Linus followed Claus back through the camp, camera in his hand and began taking photos.

****

Portsmouth

'We need to get him back on the ship.' Bill was unconscious, his head on the table and Tom was surprised he hadn't been robbed. It had taken him and Gerry over an hour to find Bill. They had started searching the Hard in Portsea in the most obvious pubs, *The Ship Anson*, *London Tavern*, *Queenshead* and *Victoria and Albert*, the four pubs were next to each other, but he wasn't in any of them. They had finally found him in one of the *Army and Navy* in Half Moon Street after an exhaustive search of the more popular places.

The two men lifted him carefully, supporting his arms and leading him through the maze of busy tables and out through the door.

'He doesn't have much luck, does he?' Gerry sighed as he manhandled Bill's deadweight down the cobbled road. Fortunately, Bill was quite thin and wiry and not that heavy.

'Don't you start.' Tom snapped. 'There's a war on. I bet you could find loads more sailors who've been on more than one ship that's sunk.'

Gerry shrugged. 'Yeah, you're probably right.' He sighed. 'He's really tanked this time.'

Tom nodded. 'Yeah, we'll have to try and smuggle him back on board without any of the officers seeing.'

'She was a pretty girl, wasn't she?'

'Abigail? Yeah, I saw the photo he had of her. Poor lass. We're in the forces, we can expect to get killed, but when the bastards deliberately target civilians...' Tom shook his head.

'They'll get theirs. The RAF are bombing the shit out of Berlin and other German cities. And it can't be long before we invade Europe.' Gerry was relieved to see the harbour coming into view.

Tom nodded. 'Let's hope you're right or more innocent civilians will die.' He peered ahead and breathed a sigh of relief. *HMS Keats* was in sight, now they just had to find a way to get aboard without anyone seeing them.

****

Majdanek

Jacob had no idea how he managed not to react as he walked from hut to hut, photographing one prisoner after another. As he saw one atrocity after another, the sicker and more disgusted he felt, and it was even harder not to show what he was feeling, to keep his face impassive, to pretend indifference. Inside he was in turmoil, hating himself for not being able to do anything to help the tragic victims of such a barbaric place.

'Have you got enough?' Claus looked uneasy and Jacob nodded. He couldn't wait to leave Majdanek and there was no point pushing his luck.

Claus gave a relieved smile. 'Good. I'll see you off the camp.' The two men walked back to Jacob's car and he climbed in behind the wheel. Claus climbed in the other side. 'Give my love to my family.'

'I will.' Jacob hesitated. 'Look after yourself Claus.' His mouth twitched in amusement as he recognised the irony of telling an SS officer to take care. But he had the feeling that Claus wasn't like the rest of the SS men, he was too much like Clemens.

He reached the gates, Claus climbed out and watched as Jacob drove carefully through the gates.

****

Off the coast of Crete,

Levi thought back to his last night with Marta and wished he'd handled it better. At first he had hoped that she would come around. He had written to her as usual when he arrived back in Scotland to train for his next mission, but she hadn't replied and gradually Levi had accepted that there was no going back. He had damaged Marta's feelings, obviously beyond repair. He had tried to explain himself in another letter, but she still hadn't responded, and he knew now that he would have to accept their relationship was over.

Levi sighed and tried to concentrate on what he was supposed to be doing, instead of his love life, but it was difficult when he loved her so much and when there was little to see except the sea. The moon was now rising into the cloudless sky, sharpening the silhouette of Crete's coast and quickening his pulse. Perhaps this time they would finally make it. He could hear the local men chattering excitedly as they identified several landmarks and the sound of the engine which seemed to grow louder, the nearer they came to the coast. Then the small launch adjusted its course, travelling east for several minutes before finally turning northwards towards the island and Levi realised they had been too far west of the landing beach. The men fell silent and the engine sounded very loud in the now silent boat. Levi hoped what he had been told was correct, that the engine noise would be muffled by the mist and dulled by the sea, whereas voices would carry a long way at night. There was a German coastal position about three quarters of a mile from where they were due to land, so it was imperative they weren't heard.

The first plan had been to parachute the men onto the island, but the attempted drop on Crete had gone wrong. The pilot had circled the designated landing ground and dropped the first parachutist but decided that the area was too small for both men, so he had flown another circuit and then become lost in a cloud. After that they had then tried several sea landings, all of which had failed. Levi hoped this time they would finally be successful.

He was still reflecting on their failures when he spotted the flash of light from the shore. 'The signal!' His whisper sounded very loud in the silent craft and he could hardly stop himself from wincing.

The commander of the group peered through his binoculars and checked as the light flashed briefly on and off through the mist. It was only as they approached the coast that it became clear the lights were morse code. Levi concentrated and then nodded. 'All correct, sir.'

The boat headed closer in shore, the lights became even clearer and then Levi could make out a cove, a sandy beach surrounded on three sides by a steep cliff and see several figures moving around. He glanced around the ship and smiled briefly. The Cretans, their rucksacks, Marlin guns and ammunition belts on their shoulders, were singing softly. They were obviously pleased to be home.

The boat eased closer to the cove and then Stan gave the order to cut the engine. A dinghy was let down into the water and a couple of the crew climbed aboard and headed to the shore, letting out the tow line as they went.

Levi waited for the second dingy to be lowered before he began piling their kit into it, ignoring the water that was already seeping in. Eventually they received the all clear from the shore that the tow line had been secured and Levi climbed down on top of the kit and found himself being pulled towards the shore.

Within minutes Levi had been hauled ashore, helped out of the dinghy and was watching as several heavily moustached men with dark faces, turbaned heads, dark shabby clothes with either bare feet or tall boots, began emptying the contents of the dingy onto the sand. Levi stood still, hands on hips and began scanning the area. After several failed attempts he had finally arrived in Crete and although he was sure the Cretans would have secured the perimeter, he had no intention of taking any chances.

****

Manchester

'Francis?' Nora stared up at him in astonishment and confusion.

Francis was just as shocked. Nora looked awful, her eyes red rimmed from crying, her clothes wrinkled and dirty and there was a strong smell of stale urine. He sat down at the table opposite her. 'What on earth have they done to you?'

It took Nora a few moments to recover then she quickly explained.

Francis listened patiently and then shook his head. 'What on earth possessed you to pull a gun on them? I understand you were distressed but…'

'They were stealing my child. What else could I do?' Nora blinked the tears away and took a breath. 'If they'd let me leave…'

Francis sighed and tried to hide the fury rising up inside him, anger at her treatment but also because he couldn't do anything legally to help her. 'I'm so sorry Nora… I have looked into the charges against you, and it seems that unfortunately you did sign a contract when you entered the Home. That means that however unfair or immoral this situation is, they were within their *legal* rights to take your daughter and have her adopted. I know that doesn't make it any easier to bear.'

Nora shook her head and glared at him. 'I lost everything because I helped you. I had a job I loved but they thought I was a security risk because of you. Then I couldn't get another job on the Island because my reputation was ruined, so we had to move.'

Francis didn't answer for a moment, mainly because he knew what she was saying was true. He had not been able to tell everyone what she had been doing because of the security risk to Tilly and Jacob, so other than clearing her with the Island's security he hadn't done anything, and the damage was done. He tried to change the subject. 'But you were happy on the US Air base weren't you?'

Nora hesitated then looked down at the table. 'I was until I was raped. That was how I got pregnant.'

Having read her pleading letter to Tilly Francis already knew what had happened, but he didn't think it would be wise to let Nora knew he had read her letter. It would have led to more questions that he couldn't answer, including why he hadn't tried to help her then. Francis was feeling extremely guilty. If only he had acted when she had first begged Tilly for help... His only option was to pretend ignorance and horror. 'For heaven's sake...I'm so sorry Nora. I don't know what to say.' He took a breath. 'Did they catch the person responsible?'

To his relief Nora didn't seem to realise he was lying. 'No, I didn't report it because he threatened to kill me if I did. I didn't realise he had been deployed overseas the next day until it was too late.' She wiped her eyes with her sleeve.

Francis hunted in his pocket for a handkerchief. 'Here, its clean I promise.'

'Unlike me.' Nora wiped her eyes again.

'That's something I can rectify. When we've finished talking, I'll arrange for some clean clothes and a bath.' He stopped. 'I can't do anything about the contract,' he raised his hand to stop Nora interrupting, 'but I can get the gun charge dropped. That means you'll be free to leave here, go back home and back to work, if that's what you want to do.'

Nora thought about what he was offering and knew she would be wise to accept it, but the thought of losing Jennifer... 'Where's Tilly? I wrote to her care of your office. She never replied.'

Francis knew he should lie but Nora had been through enough, he didn't want her to think Tilly had abandoned her too. 'She hasn't received it. She's not in the country. I can't tell you any more for security reasons.' He gave a wry smile. 'I shouldn't have even told you that.'

Nora stared at him and then nodded. Given what Tilly had been doing when they had met she guessed her friend was some sort of spy. At least she knew Tilly hadn't ignored her. 'Thank you for telling me. I thought she just didn't want to get involved.' She took a deep breath and changed the subject. 'Is there really nothing I can do to get Jennifer back?'

Francis shook his head. 'No, I don't think so. I can ask one of our lawyers for you, but I would imagine the Home has these things well sewn up, so don't get your hopes up.'

Nora sighed. She would never forgive her parents for doing this to her. But at the moment she didn't have any option but to accept Francis' offer. At least then she would be free and she could go back to work. 'Thank you for coming to see me, I would like to accept your offer to get me out of here.' She frowned. 'How did you know I was here?'

'I imagine my name came up when they investigated you.' Francis was relieved Nora had agreed but he still felt guilty. If she hadn't become involved in the kidnapping her life would have taken a different path.

Nora suddenly remembered Halford Manor. 'What about the missing children? Did you find anything out about them?'

Francis shook his head. 'No, I haven't forgotten though. I will look into it when things quieten down a bit.'

Nora stared into his eyes and Francis looked away, his earlier guilt returning. He should probably have done something about it, even though it wasn't a priority given everything else he was dealing with. Nora misread his expression and suddenly felt exhausted. She'd had enough. She was tired of doing her bit, tired of fighting for a daughter no one thought she was capable of looking after, tired of doing the right thing when no one believed her, tired of worrying about other people when no one cared about her. Jacob had thought so little of her he couldn't even be bothered to tell her he didn't want to see her again, Francis obviously didn't think missing children were important, the nuns thought she deserved to be punished for being raped and her parents thought she was a tart. As she sat there Nora made a vow that she was not going to be a victim anymore. Never again would people take advantage of her. In future she would only think about herself.

****

Crete

Levi had packed all his kit on one of the mules, then helped to load the ammunition, explosives and various other items of shared equipment onto a second group of mules. Once that was done several Austrian deserters had been loaded onto the dingy and would be taken back to Cairo.

'The beach had been heavily mined but it's safe now.' One of the men hired to help unload and load their supplies grinned at Levi who had paled. 'It's alright, you don't need to worry. The shifting sands here mean most of the mines have drifted harmlessly away, the rest were blown up by the sheep that roam along here.'

'How long until we reach our destination?' Levi asked the man in charge.

'About an hour and a half.' Antonis responded and Levi smiled, not too long then.

Four hours later they finally arrived at the base of the mountains and began the climb, their route crossing gullies and mountain streams with fast flowing fresh water which tasted delicious and slaked their thirst. Eventually they reached the gully which would provide their hiding place for the next few hours and Levi looked around, checking its security. To his relief it was a good place to hide, flanked by rocks on three sides and surrounded by trees and thickets. He helped to unload the mules, took his blanket and found some shelter in a dried up stream bed, overgrown with foliage which made a comfortable bed. Levi was exhausted and despite the light rain he soon fell into a deep dreamless sleep.

Chapter 17

Berlin

Clemens stared at the photographs Jacob had given him in horror and disbelief. Jacob was sitting opposite him, his face expressionless. He still hadn't recovered from his visit to Majdanek even though it had been several days now. He was barely sleeping, terrified to close his eyes in case he had nightmares and he had started drinking schnapps every morning before leaving for work, unable to face the day without dulling the enormity of what he had seen.

He watched as Clemens went through the photos carefully before reading his report and then reaching for another cigarette. Jacob hoped Clemens was not going to ask him to explain anything because he didn't think he could bear to look at the photos again. His thoughts wouldn't leave Majdanek and the dreadful images that seared his brain. If he hadn't seen the horror for himself he would not have believed it, and he only hoped Francis would not think the photographs were doctored although they were so graphic, so awful he would not blame his employer for not believing what he was seeing. Once Clemens had finished with them, he would have to meet with Niklas and arrange for the pictures to be couriered back to England.

Jacob closed his eyes and thought back to the day he had driven away from the camp. He had waited until there were no other cars around, and he was sure he was not being followed, before stopping the car, climbing out and lighting a cigarette with shaking hands. A couple of minutes later he had emptied the contents of his stomach on the side of the road and tears were running unchecked down his face. If he hadn't seen the camp with his own eyes, he would not have believed it. How on earth Claus could work there he had no idea.

'I can't believe it.' Clemens eventually spoke. 'How could....?' He stopped unable to articulate his thoughts. He lit a cigarette and exhaled slowly before speaking again. 'I'm so sorry Linus. I had no idea.' He had known things were bad when Linus had returned to work and now he understood why. Linus had gone to Majdanek one man and come back another, his eyes haunted, an expression on his face that Clemens had been unable to read. He took a breath. 'Can you make some copies please.'

Jacob dragged himself back to the present and stared at him. 'Sorry? Copies...Why?'

'You are going to send these back to England by whatever means you have at your disposal... no I don't need or want to know how... I want to show them to the General Staff. I think we should also try and send them copies back to England by another route so that there is no danger of them becoming lost on the way. This is much too important.'

Jacob nodded although he had no idea how they could do that. 'I only have one contact sir.'

Clemens nodded. 'I will talk to some friends.' He suddenly slammed his fist on the desk. 'I am a soldier not a murderer. I will not be a part of this genocide. It is a slur on my country's armed forces and my son.' He stood up and began pacing the office. 'How on earth is he coping with this?'

Jacob shook his head. 'He's horrified by the things he has to do on a daily basis. I can't even imagine what he is going through. I could barely keep my feelings hidden for a few hours, to be stuck there day in, day out...' He fell silent.

'Perhaps I should see if there is any way I can get him transferred.'

'From the SS?' Jacob looked shocked. 'Is that possible?'

Clemens shook his head. 'No, probably not. At least not without drawing attention to him.' He leaned across the desk. 'Have four sets of copies made and then arrange to have your set delivered. Give the rest to me.' Clemens stared down again at the photos and fought back the bile rising in his throat. He would make sure his fellow generals knew exactly what that monster was doing, how he was dragging the good name of the German Army through the mud, if it was the last thing he ever did.

****

London

Francis replaced the receiver and wondered if he had done enough to atone for his part in Nora's downfall. He hoped so. Only time would tell, but at least this way there was a chance Nora would be reunited with her daughter at some point. But he wouldn't say anything yet, not until he was sure Nora was in the right place to look after a child.

He turned his attention to the files on his desk and sighed. He was becoming increasingly concerned about the double life Tilly was leading in the Netherlands. It was one thing being a double agent in England where his people were close enough to help her, but in occupied Holland with Kessel just across the border in Brussels, she was in permanent danger.

He picked up Jacob's file, stared down at the latest message and frowned. What the hell was Jacob doing in Majdanek? He read some more, and his frown deepened. He had heard rumours about the camps but like most of his contacts, had assumed the scale of atrocities were being exaggerated. Whilst some thought it was propaganda put out by various Jewish groups around the world, his own thoughts were that it was the Germans attempting to distract and disrupt the allied advance. If they could divert advancing troops, it might buy them some time to develop their super weapons, Hitler's so-called V (vengeance) weapons. Francis shrugged. Jacob's message said that he had sent photographs so he would soon know one way or the other.

Francis was still thinking about that when an idea began to form. He had been wracking his brains as to how to help Jacob and this could be the answer. Perhaps Jacob could find out more about those weapons. The Germans had moved everything away from Peenemunde after the allied bombing raids, and from the little intelligence he had the Germans had moved production to Mittelwerk, an underground factory in a hill called Kohnstein and were using slave labour from the Mittlebau-Dora concentration camp. It would add to Jacob's investigation into the concentration camps which might help to encourage the German generals to move faster in their attempt to overthrow Hitler. It could also push his superiors to lend some support to the German generals. Francis smiled and reached for a pen and some paper to write a message to Jacob.

******

Amsterdam

'Well done, Juliette. It looks like they've taken the bait.'

Tilly nodded and tried not to think of the night she had spent with Drescher, something that would have been easier if she wasn't due to have dinner with him again that evening. 'Good, let's hope they keep believing me.'

'Well presumably they won't expect any more names for a little while?'

Tilly shrugged. 'I hope not. I will have to make them realise that if they push too hard the resistance will guess and then I will not be of any use to them.' She fell silent. She wanted to tell him about Drescher, but she was too ashamed.

'Are you alright Juliette? Is there anything else worrying you?' Joren was watching her carefully.

'No, just worried about Martijn.' Tilly improvised quickly. 'I haven't heard anything, and I can't really ask.'

Joren considered for a moment then shrugged. 'They think you are one of them, not someone they've turned, so why wouldn't you ask? You suggested the idea didn't you so I think you should show interest.'

Tilly frowned. 'You're right. It would probably be more suspicious for me not to ask.' She forced a smile. 'I know I've been doing this for years, but it was much more clear cut in England. I am having to second guess myself all the time out here.'

Joren reached out and patted her shoulder. 'You're doing a great job Juliette and I'm always here for you to bounce ideas off, you know that don't you?'

Tilly sighed. 'Yes, thank you. I couldn't do this if I didn't have someone to talk to Joren.' She glanced up at the clock and grimaced. 'I'd better go, I'm having dinner with Drescher tonight.'

'Just think yourself German and act accordingly. You'll have him eating out of your hands.' Joren stood up, walked over and opened the door. 'I'll see you tomorrow.'

'Let's hope so.' Tilly left the office her thoughts on the coming evening, trying to suppress the glow of excitement she could feel growing in her stomach.

****

Crete

Having eaten breakfast of American K rations and various parts of cooked goat, the men discussed their plans and decided to make for

Kastamonitsa which was near Heraklion, the place they had chosen to make their headquarters. Antonis was sure they could reach Kastamonitsa by nightfall, but Levi was reluctant to accept his estimate after he had vastly underestimated the time it would take to reach the gully from the beach. Their commander also agreed that it would probably take them much longer than Antonis' estimate, so they had decided to leave immediately.

Levi was still having doubts as to the main reason they were here. The original plan had been to kidnap the Island commander, General Müller, who had been behaving towards the local population in a manner similar to that Heydrich had displayed in Czechoslovakia. But after the dreadful reprisals to the population of that country that had followed his murder, the Allies had decided against any further assassinations. However, they had decided that a kidnap was different and would cause considerable embarrassment to the occupying forces. Unfortunately, the plan had taken so long to put into action that General Müller had been replaced by General Kreipe. As far as Levi knew neither General had any specific information they needed, but the operation was going ahead anyway with precautions that were designed to protect the locals from reprisals.

Levi hoped his superiors were correct as he didn't want to be responsible for the mass murder of Cretan civilians. The plan was for them to leave behind a letter stating quite clearly that the General was now a Prisoner Of War of the British and would be treated as such. It further stated that no Cretan had been involved in the kidnap and no villages had been involved in hiding them or giving them any help whatsoever. Any Cretans acting as guides were already members of HM Forces and as such any reprisals against the population of Crete would be totally unwarranted. Levi only hoped the Germans would take notice of the official letter and leave the island's population alone. If not, he might have to come back again to complete his own task

Levi was there to help with whatever was needed but he had his own mission. He was to document the many German atrocities that had allegedly been carried out by both Generals on the island. These would be used as evidence to prosecute those responsible at the end of the war. There were several advantages of him collecting testimonies now, rather than waiting for peace, not least that the memories would be fresh.

Levi glanced down at the shabby black clothes that had replaced his battledress and shook his head in wry amusement. The change of clothes didn't really help him blend in with the Cretans or Paddy who was running the operation. But it was better than his uniform. He looked across at Paddy and grinned. He loved Paddy's embroidered Cretan bolero, corduroy riding breeches, tall black boots and the wine coloured cummerbund which held an ivory handled revolver and silver dagger. Paddy reminded him of an 18th century duke. He watched quietly as the group split into three and took turns to leave the gully. Eventually it was Levi's turn. He helped load their equipment onto the four mules and the men began their journey to Skoinia, this time not bothering to climb each peak but following tracks that avoided the steepest slopes.

******

Cairo

Clarissa finished filling in the forms in the administration office in Kasr el Nil to enable her to get her new British ID card. They would have to wait for their insurance money so they had all been given an advance of £50 to enable them to replace their luggage which was now at the bottom of the sea.

'I think I'll also go to the bank and get some funds transferred.' She glanced at Renee and lowered her voice. 'Do you need some extra money? I can lend you some if you like.'

Renee's face lit up. 'Really? You wouldn't mind?'

Clarissa laughed. 'Of course not. You can pay me back when the insurance comes through. I don't think £50 will go that far, not to replace everything you've lost.'

'Thank you.' Renee glanced around nervously, but Sandy and June were talking to someone else and not paying her any attention. 'I won't say anything.'

Clarissa smiled. 'Probably very wise. Come on, let's go shopping!' They hurried through the door and down the stairs.

****

Berlin

Jacob read the message and smiled. At last Francis had come through with something he could take to Clemens. But he would have to word it carefully. As much as Jacob trusted Clemens to work with the generals to overthrow Hitler, he wasn't sure how the German would react to sabotaging the German V weapon programme. Would it cross that fine line between treason and working for the good of the Fatherland?

He glanced at the clock and made his way to the door. He would arrange to meet Niklas that night, hand over one set of the photos and ask him what he knew about Mittelwerk. He would do that before speaking to Clemens. In the meantime, he would think about how to persuade Clemens to arrange a trip to Thuringia. Jacob would need a good reason to go there and take photographs. Jacob frowned. Actually there was little chance of taking any pictures, the V weapons programme was beyond secret, but he might be able to do some sketches. He would worry about that when he got there, but first he had to get permission to go there.

******

US Burtonwood

Nora arrived back at work and headed straight for the canteen. She was still grieving for Jennifer; it seemed a lifetime since she had held her daughter. Thanks to Francis Nora had not been arrested, but the nursing home had insisted she leave immediately, not that she wanted to stay there a moment longer than necessary. Her parents had been less than welcoming, assuming she would be delighted that they had resolved her *problem.* At first Nora couldn't believe they could be so uncaring, especially her mother. But then she had learnt about Abigail's death and decided that she didn't know her parents at all. They could have written to her in the home to tell her about her brother's fiancée, but they hadn't bothered so now it must look to Bill like she didn't care. Several times she picked up paper and pen to write to him but what could she say? It had happened weeks earlier, what possible excuse could she have for not writing to him other than the truth which she really didn't want to put in a letter. It was this that finally hardened her heart towards her parents, and by the time she was well enough to return to work she had hidden her pain deep inside.

'Nora, its lovely to see again.' Jessica's face lit up. She glanced quickly around, there was no one near, and lowered her voice. 'I was so worried about you. When did you get back?'

'A week ago. I would have come back sooner but... well you know.' She wanted to say more but two servicemen came in and she plastered an automatic smile on her face. 'Can I help you?'

'Sure honey, some ham and eggs please.' The man turned back to his companion and he continued his conversation. 'Gee brother, did I tell her what's what. To think…'

Nora tuned out, served the breakfast and handed the plate over the counter.

'Good morning. I haven't seen you for a while.' The tall handsome man with clear blue eyes smiled across the counter. 'You been away?'

'Yes, something like that.' Nora made an effort and smiled back. She vaguely remembered speaking to this man before.

'How about coming out for a drink tonight?'

Nora was about to refuse when she thought about spending another evening with her parents pretending nothing was wrong. If she met him in a public place and made sure she was not on her own with him she would be quite safe. 'Yes, why not. Where shall I meet you?'

'I could drive you home?'

Nora shook her head and winked. 'No thanks. I don't know if I like you yet! I'll meet you in one of the pubs in town. Which one?'

He laughed. 'The even Stars in Bridge Steet seems ok. My name's Hank by the way.'

'Nora. I'll see you at eight.' She leaned over the counter and whispered suggestively. 'Don't be late.'

Jessica stared at her in surprise. Nora saw her expression and shrugged. 'Being a nice girl hasn't done me much good has it? Do you want to come with me?'

Jessica hesitated and then nodded. 'Yes, thanks. We could get there early and have a good chat.'

Nora nodded and turned back to serve the growing queue. If Jessica thought she was going to pour her heart out in the pub she was in for a shock. Nora had already decided that Jennifer was part of her past, a past she had no intention of ever returning to.

****

HMS Keats

Bill lay on his hammock as the ship made its way to the area around Larne where they were due to form up with Escort Group 5 ready for next convoy duty. He wasn't particularly looking forward to being back in the Atlantic which he had heard one of the Canadian sailors from the RCN who had described it as the most miserable sea in the world. Bill could understand why. It was hard enough on a large ship but being on one of the small Canadian corvettes which the Canadians described as so unstable they would roll in wet grass would have been awful. Add to that the wet mess decks where tables and clothes floated in the sea water which was permanently knee deep. Bill shuddered as he remembered the sailor telling him how they were wet from the moment they left shore until they arrived at the other end, provided they survived the black pit, the area in the middle which was out of range of allied aircraft and the place most likely to be sunk by U-boats. Bill sighed. Perhaps he should stop feeling so sorry for himself. At least he was on a large ship and he would be so busy once they started across the Atlantic, he would have less time to think about everything he had lost. He reached for the last letter he had received from Abigail, held it over his heart and closed his eyes. He didn't need to read it to remember the words which were firmly imprinted on his brain. At first, Bill would have sworn that the letter smelt of Abigail, the shampoo she used on her hair, a faint aroma of her perfume, but not any longer. He had held the letter and cried copious tears so many times that it no longer smelt of anything, if it ever had.

He stared up at the ceiling and wished he could have a drink. He had tried to drink himself into oblivion as often as possible while they were in Belfast, but now they would be at sea for some time which meant the alcohol in his blood system would soon dissipate and then he would be stone cold sober. The thought depressed him, and he wondered yet again if he should have gone missing while in port. While he had wandered around the streets of Belfast, he had realised just how easy it would have been to cross the border into Ireland and then he wouldn't ruin the lives of any more of his friends. It had been so tempting, and now he was back at sea he didn't know why he hadn't taken the opportunity. Then he remembered why. If he had run away to Ireland and made friends with other people what was to stop them being affected by his curse. Bernie had died on land so had Abigail, her brother and mother. The curse didn't just affect his friends at sea it affected anyone he had contact with. Thank goodness he hadn't been home very much. Then he remembered how Nora had lost her job on the Island and how the family had been evicted and had to move to Warrington. Perhaps it didn't matter whether he was there or not, the outcome was the same.

Somewhere deep inside Bill knew he was not being logical and that not everything bad that happened was his fault. But he was beyond listening to the sensible voice in his head, the one that only spoke occasionally. In his state of absolute despair, it was much easier to listen to the other voice.

Chapter 18

Warrington

Nora finished another half pint and laughed loudly at Hank's joke while Jessica watched her with growing concern.

She leant forward and lowered her voice. 'Don't you think you've had enough Nora?'

Nora laughed loudly again and shook her head. 'Not yet Jess. Come on drink up or our friends will think we're lightweights!' She raised her empty glass in Hank's direction. He took it and stood up.

'Another one then? What about you Jessica?'

'I'm alright thanks.' Jessica shook her head.

'Its just you and me then Hank.' Nora stood unsteadily and took a step towards the ladies toilet.

'Can you manage?' Hank had taken her arm and for a split second she was back in the hut. She was about to pull away when she returned abruptly to the present. Hank was looking concerned and she moved closer to him, he smelt different, of after shave and beer and just as suddenly as the past had appeared it vanished. Nora relaxed and put her arms around him. Maybe this would help her forget, especially as this time she would be in charge of anything that happened to her, she wouldn't be a victim again. If men wanted to sleep with her, they would have to pay for the privilege and that money would go towards her new life. Nora had finally decided that she was going to find her daughter and then disappear and start again somewhere else. She hadn't decided where yet, or even when, she had to find Jennifer first. Perhaps she could go to America if the war was finished, but one thing she was sure of, she wouldn't be telling her parents where she was going.

Nora pulled herself back to the present, she could feel Hank's mouth on hers and she responded with passion.

Eventually she pulled away and grinned. 'I really do have to go to the ladies...' She pointed to the door and Hank laughed.

'This way honey, then perhaps I could walk you home?'

Nora stared into his eyes. 'I don't see why not...'

Jessica was watching Nora in disbelief. She had always believed her friend's story about being raped, but after watching her tonight Jessica was beginning to wonder if Nora had lied about the whole thing.

****

Skoinia, Crete

It was after midnight when they finally arrived at the village and, after waiting in a ditch while they sent one of the men to carefully scout ahead to ensure there were no German patrols about, they hurried down the street to a house at the far end. Levi winced as their boots echoed loudly on the cobbles, but no one came out and the two heavily armed policemen standing by a courtyard completely ignored them. The two roomed building where they were to stay overnight was owed by Mihale and his elder sister who were delighted to see them and immediately poured them wine and raki in their small living room. A noise behind him made Levi jump and spinning quickly round he trained his rifle on the door... only to see a goat. He was about to comment when the goat walked towards the fireplace and relieved itself, then wandered back out. As no one seemed to think this was strange Levi lowered his rifle and downed the rest of his drink. Several moments later they were all sitting down gratefully at a long table and tucking into sheep and lentils cooked in olive oil, hard boiled eggs and cream cheese made from goat's milk. The wine flowed freely and so did the toasts. As the Cretan custom was to make a toast whenever anyone raised their glass, the meal seemed to last for hours.

When they had finally finished eating a succession of people came to meet them, including, much to his surprise, the two policemen they had seen earlier. Levi spent several hours writing down accounts of alleged atrocities, taking names and details of corroborating witnesses and listening to dreadful stories whilst trying to remain expressionless and uninvolved. As the day wore on he found it hard not to be affected by the joy on the faces of the people who couldn't wait to shake their hands, and their delight that someone was taking notice of the awful things that had happened to them under the Nazi rule. Finally, the last of the villagers left and Levi and the others collapsed in the only bedroom while their host and his sister slept in the kitchen.

******

Berlin

Jacob grabbed Niklas' arm and stared into his eyes. 'You will make sure they get through, won't you?' The café was half empty, bomb damage piled up in one corner, the ceiling propped up with timbers. But at least it meant there was no one sitting too close to them and their conversation couldn't be overheard.

Niklas nodded, his face pale. He had glanced quickly at the photographs and that was more than enough to take his breath away. He shoved them in his pocket and licked his lips again. 'Yes, I will do my best I promise.' He hesitated. 'I can't believe...' He fell silent.

Jacob nodded. 'Nor could I, but it's true. I took the photographs myself.' He took a deep breath, and tried yet again to put away the images that haunted him. He changed the subject. 'What do you know about Mittelwerk?'

Niklas' eyes opened in shock. He double checked there was no one sitting near them again and leaned forward. 'What have you heard?'

Jacob lowered his voice to barely above a whisper. 'That its part of the V weapons project.'

Niklas nodded. 'Yes. They are using slave labour from the nearby camp, there have been lots of deaths, lack of suitable clothing, equipment, insufficient food...' His face darkened. 'I have heard that the weapons are nearly ready, but hopefully that's wrong.'

Jacob paled. Francis hadn't said that his assignment was particularly urgent, and surely he would have done if the Allies believed the V weapons were almost complete. 'How close?'

Niklas shrugged. 'I can't say exactly... maybe just rumours of course, something to keep the people happy.'

Jacob nodded, downed the rest of his ersatz coffee and winced at the taste. He stood up. 'I'm going to try and find out. If you do discover anything else, please let me know.'

Niklas finished his own drink and nodded. He watched Jacob leave and shook his head. He had hoped to survive the war, but it was beginning to get more and unlikely. He looked at the counter, shrugged and gave a wry smile. In that case he might as well have some more Schwarzwälder Kirschtorte.

******

Canal Zone

Clarissa took another bow and waved to the troops cheering in front of her. Tristram joined her for the last encore and then they were making their way back to the bus.

'I love seeing them so happy, even if it is for such a short time.'

Before Tristram could answer, Sammy snorted loudly in derision. 'Of course, you do!' Her voice carried along the bus queue and Clarissa heard some tittering behind her. She spun around.

'What do you mean by that?'

Sammy shrugged. 'Don't pretend you don't love all the adulation.'

Clarissa took a breath and tried to control her temper. 'I really don't know what you're talking about Sammy. We're here to bring a few hours of fun and laughter to these men who are fighting for our future. It's not important how we feel, it's about making them forget what's coming and encouraging them to enjoy the present.' She turned back to Tristram, gratified to hear some murmurs of approval behind her.

'And if you believe that, you'll believe anything…' June laughed.

'Just ignore them.' Tristram took Clarissa's arm and helped her climb aboard.

Clarissa didn't answer, she was sick to death of Sammy and June and their continuous sarcastic remarks. Fortunately, most of her fellow entertainers ignored them, but knowing that just one person doubted her motives for being here, made her feel sick.

'Tristram is right Clarissa, they really aren't worth worrying about. They are both just jealous.' Renee came and sat down next to them.

'Thank you, Renee, I know that deep down. But its just hard to ignore them sometimes.'

The coach began the journey back to Cairo and Clarissa stared out of the window. She loved being with Tristram and she really was enjoying entertaining the troops, but there were occasions when she missed Nathanial and Halford.

'Where shall we eat tonight?' Tristram put his arm around her. Clarissa smiled and turned towards him. She was about to speak when the coach suddenly lost its traction on the sandy road.

'Tristram..!'

The coach slid towards the edge of the road, Clarissa heard screaming and then the vehicle began to turn over and everything went black.

****

Amsterdam

Tilly crept back into her apartment, switched on the light and jumped. 'Joren! What on earth are you doing here?' Her heart was thudding against her ribs, partly from shock and partly from guilt. The meal had gone well and so had the sex afterwards much to her regret. Unfortunately, she seemed unable to resist him, and although every time she saw Drescher she was determined not to sleep with him, for some reason she still ended up in bed with him.

'I wanted to make sure you were alright. You were very distracted earlier.' Joren put his cigarette out in the ashtray and stood up. 'What is it you are not telling me?'

Tilly shook her head. 'I don't understand. What do you mean?'

'I've known you a long time Tilly and I think I can probably tell when you are lying.'

Tilly stared at the him for several seconds and then sat down. 'How do you think I persuaded Drescher to *turn* Martijn?' She didn't wait for him to answer. 'I slept with him, it was the best way to distract him. I didn't say anything because I am ashamed.' Tears formed in her eyes and she blinked them angrily away.

Joren walked towards her and put his hand on her shoulder. 'I'm sorry… I didn't mean…' He fell silent, not knowing what else to say.

Tilly gave a watery smile but didn't answer. She hadn't exactly lied to Joren, she *was* ashamed of sleeping with Drescher even if it was for the purest of motives, but the real problem was that she was enjoying it.

****

HMS Keats

Bill finished clearing the snow and ice off the deck and glanced across at *HMS Vindex*. He could just make out sailors clearing the flight deck with the help of a doodle-bug, a small vehicle used to move aircraft around the deck, and then he heard an aircraft above him. Bill grabbed the gun, spun it upwards towards the noise then gradually relaxed. It was a Fairey Swordfish, searching for any signs of U-Boats. As it circled over the carrier another smaller naval vessel appeared off the bow and fired a test depth charge near its parent vessel. Bill watched carefully, but other than a loud noise and masses of spray shooting up into the air there was no sign of any submarines. Bill relaxed his grip on the gun and watched the reconnaissance aircraft land carefully on the aircraft carrier.

So far they had not seen any U-Boats, but there was still plenty of time. Things had improved considerably now they had aircraft patrolling the whole route. Earlier in the war the middle of the crossing had been very dangerous because the aircraft were not able to fly the whole length, leaving them dangerously exposed. But the new carriers made all the difference.

He leant back against the freezing rails and shivered. Despite his thick coat it was icy cold, the sea freezing almost as soon as it hit the deck, making the ship slippery and dangerous to move about on. Even the gun froze making it essential to wear gloves or he would lose fingers. He peered into the spray, his eyes searching relentlessly for anything that indicated a U-Boat was about. In the distance he could make out the other ships in the convoy, Britain's lifeline and a brief smile crossed his face. Normally he had no idea what the other vessels were carrying but this time he had caught sight of what he was sure was a troop ship. That meant American servicemen heading for the UK, presumably for the long awaited Second Front. Obviously, that was only a guess, but that would explain the extra tight security on this trip. They hadn't even been allowed to go ashore in Belfast or write any letters.

As usual, thinking about letters reminded Bill of Nora and the lack of news. It was very strange that he hadn't heard anything from his sister. Once he had recovered slightly from the shock of Abigail's death he had expected a letter from Nora offering her condolences, there had been one from Danny, but there had been nothing from Nora. At first he had been relieved. It was hard enough reading his mother's messages of support and reading Danny's attempts to cheer him up so having to answer Nora's as well would just make things worse. But he hadn't received anything from his sister at all which was not right. Bill had eventually asked his parents if Nora was alright as he hadn't heard from her, but they had completely ignored his question, not mentioning Nora at all, which made it all the more peculiar.

Bill had thought hard and decided that the only possible explanation was that Nora had fallen out with their parents and was living somewhere else. But that didn't really make sense. His parents knew where Nora worked and even if they didn't want to talk to her, they could have written to her care of the base. Unless she had changed jobs as well. Bill resolved to write to Nora when his watch was over, then he could post it as soon as he reached port. Although his first reaction had been anger that she hadn't bothered to write to him, that she didn't care enough to offer him her condolences, he was now starting to worry.

******

Berlin

'Thuringia? Why on earth do you want to go there?' Clemens eyed Jacob suspiciously.

'There's another camp there, Mittlebrau-Dora concentration camp. If I can get photos of that the allies might be prepared to talk to you.'

'Why?'

Jacob took a deep breath. 'Because that's where the V weapons project is. They're using slave labour from the camp. If I can show them that they might agree to help you.'

Clemens stared at him for several second. 'You are asking me to betray my country… its not the same as the camps…' He fell silent.

'Yes, it is the same Clemens.' Jacob spoke with passion. 'If Hitler can deploy these weapons, and they succeed in prolonging the war, more people will die, more innocent civilians in German cities will be bombed, and the deaths in the camps will continue. You know I am right.' There was no response so Jacob continued. 'You said you wanted to stop the war, that is why you and the generals are trying to do something. Help me get to Thuringia Clemens and then hopefully the Allies will help you.' Jacob held his breath. He had eventually decided to tell Clemens the truth, mainly because he couldn't think of a lie that would be both believable and sufficient reason for him to go to Mittelwerk.

'Can you guarantee the Allies will accept our surrender if I do what you want?'

Jacob shook his head. 'No, of course not. I don't have that kind of authority. But my instincts tell me that they will. If the V Weapons are even half as lethal as Hitler keeps threatening, and there's a chance to stop the programme they will take it. They would be stupid not to.'

Clemens stood up and walked to the window. He gazed down on the city he loved, a city that was already devastated by the Allied aerial bombardment. If he and his companions didn't stop the war soon there would be nothing left for his children, assuming they even survived. And then there was Claus. If he had to carry on working in Majdanek for much longer what would happen to him? What kind of damage was it doing to him?

'What will happen to Claus when the war ends? Will the Allies let him go?'

Jacob was thrown by the change of subject and didn't answer for the moment. 'I don't know. I can't answer that. But I will tell them that he helped us get the proof at considerable risk to his own life. That can only help his cause.'

Clemens nodded slowly. 'Yes, I suppose so, although you being married to my daughter might work against him.'

'It proves that you were all working against the regime, that you are all...' Jacob stopped, not sure how to phrase what he wanted to say.

'That we are *good* Germans.' Clemens gave a wry smile.

Jacob looked so embarrassed that Clemens laughed out loud, releasing the tension in the room. 'Its alright Linus, I am not offended. There are lots of good Germans, we are just too frightened to speak out or do anything against the regime.'

Jacob nodded. 'I'm not surprised... and yes, I know that not all Germans are Nazis but...' He stopped.

'But we let him take power and then we allowed him to stay there, to start a war that has killed thousands, probably millions and we continue to let the SS to do unspeakable things in our name.' Clemens sighed. 'I would like to say we, the Armed Forces, aren't responsible, but of course we are. Our generals liked the idea of salving our bruised pride after the Great War, of showing the French and the British that we weren't beaten. Yes, there were those who objected, and they were removed from their posts, a good reason for those remaining to stay quiet and support the resurgence of German military power. I could say we didn't know about the extermination of the Jews, but I would be lying.' He saw Jacob's shock and he hastened to explain. 'I don't mean me personally. I had no idea about that. I swear on Eve's life. But I am reasonably sure the top brass did know, although they might not have thought it was so...' He paused, hunting for the right word.

'Industrialised?' Jacob suggested, his face still pale, his expression unfathomable.

'Yes.' Clemens frowned suddenly. 'Can I ask you something Linus?'

Jacob nodded. 'I think you will anyway.'

'You are of German extraction, aren't you?'

'Yes, I told you that.' Jacob wondered where the conversation was going.

'Are you also Jewish?'

There was a long silence while Jacob tried to decide what to say.

Clemens smiled. 'Its alright. You don't have to answer.' He changed the subject. 'I will find a reason for you to visit Thuringia.' He glanced at the clock. 'Why don't you finish early. I am sure Eva will be delighted to spend some time with her new husband.'

Jacob smiled. 'Thank you.'

Clemens shrugged. 'I don't really have a choice, do I?' He watched Linus leave the room, closed his eyes and sighed. What possible reason could he have to send his secretary to Thuringia.

Chapter 19

Kastamonitsa, Crete

On arrival in the village at daybreak Levi and the other men went straight to the Zahari's house where they were greeted with such a large meal that after eating it they lay down and slept until noon.

After lunch they met the chief agent in Heraklion, 'Micky' Akoumianakis. Micky owned a house in Knossos which was next door to the Villa Ariadne, General Kreipe's sleeping quarters, so was able to provide good reconnaissance on the activities of the General.

'At least we won't be bothered by too many visitors.' Paddy spoke quickly while laying out the maps on the floor.

'Why?' Levi looked concerned. It would be hard for him to do his job if there were no visitors, although better for the security of the main mission.

'There's a large German convalescent home on the other edge of the village so its not safe to keep visiting the house.'

'The bastards also keep trying to buy eggs and vegetables from the villagers.' One of the family interjected. 'They congregate on street corners or walk around in groups seeing what they can pillage.' He spat on the floor.

Levi nodded. He would have to find some other way of getting the information he wanted. He was about to say that when another member of the family came into warn them that Germans were approaching.

'Quick get away from the windows…'

They all moved quickly and a few moment later they heard the sound of numerous German boots echoing on the cobbles. Levi could feel the sweat forming on his upper lip and he tightened his grip on the rifle. He glanced at their hosts and was reassured by a smile from Zahari's father although his wife seemed visibly upset, her lips trembling, her eyes wide with fright.

'My eldest brother was killed by the Germans three months ago.' Zahari whispered. 'As was Micky's father.'

'I'm sorry. Perhaps you could give me some details once the danger is passed?'

Zahari frowned and Levi hastened to explain. 'As well as our main task I am here to get information about German atrocities so they can be used at the end of the war to bring those guilty of war crimes to account.'

Zahari's face cleared, he smiled and began talking quickly. Levi pulled out his notebook and started taking notes in Hebrew. He knew it would not help him if he was caught, but it would be harder for the Germans to translate if he was captured and this would hopefully protect the people who had spoken to him if he wasn't able to destroy his notes. Several moments later the danger had passed, Paddy handed out some blank identity cards and some maps, Levi put away his notebook and turned his attention back to the main mission.

'I'll go back with Micky and watch the General myself Levi. You take the rest of the men and establish an HQ in the mountains which we can use as a rallying and jump off point for the operation.'

Levi nodded. As much as he had enjoyed staying in Zahari's house he would feel safer once they were back up in the mountains, and not in such close proximity to the enemy. 'We'll need mules to move our kit, so we'll stay here until late this evening… if that's alright Zahari?'

Zahari nodded. 'The streets should be deserted then.' He turned to Paddy. 'Here are some fresh clothes for your journey to Heraklion and a cap to hide your hair.' Zahari handed Paddy a small bundle and some burned cork to darken his moustache and eyebrows. A few moments later Paddy was barely recognisable, and the men said their goodbyes.

Several hours later Levi and the other men followed Zahari's father along a little known path out of the village and up into the mountains. It was a fine night with no clouds and a full moon and to start with they made good progress as they followed the steep footway up the mountain. It was only after they left the track and began walking on bare rock that they slowed down, the mules continuously slipping and sliding. 'We'd better stop in that cave until it gets light, the path is too steep to carry on in the dark.' Zahari whispered.

Levi helped unload the mules before laying down beneath an overhanging rock in the bitter cold and trying unsuccessfully to sleep.

******

Cairo

'Thank goodness Clarissa. I was terrified when I saw you lying there unconscious.' Tristram was gazing down at her with such love that she almost forgot that she had no idea what had happened and why she was lying in a hospital bed. She raised her arm and winced as pain shot through her arm bringing her abruptly back to the present.

'What happened?'

'The coach turned over, several of the entertainers were hurt…' he hesitated, 'Cherie had her fingers crushed,'

Clarissa gasped. 'That's awful, she's an acrobat…how will she work?'

Tristram shook his head. 'I don't think she'll be able to, not doing the same act anyway.' He changed the subject. 'There were a few injuries from glass after the windows shattered, and you were knocked out. How do you feel?'

'I'm alright, bit of a headache but otherwise I'm sure there's nothing serious.' Clarissa reached out for his hand. 'I'm glad you're not hurt. Is Renee alright?'

'I'm fine.' Clarissa turned to her left and saw Renee sitting by her bed. 'I'm glad you aren't hurt.'

'I bet Sammy and June will be disappointed.' Clarissa smiled.

'Funny you should say that…' Renee laughed and stood up. 'I'd better get back, we've got a rehearsal in a couple of hours. Apparently, Sammy doesn't like something about the act,' Renee grimaced, 'no idea what, the audience seemed happy enough.'

Clarissa watched her go before speaking. 'She's much better than either of them. The soldiers were lapping her up. Sammy probably wants to cut her part down.'

'You can't interfere Clari. It will cause problems.'

Clarissa shrugged. 'She's my friend Tristram. I won't let them treat her badly. This profession is hard enough without people like Sammy.'

Tristram stared at her for several seconds before smiling warmly. He could hardly complain about her generosity, it was one of the things he loved about her. 'At the moment all I am concerned about is you. I couldn't bear to lose you.' He leant over, his lips over hers and Clarissa forgot all about Renee's problems with Sammy.

******

HMS Keats

Bill handed over the letter to be posted and was assured it would go as soon as the ship docked. He had not written very much, just a quick note asking Nora if she was alright as he hadn't heard from her in ages. He had debated whether to mention Abigail and then decided it would be odd not to. But he had tried not to make it sound like an accusation that she hadn't written to him.

They had almost finished escorting the latest convoy across the Atlantic and Bill was looking forward to some shore leave before the next trip. His thoughts returned to Nora and he sighed. It was so very odd that she hadn't written to him. Even Danny had written to him and Danny hated writing letters. He couldn't think of any reason why his sister wouldn't offer him her condolences unless she was in trouble of some kind. He frowned. There had been something odd about her losing her job on the Island, when he'd mentioned it Nora had changed the subject. He reached his bunk, lay down and closed his eyes and thought about Abigail. If only she hadn't gone to London. He was still struggling to accept that he would never see her again. His dreams were full of her and he would wake up believing she was alive, his spirits would soar and then the truth would hit him and he was plunged into the depths of despair again. Bill sighed. Although he was worried about Nora, the real reason he wanted to hear from her was because he needed someone he could talk to, someone who would understand how he felt. He couldn't tell his friends, it wasn't something men spoke about. They had given him their sympathy when she had first been killed, but everyone had lost someone in the war. He couldn't wallow in his misery, others had lost much more. Bill knew that, but it didn't really help. They were at war. He was expected to put on a stiff upper lip and get on with his life as if nothing had happened. There would be time to mourn the dead afterwards, except he couldn't do that. The people he had lost were with him every minute of the day. They weren't at peace and nor was he.

****

Mittelwerk

Jacob arrived at the underground complex and looked around him in disbelief. It was much bigger than he had imagined with thousands of labourers. The former Wifo gypsum mine was in the Kohnstein Hill on the southern border of the Harz mountains close to Nordhausen. According to the brief history Clemens had given him, the mine had originally been opened in 1917 and commandeered by the Wehrmacht in 1936 to store poison gas and fuel and by 1942 it had been the largest oil and fuel storage depot in Germany. After the destruction of Peenemunde by the RAF, work on the rocket had been divided into three and that was all he knew other than that this was the assembly site for V2 rockets. He had gathered from Clemens that the research and design was in Ebensee near Lake Traunsee in Austria and that the testing site was in Blizna in Poland, out of reach of the RAF. The last message he had received from Francis had been adamant that he get as much information as possible. The Allies would soon be opening the long awaited Second Front and it was vital nothing happened to disrupt that. Clemens had given him some more information about the V2 and the thought of these missiles raining down unchecked on England was very disturbing.

Jacob glanced down at the information in his hand, put it back in his pocket and took a deep breath. The person in charge was SS Brigadier General Hans Kammler, the man who had also been responsible for building several other camps including Auschwitz-Birkenau. Jacob had a letter of introduction from Clemens stating that Jacob was there to see the rockets and report back to the Army on their progress. The Wehrmacht were expecting an Allied invasion soon and needed to know if they could rely on the Vengeance weapons to either throw the Allies back into the Atlantic Ocean or the English Channel, which ever was applicable, or even prevent the landings in the first place.

Jacob stepped forward and the first thing he saw was the camp. It reminded him instantly of Majdanek, the same inhuman conditions, but even he wasn't prepared for the state of the labourers, thin, emaciated, virtually no hair, pale…

'Papers?'

The guard was not much older than him, a long scar on his face, and Jacob guessed immediately from the awkward gait that he had lost part of his right leg below the knee.

Jacob handed them over and waited.

The guard opened the barrier and waved him through, pointing to a door at the far end. 'You'll find someone to help you down there.'

Jacob nodded his thanks and began walking swiftly across the open space towards the first of the large buildings, his thoughts once more on the prisoners he had seen earlier. He had thought the Nazis only treated the Jews like that, but he was obviously wrong. He had heard the few words spoken by the guards to the inmates and realised immediately that the men he'd seen were Russian, presumably Prisoners of War although they certainly weren't being treated as such.

******

Crete

Levi gazed out at the huge mountains towering above them and listened as Zahari pointed. 'That's Afendis Christos and over there to the east, Mount Ida and over there, in the distance, the White Mountains.'

'It's a beautiful view.' Levi breathed in deeply 'The air is so clean up here.'

Zahari smiled and then indicated a cluster of tiny white dwellings in the far distance. 'That's Heraklion. We'll find somewhere to camp a bit closer. There's no real track now so be careful.'

Levi nodded. 'At least there's not much danger of German patrols then?'

'No.' Zahari's smile broadened. 'And we would have plenty of warning so we could pick them off quite easily.' He hesitated before speaking again. 'Do you really think writing down the things they have done here will help punish them?'

'The Krauts?' Levi clarified. Zahari nodded.

'I hope so. I can't guarantee that obviously, but if we don't write it all down properly, they will get away with it. By recording everything now we can make sure events are clear in people's minds, the names of the Germans responsible, victims, witnesses etc. If we leave it until after the war some of those people may not be alive but we will have their written testimony.'

Zahari sighed. 'They should be made to pay, them and the Italians who are just as bad, but I bet they get away with it.'

Levi wanted to argue that he was sure they wouldn't, but he realised that he too had doubts. 'Well, if they don't, we can always do it ourselves can't we? We have all the information, and our burden of proof won't be as high.'

Zahari stared at him in astonishment then grinned. 'I'll remember you said that.'

Levi smiled back and walked off, his mind going over what he'd just said. He had not really been serious… or had he? If no government was prepared to bring these criminals to account, why shouldn't he and some of the men he had worked with do it for them? It probably wasn't legal, but it was certainly moral. He shrugged and pushed the idea away. Hopefully it wouldn't come to that.

Sometime later, after a dangerous scramble down the sheer cliff face, they reached a small cave whose entrance was virtually undetectable. It was so well hidden that Levi had to crawl on all fours to get inside. There was a rock fireplace in one corner and trampled leaves and ferns on the floor.

Levi crawled back out and made his way to the surrounding trees which provided cover from the wind and prevented them from being seen. There was a freshwater stream running below them and they had adequate supplies of food to last until Paddy came to find them with the final plans. Levi sat down, lay back on the grass and closed his eyes. It was a perfectly peaceful place to wait, and he could even get some reading done and perhaps think of a way to make things up to Marta. Not that he would be able to write to her until he returned to allied territory, as they had left their personal possessions and anything that pointed to them being British back in Britain.

******

USAF Burtonwood

'She sure is sweet.' Chester sipped his coffee slowly, his eyes on Nora who was busy serving a long queue of service men.

'Yeah, maybe, but you wanna make sure you don't catch anything.' Ira lit another cigarette and added some more smoke to the already polluted atmosphere of the canteen.

'That's no way to talk about a lady.' Hank interrupted as he sat down and began cutting his eggs and ham up.

'And she aint no lady!' Ira laughed. 'Come on Hank, everyone's been there and she's only been here a short while.'

'I'm sure that's just talk. She's a nice girl.'

Ira shook his head and blew some more smoke. 'You're kidding right? I know at least three guys who've been there.' He glanced sideways at Hank and frowned. 'Did she turn you down? Is that why you don't believe me?'

Hank smiled. 'Now that would be telling Ira, and a gentleman never tells.' He added some sugar to his coffee and watched Nora surreptitiously. Almost as if she felt his gaze Nora looked up suddenly, caught his eye and gave a quick smile. Hank raised his cup briefly and then realised his friends were watching him with a mixture of disbelief and amusement. 'She's a nice kid, so cut her some slack ok.'

'Sure Hank, whatever you say.' Ira shrugged and exchanged glances with Chester.

Nora returned her attention back to the man in front of her and tried to forget the tall American who had taken her out a couple of times. Although she had allowed him to walk her home, she had not allowed him to go any further than kissing her because she liked him. She also sensed Hank was looking for something more permanent and that would never do. Nora had no intention of making the mistake of getting involved with anyone and so had accepted several invitations from other men in the hope it would put him off. It hadn't. She knew she was beginning to get a bad reputation, but she didn't care. She wasn't looking for a serious relationship. She'd tried that and look where it had got her. She was looking for fun and the best way to have fun was to date lots of men, not get serious about any of them, especially as their life expectancy wasn't that long and assume that everything they said was a lie. No one would want her now, she was damaged goods so she might as well enjoy herself on her terms.

'Can I meet you in the Seven Stars again? Say eight o'clock?'

Nora started and glared up at him. 'You made me jump Hank.'

'You're beautiful when you look startled.' He smiled at her and she felt her resistance melting. 'I'll see you there about eight then. Bye honey.' He was gone before she could argue and she cursed under her breath. What was the matter with him? Why wouldn't he get the message? She had deliberately not gone to bed with him, despite sleeping with both his friends. What did she have to do to make him see that she was bad for him? Perhaps she should just stand him up. Surely then he would see her for what she was?

****

Port Tewfik, Egypt

Clarissa stared around the French Club where they had been sitting for several hours waiting to leave for Bombay. 'I wish we'd hurry up and leave.'

Tristram grinned. 'We'll soon be aboard.' He leaned forward. 'Your friends don't seem very happy.' He indicated Sammy and June who were both sitting at a table by the bar, faces like thunder. Renee was sitting a little distance away from them, her nose in a book. Clarissa had asked her to join them, but she had declined, worried about making the relationship between herself and the sisters even worse.

'Looks like this is it... Finally!' Clarissa stood up and they began following the others out of the club, down the long straight road bordering the canal. They changed their money from piastres to rupees, had their luggage checked and then sat down outside the post official's little cabin and waited. The sun slowly sank, the sky darkened and the air grew cold. It was virtually dark before their ship finally arrived down the Suez Canal, a small white vessel that didn't look very warlike at all. They climbed into the tugboat and chugged off through the choppy waves towards the ship. The wind grew stronger as they finally reached the gangplank and climbed aboard. To Clarissa's relief she was in a small two berth cabin this time with Renee. Her only concern was that the porthole was screwed down meaning it would be very hot when they reached the Red Sea.

The vessel was a cargo ship, carrying Spitfire parts, so there were only a couple of hundred passengers on board including some US Airforce officers, some Admiralty personnel bound for Ceylon and several wives going out to India to join their husbands. The ship would sail to Aden first where they would join a convoy to cross the Indian Ocean.

Clarissa gazed around her fellow passengers and relaxed. There were plenty of people for her to get to know which meant she could comfortably avoid Sammy and June. She made her way towards a young mother with a small child and introduced herself.

'Can you sing for us? Sorry, I'm Charlotte and this is Betty. My husband is a missionary at Port Sudan. 'Betty's never seen her father so she's very excited.'

'Yes of course.' Clarissa glanced at Tristram and then began singing 'They'll be bluebirds over, the White Cliffs of Dover...' Within minutes everyone was singing along. Tristram looked around as he joined in, a smile on his face which faded slightly when he saw the sour expressions on the face of Sammy and June.

'They don't like anyone having the limelight.' Renee shrugged and then joined in. Clarissa caught her eye and the two women exchanged smiles. Tristram suddenly felt uncomfortable. He looked towards Sammy and June, but they were no longer there and his feeling of unease increased. Then he shook himself. He was being ridiculous. They were two entertainers, not enemy soldiers. What on earth could they do to Clarissa? Other than ruin her reputation and destroy her career of course?

****

Amsterdam

Tilly closed the door and let out a huge sigh of relief. She walked over to the window and watched Drescher striding towards his car. The driver opened the door and he was about to climb in when a series of shots rang out. Tilly gasped and automatically ducked back from the window before realising that the shots were not aimed at her so they must have been for Drescher. She crouched down, leaned forward and stared down into the street. There were several Germans firing at the buildings opposite and from the flashes she could make out several resistance fighters firing back. She lowered her gaze and managed to make out Drescher crouched down by the side of the car, his driver leaning out and firing protectively every few seconds. Now the initial shock was over she was beginning to think clearly again and she wondered what the hell was going on. Why were the resistance targeting Drescher? If they killed him, he would be replaced, and they would have to start all over again. Her relationship with Drescher was proving very productive as far as intelligence was concerned so why would the Resistance suddenly decide to kill him? She was still thinking about it when she realised the handle on her door was slowly moving. Someone was trying to get into her room. Tilly's heart began to beat faster and she rolled to one side before hurrying to her bedside table, reaching for her handbag in the bottom drawer, and taking out the small pistol. She took aim and waited, her pulse racing, sweat forming on her upper lip.

****

Heraklion, Crete

The men had arrived at the T junction at eight o'clock dressed in their German uniforms and immediately taken cover. Five false alarms and an hour past the time when the General should have come along, the warning torch finally blinked.

They climbed quickly out of the ditch in which they had been crouching, stood in the middle of the junction and Stan held up a traffic signal while Paddy switched on his red light. The German car came around the bend and bathed them in bright light. The chauffeur slowed down while Paddy immediately shouted in German, 'Halt!'

As soon as the car pulled up the two main abductors walked towards it, waited until they had passed the headlights and then drew their pistols.

'Is this the General's car?' The chauffeur answered yes and then Stan and Paddy sprang into action, pulling open the doors and shining the torches into the interior. Before the chauffeur could pull out his own gun Stan had reached across and hit him and then Levi was helping him out of the driving seat and Stan jumped in. The General was struggling in the back seat with Paddy and one of the other men.

Levi watched them drive off and then hurried back up into the mountains. He would remain in the forward base until he received word that the General had been taken off the island. Then he would make his way to the rendezvous and wait to be picked up. Providing everything went to plan, his part was now over.

****

Amsterdam

'Tilly?' The door swing slowly open and Joren crept in.

Tilly relaxed her arm and took a breath. 'Joren? What the hell's going on?'

'I don't know, that's why I came to get you.'

'Am I in danger?' She was already collecting her bag and ID papers. She shoved the pistol in her coat pocket and put it on quickly. Everything else she could replace.

'I don't know. But yes, I would think so. The shooters are not our people. It would appear they are a communist group that we didn't know anything about.'

'So, they think I am a collaborator?'

'Something like that.' Joren allowed the ghost of smile to cross his lips. 'Nazi whore was the last thing I heard.'

Despite the seriousness of her situation Tilly couldn't help laughing. 'Great. Obviously I am doing a good job.' She stepped towards him. 'Come on then, lets go.' Then she paused. The firing had stopped and other than some shouting it had gone quiet outside. 'What about Drescher?'

She had barely finished speaking before he appeared in the doorway. 'I'm fine. I came back to see if you were alright.'

Tilly nodded and wondered how much he had heard. 'Yes… yes my friend heard the shooting and was worried about me.'

'Thank you…'

'Joren Varwijk. Juliette works for me.'

'Ah yes, of course.' To Tilly's relief Drescher seemed distracted and she assumed it was from the assassination attempt. But he wouldn't stay distracted and she didn't want him asking any awkward questions.

'I think you can go now Joren, thanks for coming round. I'll be alright now Bruno is here.' Joren didn't need telling twice. He disappeared down the corridor and hoped he wouldn't have any trouble getting through the check points.

Tilly walked towards Bruno, put her arms around him and held him tight. 'I'm so pleased you are alright. When I heard the shooting… I was so scared.'

Bruno tightened his own arms around her before gently stroking her hair with his fingers. 'You're safe now. My men have killed the criminals.' He closed his eyes briefly and muttered. 'We will have to find out how they knew I was here though.' He pulled back. 'Did they fire up here?'

Tilly shook her head. 'I don't think so. I was too scared to do anything but duck back in the bedroom and hide behind the bed.' She paled. She had to divert his attention from her and stop him getting suspicious. 'Perhaps they were going to kill me once they had finished with you.' She shuddered and he tightened his grip.

'You'd better stay with me tonight. We can find you somewhere else to live tomorrow.'

Chapter 20

North Atlantic

The 6th May had started the same as any other day until they spotted the U-Boat, U-765. The sea was rough, the waves crashing relentlessly against the bows as the ship ploughed towards the submarine's last known location. When the other ships from the 9th Escort group had returned to Canada to refuel a few days earlier *HMS Keats* had been deployed as close escort for the aircraft carrier *HMS Vindex*. The crew had already responded to action stations and Bill was standing by the gun, his eyes roving over the restless sea, waiting and watching for any sign of the U-Boat. He was aware that the other frigates in the convoy, *HMS Aylmer, Bligh and Bickerton*, were close, all searching for the U-Boat before it could launch its deadly torpedoes at the convoy. Bill guessed that down below the radar would be pinging madly and he gazed down at the sea, wishing he could see the enemy vessel. The roar of aircraft taking off caught his attention and he watched transfixed as the Fairey Swordfish from 825 Naval Air Squadron were scrambled, their depth charges plainly visible.

Meanwhile the other frigates joined *Keats* in firing their own depth charges, the sea boiled in a hail of explosions, the deck showered with icy cold water. Bill held tight to the gun as he felt his feet slipping, his ears ringing with the explosions. And then he saw her slowly surfacing and he aimed his gun and began firing. Above him the swordfish let loose their depth charges, Bill watched the trail in the water, the submarine exploding…, he continued to fire… and then it was all over. He stopped firing and leant back. In the water he could just make out men swimming, their heads bobbing above the oil covered water. The ships lowered their lifeboats, the men scrambled aboard, grateful to be rescued and the submarine slowly disappeared below the surface.

Bill smiled. At last he had revenge for the death of his friends, and for Abigail. The lifeboat was hauled back on board and he stared at the enemy, the first time he had been that close to Germans since Greece, only this time he was on the winning side, and it was the enemy who had been sunk. Then his smile faded and for some reason he felt cheated. The submariners didn't have horns, they looked just like him, young men, shocked, covered in oil, shivering, some injured, men relieved to have survived. As the crew took them below, Bill turned away. They would be given some rum and tea and looked after, treated much better than they deserved, much better than he and his friends would be if the positions were reversed. Bill sighed, slammed his fist against the gun and blocked out the cheery voices around him celebrating the sinking of the submarine. His pain hadn't gone away, Abigail hadn't been miraculously returned to him. The sinking of the U-Boat hadn't changed anything.

****

London

Levi finished writing up the last of his reports about German activity on Crete and sat back. The final two accounts had been told to him by Manoli while they waited at the forward base for the go ahead for the kidnap, and although he hadn't had time to verify them, it should be easy enough after the war to collect corroborative testimony from the Cretans. The first account told how all the people in a small hillside village had been lined up against the wall of the church to be shot for helping the partisans when Manoli's brother had shot the machine gunner from his hiding place on the overlooking hillside. The few remaining Germans panicked, thinking they were about to be attacked in force and had fled, allowing the residents to gather their belongings and flee to the safety of the mountains. The second account had more effect on Levi as it concerned a small child, probably not much older than Aaron, who had been crossing the road when a German staff car had sped around the corner and had to swerve to avoid him. The car ended up in the ditch and scratched the mudguard. The officer beckoned the child who smiled shyly and went towards him. The officer had grabbed the child's arm and broken it as a punishment for damaging his car.

Levi stood up and walked away from the desk. He had now written up all his notes on the German atrocities on Crete and he just had to hope that they would help to bring the perpetrators to justice when the war finished. If not... He remembered his words to Zahari and a cold smile crossed his face. At the time he hadn't really meant it, but the story of the child had got through to him more than any of the other accounts and now he had every intention of following through with his threat. Even if the Allies did go after the Nazis for their atrocities, it was most likely to be the mass murders, the dreadful events that were so big they couldn't possibly be kept hidden. The smaller crimes would probably go unpunished, and it was these he would target. It might take him several years, but he didn't care. It was his moral duty to punish those responsible, if he survived the war of course. Levi smiled. In fact he would consider his survival as a green light to go ahead and seek retribution on behalf of the small victims, those that couldn't fight back. Levi picked up the original notes, put them in his pocket and left the office. He would put them in a safe place so he could find them easily when he needed them again.

****

Amsterdam

'And he definitely doesn't suspect you?' Joren was watching her face carefully.

Tilly shrugged. 'I don't think so.' Bruno hadn't mentioned the assassination attempt for ages. When she'd finally decided to broach the subject he had seemed surprised, and said that all the perpetrators were dead so the case was closed. She hadn't been entirely convinced but she could hardly keep asking questions. 'You still don't know who it was?'

'No, it must have been a communist group.' Joren hoped so otherwise it meant there were resistance groups operating outside the main umbrella which was dangerous. The whole point of joining together was to prevent wasting resources or duplicating their efforts. He changed the subject. 'The Allies want information about German tank regiments. There's one they can't locate and they need to know where it is before they open the Second Front.'

'I'll see what I can find out tonight.' Her heart skipped a beat. She had not gone through Bruno's briefcase since the attempt on his life just in case he was testing her.

'Is that wise?'

Tilly shrugged. 'I've got to do it sooner or later or I might as well finish the relationship. I haven't found out anything since those idiots tried to kill him.'

'Be careful.'

Tilly nodded. 'I'll see how it feels at the time. If I get any inkling that he is setting me up I won't do anything.'

'Do you have enough tablets?'

'Yes, but I'm a bit wary of using them. Drescher sleeps very lightly. On the one occasion I did use them he was very suspicious that he had slept all night. I'll use alcohol instead.'

Joren stood up, stepped towards her and gave her a quick hug. 'I'll see you in the morning.'

Tilly hugged him back, pulled away and left the office, her thoughts already on the task ahead.

******

En route to India

Clarissa had soon decided to sleep on deck with many of the other passengers. Not only was it cooler and more comfortable, it meant she could sleep next to Tristram without anyone thinking anything of it. Most night there was no moon, but the sky was filled with thousands of stars and the dark water lapping gently against the ship lulled her to sleep. The only downside was having to wake quickly in the morning as the native deck scrubbers would give little warning before sloshing buckets of cold water everywhere.

Breakfast was normally crisp rolls, eggs and coffee and then the day would begin. They rehearsed every morning in a low cabin in the stern, preparing for the concert they would provide on board. Clarissa had thought she had grown used to the heat, but despite the sea breeze the weather grew hotter and hotter each day and many of the troupe spent their days laying on their bunks trying to recover from the overpowering heat. Renee had come out in a rash which she was told was prickly heat, but this hadn't reduced Sammy and June's antipathy towards her.

'Look, the island of the Twelve Apostles!' Renee stared at the strange remote, lifeless, white hills of sand and rock rising out of the sea.

'Weird.' Clarissa frowned. 'I wonder why they're called that.'

Tristram shrugged. 'No idea.' It was much too hot to speculate about anything other than whether he had enough water to drink. He made an effort to show interest and his gaze travelled further ahead. 'Look I think that must be Port Sudan.' He raised his hand and pointed, a relieved smile on his face. Thank goodness, perhaps it would be cooler ashore.

Clarissa stood up and watched as the ship sailed slowly into the harbour. Charlotte and Betty waved to her from the lower deck, and she waved back. The gangplank was lowered and they headed ashore. A short, rather stout, bearded man hurried towards them, his arms outstretched, a beaming smile stretching from ear to ear.

Clarissa was watching and she smiled. 'That must be Betty's father.'

Renee grinned. 'Obviously not what she was expecting.' Betty was clinging to Charlotte and refusing to look at the strange man with the dog collar who was visibly disappointed at his daughter's reaction.

'She'll soon get used to him... I hope she will anyway.' Clarissa felt sorry for him and then she paled suddenly. What if Nathanial was the same when she returned.

'Are you alright Clari?' Tristram was watching her with concern.

'Yes... No... I was just thinking about Nathanial. What if he doesn't remember me?'

'Of course he will.' Tristram automatically put his arms around her. 'Betty had never met her father had she? Nathanial is five, he wasn't a baby when you left and anyway, you won't be gone that long.'

The colour returned to Clarissa's face. 'Yes, of course. I'm just being silly.'

'Children do have very short memories, but in my experience they always remember people who abandon them.' Sandy's voice carried clearly across the ship.

'Ignore her Clari. She's just trying to get a reaction.' Tristram took her arm.

Clarissa didn't answer.

'Rich children don't know their parents anyway, they're always closer to the nanny. She's the one who looks after them.' June answered, her eyes on Clarissa.

Sammy laughed. 'You're right June. Of course, if rich people looked after their offspring themselves, they wouldn't have to worry about their children not recognising them.'

'True. But most of them are too busy enjoying themselves to worry about their children.'

Clarissa pulled back from Tristram and took a step towards them. 'How dare you judge me? I'm here to do my bit to end this dreadful war. If I was a man I would fight, but I'm not so I am using my talent instead.'

'You could have done that at home in blighty.' Sammy glared at her. 'You wanted an excuse to be with lover boy, a long way from home where no one knew you.'

'That's outrageous.' Tristram snapped. He moved to Clarissa's side. 'Clarissa has more talent in her little finger than either of you. Yes, she could have stayed in England and been safe. She could have put on concerts there and remained at home with her son, but she wanted to do something for the men who are fighting and dying out here for us, the forgotten front. That's why she's here, risking her life.'

'And having plenty of fun too.' June gave a harsh laugh and then gasped as Clarissa slapped her hard across the face, knocking her backwards.

****

Warrington

The airman thrust harder and harder, his breath coming in short gasps as he slammed her repeatedly back against the wall in the alleyway between the shops. Nora made encouraging noises, her eyes watching his face carefully. He was almost there. She reached down, squeezed his testicles, and felt him tense. He moaned loudly and she suddenly twisted, leaving him to spurt all over her the tops of her suspenders. He leaned against her, his breathing slowly returning to normal and frowned. 'What did you do that for? I told you I would pull out?'

'Just wasn't taking any chances.' Nora shrugged. 'You enjoyed it didn't you?'

He grinned. 'Sure honey.'

Nora pulled down her skirt and held out her hand. She should have taken the money first, but that wasn't the main reason for sleeping with them and Chester was quite handsome.

His grin widened and he handed her a note. 'See you next time then?'

Nora smiled back and nodded. 'Yes. Goodnight.' She pocketed the money and made sure her skirt was straight before walking slowly back to the pub. It was early yet, she might earn some more money before they closed.

'Hi Nora, I was hoping you'd be here. Come and have a drink with me.'

'Hank…' Nora tried to think of a reason to say no but nothing came to her, so she gave in and followed him back into the pub. After the quiet of the alleyway the noise was deafening, a mixed group around the piano singing loudly, some men from one of the local factories playing darts and arguing near the toilet. Nora ignored the ribald remarks of some airmen near the door and glanced at Hank, but he didn't seem to have noticed. Some girls near the bar gave her disgusted looks and turned away, but their disdain was lost on her.

'Two beers landlord please… sorry… a half for the lady and a pint for me.'

The publican stared at Hank and then at Nora. He shook his head, tempted to say she was no lady, but the Yanks paid well so he stopped himself in time. 'Yes sir.'

Hank smiled at Nora and raised his voice over the loud voices around them. 'Why don't you find a table?'

'Or we could stay at the bar?' She sat down on one of the stools and Hank joined her. 'Here's to lots more auspicious meetings.' He clinked her glass and drank deeply.

Nora frowned. 'What do you mean?'

'Just that I love bumping into you and I want to do it more often.' He drank some more then fixed her with a stare. 'I'm asking you to be my girlfriend Nora and I won't take no for an answer.'

Nora shook her head. 'I don't think you'd want me as your girlfriend if you knew....'

'Not taking no for an answer Nora.' He interrupted, repeating his earlier words. 'Don't care what you've done in the past. Time starts now. Drink up!'

'But...' Nora wanted to argue, but found she was transfixed by his eyes which seemed to bore into her. She sipped her beer, replaced the glass on the bar slowly, her eyes never leaving his face. She nodded. 'Ok. If you're sure?'

Hank smiled. 'Damn straight I am. You and me, we're gonna have a ball.' His eyes twinkled and Nora briefly forgot her reservations. He couldn't have failed to hear the rumours about her, she'd gone out of her way to make sure of that and yet he was still there, still determined that she would be his girlfriend. Perhaps she should take a chance after all. Anyone that was prepared to overlook her reputation had to be worth a gamble.

Hank smiled and finished his drink. He'd done his homework and Nora was perfect for what he had in mind.

****

En Route to India

There were a few seconds of shocked silence and then Sammy rushed at Clarissa and grabbed her hair, tugging it backwards. As Clarissa moaned and fell back Tristram slapped Sammy's arm making her let go of Clarissa's hair. The next second June threw herself on him, scratching and biting him while Sammy renewed her assault on Clarissa.

'Stop them someone... please!' Renee yelled, looking around for some kind of weapon. She was beaten to it by two sailors and a couple of buckets of cold water.

'Aaagh!' Sammy let go of Clarissa as the sea water hit her and gasped. June screamed then stepped forward to attack the sailors. The water had made the surface slippery and as she moved she lost her footing, falling heavily and awkwardly on the deck. Clarissa and Sammy both heard a faint crack and forgot their animosity for a moment as they realised something serious had happened. As they moved towards her June turned white and passed out. Sammy shoved Clarissa out of the way and rushed towards her sister. 'June! June!'

'Call the doctor, quickly!' Tristram yelled.

'What's happened?' Clarissa was almost as pale as June. This was all her fault. If she hadn't slapped June...

'I think she's broken a bone.' Tristram pointed to June's ankle which was lying at a strange angle.

'Oh God!' Clarissa was horrified. 'I never meant for this...'

'Its not your fault. You didn't throw the sea water.'

'But she did start the fight.' Sammy glared at her from her position by June's side. 'If she's badly hurt I'll make you pay, you mark my words.'

'That's enough.' Tristram snapped. 'Its your animosity and jealousy towards Clarissa that's caused this.' He was about to say more when the doctor arrived. He examined June's ankle carefully and then asked the sailors to take her to his cabin. 'Does she have any relatives?'

'I'm her sister.' Sammy spoke up.

'You'd better come with me.' The sailors reappeared with a stretcher and began strapping her onto it.

Sammy watched in increasing horror. 'What's the matter? She will be alright won't she?'

The doctor smiled reassuringly. 'It looks like she's broken her ankle. It will take a while to heal, but she will be fine. It's not life threatening.' He began to follow the stretcher.

'But she's a dancer...' Sammy paled and shook her head. 'Will she be able to dance when it heals?'

The doctor stopped, a frown on his face. 'I can't say at the moment. It all depends on how it heals.' He took a breath and looked into her eyes. 'But even if it does heal completely, it will always be weaker than the other one. It won't affect her normal life, walking about and such like, but I'm not sure of it will take the strain of a professional dancer. I'm sorry.'

He turned and walked in the direction the sailors had gone. Sammy didn't move for several seconds then she suddenly reached out and grabbed Clarissa's wrist. 'You'll pay for this,' she spat before following the doctor.

'I didn't mean...' Clarissa stared after her in shock. Tristram put his arm around her but she barely noticed.

'It wasn't your fault.' Renee had taken her hand. She realised Clarissa wasn't listening and stared up at Tristram. 'But Sammy won't see it like that.'

Tristram stared at her. 'What do you mean?'

'She won't stop until she's got her revenge. I think you need to get Clarissa away from here as soon as possible.'

Chapter 21

Amsterdam

Tilly lay in bed and watched Bruno leave, her heart thudding uncomfortably against her ribs. She had done her best to get him drunk the previous evening, but he had only had a couple of glasses of schnapps before insisting on taking her to bed. She waited until she heard the door close and then breathed a sigh of relief followed by a deep frown. She was wasting time but she couldn't risk being caught. She was still mulling over how to carry out her job properly when there was a knock on the door. She pulled on a dressing gown and hurried to answer it, her heart beating even faster than earlier. What if Drescher suspected her and had sent his men to arrest her?

'Joren? What on earth...? He's only just gone.' Tilly breathed a sigh of relief and stepped back to let him in.

'Yes, I know, I waited until I saw him leave. Did you get anything?'

Tilly shook her head. 'No, nothing. He wasn't interested in drinking and I didn't dare risk going through his papers unless I was sure he wouldn't wake up. I'm really sorry...'

'It doesn't matter anymore. You've got another assignment.'

Tilly frowned. 'For the newspaper?'

He smiled. 'Yes and no. You can use your cover with the newspaper. Our mutual friends want you to go to Austria.'

'Austria?'

'To a place called Ebensee, its near Lake Traunsee apparently.'

Tilly looked puzzled. 'What's there?'

'That's what they want you to find out. Its something to do with rockets apparently.'

Tilly looked even more confused. 'I don't know anything about rockets?'

'Just come into the office, there's someone I want you to meet, they will explain more.' Joren glanced at his watch then back at Tilly. 'Get dressed then.'

'Do I need to pack?'

Joren thought for a moment and then nodded. 'Yes, good idea. It will save coming back here.'

Tilly stared at him for several seconds and then hurried to the bathroom. It would be a relief to be away from Bruno for a while, but Austria... She shivered. Everyone would be an enemy, there wouldn't be any help there if she was discovered. She would be alone.

****

Sarnaki, Poland

The farmer was repairing the broken harness in his dilapidated barn, his young son playing with some wooden soldiers on the straw covered floor when they heard the now familiar sound in the sky above them.

'Look Dad, there's another one of those aeroplanes with fires in their tails.' The two watched the progress of the aeroplane when his father suddenly realised it was coming down. 'Quick lay down son, its going to crash!'

He pushed the boy to the ground and covered his tiny body with his own. They lay still, waiting for the sound of the explosion for several seconds but nothing happened. 'It hasn't banged...' The child wriggled away from under him and sat up.

The man raised his head cautiously and nodded. 'You're right.' He hesitated a few seconds then made up his mind. Here was a chance to do something against their oppressors. 'Quick son, go and find your uncle and ask him to bring some men back here. It fell by the river. Tell them to meet me there.'

As the boy ran back to the village the farmer stood up, walked the several hundred yards through the field towards the river and began searching. When he finally found the downed rocket he shook his head in amazement and growing excitement. Most of the missile was lying on top of the earth and although the underneath was battered it, it was intact. A few moments later his brother and the other men came back with his son.

'This is what the man from Warsaw wanted.' His brother looked at him in amazement.

The farmer nodded. 'Yes, its one of those Revenge Weapons. And its intact.'

His brother thought hard. 'What are we going to do with it? The Germans will be here soon, you known they always follow the weapons once they've fired them.

'We could hide it.'

'Where? Its much too big to hide it under the straw like we did with the bits we found the other week.'

They were still trying to work out how to move it out of sight when his son yelled. 'The Germans are coming…'

The farmer thought quickly and had a brainwave. 'Quick shove it in the river.' While he looked for a suitable place, the rest of the men dragged the bomb loose, then half lifted and half hauled it towards the river bank.

'This should do it.' The farmer pointed to a place where the river flowed around a bend. 'Its deep there and the bank is quite high.' He waited until the missile was in the river before turning to one of the other men. 'Quick, go and drive your cattle into the flat part of the river upstream, get them to make plenty of mud. Everyone else go back to the village. Hurry now but be careful that the Germans don't see you.' While the men hurried away the farmer threw some straw over where the bomb had landed until all signs had gone and then took his son back to the farm. 'Not a word boy, go and play with one of your friends.' He sat down and continued to repair his harness, his heart beating wildly but for once he felt at peace. He had finally done something towards defeating the enemy. Now all he had to do was to act stupid.

****

En route to India

Clarissa watched June hobbling about the deck and let out a deep sigh. She didn't like the woman, but she would never have deliberately hurt her. Unfortunately, Sammy didn't see it that way and kept muttering veiled threats when she thought no one else could hear. At first Clarissa had tried to apologise, but her words fell on deaf ears, so she finally gave up.

She turned back towards the sea and tried to put June out of her mind. She had volunteered for submarine watch now they were crossing the Indian ocean. The ship had a maximum speed of only thirteen knots, there were no submarine detectors aboard and to make matters worse the captain had decided not to wait for the convoy so they were unescorted, apart from a solitary aeroplane which appeared overhead each day and then flew off again. After their previous experience Clarissa had decided to keep sleeping on deck as it would be easier to jump overboard if they were torpedoed. But her biggest fear was sharks. She had seen several while they were in Aden and laughed as some of the passengers tried to feed them bread, but they no longer seemed so funny now she was on a ship in the middle of what seemed like an endless ocean.

'Are you alright? You look worried.' Tristram handed her a mug of tea.

'Sorry, I was just thinking about sharks.'

Tristram leaned closer and lowered his voice. 'The human or fishy kind?'

Clarissa laughed. 'Both.' She sighed. 'Do you know how much longer before we reach Bombay?'

'A couple of days probably, maybe less. Why don't you concentrate on the concert instead?'

'I will. At least I don't have to worry about carting costumes up to the deck. Renee was really fed up earlier. She'd been up and down several times with their dresses and was perspiring heavily when a passenger, seated in a deckchair in the shade, some cordial in her hand, asked if she was looking forward to the concert!'

Tristram laughed. 'Ouch. What did she say?'

'I think she was too hot and out of breath to say anything which is probably good.'

'I take it Sammy didn't help her?'

Clarissa shook her head. 'No.' She shook her head. 'I don't like Sammy, but I do feel sorry for her. Unfortunately, she won't let me do anything to help. I offered for her and Renee to join us in some songs, but she bit my head off.'

Tristram breathed a sigh of relief, the thought of having to adjust their act to accommodate Sammy and Renee wasn't something he wanted to contemplate. He reached forward and kissed her passionately on the lips. 'Just forget about it Clari. It was an accident. Have you decided what songs you want to sing yet?'

'Yes, I thought we'd do our usual routine. Everyone knows the songs so they can join in.' She peered at the gentle sea, her heart beating slightly faster, than relaxed. 'I thought I saw a submarine.'

Tristram stared and then grinned. 'Did you hear what one of the crew said?'

'Oh you mean the rules for submarine spotting? That the ship would be hit before you were likely to see a submarine and by the time you could give the alarm the ship would be sinking? Very upbeat.' Clarissa sipped her tea and gazed restlessly over the gentle waves. 'He's probably right though, isn't he? They won't surface to fire at us so unless we're lucky enough to spot the periscope...' She fell silent and Tristram put his arm around her. He was loving his time with Clarissa but at times like this he felt guilty. If he died it wouldn't affect anyone, but there was a young boy at home in England waiting for his mother to return.

******

Sarnaki, Poland

The German army staff car pulled up sharply by the farm and a German officer climbed out followed closely by a civilian. The officer looked around, distaste on his face at having to lower himself to speak to what he considered to be illiterate scum.

'You! Come here!'

The farmer took a breath, ignored his rapidly beating heart, stood up and walked slowly toward them.

'Have you seen an aeroplane?'

The farmer shrugged. The Germans treated them all like ignorant peasants so he would give them what they expected. 'An aeroplane?'

'You idiot.' The officer swore under his breath. 'You must have seen it. An aircraft with a light in its tail.'

The farmer continued to look blank then his face lit up. 'Oh yes. I did see it.'

'Where did it go?'

The man frowned, thought hard and then replied. 'Over there by the trees.'

'That's impossible Herr Hauptmann,' the civilian interrupted. 'That's due south.'

The officer cursed again. This man was obviously stupid. He looked around and spotted the farmer's brother who had come back to make sure his brother and nephew were alright. 'You! Come here! Have you seen an aircraft fly over, one of those with lights in its tail.'

The man nodded. 'Yes, it went over the church, flying towards Sokolow.'

'That's ridiculous.' The civilian shook his head. 'That's due east.'

The Germans gave up, got back in the car and drove off. The farmer and his brother waited until the Germans were out of sight and then laughed. It was unlikely the Germans would leave it at that. They would probably come back with more manpower to search so they would just have to hope the hiding place in the river was good enough to keep its secret from the Nazis.

****

Bangor

Bill staggered back aboard *HMS Keats* and somehow made his way below deck before collapsing on his hammock. His head was swimming, his stomach rebelling against the copious amounts of alcohol he had consumed, but he was still conscious enough to feel the familiar pain. He should be married now, Abigail might even have been pregnant, carrying his child, but instead he was still single and the woman he loved was dead. He thought back to the evening and the various women his mates had tried to set him up with. But it was no good, he was not interested. So many people had died now and it was all his fault. If they hadn't known him, they would probably still be alive. Even worse he was unhurt, not even one scar to show for the numerous close calls.

'Wanna game of cards Young?'

Bill didn't even bother to raise his head to see who was asking. Whoever it was would be better off not getting too close to him. 'No, gonna sleep it off.' He shut his eyes tight and tried not to see the images of dead and dying men floating in the oil covered water that always appeared. Obviously, he needed more alcohol. He opened them again and sat up. 'You got anymore rum?'

'Here.' Someone handed him a bottle and Bill took several large swallows before handing it back.

'Cheers mate.' Everything was swaying now and he only just managed to lay back down before everything went black.

'He's drinking way too much.' Tom stared at his friend who was now snoring loudly.

Gerry shrugged but didn't answer. They all had their demons and they all dealt with them differently. Bill didn't drink when they were at sea which was really all that mattered. None of the knew how much longer they had to enjoy themselves so why worry.

******

Sarnaki, Poland

The farmer watched his son playing in the field with his friend and then looked at his brother. 'Do you think the Germans will be back again?' As expected, they had returned not long after his earlier encounter with the officer, and the farmer and his brother had watched surreptitiously as the Nazis had searched for hours before finally giving up

'I doubt it, they searched pretty thoroughly last time, probably came to the conclusion that one of us might have told them the truth.' The two men laughed before his brother continued. 'Anyway the Home Army have it under control. They have men everywhere making sure they won't be disturbed.'

'Who's the man in charge?'

'No idea, he's some kind of scientist.' His brother answered. 'Probably best we don't know any more. The Krauts will be fuming if they find out we've taken their rocket, we don't need to antagonise them.'

'You're right.' The farmer smiled. 'I've done my bit, let's hope it speeds up the end of the war.' His brother nodded. Their lives had been unbearable under the Nazis. He couldn't wait until they were finally defeated and he and his family were free again.

Down by the river Jerzy 'Rafal' Chmielewski, a leading Polish aeronautical scientist, had taken charge of the salvage operation. The Polish Home Army had scattered guards all around the area so they would have plenty of warning if the Germans came back and they had bought ropes and pulleys and engineers to supervise the local men who were being utilised as labour to salvage the aircraft.

While Rafal watched, two expert swimmers fixed chains to the missile and then the men pulled it slowly out of the river. They took dozens of photographs and experts took technical measurements and external details in case anything happened. The army engineers examined the warhead and eventually managed to immunise the charge before proceeding to take it to pieces. Rafal was still examining the missile a few days later when he received a message from the Polish General Staff. He read it in disbelief, shook his head and grinned. Didn't want much did they? *London are delighted with the information, but would it be possible to send the bomb itself back to England?*

Chapter 22

Liverpool

The rain was hammering down, the wind howling. Bill stood on deck, stared out across the busy harbour and sighed heavily. It was most unlike early June, cold, wet and windy. If only he was back in Bermuda with the calm blue seas, sunshine, sandy beaches and endless heat. He smiled. It seemed so long ago, his memories clouded by months of cold winds and the icy seas of the Atlantic. The journey from Bangor to Liverpool the previous day had been uneventful despite rumours about the second front. Bill shrugged. All the time the weather was like this he couldn't see any invasion happening. One of the sailors on another ship said there were troops camping everywhere on the south coast so if they were going to be involved in some way surely they would have to be further south. More believable rumours suggested they were just waiting for yet another escort duty across the Atlantic, which made a lot more sense. Bill shrugged. Whatever their next job he wouldn't have any say, so why bother worrying.

He had more important things to think about. He still hadn't heard from Nora and the ongoing silence was seriously worrying him now. It was so unlike Nora not to answer his letters. If only he could have some leave to go home and speak to her in person. But instead he was stuck on the ship in Liverpool waiting for orders to sail. There were times he was tempted to just take a chance and go, but his common sense told him that was stupid, so he had stayed put. But every day he was becoming more and more frustrated. He turned and walked back down to his bunk. He would try writing again and if she still didn't reply he would have to take matters into his own hands.

****

London

Francis handed Levi a glass of whisky and pushed some papers across the desk towards him. 'I have another job for you. Poland this time.' He sipped his drink. 'The Poles have captured a vengeance weapon intact and we're going to fly it back here.' Levi choked on his drink; Francis ignored him. 'There's an airstrip where the River Dunajec joins the Vistula. It was used by the Germans as an emergency landing ground at the beginning of the war in 1939. The RAF will land an aeroplane there to pick up the missile, and also the scientist, Jerzy 'Rafal' Chmielewski, who sent us the information.' Francis smiled at Levi.

Levi stared at him in disbelief. 'You want me to go to Poland to bring back an intact vengeance weapon that the Poles have captured? Will it even fit on a plane?' He carried on before Francis could answer. 'How on earth did they do that?'

Francis smile widened. 'Its amazing isn't it? To cut a long story short, as you know, the Polish underground forces established their own commando units called Kedyw. One of these unit commanders heard Rafal saying that he had to get closer to one of the vengeance weapons and decided to ensure Rafal was given one to examine. They first plan was to try and capture one while it was in transit between Mielec and Blizna, but the Germans suddenly increased their security and the units suffered numerous casualties when they attacked. This didn't put them off, they tried again and failed, suffering even more casualties. They were busy planning yet another assault which probably would have failed as well when their luck changed and one dropped right into their laps. Landed in a field without blowing up.' Francis shook his head and then continued. 'The villagers hid it in the river so the Krauts couldn't find it, and when they'd given up looking Rafal and the Home Army diffused it, took photos and technical specifications and sent us the details.'

Levi was still staring in amazement. 'Its an incredible achievement, but I don't see how on earth we going to get a missile across Poland, let alone fly it back here?'

'Its in pieces, all parcelled up ready to go. I did say we need the scientists as well didn't I?'

Levi nodded and Francis topped up his whiskey while he mulled over what Francis had said. 'I assume you have a plan to get it across Poland, or do we have to work it out from there?'

'We have a plan, that's why you are going. You speak fluent German as well as Polish. Rafal speaks fluent German too and we'll provide you with a driver who is also fluent.'

'Ah, so this plan involves pretending to be a German?'

Francis smiled again, topped up their drinks and began speaking.

****

En Route to India

Clarissa finished her song to an enthusiastic round of applause, took a bow and left the makeshift stage, perspiration dripping off her face and body, her hair limp and wringing wet, her face beetroot red from the heat. Behind the curtains the stale air was even hotter than on the stage and she was relieved to step out into the main saloon and wait in front of them for her last song.

'That was brilliant. I'm sure your voice has grown even better over the past few weeks.' Tristram smiled at her.

'Perhaps it's the sea air...' She sighed, wondered briefly how he managed to stay looking so unruffled and cool despite the temperature, and then resumed fanning herself frantically with the programme. 'God its hot in here,' she continued, 'if a torpedo hit us now, we'd never get out.' The show was taking place in the not very large dining saloon which was packed with people. The portholes had been screwed shut as usual after sunset and the overhead fans were just circulating hot air. She could feel her make up running and she was grateful that she only had one more song to perform before she could go up on deck, unlike the dancers who had several more routines to perform. 'I do hope India is not this airless.'

'Moaning again?' Sammy gave a theatrical sigh that was loud enough to be heard by the first few rows of the audience.

Clarissa ignored her and to her relief the performer on stage finished and any further comments Sammy might have made were drowned out by the audience response.

Clarissa took the opportunity to climb back up on stage and lead the audience in *God Save the King* followed by the *Star Spangled Banner* because half the audience was American.

The music eventually finished, and everyone began to leave. Clarissa and Tristram made their way slowly up on deck. The air was warm and sultry and there was a gentle sea breeze. Clarissa sat down and closed her eyes. They were due to arrive in India in the next few days. Then the cast would split up and go their separate ways and she would be free of Sammy and June. She was sorry about June, but her sympathy was now overtaken by irritation that Sammy wouldn't accept her apology. She couldn't wait to see the back of them, especially as Renee had indicated she intended to stay and take up Clarissa's offer to sing with her. Hopefully, the sisters wouldn't find that out until they were on their way home.

****

Ebensee, Austria

Tilly stared at the hills near Traunsee Lake through the binoculars for several moments before handing them back to her contact. 'So they aren't building rockets there then?'

'They aren't doing anything in them at the moment. Originally it was going to be the Luftwaffe's underground headquarters. Then they were going to research and test an anti-aircraft rocket called wasserfall and the intercontinental Amerika Rakete, but so far none of it has happened. Believe me we've been keeping a very careful eye on them.'

'How have you managed that?'

Luca shrugged. 'I have some people on the inside.' Tilly didn't bother asking any more. The less she knew the better. She didn't know much about Luca Ebna except what he had told her on her arrival, that he had been in place for ten years, since the Austrian civil war in fact, when the Nazis had first tried to annex Austria. Having been a member of the Austrian Nazi Party since 1934 he was, therefore, above suspicion he had told Tilly with a wry smile, adding that at least he hoped he was. Tilly had warmed to the small balding man who had been living and fighting the enemy for so long and she didn't doubt his information. But she did wonder why Francis had sent her there when he could have just asked Luca about the weapons.

Luca was talking again and pointing in the direction of the town. 'That's Analage A, its the bigger of the two, larger tunnels.' He pointed to the southwest. 'The other site is Analage B and is next to the camp, over there to the south west.'

'But there's definitely no V weapons being built there?'

Luca shook his head. 'No. Not yet anyway, but neither is finished so maybe they will use them once the tunnels and storage areas are completed. Although it seems unlikely to be honest.' He saw her expression. 'It's not the best testing ground here is it? Look around you. Too many mountains and steep valleys. It takes ages to get anywhere. They'd never be able to see where a rocket went down without wasting hours driving around tiny mountain roads.'

Tilly sighed. 'Looks like I've had a wasted journey.'

Luca shook his head. 'No, time spent in reconnaissance is seldom wasted, as they say. Even a negative answer is useful. Although I could have told London this if they had asked.'

Tilly nodded. 'That's what I thought. It seems pointless sending me out here although if I'm honest its rather nice to be away from Amsterdam.'

Luca didn't answer for a moment as an idea came to him. Perhaps Francis did have a reason for sending her. 'Why don't you stay here?'

'In Austria you mean?' Tilly shook her head. 'I couldn't do that.'

'Why not? I need a new radio operator and we could find you a cover job with a newspaper in Salzburg.'

Tilly stared at him. It was the answer to her problems in Amsterdam. Since the renegade group had tried to assassinate Bruno she hadn't been able to find out anything and she was beginning to feel increasingly unsafe there. She would miss Joren, but a change of scene might be exactly what she needed.

******

Mittelwerk

Jacob finished the last of his sketches and placed it carefully in the briefcase with the other drawings. He was due to leave today but first he had to dine with Hans Kammler, something he really wasn't looking forward to. He had been convinced that the Brigadeführer had been suspicious of him when he arrived, but to his surprise he had been left pretty much to his own devices. Other than a guard to show him around, nothing had been out of bounds and he had very quickly acquired a comprehensive understanding of the complex. The main purpose of Mittelwerk was storage of the weapons and that was what the mass labour was all about. He was stunned by the size of the underground caverns and horrified. The thought of them being filled with weapons was appalling especially as there was no way an RAF strike could destroy them. The caves were too deep underground. The only way to destroy them was by sabotage and that would mean careful planning. Somehow, they would have to get men into the caves and with explosives. He had no idea how they would manage that as security was extremely tight. Fortunately, that wasn't his job, his role was to get as much information as possible and relay it back to Francis.

He had finished packing and was checking to make sure he hadn't left anything behind when there was a knock on the door.

'Brigadeführer Kammler is expecting you.'

Jacob nodded. 'Thank you Unterscharführer.' He picked up his bag and briefcase and followed the corporal to Kammler's office, his thoughts on whether there was anything else he needed to find out. This would be his last chance.

******

Warrington

Nora glanced at the envelope and sighed. She loved Bill but she wished he would stop writing to her. She hadn't answered any of his letters because she didn't know what to say. She didn't want to lie to him, but she couldn't tell him the truth either, so her only option was to ignore his letters. Reluctantly she opened the envelope, pulled out the letter and began reading.

Dear Nora

I am not sure if you have received my last three letters, but I am getting very worried that I haven't heard anything from you in months. I tried to tell myself that my letters have gone astray but then I realised that even if they had, you would have written to me to find out why I wasn't writing to you. The fact that you haven't tells me that you have received my letters and for some reason are not answering them. You are my sister, I love you. I have lost my fiancée, yet not a word of condolence from you. I want to be angry with you, but this is so unlike you that instead I am frightened, scared that something terrible has happened to you. I don't fear that you are dead, because if you were Mum would have told me, so that just leaves the door open to my imagination. Have you run off with some unsuitable man? Maybe he's married which is why you aren't replying to me. If you have found someone you love I don't care if he's married. I only care that you are happy. I am starting to go out of my mind with worry, so if I don't hear from you soon, I will jump ship and come looking for you.

If you care anything for me at all, please at least let me know you are alright. If you don't want to explain the months of silence, I will accept that, but please answer me.

Your loving brother

Bill.

Nora screwed the letter up and threw it across the room. Damn him. She couldn't let him jump ship, he would end up being imprisoned or shot as a deserter or something and that wasn't fair. She rummaged in the drawer for some paper and a pencil and quickly scribbled a reply. She didn't bother reading it before putting it in an envelope and putting it by her hat on the bed side cabinet. Bill wanted a reply, well now he had one. She would post it on the way to work.

****

Ebensee, Austria

Tilly took down the aerial and hurriedly put the rest of the wireless set back in the suitcase before handing it over to Luca who had been witing patiently for her to finish. 'Well? What did he say?'

Tilly smiled, followed him out of the loft and down the stairs to the landing and then downstairs to the sitting room. 'Give me a few moments to decode it.'

Luca laughed. 'Sorry. I'll go and make some coffee.'

Tilly took out a pencil and her notebook and concentrated on the letters in front of her. A few moments later she was sitting back, the coded message and the translation torn out and burning in the ashtray, the notebook back in her bag.

'Well?' Luca handed her a cup of strong coffee and a couple of biscuits.

Tilly thanked him for the refreshment and then nodded. 'Yes, I'm to stay here, at least for the time being.' She hesitated. 'I don't know whether I need to change my identity though? If I just disappear from Amsterdam it could cause problems for the people I've been working with there.'

Luca thought hard and nodded. 'You're right, I think you should keep your identity. We will have to find a good reason for you to stay here.'

Tilly sighed. 'Like what. It was hard enough finding a reason to suddenly go to Austria. Eventually Joren, my editor, decided to send me to cover the Salzburg Summer of Theatre and Music. Obviously, I'm a bit early but I could get round that by saying I was coming here to learn about its history.'

'I am sure we can work something out, and there's no rush, we don't need to come up with something immediately.'

Tilly breathed a sigh of relief. She didn't have to go back to Amsterdam, and she could keep her identity. Bruno knew she was in Austria and when she didn't come back he was bound to check-up. It would look very suspicious if she wasn't there. Heinz Kessel would also be suspicious once he knew she had moved. Tilly's heart began to race. Kessel would definitely want to know why she was in Austria, especially as she was supposed to be spying for him. 'There's another problem.'

Luca stared at her.

Tilly took a breath. 'It's a long story.'

****

Sarnaki village, Poland

Levi arrived at the small village, secreted himself amongst the trees on the edge of the forest bordering the settlement and waited for someone to come and collect him. His job was to liaise with the local Polish Home Army (Armia Krajowa) who would bring him up to date about the rocket testing that was being carried out from Blizna in southeast Poland and then take him to Rafal. It was getting dark, and he hoped someone would come before the light faded completely. It was easier to spot if someone was lying when there was enough light to see into their eyes. He hoped whoever they sent spoke English or German. His Polish was adequate and had definitely improved after months of conversing with Marta, but he wasn't entirely sure it would stand up to anything too complicated or scientific. He thought back over the last conversation with Francis and sighed. His orders were to take the V2 across Poland and then put it on an RAF aeroplane which would fly it back to England. It sounded far-fetched to say the least, but Francis appeared to have worked out a plan with the Polish High Command so who was he to question them.

The crackling of twigs behind him made him spin around and he found himself face to face with a man of about his own height with a swarthy complexion, dark eyes and holding a Polish issue Mauser. Levi raised his hands slowly and spoke in Polish.

'I was looking for Pustków, but I am lost. Can you help?'

'Its too late to travel there now, you should sleep and travel there tomorrow.'

'I have nowhere to stay. I will have to go anyway.'

'There is a curfew, you should rest first.'

'I can't do that, its too urgent.'

The man lowered his rifle and indicated Levi follow him. 'I'm Denis Kois.'

Levi gave him the name on his forged documents. 'Bonifacy Ploski.'

A few minutes later they were in a small wooden hut on the edge of the village and Levi was being introduced to two other men and given a small glass of vodka.

'If you are ready we can start out now. The sooner you get the rocket and Rafal out of the country the better. The longer it remains here the more danger of someone finding out and informing the Germans. Its better to go now while its dark.' Denis was already blowing out the candles.

Levi would have liked to eat first, it was hours since he'd had any food. But the vodka had revived him, and he could see the sense of travelling through the countryside at night. He was also growing more and more excited by the prospect of seeing a V2, even if it was in pieces, and being able to put a stop to the threat they posed the Allies. He followed

Denis back into the forest, the other two men, Urban and Serafin, close behind him.

Chapter 23

North Sea

'I wish we'd been involved.' Bill had just finished listening to the latest briefing on the Second Front.

'At least we know its going well and what we're doing is just as important.' Jim shrugged. He was older than Bill and one of the new members of the crew, having transferred from another ship that had been sunk during escort duty in the Atlantic.

Bill didn't look convinced. Instead of being in the action they were escorting yet another convoy across the Atlantic and he still hadn't heard from Nora.

'I've had enough action thanks. Its not exactly quiet out here.' Jim saw his expression and frowned.

Bill shrugged but didn't answer. How could be explain that he felt better when there was something going on and that the quiet times put his nerves on edge.

'Looks like this trip might be a bit quieter anyway.' Jim continued. 'They've lost loads of U-Boats this month.' He smiled. 'You never know it might be the first trip there and back without any dramas.'

'Let's hope so.' Bill tried to sound enthusiastic. He had to be mad wanting the convoy to be attacked but at least when they were under fire, he was doing what he'd trained for. He stared out across the unusually calm waters of the Atlantic and for the first time in ages wondered what he was going to do when the war finished. He couldn't see himself settling for a job in a factory or working in a farm, it would drive him mad. Perhaps he could stay on in the Navy?

'Penny for them?' Jim was watching him closely.

'Oh I was wondering what I was going to do once the war is over.'

Jim looked thoughtful. 'Good point mate. I can't wait to be back home with my wife and children. I think it will be really nice knowing I can go to work in the morning and come home again at night with no one trying to kill me.'

'What sort of job are you going to look for? Won't you be bored?'

Jim laughed. 'You're joking right? After the shit we've been through peace and quiet sounds wonderful to me. What about you?'

Bill shrugged. 'I don't think I could settle in some boring mundane job, but I don't know if the Navy will let me stay on.'

'I doubt it. They'll probably cut the armed forces right back.' Jim thought for a few moments. 'You could always try the Merchant Navy. They'll probably be looking for people once trade is up and running.'

Bill stared at him. 'I hadn't thought of that. Yeah, maybe I'll give that a go.' That way he would still at sea and not stuck on land in a boring job.

****

Poland

'You know the plan?' Rafal eyed Levi cautiously.

Levi shook his head. 'No, just that we are going to be dressed as Germans.'

Rafal grinned and handed him a brown paper parcel. 'Get changed. I'll tell you everything on the way.'

'We're leaving now?'

'You have something better to do?'

Levi shook his head. 'No, I just wasn't expecting to be leaving so quickly. Sorry…this sounds like a moan, but I haven't eaten since I left England…'

Rafal looked horrified. 'Good God. That's dreadful. You get changed and I'll sort out some food.'

Levi relaxed slightly, took out the German uniform and began changing. He was amused to find he was a German Officer, there was something deliciously ironic about being a Major.

'Here, don't spill it down you.' Rafal handed him a bagel and kielbasa.

Levi ate quickly while Rafal changed and then there were several knocks on the door. Levi froze but Rafal hurried over, opened it and spoke to someone in a German uniform. 'Come on, let's go.'

Levi put what was left of the food down reluctantly and strode towards them. He walked through the door and stared at the large German truck.

'Get in the front. I'll sit in the middle.' Rafal was already climbing in and Levi followed suit.

'This is Feldwebel Georg Schmidt... well it isn't, but you don't need to know his real name.' Rafal grinned. 'He's our driver.' Levi nodded and then realised that Rafal had spoken in German.

'Best to speak only German now, less chance of forgetting.'

Levi smiled and replied in the same language. 'Good idea.'

Georg started up the lorry and drove slowly out of the yard and onto the main road.

'We're delivering some urgent and top secret material to a base near Lublin.' He handed Levi some papers. 'These are our documents, signed by the Führer himself.'

Levi stared at the signature in shock and shook his head. 'Isn't that a bit risky?'

Rafal smiled. 'No, its well known among the troops that he was in Blizna a few weeks ago visiting the V2 project so what is more normal than for him to order supplies south away from the risk of RAF bombing. Sit back my friend and enjoy the ride.'

Levi smiled back and tried to hide his own unease. Rafal seemed far too confident for his own good, or maybe it was him. Perhaps it was the lack of food, but he was sure he wouldn't be able to relax until the missile was on the aeroplane and winging its way westwards to Britain.

****

Berlin

'I've missed you Linus.' Eva flung her arms around him and hugged him tight.

'The feeling is mutual.' Jacob closed his eyes and breathed in her perfume. He wished he could tell her his real name, but it would be much too dangerous. He only hoped she would understand why he had lied to her when he was finally able to tell her the truth. 'I see the British and Americans have been busy.' He had been shocked by the increase of bombed out buildings.

Eva shivered. 'Yes, we spend much of our time underground now. Like moles, hiding from the daylight, only we don't come out at night either.'

He held her tight and didn't answer.

'The worst day was the 21st June. I've never seen so many aeroplanes Linus. There was over a thousand. I've never been so scared. We sat in the shelter all day, too terrified to go out and see what damage they had caused.'

'I'm sorry, I should have been with you.'

Eva shook her head. 'No, you were doing something to try and end the war weren't you? Papa told us.'

Linus frowned. Clemens shouldn't have said anything to his family, it was too risky.

Eva sensed his reaction, pulled back and saw his expression. 'He didn't tell us anything Linus, just that you were working for us, to save us. That's all I needed to know.'

Linus relaxed slightly. He should have known that Clemens wouldn't say anything stupid. He had too much to hide.

Eva smiled and then looked up into his eyes. 'I have something to tell you.'

Jacob smiled. 'You've found something to eat other than potatoes?'

Eva laughed but Jacob could hear the nervousness in her voice. 'Eva? Is something wrong?'

'No, well at least I don't think so... I'm going to have a baby.'

Jacob stared at her in shock and disbelief... a baby, with Berlin so dangerous, with Clemens and the plot to assassinate Hitler... with him a British spy... not to mention being Jewish and his wife not even knowing his real name. Then he felt a growing sense of excitement, of wonder...

Eva had watched his face and tears formed in her eyes. 'I'm sorry Linus, I thought you would be happy...'

Jacob took her chin in his hand and stared onto her eyes. 'Eva, it's me who should be apologising. I'm sorry. I started thinking about how I could protect both you *and* a child and I panicked, what with the war and everything. Its not exactly the greatest time to have a baby but don't be sorry... ,' a smile lit his face, 'other than the war I am so happy I could burst. I can't believe...' He placed his hand on her stomach. 'Have you told anyone else?'

'No, I wanted you to be the first to know.'

'When is it due?'

'Not for ages, not until the end of the year.'

Jacob leant forward and kissed her gently. 'Have I told you how much I love you?'

'Not recently…' Eva smiled up at him, her earlier tears forgotten.

'Well, I do… love you very, very much.' Jacob pulled her into his arms and held her tight. He closed his eyes and tried to think clearly. With her father being involved in some plot against the Führer and his own secrets it really wasn't safe for Eva to remain in Berlin any longer. He would talk to Clemens and see if they could sent her somewhere else.

****

Bombay, India

As they approached the harbour the water gradually changed from the clear glistening waters of the sea to a muddy greenish yellow colour. Everywhere she looked she could see numerous native crafts sailing in and out of small islands. In the distance she could see hills rising into the sky and to their left the houses and domes of Bombay Island came slowly into view. The great arch of the Gateway of India dominated the waterfront and further along Clarissa could see the high dome of the Taj Mahal Hotel.

'Finally.' Tristram took her hand. 'I can't wait to step ashore. I can hardly believe we are in India.'

'No, nor me. It seems like a dream, doesn't it?' Clarissa stared through her sunglasses and lowered her hat to shield herself from the sun. Now they had entered the harbour the heat was increasing and she gave an inward sigh and promised herself that once the war was over she would stay in the more temperate climate of England. For a brief moment her pain at missing her son and Halford Manor was like a physical hurt and she gasped. Nathanial would be nearly seven when she went home. What if he didn't remember her? With an effort she pushed her thoughts away and concentrated on the sights and sounds filling her senses. The port was swarming with activity. Her eyes were drawn to the hundreds of men and women trudging back and forth carrying heavy sacks on their heads, the dust hanging in the air. But it wasn't the activity that caught her attention or the oppressive heat, it was the expressions of loathing and bitterness etched on their exhausted faces. Clarissa turned away, unsettled by the misery and anger she sensed and watched the mass exodus as everyone left the ship instead.

'Shouldn't there be someone here to meet us?' Tristram frowned, unaware of her unease. 'I'll go and see if I can find out what's happening. There's no point both of us going, you might as well wait here.'

Clarissa nodded. She watched him head to the gangplank and then found a place to sit down. Other members of ENSA were already sitting down and grumbling about the heat and lack of any reception. Clarissa closed her eyes and wondered how she was going to cope with the heat. Perhaps it would be cooler ashore?

She had been sitting on the deck in the burning heat for several hours when Tristram finally returned. 'Apparently they weren't expecting us for another few days so they hadn't prepared anything. But they've got some vans now so let's go and see Bombay!'

Clarissa breathed a sigh of relief, stood up and joined the queue of people already making their way aboard the waiting vans, while their luggage was loaded onto a lorry.

******

Berlin

'Congratulations Linus. So I will be soon be a grandfather.' Clemens poured them both some schnapps and handed the glass to Jacob. The two men clinked glasses and downed their drinks.

'Is it me or are you not as pleased as you should be?' Clemens voice took on a hard edge.

Jacob shook his head. 'We're in a war, Berlin is being bombed daily, I'm a British spy and you're planning to assassinate Hitler. What on earth could be wrong?'

Clemens gave a wry smile. 'When you put it like that…'

'I want to get Eva out of Berlin, maybe out of the country.'

Clemens poured them both some more schnapps and sipped his slowly. 'Where to? If we fail and get caught none of the occupied countries would be any safer.'

Jacob stared at him in shock. 'You want me to get her to Britain?'

'Can you?'

Jacob shook his head. 'I doubt it.' Francis had always been very helpful and amenable, but the thought of his superior's face if he asked them to send an aeroplane to pick up his German wife because she was pregnant was enough to bring him out in a sweat. 'What possible reason could I give?'

'She's my daughter and I am risking my life to remove the dictator so we can end the war. If nothing else it will show them we are serious.' Clemens drank some more then stood up. 'If they did agree, do you think they would take Ursula and Anton too?' He saw Jacob's face. 'The Gestapo won't leave my family alone if we fail. I would be much happier knowing they were all somewhere safe.'

Jacob sighed. 'I can ask.'

Clemens smiled. 'That's all I require. Now let's drink to the success of our mission and to the safety of my family.' He raised his glass and Jacob did the same while his brain sought answers. He had no idea how to persuade Francis to take Clemens' family out of Germany. Perhaps he should ask Niklas for some forged papers and provide the supporting documentation himself without involving London?

'I think the first thing we should do is to get them all out of Berlin while your authority holds. If they leave now for somewhere in western Germany…?'

Clemens thought for a moment and then nodded. 'I agree. But they will need some different papers to use once they are out of Berlin, won't they?'

'Yes, I can get those, but we need to have a proper plan. It can't be rushed or we'll put them in unnecessary danger. How long have we got?'

Clemens stared at him. 'I can't answer that, I won't be told until the last minute.'

Jacob sighed. 'Then we need to make our plans and as soon as you know when, they can leave. If the plot fails, it will look suspicious whenever they leave, so it doesn't really matter. But we don't want to draw attention to you before anything happens. No one is supposed to leave Berlin unless they have a good reason so if they leave too soon and then disappear it could actually cause things to go wrong.'

'You're right. As much as I would prefer them to leave immediately, they need to stay until the last minute.' Clemens finished his drink and smiled. 'Let's work out a plan.'

Chapter 24

Nowy Korczyn, Poland

To Levi's relief the journey south was reasonably uneventful. They were stopped at checkpoints a couple of times by the Military Police who took one look at their papers and waved them through without question. They even stopped to give a lift to some German soldiers who were on their way to Kraków. Eventually they arrived near a small village. George pulled over and Rafal climbed out.

'What now?' Levi joined him and took the offered cigarette.

'We'll be met by...' He stopped and spun around in response to a rustling sound behind him, then grinned.

'Wlodek!' Rafal shook hands with the Polish Air Force officer and quickly introduced him to Levi.

The three men climbed back in the truck followed by Wlodek who was squashed up against the door. 'Fortunately, its not far. Turn left and follow the road...' A few moments later they reached the airstrip, code named Motyl (butterfly). Levi climbed back out and stared at the airstrip in dismay. It wasn't what he was expecting at all. The field was on the edge of a wood, the grass area fairly smooth, but it wasn't an airfield, just an emergency landing ground for fighters. How on earth they would land a substantial aircraft on the field and get it to take off again he had no idea. He was about to say so when Rafal began speaking.

'There are German troops billeted at Marcinkowice, under a mile away but they have just returned from a hammering on the eastern front. They are recuperating, getting ready to go back to fight, so the last thing they will be looking out for is an enemy operation going on right under their noses.' Rafal didn't wait for Levi to comment, instead he continued. 'There's a peasant cottage on the edge of the forest. The villagers have tree cutting rights because the forest is communally owned, but he has the task of indicating which trees can be cut down. He also cuts timber for himself and stacks them for sale in the market town a few miles away. That's where we're going to hide the parcels.'

A few hours later the missile had been safely stowed under piles of logs and George left to take the German truck back to Warsaw. Wlodek made radio contact with the Polish General Staff in London and then they settled down to wait.

****

Salzburg

Tilly listened to the radio in astonishment and not a little disappointment. If only the German officers had succeeded the war might be over now, but instead Hitler had survived, seemingly unhurt.

'You've heard the news then?' Luca opened the door to her office and stepped inside.

'Yes, I've just been listening.' She lowered her voice. 'Bloody shame they failed.'

Luca gave a wry smile. 'Yes it is, unfortunately that isn't the newspaper's view of course. Everyone downstairs is busy denouncing the cowardly army officers for treason, just wanted to make sure you didn't say the wrong thing!'

Tilly smiled. 'I won't. I hadn't forgotten where I was, it's a bit difficult to do that with swastikas and Nazi uniforms everywhere.'

'Just keep your head down and don't draw attention to yourself. Security everywhere is being tightened, but its mainly military personnel that are under suspicion.'

'I thought the broadcast said they had caught and executed the conspirators?' Tilly looked confused.

Luca shook his head. 'Only the main ones, von Stauffenberg and three other officers were executed by firing squad and Henning von Tresckow committed suicide. But the others were taken alive and interrogated, poor bastards, and they've now started to look for anyone who was connected to the plot, however remotely.'

Tilly sighed. 'Are they likely to be looking for conspirators in Austria too?'

'All over. As I said it seems to have been an army plot, so the Gestapo and SS are concentrating their attention on the military, not civilians, but its best to keep a low profile given your background.'

Tilly frowned. 'What do you mean?'

Luca smiled. 'Apart from what you yourself told me, you don't think I would have accepted you here without knowing something about your background, do you?'

'I thought it was best not to know anything about the people you worked with.'

'It isn't usually, but I needed to know who you were. Kessel will vouch for you, won't he?'

'Let's hope so.' Tilly wondered how much Luca knew about her, but it was hardly the right place to ask. On the other hand he was a trusted member of the Austrian Nazi Party so perhaps she should stay close to him until things died down. 'Perhaps we could have dinner tonight?'

Luca's grin widened. 'I was just going to suggest that. I'll pick you up about half seven.' He turned and left. Tilly stared at the closed door and shook her head slowly. Perhaps she would be better returning to Amsterdam?

******

Berlin

'I can't believe we failed.' Clemens paced back and forth in his living room, a pale sheen of sweat on his face.

'Is there anything to connect you with von Stauffenberg?' Jacob was equally concerned. The SS and Gestapo were already arresting people and he was wondering whether he should leave Berlin for a while. Unfortunately, he couldn't leave Eva, not only because he had promised Clemens, but because he loved her.

'I don't think so, but that may not be enough to save me. Everyone is under suspicion, so I assume that means me too.'

'Do you want me to take Eva and leave?'

Clemens shook his head. 'If you leave now, it could draw attention to me. We'll try and carry on as normal.'

'If we wait too long your signature may not be enough for any of us to leave.' Jacob knew he had more to lose than Clemens. 'At least tell me the fake documents are ready?'

Clemens nodded. 'In my desk drawer.'

Jacob stared at him in disbelief. 'In your desk drawer? What if someone finds them?'

'In the cellar, not at work.' For the first time in days a slight smile crossed Clemens' face. 'I'm not that stupid.'

Jacob relaxed slightly and smiled back. 'I'm sorry, of course you aren't. How will we know when to go?'

'I don't know. I am hoping I will get some warning, but I think you and the family should be ready to go at a moment's notice.'

'Why don't you come with us?'

Clemens stared at him. 'I can't do that.'

'Why not?'

'I am a German officer. I can't desert my country.'

Jacob shook his head in exasperation. 'You've just been involved in a plot to kill Hitler for Christ's sake!'

Clemens frowned. 'You wouldn't understand.'

Jacob tried to hide his frustration. He had grown fond of Clemens and he didn't understand why he was trying to be a martyr. 'If you stay here, they will kill you.'

Clemens shrugged. 'I can't leave. Its not an option so let's change the subject.' He put the wireless on and beckoned Jacob to come closer. 'You're right, we've waited long enough. I think you should take Eva on a holiday. You only had a brief honeymoon so you can tell people it's the rest of it.'

'What about Ursula and Anton?'

'I'll try and find a way of sending them out of Berlin. Ursula's family live in Hamburg, I could draw her papers up to go there and then, once she's out of the city she could head towards France.'

'Perhaps we could meet her somewhere?'

'No, I would love you to do that, to know that you were all safe together. But I think its best you keep to your story and go one way and they go another. If anything goes wrong at least I know Eva will be safe.'

Jacob nodded. 'When do we leave?'

'Go down and get the papers. I'll tell Eva to pack. Ursula and Anton will have to wait a couple of days or it will look suspicious.'

Jacob walked to the study door but before opening the door he turned. 'Are you sure you won't leave too? You could go and visit Claus.'

Clemens frowned. 'The Russians were very close to Majdanek the last time I heard.'

Jacob shrugged. 'All the more reason to go. You are going to check up on your son… and the SS aren't likely to follow you. Too busy saving their own skins.'

Clemens nodded. 'I think you could be right. Alright, I'll take Ursula and Anton to Poland. It has to be safer than here at the moment.'

****

Nowy Korczyn, Poland

They were listening to the tiny radio yet again when they finally heard the few bars of Chopin's Nocturn, Op 15. 'Good, its set for tomorrow.' Wlodek smiled. 'I'll need to check the airstrip tomorrow morning; we've had a lot of rain and the ground is quite soft.'

'Can you stop the operation if you have to?' Levi looked concerned.

'Yes, in an emergency, but I'd rather not. The sooner your parcels are away from here the better.'

Levi nodded. He didn't want the aircraft cancelled either. Knowing how close he was to the Germans was making him uneasy.

The following morning Wlodek checked the airstrip.

'Well?' Levi and Rafal watched him.

'The ground is soft, but as they are only sending a light aircraft it won't matter.'

'A light aircraft?' Levi frowned.

'Yes of course. They know it's a field, not a proper runway. They aren't stupid in London, its not like they're going to send anything heavy, is it?'

'Will it be big enough to take both of us as well then?' Levi was starting to feel better. For some reason he had thought the RAF were going to send a heavy bomber.

'Should be, if not we can get you out another way. Can't wait to leave us?'

Levi laughed. 'Nothing personal.'

Rafal joined in then looked at his watch. 'I've got to organise the men. We'll use two platoons of Home Army partisans to guard the outer perimeter and we have four hundred local volunteers to help.'

'Won't the Germans notice?'

Rafal shrugged. 'The locals are cutting down their timber allocation. The more men we have the better. If the Germans get suspicious we only need to hold them off while the aircraft takes off, so its better to have more men than not enough.'

Wlodek and Levi walked back to the cottage and had begun eating their lunch when a man came rushing in.

'Wlodek, come quickly!'

'What's the matter?'

'Two German aeroplanes have landed in the field.'

They hurried outside and back to the field. To their horror he was right, there were two German fighters parked in the middle of the field.

'Have they done this before?'

Wlodek shook his head. 'Not for ages.' He spoke quickly to the man who had warned them. 'We'll mobilise the neighbouring Home Guard. We can overpower them easily, but we must do it quietly.' He was about to say more when another fighter came over. Its wheels touched the earth and then it took off again. A few moments later another came over and did the same thing. Wlodek began to relax. 'Its alright. I think they are training. If that's the case they'll be gone by dark.'

'And if they aren't?'

'We'll make preparations to overpower them. Hopefully we won't need to. Although we have plenty of experience the slightest noise could alert the soldiers at the barracks.'

Levi watched as more aircraft landed and then took off. If Wlodek was wrong the night would be even more complicated than it already was. The RAF aeroplane wasn't expected until after midnight so they weren't planning to move the missile pieces until well after dark. The only good thing Levi could take from the unexpected events was that if the Luftwaffe could land on the field, then presumably so could the RAF.

****

Somewhere in the Atlantic

Bill threw in his cards and stood up, a wry smile on his face. Fortunately, he hadn't bet very much, or he would have lost it. He really should know better than to play poker with Jack. The cook was lethal, so good that he struggled to find anyone to play most of the time. If Bill hadn't been fighting his demons he wouldn't have agreed to a game, but anything was better than the black thoughts swirling around his brain. The voyage to Murmansk had been quiet, no U-boats, no Luftwaffe flying out of Poland, no sudden dispersal orders because of Nazi wolfpacks. He should have enjoyed it but despite the lull in activity his brain was still on high alert, a kind of hyper vigilance that wouldn't let him sleep which is why he'd ended up playing cards with a man he could never hope to beat.

'Next time Bill!' Jack pocketed the small amount of cash and waved to him.

Bill grinned. 'Perhaps we could play for matchsticks?'

Jack laughed. 'Don't think so mate, no fun in that.'

Bill hesitated. 'Doesn't it ever worry you? This quiet I mean.'

Jack frowned. 'No, just make the most of it Bill. Even the weather is good for a change. Perhaps we've finally got those bastards under control.'

'Yes, you could be right.' Bill tried to sound enthusiastic but failed.

'Get some shut eye mate. God knows there enough misery on these convoys normally, try and relax.'

Bill nodded and made his way back to his hammock. If he could at least sleep he would feel better. But night after night, laying awake and listening to everyone else snoring, not a care in the world... Surely it couldn't just be him that felt like this?

His thoughts turned to Nora and her strange reply to his letter. It was so short, and he had read it so many times, he knew it off by heart.

Dear Bill

I am fine, thank you for worrying about me, but there's nothing to worry about. My job keeps me busy, there's no married man, no secret, just a selfish sister who should have been more supportive when you needed me. I don't know if you can forgive me for not writing to you before, I hope so. Life sometimes throws things at us that we think we can't cope with, but we invariably do, however much we might not want to. Please don't do anything as stupid as jumping ship. It won't help anyone. I hope things soon change for you and you meet someone else. Unlike me, you deserve to be happy.

Love Nora

Bill sighed. If Nora hoped to put his mind at rest she'd failed miserably. He was even more worried about her now.

Chapter 25

Berlin

Jacob and Eva left the house a few hours later. Eva stood outside and stared up at her home, tears streaming down her cheeks. Jacob out his arm around her. 'It won't be forever my love, the war will soon be over and then you'll all be back together.'

Eva wiped her eyes. 'I hope you're right, but what if they are captured before they reach the border?'

'We'll just have to hope they aren't. I know its difficult, but we have to believe they will escape, the same as we will.' He took her arm, but she resisted.

'Do you really think we can get to England?'

Jacob looked into her eyes and wished he could tell her the truth, but he couldn't until they were safe in England. Instead, he shrugged. 'We've got to try. It's the best place for us and its where your father will be looking for you after the war.' Jacob hoped she wouldn't ask anymore, but fortunately she seemed too preoccupied with her own sadness to wonder why both her father and husband were so keen on her going to England. 'The British and Americans have broken out of Normandy and are taking back swathes of France. Sooner or later we'll meet then coming eastwards.' He didn't mention that to do that, they would have to cross enemy lines, he would worry about that when the problem arose. 'Come on, get in the car.'

Eva climbed in and they began the slow journey across the city. Jacob was horrified by how much of the city was now in ruins, but more concerned by the number of checkpoints that seemed to have sprung up overnight. The first few took little notice of their papers, just glanced at the signature and waved them through. Jacob began to relax slightly. Perhaps this would work after all.

'Shall I get a newspaper?' Eva indicated a newspaper vendor standing by the entrance to the station, a pile of papers by his side.

Jacob nodded. It would be a good idea to keep abreast of the invasion, not that he was sure the details would be very accurate, but it would give them some idea. He pulled up and waited while she ran across the road and paid for a paper. He glanced in the mirror, no SS cars in sight thank goodness, and then a loud hooting made him jump. He looked back across the road. Eva was the colour of chalk, heading towards him at speed, ignoring the man in a saloon car who was yelling at her. He was about to get out when she reached him and thrust the paper in through his open window. Jacob read the headline and clenched his fist. 'No!'

Eva climbed in beside him, her features contorted in shock. 'Claus…'

'They probably abandoned the camp before the Soviets got there Eva.'

'But what about my parents and Anton? They were going there.'

Jacob sat in silence for a moment then started the car. 'We can't do anything Eva, I'm sorry. We have to keep going or we'll get stuck in Berlin.' He pulled out and joined the line of cars heading towards the next checkpoint, his heart racing. Hopefully, they would be luckier than Clemens.

****

Bombay, India

Clarissa loved Bombay. The leaves on the trees lining the streets were startlingly green, punctuated by incredible flushes of colour from gardens of properties whose windows were set well back from the road behind wide wooden verandas that prevented the sun from shining directly into the houses. Other roads were lined with British Victorian architecture, the pavements thickly populated with white suited Indians of superior caste, poorer Hindus wearing loose cotton shirts and half naked beggars. Beautiful women in colourful saris mingled with British civilians and members of the British and US forces. It reminded her of the mix of people she had seen in Cairo, but it was somehow different. The hostel where they had spent the first few nights was rather dingy and very crowded, but at least it hadn't been a brothel. Clarissa and Renee soon arranged to move to a flat belonging to a friend of the billeting officer and Tristram found another apartment in close proximity so he could visit without the prying eyes of the rest of the cast.

Renee had found out that Sammy and June would be catching the next ship back to England, but in the meantime, they too had an apartment not far from hers.

'No news of the next ship back to blighty then?'

Tristram shook his head. 'No, but all the time Renee is here you don't have to worry about your reputation.' He stopped and hunted through his pockets, eventually pulling out something before falling on one knee. 'Will you marry me Clarissa?'

****

Nowy Korczyn, Poland

To Levi's relief the German aeroplanes had taken off in the late afternoon and soon after dark they had helped Rafal to salvage his parcels from the wood pile and stacked them on a small handcart. The underground fighters had also arrived and were in position, their orders to quietly and swiftly despatch any German found in the vicinity. Now all they had to do was to wait.

Just before midnight two other men arrived, M Tomasz Arciszewski, the veteran socialist leader and his companion, M Retinger, who said they too were to go back to England to join the Polish government in exile. Levi's earlier misgivings returned. That made four men plus all the missile pieces on a light aircraft. 'They'll never get all of us on a small plane Wlodek. Are you sure they aren't sending a bomber?'

Wlodek stared at him in horror. 'The field will never take a heavy bomber. It will sink in the mud...' The two men exchanged glances and Levi offered up a small prayer that he was wrong. If he wasn't their chances of pulling this off successfully were diminishing by the hour.

The radio operator was listening hard and the confirmation they had been waiting for finally came. A single letter O, to which he replied R.

'That's the signal.'

Levi and the others rushed outside to join the men gathered around the edge of the clearing with torches and lanterns. Others were guarding the outer fringes of the forest and the brook. Levi watched as the men lit the three green lights which indicated the best makeshift runway and part of the field on which to land. There were three red lanterns at the end and the runway was marked every seventy five yards by a stable lantern. Levi could hear the aeroplane approaching and he looked up and his heart sank. He recognised the aeroplane. It was a Dakota. He was no expert, but he had a horrible feeling it was too big for the muddy field. He watched as the Dakota made one exploratory flight over the field and then came into land.

There was no time to waste. The Germans were sure to have heard the aeroplane flying over. The volunteers sprung into life. The aircraft was carrying passengers and nearly half a ton of essential supplies. These were rapidly offloaded while another gang rapidly loaded Rafal's parcels. Within five minutes the exchange was complete, Levi, Rafal and the other two men were aboard and the aircraft was ready to go. The pilot prepared the engines and pressed down on his controls. Nothing happened. The aircraft wasn't moving.

****

Bombay

'I thought you'd never ask!' Clarissa flung her arms around him. 'What took you so long?'

Tristram laughed. 'I was worried you would say no. And I didn't know what a respectable interval would be... Oh God I've wasted so much time.'

Clarissa kissed him passionately. 'It doesn't matter, not now. But I don't want to waste another moment. Please let's make the arrangements as soon as possible.'

'Yes, of course we will.' Tristram kissed her back and placed the ring on her finger. 'We won't waste another moment I promise. I'll be back later.'

Clarissa hugged herself in delight. She glanced at the clock. Renee would be back soon, but Clarissa wanted to savour her news. She would walk down to the harbour, enjoy the cool evening air and watch the little boats weaving between the islands on the calm water. She finally felt as if her life was complete. They would get married, finish the tour and when they returned home she would be with the man she loved.

****

Warrington

Nora finished her drink and smiled at Hank. She still couldn't quite believe he had insisted she become his girlfriend and she wondered briefly why his friends didn't seem to have warned him off her. Perhaps they had and he really wasn't interested in her reputation.

'So, what did you think of the film?'

They had just been to see *Double Indemnity* at the Grand Cinema, a favourite with courting couples because it had double seats without an arm rest getting in the way of any kissing and cuddling.

Nora's smile broadened. 'It was brilliant. Shame they didn't get away with it though.'

Hank laughed. 'You think they should have escaped with the money?'

Nora shrugged. 'Why not?' She finished her drink. 'They would have done if he hadn't cheated on her with her step-daughter.'

'Ah so its all his fault.'

'Well it was. He messed it up. She was doing alright until he came along. She chose the wrong man.' Her face fell and for a moment she thought back to her own choices. She hadn't done anything wrong but look what had happened to her. 'It happens to women all the time.'

'That sounds very personal Nora, do you want to tell me about it?'

Nora shook her head. 'No, you'll judge me like everyone else did.' She held out her empty glass. 'How about a refill?'

Hank nodded, took her glass and stood up but before he went back to the bar he leant forward. 'I would never judge you Nora, you should know that by now.'

She watched as he queued up at the bar and waited to be served. There was a certain amount of truth in that. If he had been critical of her behaviour, he would never have asked her to be his girlfriend. Perhaps she should tell him. It would be best to have it out in the open before she grew too fond of him, then if he didn't like what she heard she could walk away before she got hurt.

****

Levi stared out the aircraft window at the field in dismay. What the hell was happening?

'You'll have to get off, we're stuck in the mud. We'll have to destroy her.' The pilot sounded desolate.

The passengers climbed off the aircraft and were watching Wlodek's men unloading the parcels when several other men in ragged clothing appeared from deep in the forest carrying spades. Within second they had begun digging out the wheels out while the four passengers, Levi included, watched and waited. Wlodek had told Levi that the whole thing should only take five minutes. Any longer than that and the Germans would be on them.

Half an hour passed and they were still on the ground. Fortunately there was no sign of the Germans, but Levi was convinced they would arrive at any moment. Eventually the men stopped digging, declared themselves satisfied and the passengers climbed hastily back on board while the parcels were swiftly reloaded. Again, the pilot boosted the engines and tried to take off, but again nothing happened.

'The Germans are too close. We need to destroy the aircraft.' The second pilot, a Pole, muttered urgently. Preparations were made to destroy the aircraft once more and one of the men began pouring petrol over the wheels.

'No, please. Just one more try.' Wlodek implored him.

The pilot glanced at his watch and nodded. Wlodek's men dug some more, the clock ticked on.

Everything was reloaded, the passengers climbed back aboard and the pilot prepared to try again.

'A German patrol is coming.'

'There are tanks coming!'

Levi heard the urgent shouting, leant back in his seat, closed his eyes and prayed. Other than his brief prayer earlier, it was a long time since he'd spoken to God, but if ever there was a good time to reconnect with his religion, it was now.

He was vaguely aware of the pilot finishing boosting the engines and then, to his relief, the machine began to move slowly forward. Levi held his breath, stared across the aisle and caught Rafal's eye. The scientist smiled at him as the machine speeded up, then taxied around the landing field twice before rushing forward across the grass.

'Yes!' Levi expelled the air from his lungs and breathed deeply as the aircraft finally left the ground and left the muddy field behind them. He sat back in his seat and his heart rate slowly returned to normal. They had some way to go, and they weren't safe yet by any means, but he was on his way home and more importantly, so was the missile.

****

Warrington

'You can trust me Nora I promise.' Hank took a deep swig of his beer and stared into her eyes.

Nora sipped her own beer in the half pint glass and tried to make up her mind. Why was she vacillating? It wasn't as if she cared that much about him… or did she?' She took a breath and stared down at the table. 'One of the soldiers guarding the base asked me if he could walk me home. It was just before they were sent overseas but I didn't know that.' She stopped, realising she was in danger of confusing him. 'I said yes, he seemed nice. We didn't even get off the base, he shoved me into one of the huts and raped me.' She heard him gasp but didn't look up at him, she continued in a monotone. 'I didn't tell anyone, he threatened that he would kill me if I said anything. A few days later I found out that he had gone overseas but it was too late by then. I didn't think anyone would believe me because I had left it so long. Then a few weeks later I found out I was pregnant. I didn't tell anyone but eventually I was starting to show so I told my friend Jessica and she persuaded me to tell my parents. She was trying to help, I don't blame her.' Nora fell silent for a moment as she remembered the awful scenes at her parents. With difficulty she pushed the memories away and continued. 'They didn't believe me, said it was my fault and that I had bought shame on them, then put me in one of those homes for unmarried mothers...' her voice shook and she fought back tears, 'and they took my baby away. Even though she was a result of being raped, I had grown to love Jennifer... that's what I called her. I wanted to keep her, but they wouldn't let me.' She drank some more beer, but it didn't dull her pain and she struggled to control her tears. There was no reason for her to tell him how she had pulled a gun on the doctor and the nun in charge.

'I'm sorry Nora, that's terrible.'

Nora looked up at him. There was nothing but compassion in his face, none of the contempt she had expected. 'You believe me?' She sounded so surprised that he reached across the table and took her hand.

'Of course, I do.'

She nodded and wondered if she should explain why she had slept with so many of the other men on the base, but he spoke before she could say anything.

'So you thought that if they wanted to treat you like a slut you might as well behave like one.'

Nora almost dropped her glass in surprise. She could feel herself blushing furiously as she nodded and lowered her gaze.

Hank squeezed her hand. 'Why didn't you sleep with me then?' His voice was gentle, caressing her.

Nora was mesmerised. She raised her eyes to his and finally told him the truth. 'Because I liked you and I didn't want to get hurt again.'

Chapter 26

London

Levi finished writing up his report, sat back and read it through quickly. The Dakota had landed safely in Brindisi and the two Polish politicians had been escorted to the airport buildings leaving Levi and Rafal with the parcels. An RAF intelligence officer had then come aboard and asked to see the missile and said he was there to take charge of it, but Rafal had refused. 'My orders are to hand them over to the Polish General Staff in London.'

The officer had been astonished. 'Don't you want a meal and a rest?'

Rafal shook his head. He hadn't risked his life to bring the missile out of Poland to lose control of it before he had handed it over properly. 'No.'

Levi smiled to himself as he remembered the officer then making arrangements for Rafal, himself and the parcels to travel by aircraft to London via Algiers and Gibraltar. The RAF pilots had been curious about Rafal and halfway back home they had decided to have some fun and to see if Rafal was genuine about guarding the parcels. One of them opened the passenger door and told Rafal and Levi that the port engine was on fire and to put their parachutes on and be prepared to jump. Rafal had refused unless he could take his parcels with him.

On their arrival in London Rafal had again refused to hand over the parcels to anyone. Eventually a Polish colonel was bought to the airfield and only after he had produced his credentials, Rafal handed over the precious cargo.

Levi stood up and poured himself a drink. A lot had happened while he had been in Poland. The allies had finally opened a Second Front and the Russians had reached Warsaw. Strangely enough they had done that on the same day he and Rafal had flown out of Poland. According to Francis one of the men who had flown into Poland on the Dakota, Jan Nowak, had gone to help the Poles rise up against the Germans. Unfortunately, the Russians hadn't done anything to help. They had sat on the other side of the Vistula and watched as the Poles and German fought it out. They were even refusing to let the British and Polish airmen refuel on Russian airfields after their dangerous seven hundred mile flight from Italy with supplies. Levi sighed. Obviously, the Russians had some other agenda, although he couldn't work out what. If they didn't intervene soon the Poles would be overrun and the Germans would take back control and then the Russians would have to fight the Germans. It didn't make any sense to him or it hadn't until Francis had explained that Churchill, Roosevelt and Stalin had met in Tehran and agreed that Poland should be a strong and independent nation after the war. Presumably the Russians had no intention of allowing that, hence their refusal to help the uprising. Levi sighed. The way things were going they would be fighting the Russians next, once they had defeated the Germans. The thought didn't fill him with confidence. The Russians had recovered from their earlier defeats and were becoming unstoppable. Even with America on their side he wasn't sure they could beat the Russians. He pushed his depressing thoughts away and glanced at his watch. He would drop the report off with Francis, then take some well earned leave and go home to see his son and Rachel.

******

Warrington

Hank lit a Lucky Strike cigarette and watched Nora getting dressed. 'I wish you could stay a bit longer. Are you sure you can't call in sick?'

Nora paused while doing up her bra and smiled back at him. 'No, of course I can't. I only get paid for the shifts I do. My parents need my rent money.' She fell silent, a frown on her face, as she realised for the first time that she was mainly working to keep a roof over her parents' heads.

'What's the matter honey?' Hank was watching her closely.

'Nothing.' She would think about it more later, but at the moment she wasn't ready to discuss it with Hank. She stepped towards the bed, leaned over and kissed him passionately. 'Thank you. I can't believe…' She fell silent.

'Nothing to thank me for honey. Just forget about the past and look forward to the future.'

Nora sighed. 'I have no idea what my future holds so I'll just settle for enjoying the present.' The war would end one day and Hank would go back to America leaving her to carry on with her life. Perhaps she was stupid to let herself fall in love with him, but it was much too late to worry about that now.

'Will you marry me Nora?' He saw the shock on her face and wondered if he'd spoken too soon. He had been intending to wait until she was pregnant but there was something about the wistful expression on her face that had made him speak sooner than he'd intended. 'Not now obviously, when the war ends. Then you can come back to the States with me.'

'You really want to marry me?' Nora had stopped dressing and was staring at him in astonishment.

'Yes of course I do.' Hank began to relax now he could see she wasn't likely to say no. 'You must have guessed that I'm in love with you.'

Nora was still trying to control her growing excitement. She had to make sure the US Army Airforce couldn't stop them thought before she let herself enjoy the moment. 'Will they let you marry me? Your commanding officer I mean? I thought there were rules…?'

Hank shrugged. 'I'm sure there are, but I won't let anything stand in our way… that is if you do want to marry me, of course…?'

'Yes, yes I do. But what about the Airforce?'

Hank leapt out of bed and pulled her into his arms. 'If they won't agree we can wait until the war ends and I'm out of the Air Force, but there's no reason for them to say no is there?'

Nora sighed. 'What about my reputation?'

Hank laughed. 'I'm sure that won't make any difference. I will ask today…' He stopped and thought hard. Having deviated from his original plan he was having to improvise. 'I need to ask your father for permission, don't I? Perhaps I should meet your parents first, before asking my CO, I mean.' He held her at arm's length and looked into her eyes. 'Can you bear to keep it a secret until we've sorted all the legalities?'

Nora nodded. 'Yes, of course.' She leaned forward and kissed him. 'Although it will be difficult.'

Hank laughed. 'It won't be for long, just until we've got all the formalities done.'

'I have to go, or I will be late.' Nora pulled away reluctantly, sat on the edge of the bed and put her shoes on. Her heart was pounding, partly from excitement at the thought of marrying Hank, and partly from fear that because no one would know they were engaged he could always change his mind.

'Before you go, take this.' Hank handed her a small jewellery box. 'You can't wear it on your left hand of course, but you could put it on the chain with your crucifix if you want.'

Nora could barely stop her hands trembling, her fingers felt awkward, and it took her a few seconds to clumsily open the box. She gasped. 'Its beautiful Hank.' She took out the simple gold band with a solitary diamond and couldn't resist putting it on her third finger.

'Phew, I'm glad it fits ok. I had to guess.' Hank was beaming. He reached out and stroked her finger gently. Nora reluctantly removed it, undid the gold chain around her neck and added the ring to her crucifix.

'I'll see you at lunchtime.' Nora kissed him again, grabbed her coat and hat and hurried out of the door.

Hank watched her go before closing the door and smiling to himself. It was all falling into place nicely.

****

Douglas, Isle of Man

Levi sat on the bench and laughed as he watched Rachel playing with Aaron. His son was so big now. He had missed so much of Aaron's short life, but hopefully not for much longer. The war looked like it was finally going to end which meant he could start a new life, a new adventure, only this one would include his son, and Rachel of course.

'Penny for them?' Levi looked startled and Rachel hastened to explain. 'You were lost in thought?' She flopped down on the seat beside him, handed Aaron a sandwich and stared at her brother.

'I was thinking about the end of the war, about what I was going to do.'

'Do your plans include Aaron and me?'

'Of course, they do.' Levi took her hand. 'Thank you, Rachel. For being there for Aaron and me. I couldn't have managed after Sura was killed without you.'

'That's what family is for Levi.' Her face darkened. 'Is it true? The rumours that I've heard…'

'What rumours?' Levi stared ahead, his face expressionless.

'That the Nazis have killed millions of Jews.'

Levi nodded. 'Yes. I haven't seen any proof, but I have heard enough...'

Rachel shuddered. 'If Jacob hadn't rescued us from Germany, we would be dead then.' It wasn't a question and Levi didn't treat it as one.

'We owe him our lives Rachel... and Sura. Without Sura Jacob would not have come to Berlin.'

'Have you heard from him?'

Levi shook his head. 'No, nothing. I don't even know if he's been told about Sura.'

'I thought your friend Francis was going to tell him.'

'Yes of course.' Levi fell silent. He couldn't tell Rachel that Jacob was probably a spy somewhere in occupied Europe.

'Strange that he hasn't contacted you then, isn't it?' Rachel was staring at him and Levi sighed and nodded. He hated lying to Rachel, but he couldn't tell her the truth, not now, perhaps never.

'What will happen to the Nazis when the war ends? Will they be punished for killing the Jews?'

'I don't know. I hope so.' Levi frowned. He hadn't given it much thought since Crete, but Rachel was right. Those responsible should be punished, they shouldn't be allowed to walk away and live their lives in peace. But that wasn't his problem... or was it? Levi took a sandwich from the box and ate slowly, his mind churning over everything he had seen and heard in the past few years. Hitler wasn't the only person responsible for the mass murders of Jews and Poles and Russians. While he was waiting with Rafal, Levi had learned about the savage occupation of Poland, had read numerous reports about concentration camps and spoken to several people who confirmed the existence of the camps and the mass extermination of Jews and Romany's, Poles and Russians. Surely the world would not just ignore these obscenities. And if they did? Levi knew he couldn't just look the other way. He couldn't right every wrong, but there were bound to be people who felt the same as him. As he sat and watched his son Levi made a decision. If the authorities didn't make some effort to punish those responsible then he would take matters into his own hands.

****

Bombay

Clarissa was growing used to the daily rehearsals ready for their first performance at an RAF depot. The heat was still a problem but at least her main role was to sing with dancing only secondary. She rehearsed several songs with Renee who was an excellent dancer and then discovered by accident that Renee also had a good voice. They were walking home with Tristram and Clarissa was singing one of the songs she had been rehearsing when she realised that Renee was harmonising with her. Clarissa stopped in surprise and turned to her friend. 'Renee, why didn't you tell me that you could sing?'

Renee blushed and looked embarrassed. 'I can't... not really. I was happy so just wanted to sing along.'

'It was very melodic. How long have you been practicing it?' Tristram smiled.

Renee looked confused. 'Practiced? Oh I haven't done that before, it was the first time.'

Tristram looked at Clarissa, saw the enthusiasm in her eyes and turned back to Renee. 'Can you do that with every song?'

Renee looked slightly embarrassed. 'Yes, well... I mean I try to do it with all songs. Its something I've always done.'

'Its perfect, we could incorporate it into most, if not all of our songs, couldn't we?' Clarissa was brimming over with an excitement she hadn't felt in ages. She had begun to feel that their performance was stale and this would make it fresh and exciting again.

'Do you mean it?' Renee was in shock.

'Yes of course we do. If it works, we can split any money we earn three ways. What do you say?'

'Really? You would really let me sing with you?' Renee could hardly believe her luck. Sammy and June would never have offered her anything as amazing. In fact Sammy had made a point of telling her that she couldn't sing and that her dancing was barely tolerable, but because they had taken her in they would stick to their promise.

Clarissa was watching her in amusement. 'Of course I will Renee. I don't understand why Sammy didn't utilise your talents instead of just giving you minor roles. She can't have failed to notice how talented you are…' She trailed off as she saw the expression on Renee's face. 'Ah she didn't tell you did she?' Clarissa shook her head. 'I bet she told you that you were useless?' When Renee nodded Clarissa sighed. 'Unbelievable. She was just jealous of you Renee, jealous of your talent because you are so much better than either of them.' She took her arm. 'Come on let's go back to the rehearsal hall and try some songs out.' She winked at Renee. 'I'm going to make you a star!'

Renee laughed but she still looked uncertain.

Tristram smiled. 'She's right Renee, you do have lots of talent and you were wasted with the sisters.'

'Exactly so come on let's go and rehearse!' Clarissa couldn't wait to get started.

'What about dinner?' Tristram looked amused. It was a while since he'd seen Clarissa so enthusiastic about her singing.

'It can wait. This is much more important.'

Tristram shrugged and then smiled at Renee. 'Looks like you've given Clarissa back her enthusiasm.'

Clarissa smiled. 'He's right. I wanted to make some changes to the act, but I couldn't think what to do to. Your harmonising is perfect. The three of us together will be amazing, I know we will.'

Renee couldn't keep the smile off her face as they headed back to the hall they were using to rehearse in. When June had been injured and Clarissa had invited her to join them, she had been excited and relieved to be away from Sammy, but this was beyond anything she had imagined.

'Thank you.'

Clarissa laughed and linked her arm through Renee's. 'Don't thank me yet, I'm a real slave driver. You think Sammy was bad, I'm the ultimate perfectionist!'

Renee laughed. 'You would never be as bad as Sammy.' Her face fell. 'Don't underestimate Sammy, she's really not very nice Clarissa. I've seen her planning revenge on people for things that happened years earlier. She never forgets a slight and in her eyes you are responsible for ruining June's career. She won't ever forgive you and if she can get revenge she will do.'

Clarissa paled and seeing her concern Tristram spoke. 'Sammy and June will be on their way back to England soon Renee. They can't hurt us. Just forget about them and concentrate on helping us perfect our new act.' He hoped his words would stop them worrying but he could see that it wasn't working. He needed to give them something else to think about. An idea popped into his head. 'I think we should call ourselves something different now there are three of us. What do you think?'

As he'd hoped Clarissa immediately started thinking about the act again. Renee still looked concerned but as Clarissa began coming up with new names and Tristram suggested his own humorous alternatives, she relaxed and joined in. They were so busy laughing they soon reached the hall and went inside, still laughing at some of Tristram's more ludicrous names.

Sammy watched from a safe distance, her face contorted in rage as she watched them laughing and joking, her anger fuelled by seeing Renee so obviously enjoying herself. She was determined that Clarissa wouldn't get away with injuring June, but she didn't have much time before she and her sister were shipped back home. Sammy was also determined to make Renee suffer for betraying them. She and June had given Renee her opportunity and how had she repaid them? By becoming friends with their enemy and when they really needed her, Renee had turned her back on the sisters, put her own career first and made herself part of Clarissa's act. Sammy clenched her fists and walked slowly back to the overcrowded hostel. There had to be a way of getting her revenge, but it had to be a way that didn't lead back to her.

Chapter 27

Tilly walked into the editor's office, closed the door and sat down.

Joren looked up, his face lit up and he smiled. 'Juliette, its lovely to have you back. How was Austria?'

'A waste of time from our point of view although some of the other information might be useful.' Tilly shrugged. She could only hope people would be made to pay for the things she had found out. 'According to Luca they aren't using the underground tunnels at Ebensee for the V weapons. It has become a sub-camp of Mauthausen which is a concentration camp near Linz. The camp is located in a forested area near the town and the main purpose is to provide slave labour for the construction of the enormous underground tunnels in which they were planning to house the armament works.' Tilly's face hardened. 'Luca says the prisoners rise at 4.30am and work until 6pm. The accommodation isn't suitable for the cold of the Austrian winter so men are dying all the time. Bodies are piled up in heaps in huts and every few days taken to the crematorium at Mauthausen. Apparently, many prisoners are barefoot because their clogs have fallen apart, the camp is infested with lice and rations are reduced as low as possible to save money, contributing to a massive death toll.' Tilly fell silent. Joren was staring at her in horror and disbelief.

'Are you absolutely sure about all this?'

Tilly nodded. 'Yes, no doubts at all. Unfortunately, I've seen photos.' Luca had shown her everything he had and told her what she wanted to know before she left. Tilly quickly realised that he had been telling her the truth. She had hoped she was going to be his new radio operator but for some reason Francis had suddenly changed his mind and ordered her back to Amsterdam. Tilly wasn't sure whether she was pleased or not. She had rather liked Luca and had been looking forward to being somewhere new, but orders were orders.

She glanced back down at her notes 'The Ebensee works are being used for petroleum refining and the manufacture of motor parts for tanks and trucks, by the Steyr-Daimler-Puch works of Linz and the Nibelungenwerk factory of St. Valentin. No V weapons. From what I can gather, most of those are being manufactured and tested in northern Germany and Poland.' Tilly put her notes away and asked the question she most wanted to know the answer to. 'Why was I told to come back here?'

Joren sighed. 'There's someone important escaping from Germany. You are to get him out of Amsterdam and back to England.' He shrugged. 'I don't know any more than that.'

Tilly frowned. 'That doesn't make sense. Why bring me back for that? Surely one of the other groups could have arranged this man's escape?'

Joren smiled. 'I don't know Juliette, but I am very pleased to have you back, even if its only for a short while.'

Tilly smiled back. 'I am pleased to see you Joren, but not over enthusiastic to be back in Amsterdam if I am honest. I am already getting called *moffen hoer* in the streets and I am not sure whether Drescher suspects me or not, so the idea of staying in Austria was rather appealing.'

Joren looked concerned. 'I can understand that, but its only for a short while, until that man arrives.'

'Ah yes the mysterious man from Germany.' Tilly laughed and then gave a theatrical sigh. 'In the meantime I had better go and see our German friend and let him know that I am back.'

'Be careful Juliette, the *moffen* are on high alert still, not only after the assassination attempt, but because they are expecting the Allies to arrive at any moment.'

Tilly's face lit up. If the allied troops arrived it would solve all her problems, no more Drescher and the resistance could let the population of the city know that she had been risking her life for their country while they had behaved like model citizens, obeyed the German oppressors and kept their heads down.

****

Warrington

Nora couldn't understand why she felt so nervous. Her parents would be delighted that someone wanted to marry her, at least she thought they would. She had already written to Bill to tell him. She had wanted him to be the first to know. Not that it would make up for not supporting him when Abigail was killed. She hoped he was happy for her and it didn't bring back too many unhappy memories.

'What on earth's the matter Nora?' Mary was watching her daughter uneasily.

Nora jumped. 'Nothing mum. I just want you to like him, that's all.'

'Mmm, we'll see.' Mary was sure Nora was lying and she wondered what new mess her daughter had got herself into.

Nora was about to say something else when there was a knock of the door. 'I'll get it.' She was gone before either of her parents could say anything.

'I hope you're not as nervous as I am.' Hank gave her a quick kiss. 'Is my tie straight?'

Nora laughed. 'Yes, its perfect.' She took his arm and led him into the small sitting room. 'Mum, Dad, this is Hank.'

'Hello Hank, I hope you like spam sandwiches and Victoria sponge cake.'

'That sounds swell Mrs Young.' Hank handed her a bag. 'I thought this might be of use to you.'

Mary took the bag and looked inside. Her face lit up as she saw food that she hadn't seen since the war had begun. Meanwhile Joseph shook Hank's hand and indicated he sit in the armchair opposite his on the other side of the empty fireplace. 'Do you smoke lad?'

'Here, have one of mine.' Hank offered him a Lucky Strike and Joseph laughed. 'My son smokes those, won't touch anything else since he was in Egypt. He's in the Navy... but then I'm sure you know that. Nora and Bill have always been very close.'

He was about to say more when Mary cried out. 'Oh, this is marvellous, thank you so much Hank.' Mary was still looking through the bag of goodies he had bought with him. 'I'll put everything in the larder, you can come and give me a hand Nora.'

'I'm pleased you like them Mrs Young.' Hank returned his attention to Joseph and smiled. 'Yes, she has spoken about her brother.'

Nora winked at him and helped Mary take the bag into the kitchen. So far so good. She began to relax. The plan was to have tea and if things were going well Hank would ask for her father's permission afterwards.

****

Bielefeld, Germany

Jacob pulled the car over to the side of the road and looked at his map. 'We should be approaching the city soon. Did your father ever mention knowing anyone here?'

Eva shook her head. 'No, not that I can remember. Why?'

Jacob shrugged. 'Just trying to work out whether your father's signature will get us through the city without any problems. There are several barracks around here, so we'll probably see lots of soldiers.'

Eva frowned. 'Don't you think they will be looking for him by now?'

Jacob thought for a moment, then nodded. 'Yes, you're right. I'm sure they will be. I think we'll swap our documents over.' He reached under the seat and pulled out an envelope. 'Read through this and learn your new identity. Its not complicated, we've kept our first names, its easier that way.'

Eva scanned the papers. 'I'm Eva Weiss, you're my husband Linus Weiss?' Jacob nodded and she went back to the paperwork. 'We have family in Amsterdam.' She stopped. 'Is that where we're going?'

'Yes. My sister is Dutch. I am taking you there because you are pregnant. I have a weak heart so I am exempt from military service, but once I drop you at my sister's I am going back to Berlin to fight for the Führer. That should prevent me from being drafted into local service which would be harder to escape from.' Jacob hesitated before continuing. 'If they don't let me through you are to go to this address in Amsterdam and ask for Juliette. She will be expecting you.' This wasn't strictly true, she was expecting him, but he hoped that once Eva explained she was his wife Juliette would take Eva out of the country.

'And what then?' Eva fought back tears. She couldn't bear to think of being separated from Linus.

'She will see you are safe.' Jacob was reluctant to say anymore. It was better she still didn't know the truth. If he didn't get through then Juliette, whoever she was, would explain everything.

'And what about you?'

'I will do my best to get away and then I will join you.'

Eva stared at him. 'Is that likely?'

'I will do everything I can do join you Eva but... well... you know how difficult that could be.' Jacob stared into her eyes. 'I love you Eva, your safety is all that is important to me. You and our child must be safe.'

'And I feel the same about you Linus. I don't know if I want to carry on without you.'

'Hopefully it won't come to that Eva.' Jacob took her hand and glanced at his watch. 'Right, time to go.' He checked the mirror, pulled out and headed towards the city.

****

Warrington

'Marry Nora?' Joseph looked shocked and reached for his cigarettes. 'When did you decide this?' He frowned. 'She's not pregnant, is she?'

Hank looked horrified. 'Of course not, sir. And before you say anymore, Nora has told me all about her past and the baby.'

Joseph looked even more astonished. 'And you don't mind?'

Hank shook his head. 'No, it wasn't her fault.'

Joseph snorted. 'You believe her story then?' The word were out before he could stop them, and he cursed under his breath. He should be delighted this man wanted to marry Nora and wasn't worried about her past. 'Of course, it's the truth...' He realised he was digging himself a hole and stopped.

'So, do I have your permission sir?'

'Yes, of course.' Joseph pulled himself together. Then he frowned. 'What about the air force? And if they agree, where will you live?'

'In the states sir, once the war is over of course, and I'm sure the air force won't have a problem with me marrying such a lovely girl as Nora.'

'And what will you do for work after the war?'

'I'm not sure yet sir, but they'll be plenty of things I can turn my hand to. America is a big place, it will be booming after the war. I will look after your daughter in the manner she deserves, I promise.'

Joseph stared at him for several seconds. There was something… then he shrugged, pushed his concerns to the back of his mind and held out his hand. Nora would struggle to start a new life in England, no one knew her in America, it was the best thing for her. 'Congratulations then Hank. Welcome to the family.'

****

Bielefeld, Germany

The guard at the checkpoint seemed to be taking an age to check Jacob's papers and he was struggling to control his nerves. 'And you say you are returning to Berlin once you have taken your wife to your sister?' The soldier stared into Jacob's face and then back down to the papers.

'Yes.' Jacob sighed. 'I appreciate you have a job to do but I have been away too long already. Can you please hurry up and wave us through so I can drop Eva and get back to defend my country.'

The soldier still hesitated, then finally handed back the documents and stepped back.

Jacob climbed back into the car, started it up and drove slowly through the checkpoint, praying that they wouldn't be stopped. It was getting harder and harder to get through now. 'I think we should dump the car a little further on and then walk. It will take longer but we can avoid the checkpoints.'

'But its miles to Amsterdam?' Eva looked aghast.

Jacob sighed. 'Yes, I know.' He drove in silence for several miles, one eye checking the mirror continuously, half expecting to be chased and stopped at any moment. He thought hard and realised that he was the problem, not Eva. He was a man of the fighting age who should be fighting. Without him she might stand a chance. 'I have a better idea. You must take the car and travel on your own. I will walk, you can tell Juliette I am on my way but that she is not to wait too long for me.'

Eva shook her head. 'No, I won't leave you. I refuse to go on my own Linus.'

'You have to Eva, it's the only way. I can cut through woods and use farm tracks, I can keep out of the way. You shouldn't have any problem travelling through checkpoints. You're pregnant, hardly fighting material.' He pulled the car over and took out the map. 'You just need to follow the map and stick to the story.' He leaned over and pulled her close. 'I love you Eva and I promised your father I would get you out. Now leave before I change my mind. I will find you I promise. Look after yourself and our baby.' He touched her stomach briefly and then climbed out of the car and began walking. Eva stared after him in shock for several moments, unable to believe he had left her alone. Then she climbed across into the driving seat and drove after him with the intention of making him get back in the car.

The sound of a car behind her made her slow down. It sped past her, the driver glancing at her briefly before returning his attention back to the road. She breathed a sigh of relief that it wasn't the Gestapo or SS and then looked for Linus. He was nowhere to be seen.

****

London

Francis reread Levi's report and then glanced at the reports from Tilly and Jacob. They had both done more than enough and were now in danger.

It was time they both came home. Jacob was already on his way, although how he would get out of Germany with the SS hunting for anyone involved in the failed assassination attempt, Francis didn't know. Tilly had consistently refused to leave Amsterdam despite the danger he was sure she was in. From other reports he had received Francis was convinced Kessel and Drescher were both suspicious of her and it was only a matter of time. But that wasn't the main reason he wanted them both back in England. The war was approaching what should be its final few months, and Francis had another assignment for both of them, something he didn't want to risk mentioning over the wireless. He hoped they wouldn't be too long as they would need a break before starting their training and learning their new identities.

******

Bombay

'I think that went really well.' Clarissa was buzzing with excitement as they walked back to their apartments at the end of their latest performance. The night air was sultry and suffused with the aroma of flowers, above them the sky was filled with shining stars. Clarissa stopped briefly and stared up, still unable to get used to the brilliance of the night sky. Tristram put his arm around her, pulled her close, kissing her passionately before answering.

'They loved us.' Tristram was ecstatic. He turned to Renee. 'And you, Renee, were absolutely wonderful.'

'She was, wasn't she?' Clarissa pulled out of his arms and hugged her friend.

Renee hugged her back. 'Thanks to you both for believing in me. I still can't grasp the fact that I am singing with the famous Desiree! And Tristram of course.' They all laughed and carried on walking.

'I am really looking forward to your wedding.'

'Not as much as I am.' Clarissa winked. 'It seems to be taking ages.'

'Not much longer now, only a few more days.'

'And you definitely don't want to invite more people?' Tristram took her arm.

Clarissa shook her head. 'No, I want a quiet wedding, just you and Renee and the witnesses. We have a performance at the RAF base in the evening, that's enough of a celebration for me.' *And that night we can sleep in the same bed, make love and wake up together without anyone sniggering behind our backs or telling the ENSA committee.* Clarissa closed her eyes briefly, the thought of finally being alone with Tristram and not having to worry about other people was the most appealing part of getting married. She was still thinking about it when she heard running footsteps. She opened her eyes and saw several young men coming towards them. Clarissa didn't take any notice until she suddenly realised that the men had surrounded them. She reached out for Tristram, but he was separated from her by one of the men who was holding a knife.

'Your purse...' The speaker was the tallest of the men.

She froze until he began gesticulating with the knife, then she reached into her handbag. 'No...' The shout made her jump, and she almost dropped the bag. 'Give it all to me.'

'Don't give them anything Clarissa.' It had taken Tristram a few seconds to shake off the shock that had paralysed him and regain his composure. He stepped towards her, elbowing the man roughly out of the way. 'Now look here, leave the lady alone.' There was a scuffle, a blur of movement... then Renee screamed.

****

Outside Bielefeld

Jacob had slipped out of the car when Eva had slowed down and disappeared into the undergrowth, expecting Eva to carry on driving. But instead she had stopped the car, climbed out and begun calling him.

'Linus, please don't do this. I am not going without you. You are my husband, I am carrying our child.'

At first he'd ignored her, hoping she would give up and do what he'd told her. But she didn't.

'I know you can hear me Linus. You haven't had time to go too far. If you aren't going to come out, I'm going back to Berlin. There's no point going on without you.'

Jacob remained where he was for a couple of minutes longer, convinced she was bluffing. He watched as she returned to the car and turned it round so it was facing the direction they had just come from. Then she climbed out and shouted again. 'I'm going back to Berlin now Linus, there's no point running away on my own. I would rather be dead.'

From his hiding place Jacob could see the tears on her cheeks and he felt sick. What was he doing? He couldn't leave her on her own. Eva was right. If they were going to escape, they should do it together even if he did think she stood more chance on her own. He was still arguing with himself when she shouted again.

'Last chance Linus. I thought you loved me. Obviously, I was wrong.'

He watched as she turned from side to side, trying to see him in the gloom. 'Goodbye Linus.' She sighed loudly, looked around one more time, wiped her tears away and climbed back in the driving seat.

Jacob leapt up and ran towards the car shouting, reaching her just as she started the engine. He pulled open the door 'I'm sorry. I thought it was for the best…'

Eva put her arms around him and kissed him passionately. 'I love you Linus. Please don't leave me. I couldn't bear it…' She stopped talking, unable to continue, tears streaming down her cheeks.

'I'm sorry my darling. I love you too. I won't leave you I promise.' Even as he spoke the words Jacob wondered if he would really be able to keep them.

Chapter 28

HMS Keats, Barents Sea

Bill peered out to sea, searching for the U-boats he was sure were out there, shadowing them as they escorted convoy JW59 to Northern Russia. According to the rumour mill that was always active if not accurate, the convoy was intended to shield Operation Goodwood and draw the Germans out from protecting the German battleship Tirpitz so instead of trying to avoid trouble they would be actively seeking it out. Bill didn't know how he felt about that. It would be great to be able to sink some U-boats but on balance he would prefer to avoid trouble. He had been torpedoed and sunk enough, the last thing he needed was to end up in the water off the coast of Russia, even if it was late summer and not the depths of winter. They were escorting the aircraft carriers, Vindex and Striker along with HMS Kite when he heard a familiar droning above them. He looked up to see some German aircraft and his heart sank. Not long then before the U-boats appeared. His muscles tensed and his grasp on the guns tightened.

****

London

'Scientists? The ones who have been trying to kill us for nearly five years. You want me to rescue them?' Levi was struggling to keep his temper.

'I know its sounds ridiculous and I find it just as distasteful as you do. But if we don't find these scientists the Soviets will.'

'Ah, I see. You're already planning the next war. Not you obviously, the politicians.'

'God forbid.' Francis looked horrified. 'We are in no position to fight the Soviets, even with American help. Now they've mobilised they are considerably more formidable than we are.' Francis cursed. 'That's top secret by the way so don't repeat it anywhere.'

Levi nodded and sighed. 'So, you want me to find German scientists and bring them back to England. Are we sharing this with the Americans or is this top secret from them too?'

'The Americans have their own plans.' Francis sighed and lit a cigarette. 'After the war the Americans will be the dominant power in the west, as the Soviets will be in the east. Its vital we have control over our own defence and foreign policy and are not totally reliant on the Americans because there will be times when our interests don't coincide. We need to be independent, or we will lose what power we do have.'

Levi nodded. 'It makes sense. I don't disagree with what you are saying, and I think its important that Britain retains its world role, I just find the idea of saving any German repugnant, whether they are a scientist or not.' He sighed. 'You said the Americans and Soviets are doing the same so presumably that means I will be in competition with them? Does that mean I have to offer these scientists some incentive as well as their freedom?'

Francis looked surprised. Levi had identified the problem quicker than he'd expected. 'Yes, probably. We don't have the same resources the Americans have, so I am hoping their freedom will be enough.'

'And if it isn't?'

'Then find out what they do want and let me know. Don't agree to anything off your own back do you understand?'

'Yes Francis. Anything else?'

'Don't get involved in an auction either. If they say they are talking to the Americans, then let it go. We won't be able to outbid them, and I am not prepared to give any Nazi scientist the satisfaction of bidding for him.'

Levi smiled. 'Understood.'

'Good, we'll sort out a list of the ones we most want, together with their last known locations and then you can make plans to go and get them. I only have a small team at my disposal so keep the plans in line with my resources.'

Francis watched Levi leave a wry smile on his face. If anyone could succeed on limited resources, it would be Levi.

****

HMS Keats, Barents Sea

Bill's clothes were already covered in freezing spray, icicles formed on his outer clothes and he was struggling to keep his eyes open, the water freezing on his eyelashes. He wiped his face again and peered out to sea convinced the danger was not yet over. One of the U-boats had been sunk by Fairey Swordfish aircraft from one of the carriers and two more had been sunk by other destroyers but Bill's instincts told him the rest of the pack were still out there somewhere. He was about to say something when he noticed that HMS Kite had slowed right down.

'What the hell's the matter with Kite?' Bill yelled.

'Fuck knows but at that speed she's a sitting duck.' Larry answered.

No sooner had he spoken when they heard two massive explosions and to their horror HMS Kite began to sink.

'Fuck!' Bill waited for them to slow down and pick up survivors but nothing happened, HMS Keats continued at the same speed.

'They don't stand a chance in the icy water.' Larry said looking away from the cranage behind them.

'We can't just leave them...' Bill felt sick.

'They're probably dead by now, two minutes tops in that water. HMS Keppel is slowing, they'll pick up any survivors.'

Bill found he couldn't look away from the dying men, there was too much noise for him to hear anything, but his imagination played the sounds anyway, screaming for their mothers, yelling for help. He fought back the nausea and tried to concentrate on his own job, but his brain wouldn't let him settle, constantly replaying the sound of the men drowning all around him.

****

Amsterdam

Tilly hid the wireless set under the straw in the barn, checked it couldn't be seen and crept to the door. She peered carefully all around, but there was no one about, everything was quiet, it was safe to decode the message from Francis and then leave. She had acknowledged the message and then let Francis know that the German contact hadn't arrived yet, although it had been weeks since she'd been warned to expect him. She climbed on her bike and began pedalling quickly back towards Amsterdam, her thoughts on the decoded message. Francis wanted to know if there were any large German troop movements planned in the next couple of weeks, or if any had already moved. Tilly would pass on the message to the main group who would scout around the area and report back to her.

She glanced at her watch, if she didn't hurry she would be out after curfew and that would mean finding a good excuse. It was much easier to just get back on time, especially as Bruno was coming to see her that evening. Tilly put her head down into the wind and tried to ignore the conflicting feelings that always arose in her when she thought about the German. She hated him because he was a Nazi, her enemy, the man who had ordered so many deaths… yet somewhere under that hatred was something else, something she didn't want to acknowledge. Since she'd come back from Austria he had been particularly attentive and generous, taking her out for meals and buying flowers and jewellery. She didn't mind the flowers, they brightened her apartment, but she didn't want bracelets, necklaces or rings. Some pieces looked very expensive, much too pricey even for someone in his position, and she was worried they might be heirlooms looted from Jewish families or other people the Nazis had arrested and murdered or sent to camps. She wanted to refuse them, but that might make him suspicious. Also, if she gave them back to him, he might give them to someone else. At least if she kept the trinkets he gave her, she might be able to return them to their owners when the war finished. It was probably wishful thinking, but it was the only way she could bring herself to accept them.

Tilly had eventually decided that he was no longer suspicious of her and had resumed her search of his papers when he fell asleep, cautiously at first and then with more confidence after the intelligence she had learned had saved the lives of a couple of resistance men. They had also learned some useful intelligence which they had passed onto the Allies. Tilly sighed and wondered how much longer it would be before they liberated Holland. In the distance she could see Amsterdam and she yawned. It must be the warm weather wearing her out, she had felt exhausted for the last couple of days. She hoped she wasn't sickening for anything. There was too much to do.

****

Bombay

Clarissa hadn't moved from the bedroom for a week and Renee was beginning to despair. 'Perhaps you should go home Clarissa. Nathanial will be delighted to see his mother and at least there won't be any memories...' Renee stopped at the expression on her friend's face.

'I can't go home... I won't go home. Tristram wouldn't have wanted me to give up.'

'No, he wouldn't.' Renee fell silent again, not sure what to say to comfort Clarissa. She was still in shock, so heaven only knew how Clarissa felt. They had been so happy, laughing and joking and then... those men... It had all happened so quickly. One moment Tristram was intervening between Clarissa and the robber, the next he was falling to the pavement, the man who had grabbed Clarissa's bag running off into the darkened streets with his accomplices. Renee could still hear her scream echoing through the empty streets and Clarissa kneeling down by her fiancé, tears falling silently down her cheeks as she hugged him and begged him not to die. His blood had soaked her clothes, but Clarissa didn't notice. Nor was she really aware of the police arriving and pulling her gently away from the body. Unfortunately, Renee could remember every moment, it kept replaying itself in slow motion, again and again. She wouldn't have minded if she could change the outcome, but it was always the same. Tristram was dead, his life blood draining away into the gutter of a Bombay street leaving Clarissa alone.

'There's more flowers and cards for you.'

Clarissa shrugged. 'That's very kind of people, but it doesn't help.'

'No, but it does show that people care.' Renee fell silent, not sure what else to say.

'Have the police any idea why they targeted us? None of the other ENSA members have been attacked.' Clarissa turned towards her. 'I know it sounds stupid… but you don't think Sammy had anything to do with this do you?'

Renee's mouth fell open, her eyes widened in shock. 'Surely not? I mean how…?' She shook her head. 'It was just an accident Clarissa, no one's fault, we were just in the wrong place at the wrong time.'

Clarissa snorted in derision. 'I don't believe it.' She suddenly stood up and reached for her hat. 'I am going to find out why my fiancé was murdered.'

Renee watched Clarissa walk purposefully towards the apartment door and followed at a distance. She was relieved to see her friend finally leave the bedroom, but she wasn't sure her reasoning was sound. On the other hand if it served the purpose of motivating Clarissa again then perhaps it wasn't such a bad thing. As long as it didn't get out of hand of course.

****

London

'I've been through the list and done some research and have come up with a couple I think would be reasonably easy to extradite from Poland, providing we get there before the Soviet advance which seems to be moving quite quickly westwards.' Levi handed Francis a sheet of paper.

Francis glanced at it and quickly skim read through the details. 'Excellent. I am currently waiting for my team to return from Europe and then you can go.' Francis hesitated and wondered whether he should tell Levi who they were.

'Do you know when that will be as I think we should move quickly.'

'No, at the moment one of them is supposed to be on his way to Amsterdam...' Francis stopped. 'You might as well know. I was going to use Jacob and Tilly. You remember them?'

Levi stared at him in astonishment, then his face lit up. 'Jacob is alive, that's marvellous. Thank God.' Then he frowned. 'Tilly?' He thought for a moment then grinned. 'Yes, of course. Tilly from the internment camp!'

Francis smiled. 'Yes. I am glad you remembered.' His smile faded. 'Jacob should have been in Amsterdam weeks ago. That's where Tilly is. I was going to get them both out together. But he hasn't turned up.'

'Where was he coming from?'

'Berlin. He was working with someone who was involved in the assassination attempt, hence his rather rapid exit. But he hasn't arrived and I have no means of finding out where he is.'

'Do you want me to go over and look for him?'

'No, I wouldn't know where to send you. He could be anywhere... anywhere except Amsterdam anyway.'

'Then we wait?'

'Yes, I'm sorry.'

'Indefinitely?'

'No of course not.' Francis sighed. 'You're right. This is too important to put on hold. We'll give them another week. If I haven't heard anything by then you'll have to go in on your own.'

Levi nodded, his earlier jubilation that Jacob was alive had been tempered by his friend's disappearance. On the other hand, Jacob had survived this long so he had probably just had to change his plans. Tilly was obviously still in Amsterdam and safe or Francis would have bought her out earlier. He was looking forward to seeing them both again, but he would use the week he had to make arrangements so that if he had to he could carry the extractions out on his own.

****

Amsterdam

Tilly and Joren listened to the radio in despair. A few days earlier they had joined the rest of the population in celebrating what appeared to be the Allied invasion of the Netherlands. Germans and members of the Dutch Nazi Party had fled various cities, but the radio reports were false. The Germans were far from defeated and they were still an occupied country.

Joren eventually switched off the radio and looked at the latest instructions from London that Tilly had decoded. 'All resistance groups are to co operate and operate under an umbrella group called the Internal Armed Forces (BS) headed by Prince Bernhard.'

Tilly dragged her attention back to the message. 'It makes sense. After Mad Tuesday we have lots of people wanting to join in the resistance. If we're not careful we'll be treading on each other's shoes.'

Joren sighed. 'Ah yes, the September flies.'

Tilly smiled at the derogatory term. 'Rather surprising when the Nazis have orders to shoot anyone suspected of being in the resistance, whether they are armed or not.'

'They just want to make sure they won't be accused of collaboration.'

'We need to make sure they all abide by our rules that we are only fighting against real fascists, not innocent people or children.'

Joren nodded. 'You're talking about the plot to kidnap Seyss-Inquart's children?'

'Yes, I know he's the Commissioner of the Reich of the Netherlands, but his children aren't to blame for that. Its really important we don't get drawn into Nazi ways or we become just as bad as them.'

'You're right although I can understand why it would have been suggested.' He saw Tilly's expression and he raised a hand. 'I said I could understand it, not that I agreed with it.'

Tilly relaxed and changed the subject. 'What about troop movements? Francis has asked for information regarding certain areas as a matter of urgency.' She frowned. 'Do you think they are planning an attack in those areas?'

'Probably, I can't see why else they would want the information, although we are talking a long way east of the country...' He shrugged. 'Ours not to reason why.'

Tilly stood up. 'I'll leave now and get our people on to that.'

Joren watched her go and turned his attention back to the problem of the increasing numbers of people wanting to become involved. Whilst it was good his fellow countrymen and women had finally climbed off the fence, the large numbers who now wanted to fight the occupiers was bringing its own problems, not least that they all needed to be properly vetted.

******

En route to the allied lines

Eva slipped and slid down the muddy bank, coming to a halt just above the water line. 'Shit!' She cursed loudly and buried her face in her arms trying to hide her tears.

'Eva! Are you alright?' Jacob slid down the bank after her. 'You're not hurt?'

'No, I'm bloody marvellous. I'm hungry and tired, my body is exhausted and now my clothes are covered in wet mud!'

'You chose to come after me Eva. You could have been in Amsterdam by now.' Jacob snapped, mainly out of relief that she was unhurt. He put his arm around her, helped her up and began leading her carefully across the small stream. Walking had been hard going, but they hadn't had a choice. Jacob had been convinced that eventually they would be stopped at a checkpoint and their false papers discovered. Then, if he was lucky, he would be sent somewhere to fight. If he wasn't they would work out that he was a British spy, and then he would be tortured and shot. He didn't know what would happen to Eva, but being pregnant probably wouldn't save her. As they drove westwards Jacob had thought it over and as soon as they saw another checkpoint in the distance he told Eva to pull the car off the road into the woods. Once the car was out of sight Eva turned the engine off and they sat in silence until they were sure no one had followed them. Then they had packed any essentials into two bags and begun walking.

Eva shrugged his hand off. 'Yes possibly, but I would be on my own. We are married, we should stay together.'

'But you would have been safer…'

Eva stopped and stared up at him, her eyes blazing. 'You don't know that Linus. I might have been turned back at the next checkpoint or arrested for having false papers. I've already lost my parents and Anton, the Soviets have over run the area of Poland they were going to, Claus was an SS guard at a camp that has been taken by the Soviets and Konrad was in Paris which has also now been taken by the French. I have to accept that they could all be dead. I can't lose you too.' She took a breath. 'Anyway, its done now, can we please stop going on about it.'

Jacob sighed. 'Yes, I'm sorry.' She was right, there was no point continually going over old ground. It was much too late to change anything. They reached the other side of the stream and climbed up the sloping bank and into some trees. Jacob stopped, checked the map and changed the subject. 'I've been thinking. Perhaps we should head towards the coast instead?'

Eva frowned. 'The French coast?'

'Yes. The Allies will need to supply their troops and for that they will need ports. They will want to liberate them before the main cities so if we head for places like Calais or Boulogne we might stand more chance of reaching safety.'

'How far is it?'

Jacob smiled and kissed her. After a few seconds she relaxed and kissed him back. He eventually pulled back. 'Far enough. But as you have pointed out to me we are together and we should treat every day as a bonus.'

Eva smiled back. 'I agree.' She leaned forward and put his hand on her stomach. 'But *we* are hungry Linus.'

Jacob laughed. 'Judging by the size of the bump our son is growing well considering the way we are living at the moment.'

'A son?' Eva raised an eyebrow making him laugh.

'You think our child is a girl?'

Eva thought for a moment then shook her head. 'No, I think it is a boy, not that it matters. He or she will be equally loved.'

Jacob smiled. 'Yes, you are right. The most important thing is to escape so you can have our child safely.' He picked up their bags. 'Come on, let's go and try and find something to eat.'

******

Warrington

Nora stared at herself in the mirror, her face expressionless. She wasn't sure whether she was surprised that her parents had agreed to her marriage or not. Her lip curled upwards. No doubt her parents were delighted to be rid of her. And even better she would be thousands of miles away, no longer on their doorstep to cause them embarrassment. She wondered how Hank was getting on with making the arrangements. Nora clenched her fists and stared into the reflection of her eyes. She had read somewhere that a person's eyes were the window to their soul. She leaned closer and sighed. If she had to describe what she saw she would have said they were dark and brooding, reflecting an empty soul, a bottomless pit of misery. She should be happy. After all she was getting married, something every girl was supposed to dream about, but instead Nora felt nothing at all, not even despair.

Nora knew now that she didn't really love Hank even though she had initially thought she did. But she knew now that it had been more like relief that someone actually wanted to marry her, someone actually cared for her, maybe even loved her. Her heart didn't race with excitement when she thought of him, but he was kind to her and he would give her a new start, somewhere that no one knew her. She gave another long sigh. When Hank had asked her to marry him she had almost asked him if they could look for Jennifer and bring her to live with them, but her courage had failed. Hank must love her, or he would never have asked her to marry him, even though he knew about her daughter. But would a man really want to bring up someone else's child, especially one born out of wedlock? To ask him would probably be madness and she couldn't risk ruining it. Hank was her ticket out of England, a one way ticket to another life. It would be stupid to drive him away. Maybe one day in the future, perhaps when they had their own children he would be more receptive to the idea, and then she would risk asking him. In the meantime she would use what time she had left to try and find out exactly where Jennifer was, something that would be much harder once she had left England. Then she would have to find a way of keeping an eye on Jennifer so her daughter didn't just disappear.

Chapter 29

Amsterdam

'It was called Operation Market Garden.' Joren addressed the meeting. 'The idea was to surround the German army in the western part of the Netherlands, but it has not been completely successful. They've liberated some parts of southern Netherlands, and according to our intelligence several members of the NSB (the Dutch Nazi Party) have fled.'

'We told them there were tanks in the area, why the hell didn't they listen?' Martjn snapped.

Joren shrugged. 'I don't know. Our messages definitely got through.'

'I can vouch for that.' Tilly interjected. 'I have the acknowledgments.'

'There's no point going over it again, we can't change the outcome and we have other things we can do to help.' Joren glanced down at his notes. 'Gerbrandy has called for a general railway strike.' Joren repeated the message that had come from the Prime Minister of the Netherlands in exile in London.

'We can do that.' The representative of the railway workers nodded. 'But the Nazis won't like it. There may well be reprisals.'

'But we do it anyway?'

A murmur of consent went around the room and Joren nodded. 'Good. The next item is to work out how to move the people we have in hiding around the cities if the Germans tighten security. We'll need new documents and new places for them to go to.'

Tilly listened as suggestions flowed, occasionally contributing, but it wasn't her job. Since meeting Kessel she had stopped taking people across the borders and instead was concentrating on providing and accumulating intelligence.

Eventually the meeting moved onto the next planned assassinations. Tilly listened with interest as the RVV representative announced. 'We're going to eliminate the Haarlem Criminal Investigation Service. That means killing Inspector Fake Krist, Willemse and Smit.'

'That will inevitably cause more reprisals.' Joren looked concerned.

'What's the alternative? Do nothing?'

'No, of course not.' Joren exchanged glances with Tilly. He hated sanctioning actions that meant innocent people would die, but unfortunately, they had no choice.

****

London

'There's still no news of Jacob and I need Tilly where she is for the moment in case he does turn up, so I am afraid you are on your own.'

Levi nodded. He was used to working alone but it would have been nice to be with his friends. He only hoped Jacob was alright although it did seem an awful long time now. 'One of the men you want is Bernhard Tessmann, he's an expert in guided missiles. I will start with him.'

'Where is he?'

'Northern Germany, in the Hartz mountains. Tessmann was involved in the basic planning for Peenemunde. He moved there in late 1936 to supervise construction and conducted the first engine testing there at Test Stand I. From what I can see Tessmann begun working on wind tunnels, then moved onto thrust measuring systems for the V-2 engines. According to the intelligence he was evacuated after the RAF bombed the plant in August 1943 and sent to Koelpinsee. Here he designed ground equipment for the V-2 mobile units, like the ones I destroyed, and he was also involved in the planning for the 'Projekt Zement' underground V-2 facilities at Ebensee in Austria.

'Can you get him on your own?'

'I can try. If not I have memorised the names of several others who are in that area and I will go after them.' Levi thought for a moment. 'This is just an idea, but rather than have me try to get these men out on my own, wouldn't it make more sense for me to find out exactly where these people are and then relay the information back to you. Then the British can send a special task force over to rescue that scientist, or even kidnap him if he's that important and doesn't want to play ball. I can then move on to find the next one.'

Francis stared at him and then nodded. 'Other than the kidnap bit, that's actually a brilliant idea. Yes. Go and find this Tessmann and let me know where he is.'

Levi smiled. 'I will leave today. I have my new ID papers that will allow me to travel around Germany and Poland which is where most of the scientists are now.'

'Good luck.'

'Say hello to Jacob and Tilly when they get back.'

Francis nodded. Like Levi he was still sure Jacob was alive. 'I will.' He watched Levi leave and reached for the telephone. This was a job for the Army.

******

Somewhere in the Atlantic

Bill sat on his hammock and tried to forget the images of the Barents Sea that still wouldn't leave him. The U-boat that had sunk *HMS Kite* had itself been sunk the following day by a single Swordfish aircraft that had been patrolling from *Vindex*. Bill wanted to feel some satisfaction but he didn't feel anything. It didn't matter, sinking the U-boat hadn't bought back his fellow sailors. Only fourteen sailors had been rescued alive and five of those had died on board. It could so easily have been them. Why were they still alive and not those men? He looked down at Nora's letter and his spirits sank even further. What was the matter with his family? They had such bad luck. Maybe they were all cursed?

He took a deep breath and began reading Nora's letter for the second time. The first time he had been so shocked by what he was reading that he'd had to stop and do something else. He had been so grateful to have received what appeared to be a proper letter on their arrival in port that he had dived in without really thinking, so the content had caught him completely by surprise and then they had been sent out on the convoy so he'd not had much time to think about it. Bill lit a Lucky Strike with trembling hands, took a breath and tried to concentrate on the words in front of him.

My dear Bill

I am so terribly sorry for my very abrupt reply to your letters. I didn't mean to be rude or cut you out, but things have been so difficult here and I didn't want to try and explain it all in a letter. But I am now left with no choice as I don't know if I will still be here when you finally get leave. I'm not going to die or anything, but I may be living somewhere else, a long way from here and from you. But before you start reading the rest of my letter, please promise me that you won't jump ship to come and see me. I don't want you to get into trouble and in any case its much too late for you to be able to do anything to stop the terrible things that happened. But there is something you can do to help in the future, if you want to, of course. You may read this and decide I am not the little sister you used to know and that you would rather not have anything to do with me now. But

I hope not because you are all I have left, the only person I can really rely on for help.

I have reached this point and now I don't know where to start. At the beginning I suppose. Well I suppose it started while I was still living on the Isle of Man. I got involved with some people who were working for the intelligence services. Yes, me, the uneducated girl who worked in a shop. I was working in one of the internment camps and there was a girl called Tilly who was spying on some of the Nazis that we had detained there. She had a contact called Jacob Goldsmith. Yes, it was his father whose shop you broke into with Alan. But Tilly couldn't be seen talking to Jacob because he is Jewish, so I was the go between. I pretended to be going out with him and this allowed her to pass messages by me to him and therefore out of the camp. I really enjoyed doing that and became good friends with both Tilly and Jacob. We were told there was a plot, I can't tell you what it was, but it was something that would have helped the Nazis a lot and I helped to foil it. But because I was involved in that my colleagues in the internment camp thought I was behaving suspiciously and notified the security services, a different branch from the ones I was working with. The people I was working for quickly cleared my name, but I couldn't stay there so I lost my job. That's when we left for Warrington.

As you know I worked in a stately home for a while with some evacuees but eventually they went home and then I got the job in the US Airforce camp. One evening a British soldier from the regiment who were guarding the camp asked me if he could walk me home. He seemed nice so I said yes. He wasn't. He pushed me into one of the empty huts and raped me, then said he would kill me if I told anyone. I was so scared I didn't tell anyone and I only found out later that he had been shipped overseas the following day so he couldn't have hurt me, but by then it was too late. I tried to forget what had happened, but then I discovered I was pregnant.

Mum and Dad didn't believe me, they blamed me and arranged for me to go into a mother and baby home and for the baby to be taken away and adopted. I tried to stop them, I threatened the doctor and one of the nuns with a gun, but they overpowered me and I was arrested. Francis, the man in the intelligence services, persuaded them to drop charges against me and I went back to work.

I have now met someone who wants to marry me. He's American and he knows about Jennifer. That was the name I gave my daughter, your niece. But I don't think he will want to look after Jennifer too and I am scared to ask in case he changes his mind about me. I don't love him, but he is kind to me and I can have a fresh start in America.

I have finally told you all this because I want to eventually have my daughter with me, maybe when Hank, (that's my future husband's name) and I have our own children, but to do that I need to know where Jennifer is. I am going to try and find her before I leave England, but after that I want to ask you to keep track of her for me so that one day I can send for her. I know this is a lot to ask and I know you must be disgusted at me, but it really wasn't my fault. This letter is the truth, whatever Mum and Dad say.

I will hold my breath and wait to hear from you. Please find it in your heart to forgive me.

Your loving sister

Nora.

Bill stared at the letter, open mouthed in shock and disbelief. No wonder Nora hadn't written to him when Abigail had been killed. He lit another cigarette and scanned through the words again. When he had finally finished he clenched his fist. Bill was convinced Nora was telling him the truth which made everything worse. Why hadn't his parents supported her? Why had they been so sure that she had lied to them? He glanced at the letter again and shook his head. No, Nora had never lied to him. But how could he help her? He was stuck on *HMS Keats* until he was either transferred or the war ended, *or it was torpedoed or bombed...* the words filled his brain before he could stop them. He pushed thoughts of sinking away and tried to concentrate on Nora. He would write back immediately, but she wouldn't get it for a while. It wouldn't be posted until they were back in port. The thought of Nora waiting patiently for a reply while they continued their duties, and his reply promising to support her, sat waiting in a sack to be posted was unbearable, but there was nothing he could do about that. Bill reached for some paper and a pen. At least if he wrote his reply now it would go as soon as they reached land and that might be quite soon. They had been at sea for ages this time, surely they were due in port soon. And if they were he might be able to telephone her, to let her know his letter was on its way.

******

En route to the coast

Jacob wasn't sure crossing into France had been one of his better ideas, but at least they were heading in the right direction to get back to England. He was hoping that by the time they reached Calais or Boulogne the Allies would have defeated the German presence in the area and liberated the ports. From what he could remember of the documents that had passed over his desk while in Germany, there were no reserve defences in the area because Hitler had forbidden their construction so with a bit of luck the Allies could roll straight through. If not they would have to change direction and head for Paris which had now been liberated.

Several hours later they were walking along the edge of wooded area when they suddenly heard heavy guns in the distance. Eva stopped dead and stared at him in horror. Jacob's instinctive reaction was to grab Eva and throw themselves flat on the ground, but the guns weren't close. 'It's alright, they're a long way off. Let's keep walking.'

'Are you sure?'

Jacob nodded. 'If I'm correct we're not too far from Calais now.'

Eva's face lit up at the thought they could soon stop walking then she frowned. 'Sounds like they are still fighting there?'

'Yes. Perhaps the garrison will surrender quickly rather than keep fighting.' Jacob fell silent trying to remember the reports he had sent back to Francis in the last few months. They had come from the garrison commander, Oberstleutnant Ludwig Schroeder, and according to him only about two and half thousand of the seven and half thousand soldiers, sailors and airmen were fit to be used as infantry. Furthermore, most of the garrison troops were volunteers or ethnic Germans born in other countries. Jacob smiled slightly as he remembered Shroeder's own description of the troops under his command, his report describing the army personnel as old, ill, and lacking the will to fight and resist interrogation. He had even less faith in the Naval personnel who he also considered to be old with a total lack of the experience when it came to fighting on land. The only troops Shroeder seemed to have any faith in were the air force A.A. gunners who were young and apparently showed signs of good morale. Jacob had hoped at the time that Shroeder's assessment was accurate, especially as the man himself was only considered a mediocre commander who had been given control because there wasn't anyone else.

As they walked on the bombardment continued in the distance, the sky alight with tracer, and the ground trembling as the heavy guns continued their assault. In the sky ahead he could just make out aircraft flying low over the city and the subsequent explosions as they dropped their bombs.

Jacob took Eva's arm. 'Let's sit down on the grass and rest for a bit. There's no point continuing until the bombardment stops. We're on the wrong side of the city to link up with the Allies, and the last thing we want is to be spotted by a German patrol and for me to be forced to fight to defend Calais.' He frowned. Or was it? Perhaps that was the best way to get across the lines? The garrison couldn't hold out for ever. Sooner or later they would surrender to overwhelming forces and if he was one of them... On the other hand it wasn't without risk. There was always the chance he would be killed by the very people he was trying to reach, unless...

Chapter 30

Bombay

'You can't just accuse people of murder without any proof Clarissa.' Renee was beginning to lose patience.

'I know Sammy was behind Tristram's murder and I intend to prove it.' Clarissa knew people were beginning to think her grief had sent her mad, but she was convinced Sammy was guilty. Her only problem was finding the evidence to support her feelings.

Renee didn't answer for a moment, then she changed the subject. 'Don't forget we're off to Poona and then onto Bangalore. The train leaves tomorrow. We need to pack or we'll be rushing tomorrow.'

Clarissa stared at her in disbelief. Tristram had been murdered somehow orchestrated by Sammy and all Renee could talk about was going to Poona. 'Do you think I care about that?'

Renee had finally had enough. 'Tristram would have done. He would be horrified that you no longer cared about entertaining the troops. You said you owed it to him to keep going. Has that changed? Because if it has you should go back home to England.'

'And what would you do if I went back home? You could hardly carry on singing on your own could you?'

Renee stared, her lip trembled and she shook her head. 'I thought you were different. I thought you genuinely liked me… But you're no different from Sammy and June. Only thinking of yourself.' She walked to the door. 'I'll take my things and go.'

Clarissa watched in silence then she stood up and rushed towards her. 'I'm so sorry. That was a dreadful thing to say. Completely unforgivable. I didn't mean it. I was just hitting out. Please try and forgive me Renee. I know I have been awful, obsessive and mean and… I just can't bear to think that Sammy has got away with it. Tristram was such a lovely man, he didn't deserve to die like that.'

Renee looked down at the floor. Clarissa sounded genuinely sorry, but would she revert back again if she thought Renee had forgiven her? Clarissa stepped towards her and took her hand.

'But that's no excuse Renee. You have been such a good friend to me. I don't deserve you and I would understand if you wanted to go on without me. And what I said about you not being capable... it was rubbish. You have a wonderful voice. Tristram was going to suggest you did some solos... would you interested in doing that?'

Renee looked shocked. She had been concerned that Tristram would see her as a threat to the act... she had misread things, obviously. She pushed her thoughts away and smiled. 'Really?'

'Yes, really. It's the least I could do after how I have been behaving.'

'And Sammy?'

Clarissa shrugged. 'I will find out what happened, I owe Tristram that. But now isn't the time.' She smiled. 'Come on, we have other things to do.'

******

Calais

'You say you're from Berlin?' Schroeder stared at him suspiciously.

Jacob and Eva had arrived in Calais the previous day and things weren't going exactly as he had planned. For some reason he had persuaded himself that he could just walk in and persuade Schroeder to surrender to the overwhelming forces outside the city. Unfortunately, Schroeder had other ideas. He seemed intent on defending the city for as long as possible, in the mistaken belief that reinforcements were on their way.

'Yes, from the Oberkommando der Wehrmacht on Stauffenbergstrasse. I work for Major Clemens von Landau.' Jacob had decided to take a chance that the garrison in Calais would be too remote to know everything that was going on in Berlin. Yes, they would know that the SS were hunting for traitors, but hopefully not which members of the armed forces they were hunting for.

'And you bought your wife with you? Why?'

'She was my cover, to prevent suspicion. I was ostensibly taking her to my sister in Amsterdam. Then when we got to the Dutch border we threw away those papers and carried on here.'

'On foot?'

'Our car was damaged, we didn't have any choice.' Jacob had been through this several times now. For a so-called mediocre officer Schroeder was becoming rather forbidding. He forced himself to concentrate.

Schroeder shook his head, his eyes cold and disbelieving. 'And your job was to tell me that I am supposed to surrender?'

Jacob took a breath and tried to sound enthusiastic. 'Yes sir.

'My last orders were to hold at all costs.' Schroeder paced up and down his office, then stopped and stared at Jacob. 'Why would Command suddenly decide to surrender such a vital port?'

'As I said, its been decided that Calais is impossible to hold and that for Germany's sake it would be better if the western Allies reached the German border before the Soviets. If Germany has to surrender, it would be better to surrender to the British or the Americans. The High Command is hoping that the western Allies will join with the Germans to fight the Soviets. The thinking is that Calais and Boulogne will fall within days anyway with the loss of valuable lives on both sides, troops that could be used to fight the Soviets.'

'But the Führer said we are not to surrender under any circumstances.' Schroeder sat down and thought about the continual propaganda pouring out of the radio telling them that the western allies were just as bad as the Soviets and that they would punish the Germans even more for the war, like they had after the previous war. 'That's not what the news broadcasts say?'

'The High Command wants to prevent further loss of German life. The war is lost, we need to save people now and the biggest threat to Germany are the Soviets.' Jacob tried to explain calmly.

Schroeder stared at him and then spoke slowly. 'You're right. The troops that are here could be much more useful back in Germany, stopping the Soviets rapid approach from the east. I could evacuate as many troops as possible back to Germany and then surrender the garrison to the Canadians.'

Jacob didn't answer. That wasn't exactly what he had intended, but perhaps it was the best he could hope for. Now he had to ensure that he remained with the troops who were surrendering. 'And what's your plan in this? Are you going back to Berlin now?' Schroeder suddenly snapped.

A glimmer of an idea came to Jacob. If he could only persuade Schroeder...

'Its supposed to be top secret sir.' He saw the frustrated expression on Schroeder's face and decided it was now or never. 'But if I don't tell you...' Jacob took a breath and hoped he would sound convincing. 'I'm to surrender with the remaining troops, ingratiate myself with the Canadians and then pass back intelligence to Berlin.'

******

Amsterdam

'The attacks on Krist and Smit have failed. One of the fighters was shot in the leg and has been arrested. The attack on Willemse failed as well. Hannie did manage to shoot him in the arm but her gun failed, and he shot her in the thigh. We got her away thank God, but the danger is increasing. It won't take them too long to realise that they must have a spy in their midst. I think you should leave Amsterdam.'

Tilly paled. 'I can't just go without a good reason. It will draw attention to you.'

'And you being arrested won't of course?'

Tilly gave a wry smile but didn't answer.

'Alright, perhaps I could find you a story somewhere else?'

'The fighting is everywhere. Brussels and Antwerp have fallen, the allies are fighting for the channel ports and they will probably fall soon. The only place I could go would be to Germany and I'm not sure that's a good idea.'

'No... no of course not.' Joren stood up and began pacing the office. 'Look I can't think of anything. I think the best thing is for you to send a message to London and ask them what you should do?'

Tilly stared at him for several seconds then she nodded. Joren was right. She knew too much to allow herself to be arrested. The lives of too many people depended on her being safe. 'Yes, alright. I'll do it tonight.' She glanced at the clock on the wall. 'Actually, I'll go now. The sooner we sort this out the better. I don't want to be responsible for any problems here.'

Joren breathed a sigh of relief. He had expected Juliette to argue, but she had surprised him. He smiled. Juliette was always surprising him, he should be used to it by now.

******

Harz Mountains, Germany

Levi climbed back into the German car, looked at himself in the driving mirror and gave a cold smile. He had decided to disguise himself as an SS Officer because that way no one would dare argue with him unless it was a more senior SS officer and Levi intended to keep clear of them. His cover was that he was looking for deserters and people in contact with the enemy.

He sighed and turned his attention back to Tessmann, slammed his fist on the steering wheel and cursed loudly. He had been too late. Tessmann had left ages ago. However, as annoying as it was, it did justify the plan he had suggested to Francis. They needed someone on the ground who could find the scientists and then the commandos or whoever the British planned to use, could come in and take them out. Levi couldn't care less how they did it. If it was up to him he would offer an escape route for them and their family, with a good salary, somewhere to live and guaranteed work for five years. If they didn't agree he would just kidnap them. It was obviously what the Soviets were doing, and they were being very successful. As far as he was concerned the scientists had lost the right to choose a long time ago.

He drove quickly back to where he was hiding in the forest, set up his wireless and sent his transmission. Francis would be disappointed, but Levi was sure he would soon find Tessmann and if not he would start on the rest of the list.

******

En route to Poona

'Are you feeling alright? You look very flushed.' Renee looked at Clarissa with concern. They had just boarded the hot crowded train and finally found some seats by an open window.

'Yes, I think its probably just the heat although I haven't felt like this before.' Clarissa began fanning herself with the newspaper she had bought before leaving Bombay.

'It will be better once the train leaves, there will be some fresh air.' Renee sat back on the seat and willed the train to move and cool them all down.

Clarissa leant back and closed her eyes trying to fight off the dizzy feeling in her head, but nothing changed. Everything was swimming around and now she was starting to feel sick. She opened her eyes and tried to focus on Renee. 'Actually, no I don't feel well at all. Perhaps I should get off the train before it leaves…' She didn't get any further before everything went black.

'Clarissa!' Renee tried to revive her, but Clarissa was limp and Renee could feel the heat from the fever. 'Help! My friend is ill!' She had to yell loudly to make herself heard but people were already moving away from them and her pleas for help were falling on deaf ears.

'What is it?' Phillip Jackson, one of the ENSA organiser suddenly appeared at her side. He took one look at Clarissa and yelled out of the window for an ambulance.

'What's the matter with her?' Renee grabbed his sleeve.

'I don't know, I'm not a doctor but it looks like malaria. Has she been taking her medicine?'

Renee shrugged. 'I don't know to be honest. Will she be alright?'

Phillip shook his head. 'I don't know. She definitely won't be well enough to go to Poona. What about you?'

Renee looked confused. 'Me?'

'Are you going on your own?'

She shook her head. 'No, I can't leave her.'

'Are you sure?'

'Yes.'

'Then you'd better come with us.' He was looking out of the window and as he spoke two men came along the platform carrying a stretcher. 'Over here!'

Renee watched as they place Clarissa on the stretcher and then followed them off the train. She had no idea what good she could do by staying, but she wouldn't desert Clarissa. The concert would miss Clarissa's act, but it could easily do without her. Her only concern now was for her friend. If she died everything would have been for nothing.

Chapter 31

Calais

'But I don't want to go back without my husband.' Eva folded her arms and glared at Helga, the wife of Major Andrea Eberl, one of the senior officers. It was two days since she and Linus had arrived inside the garrison. They had immediately been separated and she hadn't seen Linus at all. Linus had explained that their best way to get across the allied lines was to get the garrison commander to surrender. Eva had questioned how easy this would be, but Linus had told her he had a plan and all she had to do was to stick to the story they had agreed. That she was there as Linus' cover on an important mission for her father. She hadn't been told anything else and had agreed to come along because she wanted to spend as much time as possible with her husband as they hadn't been married very long.

'You don't have a choice. All the civilians are being evacuated.' Helga shook her head. 'Now go and join the others downstairs and get on the lorry.'

Eva stood her ground. 'Can I at least speak to my husband?'

'No. He's rather busy... fighting the enemy with my husband and the husband of every other woman on that lorry. Don't worry, he'll be told you've gone. No doubt he'll be relieved to know you are safely on the way back to your father.'

Eva's eyes opened wide in shock. How could she possibly go back to Berlin? They had just spent weeks escaping. If she went back, she would probably be arrested.

'Well, what are you waiting for? We're in a hurry. The Canadians will be here soon, we have to go.' Helga grabbed her arm and dragged her to the door.

'I must say goodbye to my husband.'

'No time.' Helga was holding her arm tight and they were now halfway down the stairs and almost in the courtyard where she guessed the lorry would be waiting. The only way Eva could get free would be to cause a scene and that would just draw attention to herself and Linus and she was sure that wouldn't do either of them any good. Eva had no idea what her husband was up to, but she was sure that whatever it was, it would be in Germany's best interests, otherwise her father would not have sent her with him. She would just have to go with Helga and the other women and rely on Linus coming to her rescue before she reached Berlin.

******

Amsterdam

'I am still waiting for an answer.' Tilly lit a cigarette and stared moodily across the desk at Joren. 'Perhaps I should try and get back on my own?'

'No, you should wait until London answers. They will send a plane for you. Much better than you trying to use the escape lines to get out.'

'But I wouldn't need to go very far would I? The allies have moved so quickly I could meet up with them really quickly now.'

Joren looked concerned. 'It would be very dangerous Juliette. If you haven't heard anything by the end of the week we'll do that, but just wait a little longer. Drescher isn't suspicious is he?'

'No, if I thought he was I would have already left!'

'Then hold on a bit longer. I'm sure London will answer soon.'

Tilly nodded and tried to ignore her growing unease. She was reasonably sure Drescher didn't suspect her, but she had a feeling that her time was running out. She would give Francis another week then she was going. In the meantime she would make preparations so that she could leave at a moment's notice. She realised Joren was smiling. 'What's so funny?'

'I was just thinking that not so long ago you were adamant you weren't leaving and now…'

Tilly gave a wry smile in return. 'I know. I probably just needed time to adjust to the idea. I was sure I would remain here until the end of the war but now I've decided to go, I just want to get on with it.'

'For what its worth I think you are right to leave. Even if the Nazis aren't suspicious, there are plenty of civilians who consider you and me to be collaborators. I know the resistance will make our position clear once the war is over, but before that happens you could be in danger from some idiot who has spent the war doing nothing to upset the Nazis and now wants to be a hero.'

Tilly nodded. 'I have considered that and its one of the reasons I think I should leave while I still can.' She wondered if she should tell him about the increasingly threatening comments she received when she was on her own and then decided not to. There was nothing he could do, and he had enough things to worry about. In any case she was sure she would soon be on her way, either home or somewhere else.

****

Bombay

'Back to England?' Renee looked shocked. 'She's that ill?'

'She's on the mend but she will be vulnerable now to the virus coming back. Its best for her to go home.' Phillip smiled at her. 'What will you do? Do you want to go onto to Poona?'

'I… no, I don't think so, not on my own.'

Phillip looked surprised. 'Clarissa said you are perfectly capable of singing on your own. She seems to think you are very good and could actually replace her in this tour.'

Renee stared at him in shock. 'You're joking aren't you?'

Phillip laughed. 'Clarissa said you would say that. But no I'm not. There's room for you if you want to go. If not then presumably you'll want to go back home?'

Renee didn't answer. 'I don't think I could sing on my own, but I don't have a good reason to go home either.'

'Think about it for a couple of days, you don't need to decide now.'

Renee nodded. 'Can I see her?'

'Yes, of course. Just don't tire her out.'

Renee stepped into the corridor and walked the short distance to the private room that Clarissa was paying for.

'Renee! I'm so pleased to see you.' Clarissa was sitting up in bed looking very pale, but her face lit up when she saw Renee.

'You're looking much better!' Renee pulled up a chair and sat down by the bed. 'Phillip said they're going to send you home.'

'Yes, apparently malaria can reoccur and I will take quite a while to recover completely so he thinks its better for me to go back to England.'

'Do you mind?'

Clarissa shrugged. 'I did at first, but now I am looking forward to going back to see Nathanial and Halford. In fact I can't wait. What are you going to do? I told Phillip you could quite easily perform solo.'

Renee smiled. 'Yes I know, he told me. But I'm not sure I am really up to it.'

'Will you come back to England then?'

Renee shrugged. 'I don't know. Its not like I have anything to go back to. I don't know what to do to be honest.'

'You don't have any family?' Clarissa shook her head. 'I'm so sorry Renee, I have just realised how little I know about you. Its always been about me, hasn't it? I'm a terrible friend.'

Renee laughed. 'No, you aren't. You rescued me from Sammy and June and the time I spent with you... and Tristram... was some of the happiest of my life.' She saw Clarissa's expression and smiled. 'My life hasn't been great to be honest, and I will probably tell you about it one day...' She stopped. 'Well at least I might have done, but now there probably wouldn't be any opportunity.'

'If you decide to come back to England you can always stay with me until you decide what you want to do.' Clarissa smiled. 'I would love the company and its not as if I am short of space.'

Renee stared at her in surprise. 'Really?'

'Yes of course.' Clarissa reached out a hand. 'I was dreading saying goodbye to you, but you don't have to stay with me... I mean if you would really like to say here and join the concert I would understand.'

Renee shook her head. 'No, I would much rather come back to England with you.'

Clarissa leant back and gave a tired smile. 'Good that's settled then.'

'I'll go and tell Phillip and leave you to rest then.'

Clarissa nodded. 'I'm sorry, I just seem to tire very easily.'

'Its not a problem. You get some sleep and I will make all the arrangements.' Renee hurried out of the room. She couldn't wait to tell Phillip to book her on the same boat back to England as Clarissa.

******

Warrington

'You look worried Nora, is something wrong?' Hank looked concerned. He leaned over the counter and helped himself to cutlery before taking the mug of coffee from her.

Nora smiled and shook her head. 'No, I was just waiting for a letter from my brother, Bill. Its ages since I heard from him. But I expect its just because he is at sea and can't get to the post.' *At least I hope so.*

'I'm sure that's all it is. I guess you told him about us?'

Nora smiled. 'Yes I did. We have always been close so I would like his blessing. Hopefully he'll be back home soon and you two can meet.'

Hank felt a momentary frisson of unease which he quickly shrugged off. Why on earth should Nora's brother be a threat? Bill would come back to Great Britain to live when the war was over, while he would take Nora to America, thousands of miles away. There was no way Bill could interfere in their lives from that distance. Hank forced a smile and made some more small talk, eventually arranging to pick Nora up after her shift. Everything was working out well although he had hoped that Nora would be pregnant by now. It seemed strange that she wasn't, not when she'd fallen immediately after the rape. For a brief moment he wondered if Nora had been lying, not about the rape, but about being a virgin before it happened. Then he pushed that thought away. He was sure Nora was telling him the truth. He frowned. In which case… he stopped and pushed that thought away too, the one that said he couldn't have children. The doctor had lied to him, trying to cover his own back. There was no reason to take notice of him. He smiled. Obviously, he would just have to try a little harder to get Nora pregnant. It wasn't as if the work was too arduous.

****

Calais

Jacob forgot about the constant bombardment going on all around him and stared at Major Andrea Eberl in disbelief. 'What do you mean they've sent all the women back to Berlin?'

'All our wives were evacuated a couple of days ago. Don't worry Helga, my wife, will look after her.'

Jacob was horrified, and for a moment couldn't think of anything to say. There was no way he could rescue Eva if they had been gone two days. What on earth would happen to her once she could back to Berlin? He had promised Claus he would look after his daughter and now… thanks to his idea of surrendering to the allies, he'd put her in danger and she was heading back to Berlin where she would probably be killed. She might even be used to make her family come out of hiding, providing any of them were still alive of course.

'For heaven's sake man, you wouldn't want her here at the mercy of the enemy, would you?' Andrea looked astonished.

'No… no of course not. I would have liked to say goodbye, that's all.' A shell landed rather close, knocking them both on the ground, the surrounding buildings trembled and some of the masonry fell, missing them by a few feet. Jacob winced and picked himself up, but his thoughts were still on Eva.

Andrea glanced at his watch and shook his head. 'Looks like this will be the end of it.'

Jacob looked at his own watch and breathed a sigh of relief. In a few moments Schroeder would raise the white flag. Unfortunately, it was too late for Eva. Jacob tried to concentrate on himself. In a little while he would be back on his own side. He would no longer need to look over his shoulder all the time, he would have done his bit and be on his way back home. He should be delighted, but all he could think of was Eva. She must be terrified and there was nothing he could do. Not at the moment anyway.

Once the war was over he would be able to go and look for her, but by then it would possibly be too late. Jacob clenched his fists. He couldn't just give up on Eva and his child. There had to be another way. Obviously he couldn't leave now, but perhaps when the Canadians came he could go back to Germany and look for her. He was still thinking about how he could persuade the Canadians to let him go back to Germany when another shell came over.

'Linus…!'

Jacob vaguely heard Andrea yelling his name and then everything went black.

Chapter 32

Warrington

Nora stared at the letter for ages. What if Bill didn't want anything else to do with her? What if he was disgusted by what he'd done? She couldn't bear to lose him, he had always been there for her... Eventually she took her courage in both hands and opening it with trembling fingers.

My dear Nora

I am so sorry to hear the terrible things that have happened to you and I wish I could have been there to help and support you. Of course I will help you find your daughter, and do anything I can to reunite you both. I am still reeling from everything you have told me, and I completely understand why you didn't write to me so please don't give that another thought.

I am rather proud to know that I am an uncle, shocked by the circumstances of course, but amazed that somewhere in England there is a miniature version of you. There is one question I want to ask if you don't mind? That is why you wanted to keep the baby when it was a result of something so dramatic. You don't have to explain if you don't want to...

Actually, just ignore that, I am a man so what would I know? Its good enough for me that you want to find Jennifer and I will do my utmost to help, as much as I can, although it may be difficult until I can leave the Royal Navy.

I want to finish this now so that as soon as we are in port it will be posted but rest assured, I will always be there for you. You are my little sister and I love you.

Your big brother

Bill

Tears streamed down her face and she wiped them away. She should have had more faith that Bill would support her, of course he would. How could she have ever doubted him? She wondered how much longer she would have to wait for him to be back in port so she could hug him. She placed the letter back in its envelope and then into the drawer with his other letters and those from Alan. She still read his letters from time to time but although they bought back happy memories, they also reinforced her loss and made her sad for what could have been. If she'd married Alan her life would have been so different. 'Damn this blasted war!' The words echoed around the room and she sighed. She couldn't turn back the clock, she could only try and make things better from now on. And the first thing she needed to do was to find Jennifer.

******

Calais

'Welcome back.'

Jacob was sure he could hear someone speaking, but the voice was coming from a distance and he didn't really want to leave the warm comfortable space he was in.

'Mr Goldsmith... can you hear me?'

Jacob sighed. Why wouldn't the man go away and leave him in peace... then he frowned. The voice had called him by his real name. It was a long time since he'd been addressed as Mr Goldsmith... perhaps he should make the effort. He opened his eyes and immediately closed them again. The light was much too bright.

'Mr Goldsmith, please try and open your eyes again.'

Jacob automatically responded and this time kept them open until his vision adjusted. He moved his head slightly and found himself looking at a tall thin man in a white coat.

'Where am I?'

'Its nice to have you back Mr Goldsmith. You are in a hospital in Calais and I am Dr Carlson.'

Jacob thought for a moment. They were speaking English although the doctor sounded American... no it was a Canadian accent. 'Are you Canadian?'

The doctor smiled. 'Yes. We took Calais. The Germans have surrendered here. You're quite safe.'

Jacob didn't answer straight away. What if it was a trap? Then he realised that he had been answering in English and that they knew his real name.

'You know who I am?'

'Yes, but that's not my field of expertise. Someone will be down to speak to you in a little while but first I need to check you over physically.'

'Why am I in hospital?'

'You were injured in the shelling when we took the city.'

Jacob's heart sank. 'Badly?' If it was too bad he wouldn't be able to go after Eva. 'How long have I been here?'

'You've been unconscious for three weeks. You have severe injuries to your left leg and left arm.'

Jacob immediately tried to move his limbs, but nothing happened. 'Will they heal?'

The doctor sighed. 'Your arm will recover probably although you may not have full functionality.' He stopped.

'And my leg?'

There was a long pause and Jacob feared the worst. Eventually the doctor spoke again. 'We have had to remove the lower leg from the knee down. We did everything we could to save it, but we couldn't. I'm so sorry.'

Jacob stared up at him, thoughts of Eva momentarily forgotten as he took in the enormity of what had happened. His life would never be the same.

'Can I sit up?'

'Yes of course, here…' the doctor helped him up and was helping him get comfortable when another voice greeted him. This time he immediately recognised the voice and he stared at the new visitor in astonishment.

'Francis?'

'Hello Jacob. I am so sorry about your injuries.'

Jacob shrugged. 'I'm alive so I suppose I should be grateful.'

Francis nodded at the doctor who walked away. Francis pulled up a chair and sat down next to the bed. 'You did a brilliant job persuading the garrison commander to surrender.'

Jacob gave a wry smile. 'It worked then. I was worried he would change his mind and fight on.' He frowned. 'How did you know it was me?'

Francis smiled. 'He couldn't wait to surrender and to tell the Canadians all about the plans to join us and fight the Soviets. He said that the whole thing was your idea and you had arrived from Berlin specifically to pass the message onto him and to the British, Canadians and Americans. They CO finally managed to find you in here, but you were unconscious. The idea of us stopping the war against the Germans and joining forces with them to fight the Soviets was so ludicrous he wondered if you were a spy so he sent out some messages to the intelligence community to try and identify you. That's when the report came across my desk and of course I recognised your German name. The rest, as they say, is history.' Francis frowned. 'I thought you were going to Amsterdam. I had made all the arrangements there for you. How did you end up here?'

'It was impossible to get through so we change direction and headed for Calais.'

'We?'

'My wife Eva. She's pregnant. Schroeder evacuated all the civilians and wives back to Germany. I didn't know until two days later. I have to get her out. Her father was involved in von Stauffenberg's assassination plot. He took his wife and youngest son east to escape the Gestapo and SS. Eva came with me, but now she's gone back to Berlin. I have to find her.'

Francis tried to adjust to the idea that Jacob had married a German and that his wife was pregnant. Then he shook his head. 'I'm sorry but there's nothing you can do. You aren't well enough to do anything at the moment, even if it was possible to go back to Berlin.'

'I can't just leave her!' Jacob shouted. Doctor Carlson turned around and began walking back towards them.

'I'm not asking you to do that Jacob.' Francis rested his hand on Jacob's shoulder. 'I will try and send someone else.'

'Someone else?'

'Yes, you're not my only agent.' Francis smiled but Jacob didn't respond.

'You promise?'

'You have my word.' Doctor Carlson reached the bed and Francis spoke quickly. 'It's alright, I'm going. Look after him.' He turned back to Jacob. 'I will go and sort something out now and then I will come back to you.'

Jacob nodded. 'You will find her, won't you?'

'I will do my best Jacob. Now rest and think about what you would like to do with the rest of your life.'

Jacob frowned. 'What do you mean?'

'Your days of working for me are over Jacob, but I have some ideas that you might be interested in.' He raised his hand and turned to walk away.

Jacob watched him go, his thoughts on Eva and whether Francis would really risk another agent's life to rescue his wife. Then he sat back and closed his eyes. Francis had never let him down yet. His thoughts wandered to Francis' last comment and he frowned. He had lost part of his leg, what kind of work did Francis have in mind? He was still thinking about that when he fell asleep.

****

Bombay

'You look so much better Clarissa.' Renee finished clearing away the lunch tray and sat down.

'I feel much better too. Come on, don't get too comfortable, let's go for our walk. A little more each day the doctor said.'

Renee laughed. 'Its nice to be back at the apartment isn't it. Walking around the hospital corridors is not the same as exploring the streets and gardens.'

'My thoughts exactly. I feel almost normal again and it hasn't taken too long, has it?' They left the apartment and made their way down the stairs and outside.

'No. You'll be completely well by the time we leave.'

'Only another week and we'll be on our way home.' Clarissa smiled. 'I like India, and I love the people, but I must say I can't wait to get home.'

'At least it won't be so hot.'

'I'll remind you of that when its been raining for days or when its freezing cold in the winter.' Clarissa laughed.

'I can hardly remember what its like to be that cold.' Renee sighed.

'Nor me, but no doubt we'll soon get used to it again.' Clarissa stopped to look at some material in one of small shops. 'I'd love to take some of this home with me, but we'd look completely out of place wearing it in England wouldn't we?'

'You said you were planning on going back to singing again didn't you?' Renee asked.

'Yes of course, I was planning on both of us singing once we get settled back in. Why?'

'Well, it would be nice to use these materials for our costumes perhaps? That way we could still wear all these beautiful materials and not look out of place.'

'That's a brilliant idea Renee. Come on let's pick out a selection to take home with us.' Clarissa began talking to the merchant and Renee smiled. She was really looking forward to her new life in England. The only fly in the ointment that she could see was that Sammy and June were booked on the same ship back to England. Clarissa hadn't mentioned them at all lately and as they were living in different parts of the city their paths hadn't crossed. She hadn't told Clarissa yet as she didn't want to upset her friend, but she couldn't keep putting it off.

****

Amsterdam

Tilly stared at the message she had just decoded and shook her head in disbelief. Francis wanted her to go to Berlin to look for some woman.

Other than her name and the fact she was the daughter of Major Clemens von Landau, one of the von Stauffenberg conspirators, there was no other information.

Joren looked horrified. 'Things are bad here, but going to Berlin…'

'Yes, my thoughts exactly.' Tilly sighed. At least it would get her away from Drescher. 'I need a cover story Joren.'

'Visiting the glorious Reich to report how they are succeeding in fighting off the advancing Soviets?'

Tilly grinned. 'Because they are winning of course.' She laughed. 'That should work. I can't see Drescher objecting to that. I'll ask him to draw up the necessary paperwork tonight.'

'Won't he ask why you suddenly want to go to Berlin?'

Tilly frowned and then smiled. 'The Nazis have just fought back against the Allied attack in the Netherlands. I want to show how they are fighting back against the Soviets too, just in case the dreadful resistance people here think they can rise up and force the Germans out. How does that sound?'

Joren smiled. 'I think that will work.'

'Good, if it doesn't I will have to think of some other reason to go there which will probably look very suspicious so let's hope this works.'

'Can you think of another reason to go there?'

Tilly nodded. 'Yes, but I would rather not use it because it might get complicated. Keep your fingers crossed for me.'

'I will. I'll see you in the morning.'

Tilly left the office her mind buzzing. She did have another reason she could use but it might open a can of worms. Hopefully Bruno would accept her reason and then she wouldn't need to worry.

****

Somewhere in the Atlantic

The U-boat had escaped them again, disappearing into the frothy waves and Bill cursed loudly, slamming his hand against the machine gun in irritation.

'Never mind we'll get him next time.' Tom began picking up the spent ammunition.

'Yeah, but all the time the bastard's out there he can do a lot of damage.' Bill snapped.

'Not as much as they could do. Most of them have been sunk now, very few left and the war will soon be over.' Much to Bill's annoyance Tom sounded infuriatingly cheerful. He fought down his irritation and wondered what Nora had thought about his letter. He hoped it had put her mind at rest, but until he was back in port again and had some leave he wouldn't know.

His thoughts drifted to Jennifer, the niece he didn't know he had and had never met. He wondered if she looked like Nora, his irritation slowly dissipated, and he smiled. He hoped Nora had been able to locate her as he rather liked the idea of having someone to watch over, even if it was from a distance. His face darkened again. Why on earth had his parents made her give up the child? Yes, it might have bought disgrace on the family, but it wasn't as if they had a spotless reputation, was it? In any case the world was changing and so eventually would people's attitudes. The war would surely see to that. He would bet money that Nora wasn't the only woman to have a child out of wedlock. There would probably be plenty of men returning home after the war to children who had been born while they were away, and he would bet some of the ages of those children would be questionable as well. And how many of those men had fathered children on women who they weren't married to while they were away fighting? He didn't agree with it, but he understood why. When you might be killed at any moment you took your pleasure when you could. There would be a lot of secrets after the war.

Bill sighed, secrets like Jennifer that people would do anything to protect. Perhaps it was a good thing he wasn't married. At least he could do what he wanted without feeling guilty.

****

Dusseldorf, Germany

'Have you seen this man?'

The man was thin with a sallow complexion, an unpleasant odour, foul breath and at least two day's stubble. He shook his head nervously. 'No sir, I haven't.' He swallowed, cleared his throat and spat on the street.

'But you will find him, won't you?'

'Yes sir, if he's here…'

'Good. This is the hotel I am staying in. Just leave a message and I will come back. You won't let me down, will you?'

'No… no sir. If he's here I will find him.'

Levi walked away with a smile on his face. When he had started looking for Karl Weiss he had not known where to start. The latest information he had was that he had gone on the run and was hiding somewhere in the city. Levi had no idea how he was going to find him, but he had quickly learnt that people were very eager to ingratiate themselves with the SS. He had decided to go into the less salubrious areas of the city and see if he could find someone to lean on. It had not taken him very long to find the local black marketeer and once he had found him he had not had too much difficulty in getting him to help.

Levi walked back to his car and headed back to the hotel. So far he had found and identified four scientists for the task force and to his knowledge all the men had ended up back in England. Karl Weiss would be number five, providing the little weasel he had just threatened managed to find him.

****

Calais

'There's something I need to tell you Jacob before you return home.' Francis had been dreading this moment, but he couldn't put it off any longer. Jacob had been told not to write home until he was given permission, but there was no reason now for him not to write to his parents.

Jacob looked up expectantly then his face fell. There was something about Francis expression that warned him something was wrong. 'Are my parents alright?'

'Yes, they are fine, it's not them. Its your cousin Sura. I am afraid she was killed in an air raid on London in early 1943.' Francis quickly explained about the tube station.

Jacob's mouth fell open in shock. He felt dizzy and fought to keep conscious. Eventually he shook his head. 'Why didn't you tell me?'

'You couldn't have done anything, and it wasn't fair to disrupt your concentration.' Even as he spoke the words Francis thought how hollow they sounded.

'But she was my cousin. I risked my life to get her out of Germany.' He gasped. 'What about Levi and her child,' he frowned, 'she did have a child didn't she?'

'Yes, she did. His name is Aaron and he survived the accident in the tube station. He is being cared for by Rebecka.'

'And Levi?'

'He has been busy working for the war effort. I can't tell you anymore, I'm sorry.'

Jacob closed his eyes and tried to come to terms with the death of his cousin. Francis waited a few moments then decided to change the subject.

'I've arranged for someone to go to Berlin. She should be on her way by the end of the week.'

Jacob forgot about Sura for a moment and opened his eyes in astonished. 'Really?'

'Yes, although I obviously can't promise anything. But she's very good.'

Jacob frowned. 'You're sending a woman to Berlin?'

'Women draw less attention than men, especially at the moment. I have already sent a message to your contact so he can begin looking before she gets there.' Francis changed the subject. 'Doctor Carlson says you are doing very well and will soon be able to travel back to England.'

'I'd rather wait until Eva is safe so we can go together.'

Francis sighed. 'We have no idea how long it will take to find your wife, it makes more sense for you to return home and begin planning for the future. Much better for Eva to have a husband who is working and has a home ready for her to move into. Especially as she is expecting a child.'

Jacob frowned while he considered Francis' words and then he nodded. 'You're right. It would be much better. You said something about a job when I got home?'

Francis smiled. 'I've got two ideas, the first would involve mainly paperwork, a desk job working with my organisation.' He saw the expression on Jacob's face and continued quickly. 'The other might be more to your liking, I can arrange for you to join the police force,' he saw Jacob's look of disdain and he hurried on, 'not as a constable, but as a detective. Given your wartime experience you would go in at the rank of Inspector. You would have your own team working for you and you wouldn't be stuck behind a desk.'

Jacob looked surprised. 'I have never been in the police force; I don't have any experience. Would I be capable of doing the job?'

'You'd never been a spy either before the war. You had no trouble picking that up.' Francis smiled. 'You don't have to make a decision now, think about it.'

Jacob didn't answer for a moment then he nodded. 'I don't need to think about it. I think I would love to be in the police. Where would I be stationed?'

'One of the bigger cities probably, at least to start with. That way you would get plenty of experience quickly. After that it will be up to you.'

Jacob smiled. For the first time since he'd heard that Eva had been sent back to Berlin, he could see a future. He would have to learn to walk again and get used to a false leg as well as learn to be a policeman. But he could make a start now. 'Do you have any manuals I could read. I imagine there are lots of legal procedures I would need to know and understand. I might as well make a start now while I am laid up.'

Francis smiled. 'I will arrange for them to be sent to you.' He was surprised Jacob had accepted so quickly, he had fully expected that he would have to persuade him.

Jacob read his mind. 'You didn't think I would agree did you, not without some persuasion? I've had plenty of time to think about my future lying in bed and none of the things I came up were half as exciting as being in the police force.' He smiled. 'Thank you. I know you are doing more for me than you have to, not only looking for Eva, but also finding me a job.'

Francis looked slightly embarrassed. He could say nothing but eventually he would have to tell Jacob the truth if he wanted his help. 'Its

kind of you to say so, but… actually I do have a bit of an ulterior motive.'
He stopped. 'There is something I would like investigating, something I consider very important but for which I have no real proof. But if you investigate it you will be helping Tilly,' he saw Jacob's face light up, 'and Nora.'

Jacob was looking even more surprised. 'Can you tell me about it?' Jacob saw his hesitation and indicated his bed. 'I have nothing else to do but think, even if I can't do anything practical.'

Francis nodded. 'Tilly's younger sister went missing from the house she was evacuated to at the beginning of the war. The circumstances were suspicious and after Nora lost her job at the detention camp she went to the house and worked there and discovered several other children had also gone missing. Because the children came from different areas in the country and from different backgrounds there was no follow up by the police. Nora was convinced something strange was going on. She can give you the details, but I also have a file on the case that you can have. I promised Nora that I would investigate but I haven't had time.'

'And Tilly? Can I speak to her as well?' Jacob tried to ignore how happy the thought of seeing Tilly again, was making him. It was because she was a friend, nothing else.

'That might be more difficult, certainly at the moment… the war you know.'

Jacob sighed and then a thought struck him. Given Tilly's background… 'Ahhh… She's working for you isn't she?'

Francis was about to deny it when Jacob paled. 'Please tell me it isn't Tilly you've sent to Berlin?'

'You know I can't answer that, Jacob.'

Jacob shook his head. That was confirmation enough for him. He closed his eyes and cursed out loud. Now he had two people he loved adrift somewhere in Berlin, the capital city of their enemy that was currently in the path of an avenging Soviet army. And if that wasn't bad enough, both would be targets of the Gestapo.

****

Amsterdam

'Berlin? Why on earth would you want to go to Berlin?' Bruno Drescher stared at Tilly in surprise. He had called into the apartment on his way to work catching Tilly by surprise, but she had decided this was as good a time as any to ask him for the travel documents.

'Joren thinks it would be good to have a report from the capital of the Reich, showing how they are fighting off the threat from the east. There's so many people listening to allied propaganda saying the Soviets are winning that the number of resistance activities in Amsterdam and the Netherland as a whole is rising. By telling them the truth, that the Germans are winning and beating them back, I could help to stop that happening.'

Bruno didn't look convinced. 'I don't know. It might be dangerous.'

Tilly smiled. 'That's very thoughtful Bruno, but I am sure I will be perfectly safe.'

'No, I don't think you should go. There must be stories you could cover locally?'

Tilly sighed. She would obviously have to use her trump card. 'Its not just to report on what's happening. I've been asked to go there by Heinz Kessel. He telephoned me yesterday.'

'Why didn't you say so?' Bruno looked even more suspicious.

'Because he told me not to. He said it was secret and that I should make up a good reason to go to Berlin.'

Bruno looked uncomfortable. 'Is it something to do with me? Or can't you say?'

Tilly shook her head. 'I don't think so, he didn't give me that impression. I think its just Heinz being his normal secretive self. You know what he's like.'

Bruno frowned. 'Actually, I don't know him that well.'

Tilly relaxed. She had been worried that Bruno was a close friend of Kessel. They had never discussed him hence her decision to tread gently. 'Yes, he's always very secretive. Doesn't let the right hand know what the left hand is doing. I'm sorry. I didn't want to lie to you but...' She shrugged.

'Its alright. I understand.' Bruno sighed. 'I'll arrange the documents for you. They'll be ready by the end of the day. Is that alright?'

Tilly stood on tiptoes and kissed his cheek. 'Thank you. I'm sure I won't be there very long.'

Bruno smiled and kissed her back. 'Good, I shall miss you. I will have a surprise for you when you get back.'

Tilly felt a frission of unease that she quickly pushed away. She would worry about that later. 'Oooo, that sounds exciting.'

'It is, but it will keep. The papers will be in my office. I'll see you about four?'

Tilly nodded and watched him leave. With a bit of luck she would be able to leave the following day. She frowned. It was probably a good job she wasn't coming back to Amsterdam. Her complete orders were to find Eva Haas and then return to England with her. She had spent so long not trusting anyone completely that she had kept that part to herself. It was better that Joren didn't know she wasn't coming back, then if he was arrested for anything before she was back in England, he couldn't give her away. It would also be easier for him to tell Bruno that he had no idea where she was. With a bit of luck Bruno would think Kessel had kept her in Berlin.

****

London

Francis finished reading Nora's letter, sat back and closed his eyes. He was pleased Nora was finally happy, she deserved it after all the terrible things that had happened to her. It also sounded like moving to America at the end of the war was a good idea, a fresh start away from people who knew her. He could also understand why she didn't want to ask her fiancé to adopt her daughter now. It would be much easier when they had their own children and had lived together for some years. They would be closer then and hopefully her husband would want to help. Her request was relatively simple, she just wanted him to find out where Jennifer was and to keep her brother up to date with any changes so that, sometime in the future, when she was ready to ask her husband, she would be able to find her relatively easily. Francis had already asked one of the nuns to keep him informed about Jennifer's whereabouts, to make a note of who had adopted her, so if in the future Nora was in a position to have her daughter with her, he would be able to help. Finding Jennifer should therefore be quite easy, but he was now starting to have doubts. It would probably be several years before Nora was in that position so would it be fair to interfere in the child's life? What if the girl was happy? Surely disrupting her life would be wrong?

Francis thought hard. Maybe he should worry about that if it happened? He could always tell Nora that he'd lost touch with her daughter if he felt it was wrong to disturb the girl's life. There was no telephone number so he would have to write back. It wouldn't take long, he would tell Nora to ring him in a couple of weeks, by then he should have the information for her. Francis reached for some paper and his pen and quickly scribbled a reply. Once he'd finished he picked up the telephone and dialled the mother and baby home in Manchester.

****

Bombay

'They are on the same ship? Why on earth didn't you say so before?' Clarissa was furious.

'It wouldn't have made any difference and I wanted you to enjoy the last few days we had in India.'

Clarissa slammed the trunk shut and glared at Renee. 'You should have told me.'

'I didn't know how to. I only found out last week and then... well there didn't seem much point upsetting you until I had to.'

Clarissa didn't say anything else so Renee tried again. 'It's a big ship, I am sure we can keep out of their way.'

'Why would we want to keep out of their way? We haven't done anything wrong. They are the ones who should be avoiding us.'

'Yes, well that was what I meant.'

Clarissa suddenly laughed. 'No, that wasn't what you meant Renee. It's alright, stop looking so pained. I know its not your fault. It was just a shock that's all. I will do my best to avoid them and I am sure you will too, but I won't let them bully me.'

Renee relaxed. 'I'm sorry for not saying anything earlier.'

'It doesn't matter now. Let's try and forget it, well maybe not forget as it will be hard to do that when they are on the same ship, but I won't go out of my way to cause trouble.' Clarissa only hoped she could do that.

Perhaps it was a good thing she wasn't completely better. If she had been feeling her normal healthy self she would have found it almost impossible to keep away from them.

On the other side of the deck, hidden by some chairs, Sammy watched Clarissa and Renee chatting and laughing, seemingly happy. She had asked around and found out that Clarissa had been ill with malaria and that she was now returning home and that Renee was going with her. Sammy's face contorted with rage. Clarissa looked perfectly happy. She had obviously forgotten Tristram already. Sammy clenched her fists and wished she could have told Clarissa that she was responsible for his death. Unfortunately she couldn't do that, because she wasn't, whatever Clarissa thought. She and June had been just as shocked about his death as everyone else, neither had particularly disliked Tristram, it was Clarissa they hated. But then, having seen the way Clarissa fell apart after his murder, Sammy had eventually decided that she was pleased Tristram was dead. Losing Tristram meant Clarissa would suffer for ever. Or at least that's what Sammy had thought, but it seemed that Clarissa had already got over Tristram's death. Given that June would never completely recover enough to be able to dance professionally again, that didn't seem fair at all. Sammy was also furious about Renee. Somehow she had wheedled her way into Clarissa's life, and given her past and the secrets she had been hiding when Sammy and June had rescued her, that was something else that didn't seem very fair.

******

Amsterdam

Tilly climbed aboard the train and found a seat facing the direction they were travelling in. It had been strange leaving the place that had been her home for so long, saying goodbye to people she knew she would never see again when they thought she would be returning soon. Her thoughts travelled to the woman she was tasked to find. Eva Haass, daughter of Major Clemens von Landau, wife of the elusive Linus Haass, the man who should have come to her in Amsterdam months earlier. She wondered what had happened to him and why she was only looking for his wife. Perhaps he had already escaped, although if that was the case why would he have left his wife behind in Germany? Tilly sighed and pushed her thoughts away. There was no point speculating, she needed to concentrate on how to find Eva and then on how to get her out. Francis had given her a contact, Niklas Konig, and told her that he would already be searching for Eva while she was on her way. He was due to meet her outside what was left of the Berlin Anhalter Bahnhof, about a third of a mile south east of Potsdamer Platz. Tilly wondered how much of the city had been destroyed by allied bombing, no doubt she would soon find out.

The train eased out of the station and Tilly stared ahead, determined not to look back.

****

Somewhere in Germany

Levi sat in his car and thought hard about what he was to do next. So far he had not had any problems. No one had questioned him and everyone he had threatened had been extremely helpful. But now he was thinking about stepping into the lion's den. The scientist he was looking for had last been seen in Berlin. Was this really worth risking his life for?

He closed his eyes and thought about the men who were left on his list. Perhaps he should go after them instead? But Willy Ritschel was more important, a chemical and biological weapons specialist. Levi hated the very idea of chemical and biological weapons, and letting this man fall into Soviet hands was not a good idea. In any case, his orders on this man were different. The British didn't want him, and they didn't want him to go anywhere else to ply his disgusting trade. Levi was to find him and kill him.

******

London

'Nora, how lovely to hear from you. I hope you are well and looking forward to your wedding.' Francis was pleased to hear from her, but he wished he had better news.

'I'm fine thank you. Its very kind of you to help me. I didn't know who else to ask.' Nora sounded nervous and Francis felt even worse. He cleared his throat.

'I'm sorry but I haven't been able to find her, not yet.' Sister Angelica, the nun he had asked to help months earlier, had seemingly disappeared, left the convent and returned to civilian life. No one appeared to know where and perhaps more tellingly, no one appeared to care. She had let the convent down, let God down and therefore had been excommunicated and therefore no longer existed. Francis was furious especially as everyone else in the mother and baby home had been surprisingly unhelpful, even when he had used his position to push for information. The person in charge had effectively told him that it was nothing to do with the government, that the child was well looked after and that was all he needed to know. Francis had enough experience of people being obstructive to immediately recognise when he was getting the run around. What he didn't understand was why. The name of a family who had adopted a child was hardly a state secret, even if the family itself was very important. It didn't make sense and Francis began to wonder what they had to hide.

In normal circumstances Francis might have turned his attention back to the war and told Nora there was nothing else he could do, but Francis didn't like people lying to him and he still felt responsible for the way Nora's life had turned out. If she hadn't been helping him, she would not have lost her job and set off the chain reaction which led to Jennifer's birth.

'I don't understand. Why would it be a secret? I can understand them not telling me but…' She fell silent.

'I don't know, but I intend to find out.'

'You don't think something has happened to her, do you?'

'No… not in the way you mean.' Francis hoped he was right, but he didn't want Nora to be upset so he told her the only other reason he could think of for the Home's reluctance to divulge Jennifer's location. 'It might just be that Jennifer has been adopted by someone important, someone they don't want to upset.'

'Do you really think its just that?' Nora sounded much happier. 'If she's happy I don't want to ruin it for her, not if they can provide her with a good life.'

'If that is the case you can make the decision then, but, in the meantime, I think I should continue to look for her. Just to make sure.' Deep down Francis was becoming even more certain that the Home was hiding something, something they didn't want coming to light. It sounded ridiculous but he was sure something was wrong, and he intended to find out.

'Thank you.' Nora wiped away the tears that were streaming down her cheeks, relieved that Francis couldn't see her.

'It's not a problem Nora. I will be in touch as soon as I know anything.' Francis changed the subject. 'When are you getting married?'

'In a couple of weeks. Do you want to come?' Nora had asked automatically out of politeness, so Francis' reply caught her by surprise.

'I would love to, if you are sure of course.'

'Yes, definitely.' She hesitated. 'How shall I introduce you?'

'Introduce me? Oh… I see.' Francis thought hard. 'How about as a friend of your brother's?'

Nora thought for a moment. 'Yes, I suppose that would work. Bill is coming to the wedding so I will have to warn him first.'

'It makes sense for your brother and I to know each other so that when your husband does agree to accept your daughter, we can work together to make that happen.'

'I don't know how to thank you.' Nora felt the tears coming again, she blinked them away and tried not to sniff.

'By being happy. Now I have to go but I will see you at your wedding.'

'Goodbye.' Nora replaced the receiver and allowed a brief smile to cross her face. Despite not having any news of Jennifer she was sure Francis would be as good as his word. Now all she had to do was to warn Bill that he was to tell everyone that Francis was an old friend.

****

Berlin

Tilly was shocked by the sight that met her as she alighted from the train. London had been bad enough during the Blitz, but this was much worse and reminded her more of Rotterdam. She was confused, not wanting to feel any sympathy for the Nazis who had inflicted this and much worse on the rest of Europe, but unable to fight off the thought that many of the people affected would not have been Nazis, not the real ones anyway. She pushed her sympathy away. What was she doing making excuses for any Germans? They had done nothing to stop Hitler on his rise to power so they were all guilty.

She walked towards the barrier, showed her papers and to her relief was waved through without any problems. Now all she had to do was to find Niklas.

'Excuse me Miss, I believe you dropped this.' Tilly spun around and found herself face to face with a nervous looking man standing behind her, a brightly coloured scarf in his outstretched hands.

'Thank you, I am always dropping things. My father said it is because my head is in the clouds.'

'Sometimes being in the clouds is a good place to be.'

Tilly smiled. 'Niklas?'

'Juliette?' When she nodded he took her arm and led her towards a side street, its damaged buildings highlighted against the cloudless sky, their ragged edges stark against the skyline.

'I have found you a small apartment, it not in a particularly good area but as you can see, accommodation is hard to come by now.'

'Thank you.' Tilly lowered her voice. 'I don't suppose you have found her?'

'No, I have been everywhere she would normally go, and no one has seen her.'

'Damn! What about her family?'

'Her father is on the SS wanted list, they don't seem to have found him yet so I can only assume they are still on the run somewhere in the east, unless they have been picked up by the Soviets.'

'And the other brother? Konrad? The one who was in Paris?'

Niklas shook his head.

Tilly sighed. 'Then there's a chance she's already left Berlin and headed east in the hope of finding the rest of her family?'

Niklas frowned. 'The chances of her finding them are pretty remote.'

Tilly shrugged. 'What else could she do? Her husband is probably a prisoner of war, she can't stay in Berlin too long in case the Gestapo pick her up and she can't really afford to trust anyone here because they might betray her. Going east was her only option.'

'If that's the case, what are you going to do?'

'I don't know. My orders were to find her and bring her back to England.' She sighed. 'I'll stay a bit longer, she might still be here. Maybe she's hiding with a friend?'

Niklas thought for a moment. 'There were rumours that some wealthy Germans had been running some kind of rota of hiding places for divers,' he saw her confusion and quickly explained, 'Its Berlin slang for Jews who have submerged to avoid deportation.' Tilly nodded while he continued. 'And any other people hiding from the Gestapo. I didn't look into it because there was no reason to and if it *was* true, then me asking questions might draw attention to them.'

'Can you look into it now?'

Niklas shrugged. 'I suppose so. What are you going to do?'

'I'm meant to be here writing an article about how Berlin is fighting off the Soviets and how high morale is here.' She gave a wry smile. 'I will obviously have to rely on my imagination.' She laughed. 'I have a contact at one of the Berlin newspapers so I will go there and try and get some information for the article.'

'Good, I will come back and see you as soon as I find out anything.'

Tilly watched him go and then pulled the piece of paper out of her pocket with the name and address of the newspaper on. It was important she kept up her cover story and anyway, it wasn't as if she could do much else.

without nly person who was likely to be able to find Eva

woman ranted attention to her. Tilly's job was to get the

would do he would let Niklas get on with his job and she

Chapter 33

Dover

Jacob arrived back in England and m[...]
He would travel first to London where h[...]
Francis before heading north to the Is[...]
home for the first time in so long was [...]
he couldn't wait to see his parents agai[...]
Sura's death. It might have happened[...]
for him it was much more recent. H[...]
Aaron, his second cousin. It would [...]
and he wondered who the boy look[...]

Jacob's thoughts turned to Till[...]
that both the women he cared ab[...]
since Francis' last visit when he[...]
find Eva. Perhaps he would find[...]

Jacob reached the statio[...]
awkwardly aboard the train. H[...]
of part of his leg, mainly be[...]
and that he had to concentra[...]
down on the bench seat an[...]
that the police force would[...]
he was right. He was actu[...]
the things he would find[...]
force he would be sent [...]
as important as Eva. W[...]

****

[...]wly to the station.
[...]brief meeting with
[...]he thought of going
[...]range, but deep down
[...]ll coming to terms with
[...]go for everyone else but
[...]thoughts to Rebecka and
[...]o see Sura and Levi's child

[...]oped she found Eva and if not
[...]safe. He hadn't heard anything
[...]cob that he had sent someone to
[...]e in London.
[...]ed to the platform and climbed
[...]nding it difficult to adjust to the loss
[...]e kept forgetting that he couldn't run
[...]o the simplest things. He eased himself
[...]a deep breath. Francis had assured him
[...]nd his disability an issue and Jacob hoped
[...]ooking forward to starting work and one of
[...]at his meeting today would be which police
[...]ut although that was important, none of it was
[...]ut her there was no future, not for him anyway.

En route to England

Clarissa stared out to sea and tried to ignore the anger pulsing through her. She knew Renee was right and that the best way to deal with Sammy and June was to ignore them, but she was finding it very difficult, especially as the woman seemed to be going out of her way to irritate her.

'She is trying to get you to do something stupid so she can blame everything on you.' Renee said calmly. 'She's tried telling everyone that you deliberately broke June's leg and although some believed her, most didn't. But even the ones who want to take her side feel guilty because of Tristram's death and because you have been so ill, so she's not getting anywhere. All she can do is to keep prodding you in the hope that you will crack and do something that will prove you are the villain of her story.'

'I know you are right, but it doesn't make it any easier.' Clarissa sighed. 'I can't believe we have weeks of this.'

'She might get bored.' Renee smiled. 'Alright she probably won't. But it is only a few weeks and then you will never have to see her again. You will be back on your estate and she will be homeless and looking for work.'

'You have become very wise Renee.'

'Not really. Its always easier to see a situation from the outside, and thanks to you I have gained so much confidence. Sammy and June made my life a misery. I won't let them do it again, not now I am happy.'

'I'll try and remember your advice next time I want to throttle her or throw her overboard then!'

Renee laughed. 'Only a few weeks and we'll be free.'

Clarissa joined in, her good humour restored.

******

Berlin

Levi sat outside the bomb damaged apartment block and waited patiently. His information was that Willy Ritschel was due to meet some high ranking German official that evening. Levi hadn't been able to find out where or who, so he had decided to follow Ritschel. He could just kill the scientist as he had been ordered to, but Levi wanted to know what the man was up to. This high ranking official might have plans for something Ritschel had produced, surely he should investigate first. There was no point killing the scientist if he had already developed some dreadful weapon that was ready to be unleashed on the British or their allies.

There was movement from the building, a tall man with glasses and a military bearing strode confidently towards the road, turned left and increased his pace until he reached a car waiting further down the road. Levi cursed. How had he missed that? Probably because the car was too far from the building, but he wasn't happy that he hadn't seen it.

He waited for the car to pull away and then followed discreetly at a distance. The car drove swiftly through the city, Levi couldn't get close enough to see if there was anyone else in the car as well as the driver. He would have to wait. The car continued its drive around and then suddenly pulled up and Ritschel climbed out. Levi stared at the building in confusion. Why was Ritschel visiting Deutsche Allgemeine Zeitung, a newspaper office. He was still thinking about it when the car drove off at speed. Should he follow the car or wait and see where Ritschel went next? Levi cursed. It was too late to follow the car now so he didn't have much choice. Obviously Ritschel's meeting had taken place in the car. There was no reason for the car to have picked him up and just driven him here. If it was Ritschel's car why park it further down the road? None of this was making sense. Ritschel had gone inside the building. Should he follow?

He was still thinking about that when Ritschel left the building and began walking back towards the apartment block. Levi put the car into gear and was about to drive off when he saw someone he knew go into the newspaper building. Levi gasped in disbelief. It had been years since he'd last seen her but he recognised her immediately. 'Tilly?'

******

Warrington

'You want me to pretend this intelligence bod is my friend?' Bill grinned.

'Yes, if you don't mind? Obviously, I don't want everyone to know who he is and why he's here, so this seemed easier.' Nora smiled at him.

Bill shrugged. 'Its fine with me sis. He sounds like a good friend.' The thought crossed his mind that Francis might be quite useful to know if he got into any more trouble, not that he was planning on that. He changed the subject. 'You're looking very well by the way. Hank must be good for you, even if he is a Yank.'

Nora laughed. 'Yes, he's kind. I hope you'll like him.'

Bill smiled. 'If he makes you happy and looks after you then that's good enough for me.' He glanced at his watch. He had been ashore several hours now and still hadn't had a drink. 'The pub's are open. Danny will be here soon so come on let me get you a drink.'

Nora shook her head. 'I can't, I have to go to work.'

'What? Even the day before your wedding?'

'Yes, the rent still needs paying. Don't forget I will be living at home until we get permission to go to America. Hank will stay with me whenever he can.'

'Are you looking forward to going to America?' Bill was curious, Nora had always wanted to go the country where they made the films she loved so much and had been very jealous of him when he had been deployed to Boston while waiting for his ship to be ready. He hoped she wouldn't be disappointed.

'Yes, you know I have always wanted to see America, but now... well now its even more important. It's a fresh start, away from prying eyes and people whispering about me.'

Bill frowned. 'You don't want to take any notice of what people say Nora. What happened wasn't your fault.'

Nora shrugged. 'You know what people are like. No smoke without fire.' She shrugged. 'And I probably haven't helped myself.' She saw his puzzled expression and gave a wry smile. 'After they took Jennifer away I wasn't very well behaved. I decided that if they wanted to treat me like I was a tart even though I wasn't one, I might as well behave live up to my reputation.'

Bill didn't answer and she could see he was annoyed. Nora felt a frisson of anger. 'Its alright for you to sleep with any number of women and not think anything of it, in fact it makes you a hero, one of the boys doesn't it? Don't you ever think about those women? They have brothers and parents too. Doesn't that bother you? What do you think their parents feel about them?'

'That's different Nora and you know it.' Bill snapped.

'Why is it different?'

'Because it is. Its what men do. Women aren't meant to behave in the same way.'

'Why? Because men say so?' Nora took a breath and turned away for a moment. She hadn't meant to start an argument with Bill. 'Look, I don't want to argue with you. You're my brother and I love you, even if you can't understand that you are being two faced.'

Bill grinned. 'I don't want to argue with you either so you go to work and I'll go down the pub and have a drink or two!'

Nora smiled. 'I'll see you later.' Her smile faded as she watched him leave. Bill was different somehow, more brittle, less relaxed than she remembered. Then she thought about all the things he had experienced, and she sighed. She probably wasn't the same person she used to be either. The war had changed both their lives. Nora picked up her hat and coat and hurried out. If she didn't hurry she would be late for work.

****

Berlin

Tilly arrived at the offices of the Deutsche Allgemeine Zeitung and introduced herself to a young woman about her own age.

'Hello, I'm Ulrika von Houten. How can I help you?'

Tilly explained why she was there and for a brief second an expression of amusement crossed Ulrika's face before disappearing.

'Not easy then?' Tilly decided to take a chance.

Ulrika stared at her and tried to work out whether she could trust her. It was treason to talk of defeat and she was already in enough trouble. She decided it was safer to ignore the girl's remark, perhaps things were not as strict in Amsterdam. 'So why come to us rather than Das Reich or one of the other papers?'

Tilly smiled. 'My editor, Joren suggested you. He said your newspaper was one of the best daily's in Berlin, with a good reputation.'

Ulrike relaxed slightly. 'That's nice to know.'

'Is everything alright? You seem... I don't know... on edge? I could go somewhere else if you want. I don't want to cause you any problems.'

Ulrike shook her head. 'No, please don't do that. If you do then it might look like we aren't... that we have something...' She fought for the right words, eventually settling on. 'We don't want our loyalty to the Reich questioned. No one is more patriotic than DAZ I can assure you.'

Tilly gave what she hoped was a reassuring smile. 'I would never have thought anything else. I too have to ensure that my articles reflect the truth.' Their eyes met and Ulrike decided to take a chance. She was fed up being suspicious of everyone and there was something about this Dutch girl that she trusted. 'I'm sorry. Things have been very difficult since the 20 July affair. As you can tell from my name I am a member of an old German family and as such I am now considered a traitor, someone who is under suspicion even though I haven't done anything. I just happen to know or be related to the right, or perhaps I should say, the *wrong* people.'

Tilly could hardly believe her luck. If Ulrike was one of those the Gestapo had under suspicion, she might know Eva. But Tilly would need to earn her fellow journalist's trust first. 'That must be awful. Nothing worse than having to look over your shoulder all the time, never knowing when they will strike even if you haven't done anything.'

Ulrika nodded. 'Yes, exactly.' She was about to say more when her telephone rang and she reached for it. 'von Houten!' She smiled. 'Hello Jutta...' Her smile faded and she sat down heavily on her chair. 'Yes, of course, come into the office.'

'Problem?' Tilly couldn't help notice that Ulrike had turned pale. 'Sorry, its none of my business, but as an outsider, maybe I can help?'

'One of my friends... she arrived home last night to find her parents missing. Their bedroom had been turned upside down as if in a robbery, but all their clothes and belongings were still there. There was no note saying where they had gone so they must have been arrested.'

'Had they been involved?' Tilly cursed herself for asking such a stupid question. 'Don't bother answering that, like I said its none of my business.'

'No, they weren't involved but they gave shelter to one of the officers who was.'

Tilly spun around to find a tall rather gaunt woman in her middle twenties standing behind her.

'Jutta! You shouldn't have told Juliette that.'

Jutta lost what little colour she had in her cheeks and looked as if she was about to pass out. 'I thought she was your friend…' She groped for the desk and Tilly immediately pushed the chair under her so she could sit down.

'You don't have to worry about me, I won't repeat anything I promise.'

'How do we know that?' Ulrike looked exhausted but there was a spark in her eye that hadn't been there earlier. Tilly glanced around the open office area and saw that a couple of the men were watching. She took a breath and made a decision. If she didn't speak now they might not believe her, and her instincts told her that Ulrike could be trusted.

'Because I am looking for someone whose family was involved in the 20 July affair, my job is to get her out of Berlin, but I can't find her. The article is just a cover.'

****

London

'You're looking well Jacob. Are you completely recovered now?' Francis indicated a chair and Jacob sat down.

'Pretty much. Leg hurts like billio sometimes, but I can manage.'

'Good. Well take a couple more weeks to recover, spend some time with your family and then we'll get you working.'

'Do you know where?'

'We'll start you in London, lots going on so you'll gain plenty of experience quite quickly. Before you start though I'd like you to do something for me. You remember Nora?'

Jacob looked surprised but nodded. 'Yes, of course. How is she?'

Francis handed him a letter. 'Its easier for you to read her own account, if you don't mind.'

Jacob shrugged and began reading. A few moments later he put the letter down, shock on his face. 'Poor Nora.'

'Yes, she was in a bit of a state when I last saw her, but she's much better now. I have tried to find the child, but I am being lied to and I don't know why. I thought you could look into it and see if you can do any better.'

Jacob's face lit up. 'Absolutely sir. Nora deserves to know where her daughter is. Do you have any idea why they are lying to you?'

'No, it doesn't make any sense, which is why I want to know what they are hiding.' Francis lit a cigarette and handed the packet to Jacob who also took one and lit it. 'Why don't you come to the wedding? It will give you a chance to meet her again and I am sure she will be delighted to know you are going to help her.'

Jacob smiled. 'I'd like that. When is it?'

'Tomorrow! Its in Warrington so you can call in on your way home. I will give you her address.'

Jacob took the piece of paper and put it in his pocket. 'Have you any news from Berlin? I know its probably too early...' He trailed off.

Francis shook his head. 'No, Tilly has arrived.' He saw Jacob's surprise and shrugged. 'You had already guessed so I can't see the point of lying to you.' He resumed his report. 'That's all I know, I'm afraid. Communication is difficult now, much of their transport network is down and we've destroyed several of their radio masts. Its best to keep wireless communication to a minimum, the city is rife with detector vans, spying on their own people mainly but still looking for agents. The city had been bombed quite heavily so Eva probably won't be able to return home which will make it harder to find her and given the other problems as well, she will probably be trying to keep a low profile so the SS or Gestapo don't pick her up. Niklas started looking for her immediately, but despite checking all the places she might reasonably be expected to go, he has not had any luck yet. But it is early days so although its difficult try not to give up just yet.'

******

Warrington

'I can't believe you've actually managed to get some leave at the same time as me!' Danny could see that Bill had drunk plenty by the time he arrived and his heart sank.

'Yep makes a change doesn't it!'

Danny ordered two more pints and stared at Bill. 'I thought you would be happy Nora's getting married. You don't seem it?'

Bill shrugged. 'You don't know the half of it mate.' He drank deeply, wiped his mouth on the back of his sleeve and sighed loudly.

'Is there a problem with the bloke she's marrying? Other than him being a Yank of course?'

Bill shook his head. 'I haven't met him yet, no its not that.' He fell silent thinking back to what Nora had said about behaving like a tart. This was all his fault. If Alan hadn't been killed she would have married him and not been attacked.

'So what is it then?' Danny knew Bill well enough to see that he was getting ready to kick off and as he didn't want to spend his leave in the clink it might be better to try and effuse whatever had set him off.

'I can't tell you… its too awful.'

Danny sighed. 'Its obviously eating you up mate. Trouble shared is a trouble halved and all that…'

Bill was about to repeat himself when he suddenly changed his mind. It was killing him not being able to talk to anyone. He took a breath and everything came pouring out. Danny listened in silence and tried to keep his face impassive until Bill eventually ran out of steam.

He thought carefully before speaking. 'I'm so sorry Bill, that's dreadful. Your poor sister… But there's nothing you can do now is there, except look for her daughter like you promised and be pleased she's found a good bloke.'

Bill nodded. 'You're right, I know, but it just makes me so mad.' To Danny's relief his anger appeared to have gone and he just seemed sad now.

'Life's full of *if only's* Bill. She's getting married to a good bloke and going to start a new life. It could be worse.'

Bill stared at him and for a moment Danny wondered if he'd gone too far, then he nodded. 'Yeah, you're right mate. Come on let's have another drink to celebrate the happy couple!'

******

Berlin

Ulrike stared at Tilly in shock, then eventually she spoke. 'You say her family were involved. Have they been arrested?'

Tilly shook her head. 'No, at least not as far as I know, although my information could be out of date. They went east to escape the Gestapo, and she and her husband were supposed to come to me in Amsterdam, but they didn't turn up.'

'Why do you think they are here? Surely Berlin is the last place they would come back to?'

'They ended up in Calais and he was taken prisoner by the Canadians, but before that his wife was evacuated back to Berlin with other civilians.'

Ulrika stared at her. 'Why are you looking for her?'

Tilly had been dreading this question ever since she'd announced why she was really in Berlin. It was one thing avoiding arrest by the Gestapo and helping others do the same, quite another to work with an enemy to do that. She had thought up a lie to cover herself, but she had no idea if they would believe it.

'I used to know her husband. That was why they were coming to stay with me. As soon as he found out that Eva had been evacuated back to Berlin he sent a message to me, begging me to find and save her. He knew that if he wasn't killed in the fighting, he would be a prisoner and unable to do anything.' Tilly managed to look sheepish. 'Like an idiot I agreed. I thought it would just be a case of coming here and taking her back to Amsterdam.'

'You are still in love with him?' Ulrike asked.

Tilly thought about Jacob and how she would feel if he had married someone else and she had to admit to the strong feelings she still harboured for him and, to her astonishment and relief, felt herself blushing. 'Yes… he doesn't know though.'

Ulrike gave a harsh laugh. 'Are you sure?'

Tilly managed to look horrified. 'You think he might know?'

Ulrike sighed. 'Probably. What's her family name? Eva...?'

Tilly hesitated. If she had got this wrong, she would be endangering Eva even more. But it was too late, she didn't have any choice now. 'Eva von Landau.'

Ulrike frowned 'And who did she marry?'

'Linus Haass. He worked for her father, Clemens von Landau.'

Ulrike shook her head. 'I don't know Eva or the von Landau's, but I can ask around if you like? I know several people who might know her.'

Tilly looked uncomfortable. 'But won't that draw attention to her? I think she's gone into hiding, that is if she hasn't gone east looking for her family.'

Ulrike's face lit up. 'If she's gone into hiding, we have several contacts who might be able to locate her for you.'

'Really?'

Ulrike smiled, but her eyes were cold. 'Yes. But if you are lying to us...'

Tilly shook her head. 'I'm telling you the truth. I was taking a huge risk telling you about her, but I was sure I could trust you.'

Ulrike smiled and this time the smile reached her eyes. 'As are we. You know our secrets too Juliette, well Jutta's anyway.' She glanced across at the editor's office and then beckoned to one of the men at another desk before continuing. 'We need to find you somewhere to hide Jutta.'

'No, I want to find my parents.'

'I'll help you pack some clothes and collect some food then you can go to the country. You can't find your parents if you are locked up can you?' The man was short, plump and looked to be in his fifties.

'Thanks Schwab.' Ulrike shook his hand, gave Jutta a hug and Juliette watched them leave.

'If she tries to find her parents she'll be arrested surely?' Tilly was confused.

'There are ways of doing it without the Gestapo's knowledge. We have lots of contacts.'

Tilly fell silent until Ulrike spoke again. 'I'll ask them to look for Eva too. And while they are doing that we'd better get you started on that article, or your cover won't stand up.'

Tilly nodded gratefully. 'Thank you. I think I probably need to start by speaking to some people who have no doubts that the Führer will bring the country victory.'

Ulrike stared at her and began laughing. Tilly hesitated and then joined in. It looked like she hadn't been wrong when she'd joked with Niklas about having to use her imagination.

****

Warrington

The town hall was busy, numerous couples queuing up to make their vows, some in white but most in smart outfits like her own. Nora glanced down at the skirt suit with matching hat and hoped she looked nice. Hank had suggested that she should get married in white, but Nora couldn't agree to do that. However bad the church had treated her, she couldn't shed herself of the beliefs she had grown up with.

'You look lovely Nora. I am so proud of you.' Bill hugged her tight. 'I hope your bridegroom appreciates how lucky he is.'

'Its me who is lucky. I am the one with the past, the secret that no one ones wants to talk about.'

Bill pulled back and looked into her eyes. 'You are more than worthy of this man Nora. Stop hanging on to the past, let it go and look forward or it will ruin your future.'

'And Jennifer?'

'As soon as we know where she is I will look after her from a distance I promise.'

'Francis still hasn't found her?' Nora felt uneasy.

'The Home is being difficult, but he is determined to find out and my money's on him!'

Nora smiled. 'I can't believe I am lucky enough to have him as a friend.'

'Well, are you ready Nora?' Joseph appeared by her side. 'Its time to go in.' He held out his arm and Nora placed her hand on it.

'Yes. I'm ready.'

Bill stepped away and joined Francis. 'Do you know anything about this man she's marrying?'

Francis frowned. 'No, I haven't looked into him. Why? Has something happened?'

Bill shook his head. 'No, just a feeling. Nora seems so sure that he is much better than her, that she is lucky to have him. I'm not sure that is healthy that's all.'

Francis didn't get a chance to answer as Nora was walking into the marriage chamber and the guests were following. They found their seats and then Bill looked at him. 'Nora thinks a lot of you. You won't let her down, will you?'

'No, I will find Jennifer despite the Home's intransigence. But if she's happy and having a good life, what will you do?'

Bill sighed. 'Worry about that if it happens.'

Francis smiled. 'That sounds like a good answer Bill. None of us know what the future holds, and it may be that Nora won't ever send for her daughter.'

Bill frowned. 'Because of Hank you mean?'

'Not necessarily. Nora might just decide that Jennifer is better where she is.'

The Registrar started speaking and they fell silent, but Bill wasn't concentrating. He was going through everything Francis had said and, perhaps more important, the things he hadn't said.

Nora repeated the words and then Hank was kissing her and it was all over. She was married. Mrs Hank Layman. She waited for the excitement, the pleasure, the love and happiness to wash over her, but nothing happened. She didn't feel any different.

Hank finished kissing her and stepped back. It was done. A brief feeling of satisfaction spread over him. Soon the war would be over and they would be on their way back to the States. Then he could put the rest of his plan into action. But none of that was important unless he could get her pregnant. He had no idea why that hadn't happened yet. Perhaps she was doing something to prevent it? Given her previous experience that made sense. The last thing Nora would have wanted was to get pregnant again without being married. But now they were wed that shouldn't apply. He would have to make sure Nora knew how much he wanted children. He smiled. But not why…

Chapter 34

Berlin

'Are you sure you can trust them?' Niklas looked concerned.

Tilly shrugged. 'No, not one hundred percent obviously, but I think they have all the contacts we could possibly need and one of them is about to go into hiding. I am sure I have done the right thing.'

Niklas sighed. 'Well, let's hope so or we could be in trouble.'

'They only know about me so you should be safe. I did have to tell them Eva's family name though.'

Niklas stared at her in astonishment. 'What on earth did you tell them that for?'

'Well she's hardly likely to be using it is she? She's much safer using her husband's surname, it's her father they are looking for.'

'True.'

'Have you had any luck?'

'I discovered that Eva, her mother and some neighbours were running a network of hiding places, but none of the people involved has seen Eva since her wedding. When she married she pulled out of the group. She didn't want to lie to her husband.'

Tilly stared at him and then started laughing. 'If only she knew.'

Niklas grinned. 'Yes, I did think that was rather ironic.' He gave a loud sigh. 'I think you are right Juliette, she's gone eastwards in the hope of finding her family. Why would she bother staying here? There's nothing here.'

'Then perhaps we're starting from the wrong place.' Tilly's face lit up. 'We should speak to the civilians she came back from Calais with. She might have said something to them.'

Niklas didn't look very convinced. 'Only if she trusted them surely?'

'She might not have told them the truth. She could have made something up… maybe something about her brother fighting in the east and being her only living relative.'

'That's what you would have done?' Niklas looked slightly amused.

Tilly flushed. 'Yes, I have been trying to put myself in her shoes.' She shrugged. 'What have we got to lose? We don't have any other leads do we?'

'No, you are right. I will start on that tomorrow.' Niklas stood up to go. 'Good night Juliette.' He glanced at his watch. 'You had better get down to the shelter or you will be in trouble.'

Tilly frowned. 'The siren hasn't gone?'

'You are expected to be in the shelter whether the siren goes or not. No point drawing attention to yourself unnecessarily.'

'No, you're right, I hadn't realised it was compulsory, the siren has gone every night since I arrived, so I just followed everyone else.'

'Yes, its compulsory, like many things.' He sighed and let himself out. 'I'll see you as soon as I have some news.'

Tilly grabbed her bag, put her coat and hat on and made her way quickly down to the shelter. The last thing she needed was to draw the Gestapo's attention to herself.

****

Warrington

'Jacob?' Nora had answered the door in her wedding suit and was staring at him in shock and disbelief.

'Hello Nora.' Jacob double checked no one else was about, and the lowered his voice. 'Francis asked me to find Jennifer. I won't let you down

I promise.' He stepped back. 'I'm sorry I missed the service, but I wanted to wish you all the best for the future.'

Nora recovered quickly, smiled and stood back, 'Come in, you must have a drink with us to celebrate. My brother Bill is here too, you can meet him. Once you have found Jennifer he will keep an eye on her.'

Jacob nodded. 'That sounds like an excellent idea. Is Francis here yet?'

'Yes, he's drinking the champagne he bought with him. You'd better hurry or it will all be gone.'

Jacob stepped into the crowded sitting room and spotted Francis immediately. He was standing with another man who Jacob assumed must be Nora's brother, Bill. Francis beckoned him over and quickly introduced him to Bill who for some reason seemed rather embarrassed.

'I'm sorry… about the shop.'

Jacob looked confused then he remembered that it was Bill and his friend who had broken into the shop all those years earlier. He smiled. 'It years ago now, forget it.'

'Thank you.' Bill relaxed. 'What happened to your leg?'

'Shell blew half of it off. Doctor's couldn't save it.'

'That's awful Jacob.' Nora was standing at his side, horror etched on her face.

'I'm getting used to it, and the alternative would be worse.'

'Alternative?' Nora looked confused.

Jacob smiled. 'I could be dead.'

'Yes, of course.'

'You're a war hero then… Jacob is it?' Hank had moved quickly to Nora's side.

Jake smiled. 'Yes, Jacob Goldsmith. No, I'm not a hero, just someone doing their job.'

Hank didn't return his smile, his eyes were cold. 'So where were you then... when that happened?' He indicated Jacob's leg.

Jacob met his gaze squarely. 'I can't tell you that I'm afraid. Official secret and all that.'

Hank looked about to argue. 'I thought we were on the same side.'

Jacob was beginning to feel irritated, but for Nora's sake he didn't want to cause trouble. He changed the subject. 'Congratulations on your marriage Hank. I'm sure you and Nora will be very happy.'

'How come I haven't met you before? Nora hasn't even mentioned you.'

Jacob sighed. 'There's no reason for her to mention me Hank. I have been away fighting for my country since 1941 so we haven't seen each other. The only reason I am here is because I bumped into Francis who told me Nora was getting married. I was passing here on my way home to the Isle of Man so I thought I would call in.'

'Everything alright Jacob?' Bill appeared by his side.

'Yes, everything is fine. Hank was just asking why he hadn't heard of me.'

Bill laughed and Jacob could smell the alcohol on him, and he began to feel uneasy. Bill's next words confirmed he was right to be concerned. 'Oh, is that all? He's probably just jealous... of your wounds and the fact that you knew Nora before him.'

Hank glared at him and took a menacing step forward. Bill laughed even more and squared up to him. The room grew quiet as Jacob stepped in between them. 'Look Hank, Nora's waiting to cut the cake, why don't you join her, its your day after all.'

'That sounds like a good idea Hank, don't want to upset the bride, do you?' When Hank didn't move Bill put an arm on his shoulder. 'Go and join the ladies Hank, leave the big boys to talk about the war and the fighting they've done.' Bill goaded. Jacob sighed. Obviously, Bill didn't like Hank either, but this wasn't the time to pick a fight. Unfortunately, both men had been drinking. Hank raised his fist, Jacob was vaguely aware of Nora screaming as he pushed Bill out of the way and grabbed Hank's arm before he could connect with anything. He twisted it quickly behind his back and forced him to his knees.

At the same time Francis grabbed Bill and held him back. 'Not the time Bill. I'm sure you'll get a chance one day, but today isn't it. Come and have another drink.' Bill tried to shrug him off, but Francis' grip was too strong.

Jacob leant forward and spoke softly into Hank's ear. 'Go and enjoy your wedding Hank, forget about me. I'm only important if you make me important.'

'What the hell does that mean?'

'It just means Nora and I are friends. It's you she's married.' He let go and Hank fell forward. Nora rushed towards him and tried to help him up while Jacob moved away. 'I don't want to cause any problems, Nora so I'll be on my way now. Goodbye.' He turned to Bill and Francis and indicated they follow him out into the hall.

'A real charmer isn't he?' Bill looked furious. 'I don't understand why Nora has married him.'

'No, I'm inclined to agree.' Jacob looked at Francis who shook his head.

'Its probably just the alcohol talking.'

Bill snorted. 'You don't really believe that do you?'

Francis sighed. 'No. I think it might be a good idea to try and talk Nora into divorcing him before they leave for America.'

'Do you think she'll take any notice?' Jacob looked unconvinced.

Francis stared at Jacob and then at Bill. 'If we don't…' He fell silent.

'What exactly are you saying Francis?' Jacob and Bill exchanged glances.

'I don't know to be honest. Its just a feeling that something isn't right.'

Jacob nodded. 'I agree.' He turned to Bill. 'I don't know how you can do it, but I really don't think Nora should go to America with that man.'

****

Berlin

Levi was still following Ritschel. He didn't seem to be getting anywhere but the last thing he wanted was to draw attention to himself. He still hadn't found out who Ritschel was meeting, but he was loathe to kill him until he did know. Obviously the scientist was up to something or he wouldn't keep meeting this man. This was the third time Levi had followed the car, hopefully this time he would find more.

As before the car drove round the city before heading back to the newspaper offices. Levi decided that this time he would follow the car when it drove off, but he didn't get a chance. It pulled up outside the building and this time the door opened and someone climbed out. Levi opened his window and heard the man call out.

Levi tried to see who he was shouting at and then wished he hadn't.

****

Indian Ocean

Clarissa was in a deep dreamless sleep when she was suddenly aware of Renee shaking her roughly awake. 'They've spotted a Japanese submarine, we have to go on deck.'

'I thought they said we wouldn't have to worry about submarines until we were nearer home?' Clarissa leapt up, pulled on the warm clothes they had been told to keep ready just in case.

'I don't know. Perhaps they are just being overcautious.'

'You're probably right.' Clarissa began to say something else when there was a massive explosion and everything shook. 'What the hell...?'

There was no time to answer before another explosion and this time the ship tilted alarmingly.

'Everybody on deck, hurry, no luggage!' The voice sounded panicked and Clarissa stared at Renee in horror.

Another explosion, the ship lurched slightly and then another voice 'Abandon ship! Abandon ship! Woman and children to the lifeboats!'

Renee opened the door to a scene from hell. Smoke and flames were pouring from somewhere above them, water was cascading down the stairs, people were crowding up the stairs.

Renee grabbed Clarissa and dragged her up the stairs where they joined the queues of people heading towards the lifeboats. Clarissa was surprised there wasn't more panic, but then she realised that most people were in shock. Up ahead she could see numbers of troops who had been on their way home to England helping women into the lifeboats. The few children on board were already on one lifeboat and it was being lowered carefully into the sea. The women in front of them were already climbing into the next one. She was vaguely aware that there was quite a thick sea mist and she wondered if that was good or not. It might protect them from the Japanese who were more likely to sink them than pick them up. But it might make it harder for the Royal Navy or the Americans to find them. It bought back memories of the last time she had been in a lifeboat. Tristram had been with her then and the Americans had rescued them.

'In you go miss, hurry now.' The voice interrupted her thoughts, a short wiry sailor helped her in, and she made her way carefully to the far end as he had directed. She sat down cautiously and looked back, relieved to see Renee making her way towards her. Renee reached her and sat down beside her and the two women held hands, trying not to think of what was going to happen next. Clarissa peered nervously over the side from time to time searching for sharks, but the sea was swirling and frothing too much for her to see anything clearly.

As the boat filled up they moved closer together to allow more women on and then, after what seemed like barely any time at all, the boat was full, two sailors climbed aboard to row and navigate, and then they were being lowered slowly into the sea.

As they reached the sea, the waves splashed over the side, but Clarissa barely noticed. She was staring upward at the ship, most of which she could hardly see anymore because it was shrouded in smoke and flames. She could hear screams, she presumed from the wounded, yells of those trying to evacuate the sinking ship and the intermittent creaking and crash of timber falling as more smaller explosions shook the massive frame. As she watched she realised the bow was already sinking down into the water, the stern rising into the sky, blocking out the stars, and she realised the ship was going down. She could hear men jumping into the water around them and see them grabbing pieces of debris to help them stay afloat or hanging onto the edges of the lifeboats despite the sailor's exhortations to let go or they would sink the boats.

'Get away! Get away!' Clarissa could hear the orders to clear the area around the vessel and she wondered why it was so important to get away from the sinking ship. She could also see the sailors rowing hard and was aware that their boat was gradually moving away. Then she finally realised why they were rowing so hard and she cried out in shock and horror as one of the last lifeboats to leave was caught in the current of the sinking ship and pulled under. She shook her head and gripped Renee's hand tighter, unable to believe the tragedy that was unfolding before her eyes. Many of the men who had jumped off at the last minute were unable to swim away quickly enough and were pulled under by the current as the ship shuddered and groaned and finally sank beneath the waves.

For a brief moment there was a strange silence and Clarissa squeezed Renee's hand. 'Oh God...Those poor men...'

'They might be the lucky ones.' Renee's voice was barely above a whisper as she pointed ahead.

Clarissa peered into the mist and shivered.

******

Berlin

Tilly was hurrying back to the newspaper office trying to ignore the exhaustion she felt after very little sleep. Evidence of the previous night's raid was all around her and with so many buildings flattened she had trouble getting her bearings, getting lost several times. She was wondering whether she should ask for directions when she finally worked out where she was. Having worked that out she now knew which direction she was meant to be going and she set off, increasing her pace to make up for the tardiness. The more she thought about it, the more she realised that given the incessant bombing Eva had probably done the right thing going east, although she had heard several people discussing how bad the situation on the eastern front really was. On the other hand Tilly had given the matter considerable thought and she still couldn't work out how Eva expected to find her family. They could literally be anywhere, that was if they had even survived the Soviet advance. She was so engrossed in her thoughts that she didn't notice the car parked outside the newspaper building until she heard a voice calling her.

'Tilly?'

Tilly's heart nearly leapt out of her body. The voice had called her real name, not Juliette. She shook her head and increased her pace. She must have imagined it... too little sleep... After all who on earth could know her in Berlin?

'Tilly? It is you, isn't it?'

The voice was closer now, and she knew there was no escape. She slowed down, trying to make her brain work so she could give a good reason for her presence. What the hell was Heinz Kessel doing in Berlin? Even as she thought the words, she realised how stupid she was being. Kessel had considerably more right than her to be in Berlin. She turned round and forced a smile onto her face. 'Heinz! How lovely to see you! You were the last person I was expecting to run into. Did Bruno tell you I was here?'

Bill's true story is written at the end of book 4 by his son Bob who has also contributed the following photos and information.

HMS Keats 1943 Boston Naval Yard

William Patrick Young

HMS KEATS
Royal Navy 1943.

H.M.S. KEATS.

OFFICER COMPLEMENT.

HMS Keats 1944

Action photos of HMS Keats at sea

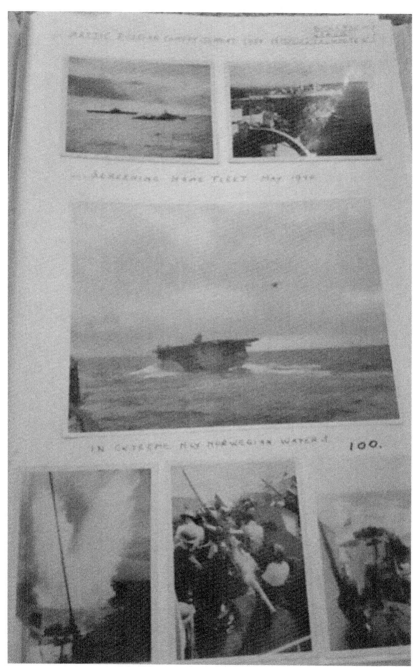

HMS Keats Arctic Convoy

Operation Goodwood (Naval)

Fairey Barracuda aircraft on board HMS FORMIDABLE during the Operation Goodwood attacks on the German battleship Tirpitz in August 1944.

HMS Nabob after being torpedoed on 22 August 1944

HMS Keats was captained by Lieutenant Commander Neil Frederick Israel, RNR.

Dad told my brother Steve he had great respect for Commander Israel. I asked his son to tell me about his father and he wrote this.

I think your Dad would find his commanding officer a very fair man with no pretensions. He would have engendered a feeling of togetherness throughout his ship and would have noticed and rewarded exceptional service such as that provided by your Dad and others. His acute sense of humour may not have infiltrated the lower decks however his sense fair play would have been appreciated by all. Your dad would have seen a very kind and generous man who put others first. He was always willing to put up members of his crew for recognition of their bravery or distinguished service and a letter I have from a crew member of "Keats" to my Dad sums up what the crew thought of him. So - your Dad and mine would have had a mutually respectful relationship where both did their respective jobs to the best of their ability, and both appreciated each other.

Dad was awarded the Arctic Star for his part in Operation Goodwood, a massive operation with the purpose of destroying the battleship Tirpitz in a Norwegian Fjord. It was carried out by British carriers against the battleship while she was anchored in Kaafjord in occupied Norway during late August 1944 and was the last of several attacks by the Home Fleet which sought to eliminate the threat the Tirpitz posed to allied shipping. Many lives were lost and it was considered a failure.

The British fleet sailed on 18 August and launched the first raid on the morning of 22 August. The attack failed, and another small raid that evening inflicted little damage. The attacks conducted on 24 and 29 August also failed. Although *Tirpitz* had been hit by two bombs on 24 August neither caused significant damage. 17 aircraft were lost, HMS Bickerton was scuttled after being partly sunk by a submarine, and HMCS Nabob was badly damaged. The Germans lost 12 aircraft and 7 ships were damaged.

The surgeon on HMS Nabob, Doctor Charles Reed Jr: *"I had already accepted the inevitability of my own death; it was not a matter of whether, only of when. In no way did this alarm me. I was deeply calm, having previously divested myself of the shackles of orthodox religion because I'd come to realise that I couldn't believe anything for which there was no proof. I did feel disappointed I was not going to do the things I'd hoped to do in the future, including having a family, live in peace, seek knowledge, and serve mankind, probably as a paediatrician. I was sorry for my parents and Anne, with whom I'd shared only two years of marriage. They would be distressed. But they all knew I had voluntarily accepted the risk when I joined the navy, and that I felt strongly that it was of the utmost importance that the forces of Nazism be defeated and that I wanted to play a part in it. I had no other regrets.*

Reproduced with permission of his daughter, Connie Reed Hippee. Memoirs of the Flight Surgeon of HMS Nabob by Charles Herbert Read, Jr. - Lammi Publishing Inc.

Printed in Great Britain
by Amazon